A Summer
at the
Castle

A Summer
at the
Castle

KATE LORD BROWN

ORION

First published as *The Taste of Summer* in Great Britain in 2016 by Orion Books
This edition published in 2021 by Orion Fiction,
an imprint of The Orion Publishing Group Ltd
Carmelite House, 50 Victoria Embankment,
London EC4Y 0DZ

An Hachette UK company

1 3 5 7 9 10 8 6 4 2

A CIP catalogue record for this book
is available from the British Library.

Epigraph extract from 'Variation on the Word Sleep'
Selected Poems II: 1976–1986 by Margaret Atwood.
Copyright © 1987 by Margaret Atwood.
Reprinted by kind permission of Little, Brown.

ISBN (Mass Market Paperback) 978 1 3987 0434 3
ISBN (eBook) 978 1 4091 6001 4

Typeset by Input Data Services Ltd, Somerset

Printed and bound in Great Britain by Clays Ltd, Elcograf S.p.A.

www.orionbooks.co.uk

For Celia

I would like to be the air
that inhabits you for a moment
only. I would like to be that unnoticed
& that necessary.

Margaret Atwood

Strawberries for Breakfast

'Tell me what you eat, and I'll tell you who you are.'

Jean Anthelme Brillat-Savarin

1

Kenmare, Ireland

Present Day

The place where her mother had been found sprawled beneath the apple tree could not be seen from the road. The spot was shielded by dense foliage, glimmering in the August morning light, fresh from the rain. *So many greens*, Darcy thought, leaning her head against the cool glass of the bus window, craning her neck to see the last of the orchard. All she saw was a blur of leaves beyond the stone walls, and a double rainbow leading her home to Kenmare Bay. The boughs of the apple trees were laden still, speckled with deep red fruit. *No wonder it took so long to find her.* Darcy shook the last strawberry from the brown paper bag into her tanned hand, bit into it. The bus wove along the silver ribbon of the coast road, overtaken from time to time by Porsches and gleaming four-by-fours speeding towards Castle Dromquinna to sample the famous lunchtime tasting menu.

'What were you thinking? Climbing trees at your age,' Darcy had said, when her mother's call woke her a couple of days before. She remembered making camps in the orchard as a child, white sheets draped over low branches glowing gold with lantern light at sunset, the smell of sausages cooking over a wood fire.

'I'm only sixty-five, plenty of tree-climbing years left in me yet,' Diana said, the transatlantic line crackling. 'I was reaching for an apple, that was all. Such an apple. The most

3

luscious, shiny red apple, just out of reach. I slipped and fell, simple as that.'

'And what if no one had found you? I heard, you know. You were half dead they said, stretched out under the tree like a corpse.'

'Well they did find me, didn't they, thanks to Conor's three-legged hound.' Diana had broken off to shout instructions to someone in the kitchen. 'It's a grand crop this year. Come home, Darcy,' she said. 'Please, I need you.'

'In the kitchen?'

'Not exactly. Conor's back now. I'll explain once you get here.'

Darcy reached across and rang the bell as the entrance to Castle Dromquinna's driveway appeared on the road ahead. 'Would you stop here for me? Thank you,' she said, dragging a large cerise suitcase along the gangway. She swung the case out and jumped down to the verge, her silver Converse splashing in a puddle iridescent with oil. The bus pulled away and she stood for a moment with her back to the Castle, letting the silence seep into her, remembering. She lowered her white Ray-Ban Wayfarers from her dark hair and waited. It smelt like she remembered, yet everything seemed changed. *Or is it me that's changed?* A breeze toyed with the hem of her white sundress, and she felt the hairs at the nape of her neck rise. She lifted the collar of her denim jacket and glanced quickly over her shoulder. A man was running towards her, his pace slowing, unruly black curls held back from his eyes by a blue and white bandana.

'Howya,' he said, catching his breath. He did a double take. 'Darcy? I hardly recognised you.'

'It's only been a year,' she said, laughing. She dragged her case across the road to meet him. Conor flung open his arms, and in their hesitant joy at seeing one another again – *is it right or left cheek first?* – she planted a kiss on his lips. A three-legged greyhound bounded from the woodland towards them. The dog circled, its tail beating their legs. 'Well I never,' he said, not stepping away. 'Still like strawberries for breakfast, eh?'

'I was starving.' Darcy blushed. *He remembered*. She reached down to smooth the hard, silken head of the dog. 'Taxi, plane, train and bus to get here and not a decent thing to eat between San Francisco and Kenmare.'

'Hole in the market there,' he said.

'Would you look at you? Conor Ricci, running?'

'New leaf,' he said, grinning, but she sensed there was a vulnerability to him she'd not seen before. 'You probably heard.'

'I'm sorry.' She held his gaze. 'How are you?'

'Better. Much better.' He wiped his brow with the arm of his grey hoodie and laughed. 'I'm getting there, day at a time. Now, will I help you with that?' He took hold of her case, dragging it along behind him. She noticed the faint tan line on his finger where his wedding ring had been. 'Tell me all about your adventures, Darcy Hughes. What's with the accent?'

'California,' she said, glancing at him. 'See they still haven't knocked your Dublin accent out of you?'

'You can take a man out of Dalkey—' he said. 'Mind yourself.' A blacked-out Range Rover sped along the driveway towards them. He shielded Darcy, taking the brunt of the muddy water splashed up at them. 'Feckin' eejit,' he said, brushing down his splattered T-shirt. The dog raced on ahead of them, barking at the car which sped past a banner reading: *Castle Dromquinna, home of 'Ireland's Top Chef'*.

'You've not changed that much, then,' Darcy said to Conor, nudging his arm.

'A man needs one vice.' He turned to her and smiled, his grey eyes creasing, and her stomach fell away. She was nine years old again, seeing him for the first time, conducting the morning kitchen with the muscular grace of a ballet dancer. She remembered hiding, sneaking a peek at him above the stainless steel counter, peering around the whitewashed brick columns, mesmerised. *Boo.* He had seen her, snuck across unseen to surprise her. He had swung her up onto the counter and insisted she try a new pudding he was working on. *Strawberries for breakfast.*

'Your ma will be glad to see you, and God knows I could do with some help around the place with her out of action,' he said, the suitcase trundling along the gravel drive behind them. 'Have you spoken to her?'

'Briefly. How is she?'

'The same, just slightly more difficult now she's in constant pain.'

'But she's resting in bed?'

'Resting?' He laughed. 'As we both know, Di's *so* good at accepting help when it's offered.' Conor glanced at her. 'I know you won't get much thanks from your ma, but it's good of you to drop everything to come and help out. I know what the job at Chez Panisse meant to you—'

'What could I do?' Darcy kept her gaze fixed on her feet, unable to look at him. 'She's taken on too much, as usual. The Castle, the TV show, this contest—'

'*Ireland's Top Chef*? The ratings just go up year after year,' he said. 'The grand final is here in a couple of weeks. We've been filming shows judging amateur cooks all over the country. Luckily most of it was in the can before she had her fall.'

'Thank God Jake found her. I hope she gave your dog a bone for saving her life, at least.'

'A bone?' Conor laughed. 'A *bone*,' he said, imitating Diana's cut-glass vowels. 'He'd be lucky. Makes good stock does a bone.' They rounded the curve of the driveway and the Castle stood before them, the grounds falling away to where the sky met the water, a shimmering land of gold and green and blue, fringed with pastel-coloured mountains. Smoke drifted leisurely from the chimney above the peat fire which always burned in the entrance hall of the hotel. They stood in silence

6

for a moment. He watched her closely. 'Forget how beautiful it is?'

'Yes. Yes I did.'

The morning light eased across the water, the mirror of the sky, clouds scudding over the still bay. She closed her eyes for a moment and inhaled, enjoying the sensation of being home – the cool breeze, the scent of the ozone and water, the good damp earth. An old stone tower sat at the corner of a later, whitewashed Georgian house with crenellated rooftops and stone mullioned windows. The tower held the family kitchen and private rooms, with Diana's suite at the very top. The Georgian end housed the restaurant and guest rooms, with a new professional kitchen at the back. Darcy smiled, spotting a skull and crossbones flying from the flagpole on the roof.

'Is that in honour of Ma's broken arm?' Darcy said.

'Nah, though I see your point,' Conor said. 'One of the chefs had their kid's birthday party here the other night so we put it up for a laugh.'

'I reckon we should keep it,' Darcy said, walking on to the Castle. She glanced back over her shoulder at him. 'Kind of suits your brigade in the kitchen.'

'Pirates are we now?' he said, following her. 'Welcome home, Darce.'

2

London

1969

Beyond the liminal reflection of her face in the kitchen window, Colleen watched a lithe red fox slinking along the end of the terraced garden. It stopped for a moment, and seemed to look back at her. *Was it daring her? What did it see?* she wondered. A grimy Underground train clanked and thundered along the tracks at the end of the garden, and she felt the tremor of the kitchen counter. The fox turned, slipped away into the long grass on the sidings and extinguished, like a flame. She wished she could do the same.

Colleen felt weightless enough, as though she had disappeared. Like an automaton going through the motions, through the dense, hot August days. Had it always been like this, with him? She tried to remember. Not at first, maybe. He kept it hidden, for a time. Then bit by bit, drop by drop, he drained the colour from her life. Sucked it from her. A vampire. She felt she was fading away, like her reflection.

More vibrations. Another train coming. This one slowed, and she could make out the hunched figures of early-morning commuters beyond the grimy windows. A young woman stared back at her from the train. *What do they see?* A lit window, a girl with long red hair warming a bottle for her baby. *The baby.* Colleen registered the rising wail, and she quickly wiped down the glass, testing a drop of milk against the inside of her wrist. She flinched as it trickled on to the fresh burn there.

'Colleen?'

Her heart quickened at the sound of his voice from upstairs. He was awake. 'Just coming.' She ran past the aspidistra lurking on its stand in the hall, her slippers padding noiselessly up the narrow brown staircase. She could hear 'Honky Tonk Women' on the radio, coming from the flats next door. Maybe the music had woken the baby. Colleen swung open the door to the dimly lit back bedroom. The air was stifling, hot, ripe with the scent of sodden nappy. The child stood in the cot, raging, hot tears scalding her cheeks. 'Here we are . . . Mammy's here,' Colleen said, gathering her daughter into her arms.

'Hush,' he said, coming up behind her. Colleen's hackles rose, her skin prickling at his touch. 'Relax. They pick up on your emotions.' She froze, terrified that his gentleness would switch at any moment without warning. 'I've a full surgery, and there's a meeting at the Lodge tonight. I won't be back until late.'

Don't look at him, she thought. Don't give him an excuse to say: why aren't you dressed yet? Why isn't your hair done? Is it too much to ask for a wife to look pretty at breakfast? 'Your porridge is on the table, Timothy,' she said. 'I'd come down, but she's hungry, and I know you don't like to be late.' She forced herself to walk slowly across the room when all she wanted to do was run. She settled back on the hard wooden rocking chair, keeping her gaze lowered as the child sucked fiercely on the bottle.

'You should still be breastfeeding – you know that, don't you?' he said.

'She bit me.'

'They all do that.'

Colleen blinked, fighting back the tears. 'No, I mean she bit me again and again, drew blood. She laughed. She knew she

9

had hurt me, and she laughed. She's eighteen months now, Timothy. Old enough.'

Still she didn't raise her face to him, but her eyes darted, noticed him lift his hand to check the time on his slim gold watch. She hated the coarse black hair over his knuckles. 'I – I'll put your dinner in the oven, shall I? Meat and veg, just like you . . .' Her voice trailed off at the memory of the beef daube she had cooked the night before, the smashed plate and stew splashed across the floor, the pain where he had pressed the hot lid of her precious Le Creuset casserole against her arm. Colleen wriggled her arm up inside the sleeve of her cardigan, not wanting him to see how much he had hurt her again.

'Good girl. None of that foreign muck, eh? Then you can shop round the corner. I don't like you going into town.'

'But I have to.' She looked up. 'It's only the Italian shops around Soho that have the ingredients I need.' He walked sharply towards her, and Colleen felt every cell in her body retreat, flinch. She hated herself at that moment, thought of a stray dog she had seen cowering in an alleyway near the market, how pathetically grateful it had been when she had given it a bit of cold meat. It had followed her home, waited outside the gate for a whole day. She longed to bring it in, but she didn't know what he would do to it. Timothy stood before her now.

'Look at me.' He raised her chin with his index finger. 'There now. All right?'

'Yes. Yes, everything is fine.'

'How about a smile then?'

Her lips trembled. 'Have a good day, Timothy.'

'I don't like it when you're hurt, you know that, don't you Colleen? You simply have to learn. What is the point in marrying your housekeeper if your home is not perfect? No more mistakes, eh? No more accidents. You're nineteen, not a child anymore. Good girl.'

'I want to be a good wife, I really do.' Colleen took the empty bottle and stood it on the table at her side. She lifted the baby up and laid her against her chest, rubbing her back. The child grizzled, lashing out at her mother's face.

'Maybe she's still hungry.' Timothy smiled indulgently, stroking the child's dark hair. 'She wants more.' He chuckled. 'There, lovely smile. She looks just like my mother, don't you little rabbit?' He began to sing: *Run, rabbit, run, rabbit, run, run, run ...* Colleen swallowed, nauseous. She'd hated that song ever since he played the old 78 on their honeymoon. She remembered the scratch and hiss of the record, how it had been a game at first, chasing her. She screwed her eyes closed. It was the first time he had hit her, when he caught her. When she tried to stop him.

Colleen fingered the fresh scratches from the tiny nails on her cheek. 'It's like a game to her, too.'

'What are you talking about? Don't be silly. She's eighteen months old, what would she know?'

'She does know, though.' Colleen stared at him. 'She enjoys hurting me. She hit me, the other day, with that rattle, and when I cried out, she just laughed.' *Like her father,* Colleen thought. *That's what I see in his face, when he hits me – not anger, just detached, curious pleasure.*

'You need a break, Colleen, no wonder you were clumsy last night. You look exhausted,' Timothy said. *His reasonable voice,* she thought. *Is that how he talks to his patients?* He reached for his wallet and handed her a note. 'Why don't you go and get yourself a new casserole, eh? Treat yourself. Go to that shop in Chelsea and replace the other one you loved so much. Such a shame you burnt yourself getting it out of the oven last night.' She flinched, remembering how he held her wrist down against the edge of the heavy metal dish, fresh from the oven. He did, didn't he? It wasn't an accident? She closed her eyes against the memory; the noise of the dish crashing to the floor, the scalding stew flecking her legs, her clothes. 'What do you say, then?'

I can't bear it, she wanted to cry out. *I can't bear it anymore.*

'Thank you,' she whispered, her voice catching. She forced herself to smile up at him, her lips trembling. 'Thank you.'

3

Kenmare

Diana Hughes strode across the gravel driveway of Castle Dromquinna, leading a scrawny black goat with amber eyes with her good arm. The hem of her orange kaftan rode up over Diana's strong, tanned legs as the goat struggled. She tightened her grip on the cerise pashmina she had tied around its neck. 'No you don't, my friend. Let's get you safely back in the field.' She dragged the goat onwards, and looked up at the stone crest above the porchway carved with DH, her silver-grey hair blowing in the breeze. Storm clouds scudded across the sky, blocking the sun. *Rain*, she thought, longing blooming in her chest for golden, sunlit days in Italy. She was counting down the days to her annual holiday.

'Let me take 'im Mrs Hughes,' the gardener said, setting down his wheelbarrow. 'Right handful this one is.'

'That would be grand, thank you Seán. Check Mephisto-pheles' fence again, would you please?' The gardener scooped the goat up into his arms, and Diana untied her scarf from its neck. 'You're a rascal, so you are,' she said, scratching the goat's bony head, its ears quivering in pleasure. She adjusted the sling at the back of her neck, her eyes narrowing.

'You've not been swimming, Mrs Hughes? Not with your arm?'

'Just a paddle with this ruddy thing,' she said, raising her arm in its plaster cast. 'I haven't missed a day since 1988 and

13

I'm not going to start now. The water is gorgeous at this time of the year. Bracing.' She picked a piece of reed from the goat's back. 'I found you down by the bay, didn't I?'

On the porch she stamped her feet, and swung open the heavy mahogany door to the reception area. At once the familiar smells of the Castle embraced her: the open fire, beeswax polish, the rich incense perfume of the stargazer lilies on the circular table at the heart of the flagstoned hall. 'Is Darcy here yet?' she asked the girl behind the desk, pulling off her wellies. A white cat with aquamarine eyes jumped down from the red velvet armchair by the fire and wound its way around her bare feet. 'Hello, Kato, have you had your breakfast?' She slipped on a battered pair of black espadrilles and walked on.

'Conor's in the kitchen with your daughter,' the girl said. 'Mrs Hughes, someone was—'

'Not now.' Diana strode through the hall, stopping to adjust a skew-whiff painting of Kenmare Bay. She knew every inch of the Castle intimately, had chosen every lamp, every rug, every picture herself. The restaurant, and the few discreet rooms above for guests who wished to stay over before driving back to Dublin and beyond, still had the air of a private house. It was classic, artfully shabby. The antiques suited the eighteenth-century architecture and anything newer she had aged. From the derelict bones of an old people's home awash with avocado bathrooms and safety handles, Diana's creation had risen like a pop-up page in a glossy magazine. She had added to it over the years, replacing make-do with make-a-statement pieces bought at country house auctions to complement those her husband had collected. At the thought of Kavanagh, she smiled, and paused to look out across the formal garden, the gravel pathways flanked with topiary leading to the walled kitchen garden with its neat brick pathways and raised beds of herbs. *We're a good team*, that's what Kavanagh always used to say. *You've got the taste and beauty, Di, I've got the balls and cheque book.* A peacock cried out, stalking across the lawns. Diana brushed a tiny strand of cobweb from the grey-painted moulding of the window frame, blowing it free from her fingertip. She made a mental note to tell the housekeeper to brush down the hand-painted wallpaper, its vines snaking up to the ceiling. *You have an eye, my girl*, she thought, imagining her husband's deep voice. *You have an eye, for sure.*

I feel old, she thought, walking on through the Castle. Her broken arm ached, and her ribs were still mending, bruised from the fall. *What would you make of me now, Kavanagh? Where's the girl you fell in love with in Porto Ercole?* She thought of the rugged Tuscan coast, the deep green and peace of the vineyards and olive groves rolling down to the shimmering sea, of her simple whitewashed cottage in the hills. *I'll take a holiday, after this.* Her expression softened and her eyes took on a faraway look. Italy was hers alone – there were no demanding customers, no arguing staff to discipline, no TV cameras, no calls from the accountant, no letters from the bank. *Perhaps I shall treat myself, book into Il Pellicano for a few days before opening up the cottage.* She thought of the hotel's sunbathing terrace overlooking the endless blue sea, imagined the warmth of the sun easing her bones, the glittering light through her closed eyelids. *But there's work to be done first.* Diana took a deep breath, and winced. *God, I hope I've done the right thing asking Darcy to come home.* She pushed open a baize-lined door marked 'Private' and strode along the flagstone corridor leading to the family kitchen in the old tower. She could hear laughter up ahead, the deep roll of Conor's voice telling a story.

'You didn't?' Darcy's voice, her soft Irish accent melded with west coast American.

'There you are,' Diana said, pausing in the doorway. Her daughter stood beside the scrubbed pine table at the heart of the yellow kitchen. The flagstone floor was covered with worn Persian carpets, and faded Liberty print cushions littered the old blue sofa by the stove. The white-painted cabinets and dresser were battered rather than distressed, and littered with pots of utensils. It was a working, homely place, and Diana's favourite room in the whole Castle. An oil painting of Diana in her prime, her arms full of fresh produce from the kitchen garden, dominated the room, gazing down from the wall between the two floor-to-ceiling sash windows. Darcy stepped towards her mother, her eyes betraying her nerves and joy. Diana tucked a strand of glossy dark hair behind Darcy's ear, cupped her cheek in her thin, dry hand. 'It's good to see you.' Darcy hugged her mother carefully. 'There, now,' Diana said, closing her eyes, breathing in the warm vanilla scent of her daughter. She pressed her lips to the top of Darcy's head.

'I was worried about you,' Darcy said, her voice muffled.

'It'll take more than a few broken bones to finish me off,' Diana said, straightening up as they stepped apart. 'You do look well. You've cut your hair since I saw you last.' *You have the look of your father,* she thought, *his dark beauty.*

'It's easier in the kitchen. How's the arm?' Darcy said.

'And the ribs,' Conor said.

'I could scream, it's so frustrating.' Diana walked to the stove, holding her side. 'Can't swim, can't cook. Shall we make a pot?' She fumbled with the tea caddy.

'Here, let me. Sit down, woman,' Conor said, pulling out a wheelback kitchen chair for her. He filled the kettle, and set it on the stove. 'Honestly, would it kill you to ask for help?'

'Yes, probably. You know me,' Diana said, wincing as she sat down.

'I was so glad that you called me,' Darcy said, sitting opposite her.

'I didn't want to bother you.' Diana gestured at Conor, who was sorting through the morning papers. 'He said it was time for the next generation to take over on the show.'

'Young blood.' Conor fished out the *Irish Times* and took down a pair of tortoiseshell glasses from his hair to read the front page. 'People have had enough of looking at our faces.'

16

'We've always assumed you'd take over running the Castle when I retire—' Diana said.

'But you're not retiring yet, are you?' Darcy said.

'Not exactly.' Diana looked at the clock. 'Why don't we talk about it later? Give you time to unpack. There's someone I'd like you to meet arriving tomorrow.'

4

London

1969

Colleen stumbled, the heel of her patent shoe slipping on the greasy pavement outside Sloane Square Tube. She was pushing a heavy Silver Cross pram, her daughter's face puce with rage beneath her thick thatch of black hair, fists balled in fury, gripping the blanket which Colleen had dutifully spent the winter nights crocheting.

'Shh, shh ...' Colleen soothed her, her own heart still racing from the journey, the silent disapproval of the commuters which cloaked her like fog. Her legs, her arms shook from exhaustion, sweat stuck her fringe to her brow beneath her grey cloche hat. She envied the carefree, leggy Chelsea girls walking past in their mini dresses. *But Timothy would never allow that.* She tried not to look at the baby, hoped the walk would settle her. Two middle-aged women talking on the corner of the street stared as Colleen hurried by, their disapproving glances piercing her like arrows. A screw of anxiety tightened in her stomach. *I'm doing my best,* she thought. *She just won't stop.* The baby's breath caught, choking on an angry sob, and Colleen stopped to check her. The child hit out at her, arms and body rigid. *The image of her father,* she thought. *The spitting image.*

Colleen leant down on the pram handle, pushing on along Holbein Place. She felt the weight of her handbag, the book inside, swinging against her wrist. She cut along Graham

Terrace, and paused on the opposite side of Bourne Street from the shop at number 46, catching her breath, enjoying the window display. Hand-forged, gold-painted letters spelling 'Elizabeth David Ltd' gleamed over an arrangement of kitchen equipment which seemed to float effortlessly in mid-air. Colleen wheeled the pram across the road.

'Are you coming in?' A tall, elegant woman paused at the door of the shop. She tucked a linen tea towel over the contents of the wicker basket slung across her arm. Her voice was feline, breathy.

'Thank you.' Colleen blushed. 'Pardon me, but are you Mrs David?'

'Yes. How do you do? Afraid there's not much room for that.' Elizabeth David raised an eyebrow, looking down at the pram. 'You can leave it out here.'

'Are you sure?'

'I'll ask one of the girls to keep an eye on it – him? Her?' She winced as the child began to scream. 'Dear me. How do you put up with it?' She pushed open the plate glass door.

'I don't. I . . . I'm not a very good mother.' Colleen clutched the handle of her handbag, relaxing only as the door swung to, drowning out the noise of the baby. 'I can't help thinking it was a terrible mistake—' She felt like she was talking too much, and Mrs David's polite smile only confirmed that.

'Well. How may we help you?'

'I need a new cast iron casserole. My old one . . .' Colleen pulled down the sleeve of her coat. 'I . . . I had an accident.'

'Happens to the best cooks. You won't regret it. Have you seen the new blue?'

'Oh, they're lovely.' The colour shone with promise. Colleen picked up a heavy oval dish. All of it – Mrs David's effortless poise, the solid goodness of the shop, the rightness of the things in it – seemed distilled in the deep blue Le Creuset pan. It was all Colleen wanted in life, all she longed for. Order. Colour. Weight. She checked the price. 'I'll take it.'

Elizabeth gestured to one of the girls to wrap the dish. 'Will you be all right carrying it?'

'I can put it under the pram.' She clicked open her handbag and lifted out a large manila envelope, holding it towards Mrs David. 'I – I hope you don't mind, I wondered if you would be kind enough to sign this book for me.'

'Of course. Do you have a pen?' Elizabeth raised an eyebrow.

'I've read it so many times,' Colleen said, searching in her bag. 'I've cooked almost all the recipes.'

'Really?' She regarded her coolly. 'What's your favourite?'

Colleen's face lit up. 'It's probably a bit simple, but I love the spaghetti all aglio e olio. My husband can't stand the garlic, but I love it.'

'He doesn't know what he's missing. The Neapolitans adore it and so do I. In fact, every decent professional cook I know eats it as a staple when they are cooking for themselves.' Elizabeth watched her with feline eyes, and nodded. It was as if Colleen had passed a test.

'I'm sorry,' Colleen said, her blush intensifying. 'I don't have a pen.'

'Very well.' Elizabeth picked up the basket from the counter and headed to the stairs. When Colleen didn't follow she paused. 'If you'd like me to sign your book, come on down.'

Colleen glanced at the pram, and followed. The shop was beautiful to her. Every item seemed to ring true. There was a simplicity and elegance to the design that resonated with her – the black and white tiles, the calm grey blue of the walls. She thought of Dr Smith's dingy, cramped kitchen in Battersea with its single ring hob and wished she could live somewhere with the order, the peace of these marble shelves with their stacks of white china. Somewhere clean, and light, and safe.

Elizabeth swung the basket on to the marble-topped table and began to unpack a greaseproof wrap of pâté, a fresh loaf and a thick slab of butter. 'Pass me that earthenware bowl, would you?' she said, gesturing at a pile of plates at the end of the table. Colleen reached over and handed it to her, and Elizabeth tumbled a paper bag of bright radishes into the bowl. She then cupped it in her hands and breathed in, her eyes closed. 'The most divine smell, so fresh.' Colleen watched, dumb with nerves, as people came and went around the table, stopping to chat to Elizabeth, to scoop up a hunk of bread and some olives for lunch, to pour a glass of wine. She envied their ease. She wanted desperately to belong in a place like this. Elizabeth waved the bottle of wine. 'Can I tempt you with a glass of Flaming Carthage, my dear? I must say, you look like you could do with one.'

'I don't . . . thank you.' Colleen took the tumbler of wine offered to her.

'Not Asher Storey's finest, but it does for lunch.' Elizabeth rummaged on the table and found a pen. 'Now, let's inscribe this book for you.'

'Thank you.' Colleen slipped the book out of the envelope, and offered it across.

Elizabeth caught sight of the bruises, the burn on Colleen's wrist, and Colleen quickly covered the livid red scar. 'It was an accident,' she said.

'It always is,' Elizabeth said quietly, raising her gaze to Colleen.

'I'm sorry, Mrs David,' one of the girls called from the stairs. 'That child is screaming blue murder. There's a crowd gathering.'

'I must go,' Colleen said.

'Who shall I dedicate this to?' Elizabeth said.

'Coll—' she began, and paused. 'No. No name. If you wouldn't mind just signing it?'

'Of course.' Elizabeth David wrote her name on the frontispiece with a flourish, and handed the dog-eared copy of *Italian Food* to her. 'Well used, I see?'

'It was my mother's,' Colleen said, smoothing her hand

over the ripped and stained dust jacket. The illustration of artichokes, a flask of wine, backed by a blue, blue sea and warm sunset promised so much – a sense of feeling alive again. She glanced up at Mrs David, the woman who was everything she wanted to be – confident, elegant, reserved. Colleen wished she could be just like her. 'She loved it, and so do I.'

'I'm glad to hear it,' Elizabeth said. 'Enjoy your cooking.'

5

Kenmare

Darcy freewheeled down the curving lane, the wind in her hair, only the slick hiss of her tyres breaking the silence. It felt good to be home. The bike ride along familiar roads had cleared the last of her jet lag, and her cheeks shone. Her striped cotton T-shirt and faded jeans sparkled with fresh raindrops, and she shook her hair dry as she hopped off her bicycle at the wide stone arch of the hotel's entrance, where two workmen were hanging a banner: *Welcome to Ireland's Top Chef.*

'Morning,' she said, seeing Conor at the reception desk, checking the bookings for the day. His greyhound lolloped over, nudging her hand with his nose, tail beating. 'Are we busy?'

'It's been too quiet for comfort. But bookings are picking up again now they're advertising the new series.' Conor tucked a pencil behind his ear and walked outside, looking beyond Darcy to where a pink Beetle had drawn to a halt just behind her.

'If you need a hand—' Darcy began to say.

'Let me guess,' a woman's voice interrupted. Darcy turned to see a red ballet pump emerge from the door of the car, followed by the full skirts of a pastel-blue tea gown. 'Conor Ricci?' The woman recoiled as the dog flattened his ears, growling at her.

'Get away, Jake,' Conor said, and the dog backed behind him, low to the ground. The woman extended her hand towards Conor. Her long peroxide-blonde hair was clipped up at the nape of her neck with a velvet clasp speckled with rosebuds, her eyes obscured by cat's eye sunglasses. She took them off and glanced at Darcy, adjusting a white cashmere cardigan over her shoulders. Her eyes were the palest blue, the colour of her dress, like a snow dog's, framed by sooty black lashes and a perfect slash of liquid liner. 'Delighted to meet you. I'm Bea Lavender.'

'How do you do?' Darcy said.

'I've just driven from London, so I'll be better once I've had a couple of paracetamol. My back!'

'Sympathies,' Conor said.

'Occupational hazard isn't it?' Bea said, smiling up at him.

'Come in and we'll get the First Aid,' Darcy said.

'Be a darling, would you, and help me carry these baskets in to the reception?' The scent of freshly baked cakes wafted out to Darcy as Bea clicked open the boot – nutmeg, cinnamon, mouth-watering and warm.

'No problem,' Darcy said, bracing as Bea loaded her up with heavy wicker trays. 'Something smells wonderful.'

'Oh good. Let's see if I can tempt you,' Bea said, locking the car, and she sauntered ahead, swinging a small basket, chatting to Conor.

'Morning,' Diana said, striding into the yellow kitchen. 'Is the new pastry chef here yet? Beatrice.'

'Is that who she is?' Darcy said, and glanced over, feeling Conor watching her. 'Little Miss Vintage, all over you like a rash.'

'Get away, she never was,' Conor said, a smile bringing dimples to his dark stubbled cheeks.

'I bumped into her in the restaurant kitchen and told her to meet us in here,' Diana said, waving her hand airily. A faded tattoo of two swallows garlanded her wrist.

'What on earth do you think you're doing taking on staff?'
Conor said, reaching over to grab a piece of toast from the battered silver Dualit toaster, tossing it on to a plate and shaking
his fingers. 'Honest to God, she's been sick with worry about
the books,' he said to Darcy. 'What do we want with a new
pastry chef?'

'We need her, for the show,' Diana said, pressing her lips
together.

'Is there any coffee?' Darcy said. Diana gestured at the
catering-size drum of instant Nescafé by the kettle.

'If it was good enough for Elizabeth, darling . . .' Diana said,
seeing Darcy pull a face.

'The sainted Elizabeth David,' Darcy said, rummaging in
the cupboard for a cafetière.

'Who is this girl?' Conor said.

'She worked for Jonny,' Diana said.

'Jonny Fish or dead Jonny?'

'It's Daffyd Fish now, did you not notice the little Welsh
fellow who dropped the order off this morning?' Diana said.
'Took me ages to find a new fishmonger. Jonny Fish sold up.
I'm talking about dead Jonny.'

'As in JJ? My best mate?' Conor looked up at the sound of a
crash from the cupboard.

'Be careful, Darcy,' Diana said. She frowned in irritation.
'You always were a clumsy child.'

'I was not,' Darcy said indignantly. She gathered up the
broken shards of glass. 'It was only one of those giveaways
from the gas station, still in its box. Why do you hoard these
things you'll never use? You can't find a thing in there.' She
winced as she dropped the pieces into the bin, and sucked at
her finger. Conor beckoned her over to the sink.

'You should see the state of your Ma's rooms—' he said.

'Don't lecture me, Conor,' Diana said.

'Piles of books and papers, every single socket loaded up
with lamps and phone chargers, cupboards full of stuff.' He

pointed at Diana. 'I keep telling her she needs a good clear out.'

'Thanks.' Darcy glanced up at him as Conor put a blue plaster over the cut. 'I wasn't clumsy, you know. But I believed it for years, because she told me I was—'

'I don't think Jonny Fish has any real friends,' Diana interrupted, and Darcy went back to searching the cupboard. 'Something cold blooded about him. Fishmongers never seem lucky in love, do they? Butchers, though . . .'

'There it is,' Darcy said, waving the cafetière triumphantly. 'I knew I'd sent you one for Christmas. What's it doing in the junk cupboard?'

'Ah, well. You might find some Blue Mountain in the fridge.' Diana gestured at her.

'Blue Mountain?' Darcy said in surprise.

'The rep left some beans for us to try,' Conor said, folding his arms. 'Your ma hasn't gone berserk at the cash and carry.' He leant back against the counter, smiling. The muscles of his forearm flexed, smooth. Diana looked at Darcy, saw something in the way she was looking at Conor. *Oh God, this could be trouble.* She remembered seeing him lift Darcy into his arms when she was a child, enfolding her. She could tell Darcy felt safe with him, then. Her gaze darted from Darcy to Conor. He'd not noticed. 'Look, about this pastry chef. I know you feel sorry for her, but I think we should try her out on probation, OK? See how she fits in. You agree, don't you?'

'Sorry?'

'I mean, what do we know about her? She says her bakery supplied Jonny's restaurant but it's not like he can give her a reference, rest his soul.' He picked up a slender, sharp knife and grabbed a lemon from the blue and white Moroccan bowl on the counter, cutting swiftly through it, perfuming the air as the thin slices fanned onto the board. He flicked one into a porcelain cup.

'If she was good enough for Jonny, that's good enough for me,' Diana said.

'Yeah, well the proof is—'

'In the pudding?' Beatrice stood in the doorway. Her chef's whites were immaculate, flaring bright in the sunlight, her blonde bunches gleaming. She carried a wicker basket covered with a linen tea towel.

'Jaysus, where's your red cloak?' Conor said.

'What makes you think I'm not the wolf?' She held Conor's gaze long enough to make sure she had his full attention, then turned to Darcy. 'I'm so sorry I didn't recognise you just now. I'm so pleased to meet you. I love your posts on *Appetite*, Darcy,' she said. 'May I call you Darcy?'

'Sure,' she said.

'Are you making tea?' Beatrice glanced over as the orange kettle let out a piercing whistle from the stove. 'Perfect timing.'

'Darcy's on coffee, Di and I are having tea. What'll you have?' Conor said.

'Camomile if you have it?' Beatrice said. 'I don't get on with caffeine, makes me hyper.' She giggled and widened her eyes, miming an explosion.

'Fascinating. Do grab a pew,' Diana said, gesturing towards an empty chair. 'How was your journey?'

'Non-stop from London, picked up the ferry at Fishguard. Not a bad crossing, very smooth, in fact. Thank you.' Beatrice looked at her hands. 'Forgive me. I'm talking too much. I'm rather nervous. You see, I'm so pleased to meet you both, at last.' She blinked. 'I mean, I'm such a fan. I grew up with your books, Mr Ricci, and yours, Mrs Hughes, in my mum's kitchen. She never stopped talking about you.'

'How charming.' Diana touched her hair. She felt embarrassed as she always did when cornered by a fan gushing praise.

'Cool tattoo,' Beatrice said, gesturing at Diana's wrist. 'Willow pattern, isn't it?'

'Yes.' *Why are the young so impolite, so personal?* Diana thought. 'It was unique at the time. Now everyone's got them.' She rubbed the birds. 'It's rather faded. Relic of another life.' She tugged her sleeve down. 'Right, shall we get on?'

The back door banged open, and a tanned, golden-haired little boy raced barefoot into the kitchen. 'Howya, Dad. Didi.' He dropped his duffel bag by the back door, and hugged Diana before going to his father. 'Is there anything to eat? I'm starving.'

'Chris? I wasn't expecting you until this evening,' Conor said, ruffling his hair.

'Mammy had a party. She said you wouldn't mind.'

'Hello, Chris,' Darcy said, swivelling around in her chair so that her eye level was the same as the boy's.

'Howya,' he said. 'Did you miss us?'

'This much,' she said, opening her arms wide.

'Who are you?' the boy said, narrowing his eyes at Beatrice.

'Now don't be rude.' Conor's hand rested on his shoulder. 'Sorry.'

'It's good to meet you.' Beatrice leant down to the boy's height, and smiled. 'I'm Bea.'

'Well I'm hungry,' Chris said.

'Why don't you come and see what I've got in here?' Beatrice said, opening her basket.

'Or shall I make him some toast?' Darcy said to Conor. She jumped up and put a couple of slices of bread into the toaster and turned the dial. 'I'm sorry,' she said quietly to him. 'I read about your divorce.'

'Been keeping tabs on me, have you?'

'Hard to avoid you,' Darcy said, smiling, not looking at him. 'All over the papers you are.'

'One of those things,' Conor said, shrugging.

'You and Alannah got together too young,' Diana interrupted, 'and she got bored waiting for you to come home from the kitchen every night.'

'No wonder she found someone else,' Conor said under his breath.

'Did she?' Darcy said.

'Didn't read that in the paper, did you?' Conor glanced over to the table where Chris was busy chatting to Beatrice. 'Can't blame Alannah for what she did, and I wasn't going to drag our dirty washing through the tabloids.'

'That was good of you,' Diana said.

'You think?' Conor said. The toaster pinged and Darcy picked the hot bread out, waving her fingers. She buttered it and passed the plate to Chris.

'So. You've met the family,' Diana said to Beatrice, gesturing that she should sit at the table. 'As I mentioned on the phone, I have a business proposition.'

'I'd love to work with you.' Beatrice blushed. 'I hope I'm not jumping the gun. I'm a huge admirer. Your biggest fan.' She looked at Diana with a clear, unwavering gaze. 'One of my earliest memories was going to a talk you did, with my mum. You signed the book for her afterwards. It was one of Mum's most treasured things—'

'How touching.' Diana tried to cut her off.

'She . . . she's just died, recently,' Beatrice said, and lowered her gaze.

'Condolences,' Conor said and sipped his tea. 'Do you have brothers and sisters?'

'No.' Beatrice folded her hands. 'I am an only child,' she said with a tremor to her voice. An awkward silence fell, and Diana looked at Conor, widening her eyes. She hated emotion, public scenes.

'Where did you train?' he said to Beatrice.

'I took the liberty of printing off my résumé,' she said, slipping a sheet of paper from the basket. 'I brought a few samples of my work, too.'

'Bea Lavender?' Diana said, running her thumb over the embossed pale purple bee on the letterhead.

'My friends call me Bumble.'

'You're Cordon Bleu trained?' Conor said. 'So why cupcakes?'

'I adore baking, it's as simple as that,' Beatrice said. 'It was my vocation to work as a pastry chef.' She looked Conor in the eye. 'I love the artistry of creating a beautiful dish, I enjoy managing a team, and I think you'll find me handy in the kitchen in plenty of ways.'

'Ma said you were working with Jonny?' Darcy said.

'Yes, my company supplied all the cakes and desserts for his cafés. I mean, obviously his team did the high-end stuff at his restaurants, but for everyday baking, he used Lavender Cupcakes. At least until . . .' Beatrice looked down at her hands. 'Look, I won't lie to you. I made a real mess of my business. I trusted Jonny's company would pay us because I liked him, I mean – who didn't?' She looked at Darcy, who was staring into her coffee cup, swirling the dregs. 'They owed us a lot of money, and I went bust. I'm normally sharper, but losing Mum was such a blow, I haven't had my eye on the bottom line.' She took a deep breath. 'But you can't live in the past, can you? I'm hoping for a fresh start.'

Diana watched her closely. 'We all need one of those once in a while.' She reached for a fork, and beckoned for Beatrice to open the cellophane box. 'What have we got here?'

'Nothing fancy. I thought I'd show you some of the basics, but I'd be glad to bake anything you want me to. I took the liberty of bringing a couple of trays of cakes for you to try out on the teatime crowd.'

'They're in the restaurant kitchen,' Darcy said.

'And here we have a Devil's Food cake, a New York cheesecake and a Black Velvet cupcake.'

'Black Velvet?' Darcy said.

'Try one,' Beatrice said. 'Guinness, sinfully dark chocolate, champagne icing and edible gold leaf. They're my signature, if you like.'

'Cupcakes, what a phenomenon,' Conor said.

'It's about desire,' Beatrice said, holding out a fork to him.

'The hell it is. It's just a cake, a little fairy cake.'

'It is *not* just a cake.' She wagged the fork at him. 'How dare you.'

'It's about people who don't want to grow up,' Diana said. 'And if that is what they want, we will give it to them.'

Beatrice laughed softly. 'Maybe you're right. People need a little comfort in this uncertain world. Who doesn't deserve a treat once in a while? People come in for a cake, and they leave with a piece of their childhood.' Conor took a fork, and broke apart the Black Velvet cake. 'They may only be little cakes but we give people a feeling of security, pleasure ...' Beatrice's voice was sibilant, hypnotic, washing over Diana. 'People associate baking with simpler, easier, sweeter times.'

Diana watched Conor's reaction. He frowned, studying the consistency, the texture, and raised it to his nose, sniffing, nostrils flaring. His eyes closed as he slid the fork into his mouth. Diana waited. At last, Conor pursed his lips and nodded.

'Oh my God,' Darcy said, her eyes rolling upwards as she swallowed a bite of the Black Velvet cake. Beatrice waited, her hands folded in front of her. Diana picked at the cake, sampling the sponge and icing without a word.

'Well?' Beatrice said to them.

'Not bad,' Conor said, throwing down his fork. 'Clearly you know your stuff.'

'I agree. More than adequate,' Diana added. She fought the temptation to take another forkful.

'Good.' Beatrice smiled at them in turn, and folded her hands in front of her, resting them gently on the immaculate full skirt of her summer dress. 'Now, why don't you tell me exactly what it is that you do need?'

Diana sat back in her chair. 'I assume you saw the last TV series?'

'*Master Baker*,' Conor said.

'It's not called that.' Darcy burst out laughing.

'That's what me and the lads call it,' Conor said. He looked at Beatrice. '*Top Chef.* We're looking for an amateur cook with real potential, someone whose dish uses the best local ingredients. Someone whose cooking has character, who makes you think of home.'

'Well, I've adored all the *Hughes at Home* series, and I like the revamped image of the TV show,' she said to Diana. 'Very natural.'

'That's exactly what we were going for with the contest, too,' Diana interrupted. 'Something fresh. That's where you and Darcy come in. Intercut with segments showing the amateur contestants for the *Top Chef* prize, we want to record pieces with the four of us demonstrating dishes. I want each of you to come up with a menu, showcasing your talents.'

'You want me to be on television?' Beatrice said, her eyes widening.

'Nothing too formal. Conor will be filmed in the restaurant. Darcy, I thought you could focus on fresh, local ingredients – put your experience at Chez Panisse to good use.' Darcy nodded. 'Beatrice, you would be doing baking, and I'll be doing pieces about easy, effortless home entertaining.'

'How exciting,' Beatrice said.

'Now, the film crew is coming here to record our segments and the last episodes of the contest over the next couple of weeks. As I'm sure you have already guessed, things here are a bit . . . difficult.' Diana gestured at her arm.

'How can I help?' Beatrice stared at her intently. Diana's stomach tightened. There was something in her gaze. She couldn't put her finger on it. *Don't be silly,* Diana told herself. *The girl's just nervous. I mean, look at her, she's just a nice young woman who needs a job and a fresh start. Everyone needs a second chance.*

'I really need someone to be me,' Diana said, looking from Darcy to Beatrice. 'Literally, in the case of social media – I don't have a clue about engaging with people online to promote the show, and I'm not interested to learn. What do you think?' Diana said.

'When can I start?' Beatrice said.

'Hold on,' Conor said. 'We'll try you out on probation. We need to check references—'

'Come on,' Diana said. 'We met her at Jonny's funeral, she worked with him, what more do you need than that?' Diana gestured at the table. 'You tasted these.' Conor drummed his fingers on his arm, frowning. 'Miss Lavender is a godsend. Welcome to Castle Dromquinna, Beatrice.'

'Do you have to give notice? What about the logistics of moving down here?' Darcy said.

'No problem. I'm travelling light.' Beatrice smiled at her. 'Is there a B and B in town or something? Just until I find somewhere.'

'Stay here,' Diana said. 'It's not the Ritz, but there's staff accommodation over the old stables by the kitchen. I think one of the rooms is free?' she said to Conor. Diana scribbled down a series of figures on a scrap of paper and slid it across to her. 'This is what we start everyone on. OK?'

'Thank you.' Beatrice looked at them in turn. 'I promise you will soon be wondering how you coped without me. I won't let you down.'

'We're selling dreams with the show, Bea,' Conor said. 'We want people to buy in to the idea of this place.'

'We need to think of the Castle's future, of attracting a younger clientele—' Diana began to say.

'I get it,' Darcy said, frowning. 'That's why you brought me all the way here, made me give up my internship at Chez Panisse just as I was about to become Garde Manger, said you *needed* me—'

'Darcy—' Diana said.

'Just so you could use me as window dressing for your TV show, like you always have?'

'Darling—'

'No, you let her have her say,' Conor interrupted. 'What if she doesn't want to run the Castle? Darcy's going to be a fine chef one day. And why should either of us have to smile for the camera with Miss Cupcake here?'

'Because cooks like Bea are having their moment,' Diana said. 'Have you seen how many followers her YouTube channel has?'

'YouTube?' Conor raised his voice. 'Feck's sake.' Diana clicked her fingers and gestured at the piggy bank on the windowsill. Conor dug in his pocket and stuffed a couple of euros in the jar. 'You go ahead though, Di, just like you always do, and I'll get on with doing what I am here for, running your kitchen. Come on, Chris,' he said, putting his arm around the boy and opening the back door.

'I am sorry,' Beatrice said, as he walked away across the yard. She glanced at Darcy. 'I hadn't realised, I mean, I thought this was just a regular job.'

'Are you up for it?' Diana said.

'Yes,' she said, nodding. 'Absolutely. I've always dreamt of being on TV.'

'Good. Now why don't you go to reception and ask one of the girls to show you where the staff quarters are?'

'Thank you,' Beatrice said. 'You won't regret giving me a chance.'

Diana waited for the kitchen door to swing closed, then exhaled, slumping down in the chair.

'That went well,' Darcy said, sipping her coffee.

'She reminds me of Mary Poppins,' Diana said.

'You always hated Mary Poppins. Called her a meddling, sinister bitch.'

Diana narrowed her eyes. 'Spoonful of sugar? Rots your teeth.' She rubbed the bridge of her nose. 'Darling, I do know what I'm doing. And I am so glad to have you here. Trust me.'

She reached across and took her hand. 'You do understand?'

'The show must go on?'

'I'm thinking about the future, for you. I'm worried that Con is washed up, burnt out. Without his Michelin stars, what do we have?'

'He looks great, though.'

'But how long until his next lapse? How many times have I picked him up? This is a young person's game and he's—'

'Washed up?' Con said, striding through the back door. He picked up his reading glasses from the kitchen table. 'I'll show youse all.'

'Con—' Darcy said, blushing.

'Is that really what you think?' He glared at Diana.

'It's nothing I haven't said to your face.' She raised her chin. 'I know you want to be chef patron when I retire. Well, prove it. Both of you. Prove that I can trust you both with Dromquinna.' Conor stormed out, slamming the back door behind him. Diana turned to Darcy.

'Is everything OK, Ma?'

'Fine, it's fine.' Diana adjusted her arm, wincing. 'You know what this place is like. It's a monster. A beautiful monster.' She thought of all that needed doing, the endless 'to do' list which seemed to grow two tasks for every one she crossed off. 'I sometimes wish it would just go up in smoke.'

Beyond the closed kitchen door, Beatrice straightened up from listening at the crack, a splinter of light illuminating her face as she stepped back into the darkness of the corridor. She sensed someone watching her, and turned to find Diana's cat sitting on a chest of drawers, his pale blue eyes glinting in the shadows. Beatrice lowered her face to his level, staring him down. The cat let out a warning growl. Beatrice edged closer, hissed, and the cat slipped away into the shadows.

6

London

1969

Colleen opened the sage-green back gate and stepped into the alleyway, balancing a tray on one hand. She glanced back anxiously at the house, listening for a cry. *Please don't wake up*, she repeated in her mind like a mantra, backing away, closing the gate silently behind her. *Please don't wake up.*

Dusty pigeons pecked among the ragged dandelions by the battered bins in the alleyway, ruffling their feathers. The air was still, fetid with the smell of old dinners and disappointment. Colleen leant against the neighbouring gate, and the flaking brown wood door creaked open. She stepped silently along the overgrown path, grass catching at her ankles. Her dull cream summer shoes slapped on the cracked paving slabs, two sizes too big. *There's no point them going to waste*, Timothy had said. Colleen felt too small for her life. Too small for the first Mrs Smith's hand-me-downs, the stiff tweed suits and taffeta dresses she had to stuff with tissue paper. The unforgiving crocodile shoes and patent leather handbags belonged to another woman, another life. She wondered sometimes what she had been like. There were no photographs of the first Mrs Smith in the house, no hint of her personality. It was like she never existed. Though Colleen walked in the woman's shoes, she had no idea what she had looked like. She didn't even know her name. She knew better than to ask again.

Colleen tapped softly on the neighbour's back door, and leant on the handle with her elbow. She pushed it open, and the scent of roses greeted her. 'Only me,' she called out. Golden sunlight filled the house, gleaming on the honey-coloured boards, the dusky pink walls. She wondered, not for the first time, how two identical houses could feel so different.

In the kitchen, Colleen put the tray on the table, and she wandered through to the living room, her footsteps softened by the faded cream rug. 'Mrs H?' she said. In the warmth of the sunlight spilling through the front window, an old woman in a gold velvet house coat lay sleeping on a tapestry-covered chaise longue. Her eyes flickered, and she turned, smiling.

'My little Irish rose,' she said, her voice rich with sleep. 'How are we today?'

'Not so bad,' Colleen said, tucking a blanket around the old woman's legs.

'Is the little one not with you?' The old woman reached, unseeing, taking Colleen's hand in her own. 'I was hoping for a cuddle.'

'She's sleeping at last.' Colleen sat on the edge of the chaise.

'Then you should be putting your feet up too, instead of taking care of me.' She raised her chin, sniffing the air. 'Is that steak and kidney pudding I can smell?'

'I had a bit extra.'

'You're a dear girl.' She patted her hand. 'You're tired, aren't you?' Colleen's eyes pricked with tears at her kindness. She was so tired. She wished she could curl up in this warm sunny window and sleep for hours. 'I can tell from your voice. You must rest. Isn't that what I always tell you? Sleep when the baby sleeps. Forget about dusting.'

Colleen laughed, her voice breaking. 'Timothy wouldn't like that,' she said.

'To hell with Dr Smith,' the old woman said. Her thin hand touched her throat, fine bones working beneath the papery skin. 'I heard him, at you again last night.'

37

'I'm sorry,' Colleen said, cringing with shame. 'It's these walls, so thin.'

'The man's a pig. All la-di-dah at the church and the surgery but I know his sort.' The old woman hesitated, feeling the edge of the bandage around Colleen's wrist where she held her hand. Her fingertips felt for the dressing, and Colleen recoiled. 'Has he hurt you again?'

'No, no. I'm fine.' Colleen tried to keep her voice steady. She wiped at her eye with the back of her other hand, holding her breath as the tears threatened to spill over.

'You poor, poor girl—'

'I can't . . .' Colleen's shoulders shook, and she caved in on herself like a cracked shell, her stomach hollow, blown. 'I can't take it anymore.'

'Hush now,' the woman said, taking her in her arms.

'I'm sorry.' Colleen screwed her eyes closed as the old woman rocked her to and fro in the warm pool of sunlight. 'I'm so sorry.'

'There, now. What are you apologising for? Even a mother needs mothering once in a while.' She smiled. 'Especially one with a baby like yours. What a set of lungs!'

'Did she wake you again? I'm so sorry. I'm a terrible mother.'

'Nonsense.' She patted Colleen's back gently. 'You're doing your best, which is all any of us can do. You're a lovely mother to that baby and don't let him tell you any different.'

'Thank you.' Colleen's breath slowed just as the high, piercing cry of the child rose up from next door. She turned, alert, but the old woman held her hand still. 'I have to go.'

'She's in her cot, isn't she? Then she won't come to any mischief for a minute or two.' The old woman squeezed her hand. 'You let it all out. Tell me everything.'

Colleen hesitated. 'I'm afraid,' she said at last. 'It's getting worse.'

38

7

Kenmare

Conor wiped his knives perfectly clean one by one, and slid them back into their battered leather roll, fastening the buckles. He tucked the roll on his shelf in the restaurant kitchen, and untied his blue and white striped apron. The room was quieter now after the frenetic lunchtime service. The stainless steel surfaces gleamed, freshly wiped down; the refrigerators hummed in the temporary, expectant lull before the kitchen kicked into gear again in preparation for the evening. He stepped out of the back door, and pulled the blue and white bandana from his hair, wiping the sweat from his face. A fine drizzle had settled on the yard, and the purple hills beyond the bay were wreathed with cloud. There was a muffled quietness to the air, and his ears rang with the noise of the kitchen, still. Behind him, he could hear someone washing up, the clatter of pots and plates. Conor closed his eyes, cricking the stiffness in his neck, and when he opened them, he blinked in surprise. A young woman in a billowing wedding dress was running barefoot across the yard, the skirts gathered up around her hips.

'Darcy?' he said as she came closer.

'Hi, Con,' she said.

'Is there something you want to tell me?'

'I can explain.' She glanced down. 'You must think I'm crazy, running around in a wedding dress.'

He pushed open the door to the kitchen corridor, and ushered her in out of the rain.

'Well, aren't you a fine thing?' he said. The soft rain sparkled on her hair, her skin like crystals. Close to, she smelt of something warm and good to him, of vanilla, of home.

'Do you like it?' Darcy walked on into the empty restaurant and gave him a twirl, the full skirt of the dress swinging after her. The intimate round tables had been covered with fresh starched linen, and they shone expectantly like a constellation beneath the panelled walls and glistening chandeliers. The light caught the crystals in Darcy's tiara, illuminated the pearls at her throat.

'A barefoot bride are you? You've been in California too long. Catch your death here, you will.'

'My feet are too small for the shoes,' she said, laughing. 'Luckily I'm so short you can't see beneath the skirts.' She lifted the veil from her cheek and smiled.

'Who's the lucky man?' he said, his gaze travelling from her ankles, upwards.

'No – oh God, I'm not. I mean, there's no one—' She broke off, blushing. 'I'm just giving Ma a hand. The model they'd booked for the new wedding brochure hasn't turned up, and the photographer is charging by the hour.'

'Better not keep them waiting; Di must be having a heart attack.'

'Listen, Con, I'm glad I caught you.' Darcy looked up at him. 'I know Ma is just trying to keep the wolf from the door with us all appearing on this TV show, but I want you to know it's not a competition between us—'

'You think you could take me on?' He folded his arms.

'In the kitchen?' Darcy said, raising her chin. She held his gaze. 'One day. But right now if anyone deserves to be chef patron, you do.'

'If this *Top Chef* business gets people through the door, we've got to do what Diana wants.' He put his hands in his pockets and shrugged. 'You know what she's like with her bright ideas.'

'Spa weekends?'

'Wine-tasting extravaganzas, cookery classes . . .' He rubbed the dark circles beneath his eyes. 'Jeez, I mean, do I look like a natural teacher?'

'And now the wedding packages,' Darcy said, gesturing at the dress.

'It's good of you to do it,' he said.

'I'm glad to help out,' Darcy said, smoothing the heavy duchess satin skirt. 'Luckily we got the outside shots done before it started raining.' She looked up as the photographer and his assistant appeared at the door, carrying the tripods and lights. 'I reckon we've just got to go through with filming this programme for her, and make the most of the publicity. It will be OK, you know? There's no way I can out-cook you – yet.'

'Yet is it?' he said and laughed. 'I'd better watch myself.'

'And as for Beatrice, however popular she is with viewers you can't compare cupcakes with Michelin-starred food.'

'Nah, your ma's right. I'm washed up on TV,' he said scuffing the floor with his trainer. 'They all want pretty young girls like you two.' He shook his head, and looked up at her through his curls. 'I can't get over you, you know. I still think of you as that little kid in dungarees hanging round the kitchen.'

Darcy turned and looked over her shoulder at him, the veil a gauzy haze around her upswept dark hair. The sudden jolt of desire he felt caught him off guard.

'Don't you reckon we always think of people the way they were when we first met?' she said. 'It's why old friends never seem to age.' She smiled, looked down at the bouquet of full-blown roses she was carrying. 'It's why when I look at you I see that twenty-year-old man who was full of passion and fire.'

'Jeez,' Conor said, raking his hand through his hair. 'I wish I could still see him.'

Darcy looked up at him, and tapped her heart. 'He's there, Con. You've just got to look harder.'

8

London

1969

Colleen checked the plain Timex watch on her wrist, and quickened her pace along the street, weaving among the crowds of people heading home from work. The shopping basket was heavy on her arm, and she struggled past the parade of shops. She saw the greengrocer was about to turn over the sign on the shop door to 'closed', and she ran towards him, waving. 'Wait! Please, I need some lemons.'

'Hello, Mrs Smith,' he said, stepping aside for her. The shop was cool, and dim. It smelt of the earth, and sawdust, made her think of dens she had built in her father's vegetable garden as a child. The greengrocer reached for a brown paper bag. 'How many do you need?'

'Just a couple, thank you.' She fumbled for her purse, wincing as the heavy basket slid onto the burn on her wrist.

'Never you mind,' he said, tucking the bag beside the tinfoil-covered dishes she was carrying. 'We can settle up next time you're in.'

'Thank you,' Colleen said, and the door swung closed behind her, its bell tinkling. She ran on along the street, the low heels of her patent shoes clicking on the pavement. Up ahead she could see a group of people milling around outside the doctors' surgery, and she sped up.

'Excuse me,' she said, pushing her way through to the reception area. She swung the basket onto the counter, and took off her coat and hat, hanging them in the office. A table had been set with plates and glasses in the waiting room, balloons strung up beside a hand-painted *Happy Retirement* banner. In the kitchen, a silver tea urn gurgled biliously among a pink sea of utility cups and saucers. Colleen quickly unwrapped the plates of vol au vents and sausage rolls, and cut the lemon into slices for the drinks. She stood behind the table, greeting the arrivals with a bright smile. 'Hello,' she said. 'Would you like a cup of tea, or a drink perhaps? Gin and orange? Port and lemon?'

She sensed rather than saw Timothy standing close behind her. As the last person turned away, he stepped closer.

'Where have you been?' he said, his breath against her ear. Her smile mirrored his, barely faltering as he pinched the back of her arm. He raised his other hand and waved in greeting to a colleague. 'Was it really too much to ask?'

'The babysitter was late—' Colleen clamped her jaw, trying not to cry out as he squeezed harder.

'Timothy.' A grey-haired man in a pinstripe suit strode across the room towards them.

'I'll deal with you later,' he said, releasing his grip on Colleen's arm. 'Dr Gardner.' He shook the man's hand. 'And the lovely Mrs Gardner. How delightful you look this evening. I always say to Colleen if she made an effort with the way she dresses she could learn a lot from you.' The woman smiled, her lips pressed together. She waited for the men to walk away, deep in conversation, and turned to Colleen.

'The food looks delightful, my dear. How clever you are,' she said. 'Dr Gardner and I do appreciate your hard work.'

'Thank you, Mrs Gardner,' Colleen said, busying herself with the plates of food, afraid the older woman would see the tears brimming in her eyes.

'No, thank *you*. It's ...' She paused. 'Mrs Smith?' She touched her arm, gently. 'Colleen.' She glanced across the room, made sure Dr Smith was not watching. 'I don't mean to pry. It's just . . . I wonder, is everything well with you, at home?'

'Yes . . . yes, perfectly fine. Thank you.' Colleen forced herself to smile. 'Can I offer you something? Port and lemon, isn't it?' She mixed the drink, ice chinking, the sliver of lemon perfuming her fingertips. *Do not. I repeat, do not forget lemons for the drinks.* She flinched, remembering how he had thumped the kitchen table the night before, running through his instructions for Dr Gardner's retirement party.

'It's just, I can't help noticing we haven't seen a lot of you, lately.' Mrs Gardner sipped her drink. 'I wondered, well, you've seemed a little down. It happens, sometimes, after a baby.'

'Thank you, but I'm fine. Absolutely fine.' Her smile trembled.

'Colleen,' Timothy called, and she started. He clicked his fingers, raising his empty glass. Mrs Gardner looked from husband to wife. She touched Colleen's arm as she went to walk away.

'My husband is retiring, but he is a good doctor,' she said, 'and a good man. If you ever need anyone to confide in, it would be in the strictest confidence.' Colleen nodded, and hurried away.

'Stay here,' Timothy whispered to her as she handed him a full glass. Colleen stood at his side, her hands clasped in front of her, her knuckles white. Timothy tapped the side of the glass. The evening sun filtered nicotine yellow through the net curtains, illuminating the halo of the rim, the amber whisky and soda. The sound of his voice, his easy charm, the rapt faces of the people crowded into the stuffy waiting room with its smell of disinfectant made her want to scream. Her heart raced, and she felt her skin prickling beneath her stockings, her white polyester blouse. She longed to tear them off, to lie down somewhere cool and quiet. She thought of Elizabeth David's shop, the deliciously cold marble shelves, the fresh starched linens. *I can't bear this.* She made herself focus on the faded posters pinned to the walls above the plastic chairs: *Do not poison the air he breathes*, she read. Colleen glanced at her husband. *That's what he does. I can't breathe around him. He's suffocating me.* She looked around the room. How could they not know? How could they not see what he was? 'So we wish Dr and Mrs Gardner a very happy retirement in Kent.' He shook the doctor's hand. 'You leave the surgery in capable hands.' Timothy led the crowd in three cheers, and Colleen forced herself to smile. Another poster caught her eye: *Life is for living. Live it.*

IF LIFE GIVES YOU LEMONS

The things you find in the backs of drawers. This morning, looking for a spatula, I found a burnt-down number nine candle. My mother never throws anything away. Her dresser drawers are like reliquaries of my childhood. I even found a little tin with my milk teeth in there. The miraculous teeth of Dromquinna – heaven knows what she's going to do with them. But seeing that candle it all came flooding back to me, how the party was spoilt because a girl from town whose family was wealthier than mine, who seemed to buy every single thing I mentioned I loved, turned up in the red shoes I'd desperately wanted for the party. And a red dress, with red ribbons in her hair, the works. I was, I believe, in Kickers and dungarees, because Ma hadn't had time to take me shopping. I didn't want the dress, just the shoes; they were a perfect patent red, like cherries. I was so upset, the birthday cake tasted like ashes to me.

I've hated people copying me ever since. Nothing bores me more than people with money and no originality. But then he came. I remember him striding through the crowd of children dancing to 'Barbie Girl', and balloons falling in slow motion. He relit the candle because he said he wanted me to make a wish, and as I blew it out, he leant down and kissed my cheek. I adored him. I didn't think he'd even noticed me, but the kitchen had baked the cake for me, and he'd taken the time before the dinner rush to come and find me. And I found that candle in a drawer, today. I remembered everything, suddenly, about that summer – how I lived for a glimpse of him. He was the most alive, the most beautiful man-boy I'd ever seen. But then one night when he sang in the pub with his band, and I sat on the bar swinging my legs, drinking lemonade through a green and white straw, I saw him kiss a girl. Really kiss her. I was happy for him, don't get me wrong, that he had found someone his age and all, but my heart broke a little that night.

Now I'm older, I know that life is full of moments like this, but that was the first. What I've learnt is: buy the damn shoes. Kiss the boy. You can lose a life in indecision, and regret is a waste of an emotion. If you are going to make lemonade, my friends, make the real McCoy. Like life – bitter sweet:

Juice four lemons, add 60 g sugar, and dilute in a litre of water. Serve chilled with lemon wedges.

Or if you've had the kind of long day when someone else is wearing your shoes or kissing the boy of your dreams, why not try an Aperol Spritz instead:

1/3 Aperol, 2/3 prosecco, splash of soda, lemon

Darcy Hughes, *Appetite* Tumblr

9

London

1969

'That went rather well,' Timothy said, pushing open the garden gate. Colleen could smell the whisky on his breath, and it scared her. She knew what it meant. She walked ahead of him, her head bowed, trying not to catch his attention. The front windows of the house were obscured by an impenetrable laurel hedge, and a single dull bulb lit the red brick porch. She let her head fall forward to the green gloss painted door frame, praying that he had drunk enough that he would just fall asleep quickly. She heard Timothy searching for the door key behind her. 'I said, it went rather well.'

'Yes. Yes, it did.'

'You could say: *Congratulations*, Timothy. I'm *so* proud of you, Timothy.' He unlocked the house, and held the door open for her. 'Is that too much to ask? Melanie, we're home,' he called, steadying himself against the door frame.

Colleen hurried through, and busied herself in the kitchen as Timothy paid the babysitter: *Thank you, Dr Smith. How kind, how generous of you.* She recognised the girl's tone: deferential, adoring. It had been hers, once. He had made her feel special, noticed, just like the young girl clutching a fistful of shiny coins. Colleen put away the bowls and plates, one by one, wiping down surfaces that did not need cleaning. She tracked his movements: the front door closing after the girl, the key turning in the lock, the bolt sliding home. His shoes coming off, soles slapping on the terracotta tile floor. The ground-glass stopper of the whisky decanter. She heard the sound of Mrs H's television through the wall, the tinny canned laughter, muffled, mocking, free. Her heart fluttered in her chest like a bird in a cage. She stood in the pool of light at the centre of the dark kitchen, the weak bulb gilding her red hair. Waiting.

'Colleen,' he called softly. She clenched her fists. '*Colleen . . .*' She screwed her eyes closed. He padded down the hall sock-footed, stealthy. The heavy cut-glass tumbler rocked as he placed it on the kitchen table. Her breath was shallow, shaky. He took the hairpins from her chignon, placing them on the table one at a time. Pin by pin. He let the heavy curtain of her hair fall, clasped the end in his fist and twisted until he held her head back, her pale neck bent, exposed.

'Please, Timothy, don't . . .' she said, her hair tugging at the nape of her neck.

'Come to bed.' His other arm encircled her waist. Colleen stumbled as he pushed her, struggling, towards the hall.

'No,' she said, fighting back, her feet dangling in the air. She reached for the table, hairpins scattering, and grabbed one, gouging at his hand. Timothy cried out, releasing her. She backed against the sink, panting.

'What a foolish thing to do,' he said, his voice low and steady.

'I'll not have it, not anymore.' Colleen's voice shook. 'I'll leave, start again with the baby.'

He sucked at the back of his hand, stemming the blood. 'No. No you won't.' He stepped towards her, his gaze relentless, focused. 'Silly girl. Who do you think people will believe? A penniless teenage orphan or me, a pillar of the community?'

'They will. They will, I'll tell them.' Colleen blinked back tears, turned her head away as he stood before her, every cell in her body turning in on itself, shrinking from him. She squeezed past him, made for the stairs. 'I won't stay and let you hurt her the way you hurt me,' she said, pausing on the bottom step.

He caught at her arm. 'I would never hurt the child.' His eyes were dark, the pupils dilated. 'She is mine, a part of me. You really think you could give her any kind of life? You'd be on the streets, penniless; she would be taken from you.' Timothy stepped round the banister, eye to eye with Colleen. 'Don't you get it? You are nothing without me, you silly, silly girl.' His fingers dug into her arm, his mouth pressed hot against her ear. 'No one will ever love you the way I do. No one will ever care for someone like you.'

'Please, Timothy, don't—' She screwed her eyes closed, turning her face from him.

'No one will ever want you,' he said, throwing her down on the hard wooden stairs. The treads bruised her spine, her head, the weight of him on her pushed the air from her throat, choked with tears. She knew better than to fight now. If she lay still, it would be over soon. Colleen heard the tearing of fabric, felt the buckle of his trousers against her leg. 'You are mine, do you hear? I will never let you go.'

A kaleidoscope of lights sparked behind her eyes, a high-pitched whine sang in her ears from the blow. Her eyes flickered open in pain as he forced himself into her. Through the fanlight of the front door, she saw the full moon. She shut out the sound of his breath in her ear, the crushing weight of him, and imagined floating free. She remembered watching the moon landing with Mrs H the month before. Timothy had wanted to watch it with his cronies at the golf club, so Colleen had pretended to be unwell. The two women had stayed up, watching the grainy images, the light from the television glimmering across the face of the child sleeping peacefully between them on the sofa. Now, Colleen imagined what it would be like to step from Apollo 11 onto the moon, weightless and free. She wondered what it would be like to simply drift away.

10

Kenmare

'Do we have to use the house kitchen?' Darcy said, her eyelids trembling as a make-up artist applied a slick of smoky grey eyeliner. She was sitting in front of a brightly lit mirror in the trailer parked up in the driveway by the kitchen door. A generator hummed in the background, powering the lights and cameras being set up nearby. 'It feels so intrusive.'

'Lovey, what we are going for is simple, home-cooked food. The restaurant kitchen is Conor's territory, the test kitchen is too austere, and besides,' Tristan, the director, waved his hand airily as he squeezed into a canvas folding chair next to her, 'little Miss Dictator has the place set up like a factory line.' He nestled down in his blue Puffa jacket, pulling his baseball cap lower.

'Beatrice. Her name's Bea. And she's very good at her job,' Darcy said. *Unlike me.* Darcy felt like a phony. She was just waiting for someone to say 'What are you doing on a cookery show?'

'I suppose she must be a great help,' Tristan said. 'So organised. Really . . .' He searched for the word. 'Focused. Where did Di find her?'

'Jonny's funeral.' Darcy's eyes flickered open. 'Ma was paying her respects at the grave, and Miss Cupcake threw down a kitchen knife among the roses and the earth.'

'A knife?'

51

'It's what JJ wanted, apparently.' Darcy shrugged. 'Anyway, before Ma knew what was happening she had agreed to a meeting with Beatrice.'

'Determined little madam,' Tristan said. 'Still, a bit of competition is just what we need.' He gestured at one of the runners for a bottle of water. 'The rest of the shows have been filmed out on location with Di, cooking at different venues with the *Top Chef* contestants. But there's a nice continuity, filming here for the finale. Older viewers will recognise the bones of the place from Di's first show, and the younger ones – the ones who know you from your column . . .'

'Appetite?'

'Exactly. They will drool over your Belfast sink and Farrow and Ball woodwork.' Darcy heard the crinkle of a packet of pills. 'God, my head.' He took the water and knocked back a couple of paracetamol.

'It's just . . . you know, it's our home.'

'Relax, lovey,' he said. 'People will love you. You've got that whole sexy girl-next-door thing going, haven't you? You're not as scary as your mother,' he whispered. 'Women could imagine hanging out with you for a coffee or a cocktail or two, and their husbands won't mind watching you because you're . . .' He waved his hand and she pinched the bridge of her nose. 'Want one of these?' He shook the packet of pills.

'No, thanks, I'm fine.' She smiled wanly. 'I just feel like it's a mistake. I'm nothing special, you know. Ma and Conor are great cooks. I'm just – well, I'm just me. I'm still learning. I keep expecting someone to pull me aside and say it's all a mistake.'

'Nonsense.' Tristan checked his notes. 'Good. We've got all the menus. What are you cooking for your pudding?'

'Apple pie and homemade vanilla ice-cream.'

'Perfect. We can do a few shots of you in the orchard, then wrapping up the apples in brown paper to lay down in the cellars. You probably remember from watching your ma when you were little, but we do it all twice – a master shot of you looking gorgeous, cooking, and then we'll do it all again for the gastroporn shot, close up and sexily lit. Everything gets spliced together and hey presto – another hit.' He leant over and pecked her on the cheek.

'You've done all the shows for Ma, haven't you?'

'Hm?' Tristan peered up over his red half-moon glasses. 'Yes, lovey, I was a friend of your dad's. We wanted to get her on TV for years, but she only agreed a short time before he died. I don't know why. Maybe they needed the financial security.' Tristan shrugged. 'I've been with Di since the first show.' He laughed, softly. 'I admire her; your mother is a re-markable woman, don't get me wrong, but there were times when I could have throttled her. Not to mention Kavanagh . . .' Tristan shook his head. 'Lord, your dad could drink. Colos-sal hangovers. Not that you'd know from looking at the first shows – it was all very *Good Life* with the hens and pigs.' His face softened. 'I remember you as an ankle biter, later on, after we lost Kavanagh. We got some lovely shots of you toddling around in your dungarees and bunches, all very wholegrain and boho.' He folded his arms. 'What we need to decide now is your USP, food-wise.'

'My US-what?'

'What makes you stand out from all the other chefs. Con's Mr Rock 'n' Roll Michelin stars, Bea has that whole vintage shabby chic, baking and bunting thing going on, and you . . . What are you?'

'I'm . . . God, I don't know.'

'Just be yourself, lovey. We'll figure it out. Relax, and let me work my magic. We'll soon see if you've got it or not. The camera and editing will amplify bits of you, of course – what goes out won't be "you" but it will be a . . .'

'Mask? A product? A brand?'

'If you're lucky.'

'Lucky?'

He rubbed his thumb against his fingers. 'Frozen foods, supermarket endorsements, cookware, column in one of the Sunday supplements—' Darcy groaned and closed her eyes. 'Don't knock it, lovey. How do you think Di has kept the Castle on the road all these years? You need to think about the future.' He dragged on a menthol e-cigarette. 'This will be my last series. I feel like one of those cops in the films, about to retire.'

'Whatever you do, don't show me a picture of your partner . . .'

Tristan laughed, and mimed being shot. At shouts from the kitchen, he jumped up. 'Madame is here.'

'Tristan?' Diana's voice boomed from the house.

'Here, Di,' Tristan said, widening his eyes at Darcy. 'Right, let's get this show on the road. Break a leg. Not literally.'

'Are we all set?' Diana said, clambering into the trailer.

'More or less, darling. We just need to zhush up the kitchen a bit. It will photograph better once the location guys have done their thing. They're giving it a quick tidy up and putting up some bunting—'

'Over my dead body,' Diana said.

'Trust me, all the kids love it. And it's a nod to Bumble Bee's YouTube channel. Nothing permanent, just dressing it, darling, giving it a bit of a spruce up to appeal to her audience.' He checked his clipboard. 'How long until Darcy is ready?'

'Ten, fifteen? Just got to get her in hair,' the make-up woman said.

'Anyone for cupcakes?' Beatrice poked her head through the door of the trailer, carrying a red polka-dot tray of cakes. 'I've baked far too many. But then you can never have enough cake,' she said, laughing.

'Ooh, yes please.' The women gathered round the tray.

'Tempt you?' Beatrice said to Tristan, her gaze steady, flirtatious.

'Not my cup of tea, if you get my drift, love.' He jumped

down from the trailer, heading for the kitchen with Diana.

'Everything going OK?' Beatrice asked Darcy.

'Yeah, fine,' she said, her foot jiggling. 'Just not good at sitting still for so long.'

Beatrice squatted down beside Darcy and took her hand. 'Are you OK?'

'I'm fine. Just a bit nervous.'

'You'll be great. You just need to relax. It's all an act, you know. You look amazing, really fresh.' Beatrice lowered her face until it was side by side with Darcy's in the mirror. 'Look, we could be sisters. Like that fairy story – snow white, rose red.' Darcy caught a flicker of something in Beatrice's expression, and her gut tightened. Then Beatrice smiled and poked her tongue out. 'Sure you're OK?'

'Really, I'm fine.' Darcy gestured at a small compressor on the counter. 'If I look good, it's thanks to this – I think they use it for airbrushing old bangers when they're not doing foundation.' The make-up woman ushered Darcy over to the hairdresser, settling her in the chair. The young man released the large foam rollers in Darcy's hair, smoothing down the glossy curls into an elegant long bob.

'Maybe I should cut my hair,' Beatrice said quietly. 'What do you think?'

'It would suit you,' the hairdresser said. 'Mia Farrow crop? With your bone structure it would be great.' He shook a can of spray. 'Right, Darce, a quick blast and you're ready to go.' She held her breath, screwing her eyes closed. 'Come on, let's get you to the set.'

Darcy paused by the door of the trailer as a text message buzzed through. 'I'll just be a minute,' she said to the hairdresser. It was drizzling, so she stepped back silently inside to read the message. She paused. Beatrice was sitting in the chair, watching herself impassively in the mirror, leaning closer, fascinated by her reflection. Beatrice bit her lip, frowning, but then her face stilled as naturally as clouds passing over the sun. Beatrice picked up a fine pair of scissors and let down her hair, the gold hanks tumbling over her shoulders. She began to cut, hair falling silently to the floor, snip, snip, snip. She turned her head from side to side, jerkily, checking the length was right.

'My god, what have you done?' the hairdresser said, pushing past Darcy, who backed away quietly. He threw down the cape Darcy had been wearing. 'They need you on set in a few minutes.'

'Finish it off,' Darcy heard Beatrice say.

'What?'

Darcy was out of sight, but she could see from the reflection in the mirror that Beatrice had turned to face the hairdresser. 'I said, finish it off.'

'I'm not here to give you freebies,' he said.

'If you know what is good for you, you will cut my hair to look exactly like that,' Beatrice said, gesturing at the test Polaroids of Darcy's hair.

'Are you threatening me?' The hairdresser put his hands on his hips.

'I'm saying if you want to keep this contract, you will do exactly what I tell you to do. One word to Diana, and you are out of here.' She handed over the scissors. 'Come on. I haven't got all day.' She eyed the crotch of his jeans, and looked up holding his gaze. 'If you're lucky, I might just give you a freebie in return.'

Darcy backed away from the trailer, and ran towards the kitchen.

'What's the craic?' Conor said, pausing by the kitchen door. He had a fresh black apron tied over his white T-shirt and chef's trousers, and wore a new pair of trainers. Darcy looked up at the sound of his voice. She wore the same apron over a white V-neck T-shirt, and faded blue jeans rolled up at the ankle. A pair of silver Birkenstocks finished her outfit, revealing blue toenails. The kitchen was rigged with lights and silver umbrellas, the freshly scrubbed island brightly lit now, a bowl of lemons and pots of fresh herbs shining. A fresh apple pie steamed on a wire rack, and the cameraman focused tightly on the pudding as one of the home economists cut it with a silver slice. In the background, another assistant was weighing out three sets of ingredients ready for filming the next segment.

'It's nuts, Con,' Darcy said quietly as she walked over to him. This is only for the introduction, and it's taking hours. 'I've got a stunt double cutting pies for me, now. I can't believe how long everything takes. A day and a half for a thirty-minute programme?'

'Away with you, your ma has it down to half that time,' he said. 'Of course you need a stunt double. Can't be trusting you with sharp objects now, can we? Ow!' Conor laughed as Darcy elbowed him in the ribs. He leant against the doorframe, his arm shielding her.

'I was rubbish, Con.' She bit at her lip.

'Have a glass of wine. It always worked for Floyd.'

'I just couldn't get the words out.' Darcy rubbed the bridge of her nose, and glanced down at her fingers, smearing the greasy make-up between her thumb and forefinger.

'Hey, relax,' he said, 'they just want you to be yourself.' She looked up at him. 'You're a knockout, Darce. They'll love you.'

'Con – you haven't seen Kato, have you?' Diana called as she strode past.

'That ratbag? No,' he said, shaking his head. 'You know what cats are like. He'll come home when he's ready.'

'I'm sure you're right.'

'We're ready for you, Darcy,' Tristan said, checking the shot. 'Shall we try again? Let's have a go with the apples.'

'Ooh – peeling apples now, are we?' Conor said to her. 'You can nail that, no problem.'

'Think you could do a better job?' she said, laughing.

'I know I could.'

'Come on then,' she said, beckoning him to follow her. 'Tris, can we try this with the two of us?'

'Sure,' he said, looking up from the camera, and stepping aside for the cameraman. 'Darcy, I don't want you to go further across than the kitchen island, OK? Con, you're good where you are. Ready? And, action.'

'Let me guess, Darce,' Conor said, 'it's going to have strawberries in.'

'Am I that predictable?' she said, putting her hands on her hips. She waited for him to look at her, and smiled. The moment he looked up at her from beneath his black curls, her nerves fell away. 'There might be a hot fruit salad involved.'

'See?' he said, pulling a blue and white bandana from his back pocket, and tying it around his forehead. 'Where do you want me?' He glanced at her out of the corner of his eye and grinned.

'Behave, will you?' she said, wagging a paring knife at him. Conor raised his hands.

'How are they?' Diana whispered in Tristan's ear as they chatted on.

'Wonderful,' he murmured. 'They've lit up like Christmas. Watch how she's looking at him. There's so much chemistry you could bottle it.'

'Started without me, have you?' Beatrice said as she swept into shot, carrying a bowl of eggs.

'Buggery bugger, trouble in paradise,' Tristan whispered. 'Cut to Conor,' he told the cameraman.

'These were freshly laid this morning,' Beatrice said, manoeuvring herself between Conor and Darcy.

'Haven't you been busy,' Conor said, not missing a beat. He glanced down at Beatrice's shoes. 'You're never cooking in those heels, are you? Look,' he said, beckoning to the cameraman. 'Can you see this?' The camera panned down to the floor, focusing on Beatrice's stilettos, the red soles picking up the tea roses on her dress.

'I can do anything you can in heels—'

'And backwards?' Darcy said, not looking up from the chopping board. Her knife flashed as she diced the apples.

'Just what I was going to say.' Beatrice's smile didn't budge an inch.

'Two's company . . .' Tristan said softly. 'And cut,' he called, signalling to the cameraman.

Conor reached round Darcy and picked up a strawberry, winking as he walked away.

'Talking of cuts,' Darcy said to Beatrice, wiping her hands on a clean linen cloth, 'nice haircut.'

'Do you like it?' Beatrice said, cupping the shoulder-length curl. 'Just thought he did such a fabulous job with yours.'

'Everything OK, girls?' Diana said, striding over to them.

'Couldn't be better,' Beatrice said, sauntering away, the petticoats of her full skirt whispering.

'Ma—' Darcy began to say.

'Yes?'

Darcy frowned as she watched Beatrice's silhouette in the doorway. 'Nothing. It's probably nothing.'

11

London

1969

'I'll take these, please,' Colleen said, breathing in the rich incense of the stargazer lilies. 'Can you deliver them this afternoon?' The bruises on her skull throbbed and her spine ached as she leant over the counter and scribbled down an address for the florist.

'Would you like to include a note?' The woman tore off a length of brown paper to wrap the lilies.

Colleen picked out a simple 'Thank you' card, and printed with a shaking hand: *Mrs H, for everything x.*

'What about ribbon?' The florist said.

'I'm sorry?' Colleen looked up in confusion and the woman gestured at the row of spooled ribbons. She thought of Mrs H, the soft pink sunlit tones of her home. 'Pink, she likes pink.' Colleen clicked open her purse and emptied some coins onto the polished wood counter.

'Wait,' the florist said as she walked away, 'that's too much.'

'Don't worry, I have to go,' Colleen said, shouldering open the door, the bell chiming above her. The sound of her daughter's cries greeted her on the pavement and she pushed her way through the gaggle of women outside the florist, cowering beneath their disapproving glances and clucks. They reminded her of a group of plump hens, fussing and chattering around the pram. 'Excuse me,' she said, swinging the carriage around.

'Shouldn't be allowed – fancy leaving her in this state,' one of them said. 'Poor little mite.'

In Chelsea Post Office, Colleen slipped the signed copy of *Italian Food* out of a large envelope, and ran her fingertips over the cover before putting it back and sealing it in. She checked the address one last time, and clasped it to her chest with one hand, rocking the pram with the other. *Please stop,* she thought, anxiety clutching at her stomach. The baby raged on, its breath catching.

'Why don't you go ahead, my dear?' An elderly gentleman ushered her to the front of the queue. 'It sounds like someone needs to get home.'

'Thank you. I'm so sorry.' Colleen's heart skipped in her chest, and she fumbled as she handed over the money for postage.

She wheeled the pram on towards the door.

'Doesn't she ever stop?' A woman said. 'She's hungry, aren't you?' She leant towards the baby.

'Please!' Colleen cried out. 'I can manage.'

'Your first, is it?' The woman pursed her lips. 'I was just trying to help.'

'Thank you. We're fine,' she said, wheeling the pram out on to the street. 'It will all be fine.'

Colleen walked faster and faster, past the Town Hall, not really seeing now as she cut across familiar roads, passing faceless people, the noise of the traffic, the child's cries fading. All she heard was her own uneven breath, the song of her blood in her ears. The pram bumped and lurched over the paving stones on Chelsea Bridge Road. She could smell the river now, felt the shimmering heat of the day radiating from the road. Colleen jogged across the Embankment, and in the middle of the bridge she took a note from the bag, pinning it to the baby's blanket. The river surged full beneath them.

Colleen lifted the child, rigid with fury, into her arms, and

61

held her close, her eyes closed. 'I'm sorry,' she whispered, her throat tight with tears. 'It's better this way.' Colleen breathed in the scent of her child. 'I love you, remember that. Whatever he tells you. I'm sorry I wasn't good enough.' She lowered the baby into the pram, and strapped her securely in. The traffic trundled on, to and fro, oblivious, the noise of a red Routemaster bus changing gear, someone ringing the bell, fading. Colleen felt quite still, far away. It was like someone else took off her black coat, unpinned her felt hat. The breeze felt marvellous. She raised her face to the sun, and closed her eyes. At the sound of a church bell tolling, she slipped off her patent shoes and clambered over the edge of the bridge, the metal cool beneath her stockinged feet. Before anyone could reach her, she was gone.

12

Kenmare

'Light my fire,' Conor sang, stamping his dusty biker boot up onto the Marshall amp. His chef's whites hung loose, and a blue and white bandana kept his wild black curls back from his eyes. The pub was packed, noisy and joyous, the younger crowd standing in front of the tiny stage in the back room where Conor and some of the lads from the kitchen were playing, singing along, while the older customers lined the walls on settles and benches, nursing their pints. Conor jumped down into the crowd, making straight for Diana. The cameras zoomed in and she played along, singing the chorus with the girls at her side. Over by the bar, Tristan watched, grim faced. Beatrice was dancing at the front of the crowd, arms in the air, a cut-off T-shirt revealing a voluptuous, curved waist.

'Chameleon girl,' Tristan said to Darcy, watching her.

'What do you mean?' Darcy said, raising her voice over the noise.

'All things to all people, haven't you noticed? Mask after mask—'

'You're exaggerating. She's just trying to fit in.'

'Darling, most people assume everyone else is like them, thinks like them, feels like them, and they project their own feelings and emotions on to them. It's why so many relationships don't work – people fall in love with who they think someone is – but can they stay in love once the idea strips away?' Tristan gestured at Beatrice. 'I've been watching her in action. I know Di thinks she's fabulous, but I've met people like her before. Strip her away and there's nothing there, trust me.'

Diana pushed her way through the crowd towards them. 'Surely that's enough for tonight, Tris? Can't we all relax?'

'Yes, lovey. Let's call it a night,' he said, signalling to the cameraman. 'We got some good footage of Con doing his Jim Morrison bit.' Tristan's face lit up. 'Fergus, you old devil, how are you?' A bear-like man with a mop of silver hair loomed towards them.

'Good God, it's bucketing down out there.' Fergus swept his damp fringe from his face. He towered over Tristan, and clapped him on the back, planting a kiss on his forehead.

'You've met Darcy, have you?' Tristan said, and Fergus stepped back to look at her.

'Is this your girl, Di? This beauty?' Fergus flung his arms wide open and embraced Darcy, lifting her from the ground in a bear hug. The air squeezed from her in an irresistible vice of soft flannel shirt, tweed and good soap.

'Put her down, Fergus, the poor girl can't breathe,' Diana said.

'Why, it's good to meet you at last, Darcy,' he said. 'Your mother's told me so much about you.' Darcy noticed the familiar way his hand rested lightly on Diana's waist. It was on the tip of her tongue to say *she's told me nothing about you*, but something in her mother's eyes stopped her.

'Fergus took over the antiques shop in town a few months back,' Diana said. 'After you left for London, and the States.'

'Can I get you both a drink?' Darcy said, waving a euro note at the barman.

'I won't hear of it,' Fergus said, beckoning to him. 'Niall, run a tab will you? What can we get you, Darcy?'

'Vodka and soda, please.'

'Diana will have a half of the black stuff and I'll have a pint and a packet of Taytos. Cabernet Sauvignon for Tris, make it a big one,' he added. 'Conor?' he bellowed down the bar, above the noise of the crowd. Conor squeezed his way through and shook Fergus's hand. 'What'll you be having? Soda?'

'Thanks,' Conor said, looking down at Darcy. Close to she felt the warmth of him through the thin cotton of her dress, smelt the heat of his skin, the fresh sweat.

'You were great,' she said. He leant closer to hear what she was saying. 'I'd forgotten what a good voice you had.' But she hadn't. She had never forgotten seeing him sing when she was nine. He was quicker back then, angrier. There was an urgent electrical quality to him, like the air before a storm. He had held the crowd in the palm of his hand pacing the stage, all leather trousers and bracelets, the most exotic, dangerous man she had ever seen. She remembered the women scream-ing, but he had only had eyes for one of them, the woman who would become his wife. Darcy remembered sitting on the bar, drinking lemonade, and how she wished one day someone would kiss her the way he kissed that girl from town.

Beatrice pushed her way through the crowd towards them. 'That was amazing!' she said, gazing up at Conor.

'Thanks, it's just a bit of craic, you know,' he said, glancing at Darcy. 'Lets off some steam for me and the boys.' He winced, stretching out his shoulder. Up on the stage a group of OAPs were tuning up their instruments, and people started clear-ing aside tables and chairs to make space for the dancing. 'See, we're just the warm-up act.'

'Come on, let me buy you a drink. What's your poison?' Beatrice smiled.

'I'm good thanks,' he said, passing the Guinness to Diana and Fergus. 'My man here's got me a soda water in.'

'Come on, you're not driving!' Beatrice laughed.

'Con has an early start,' Darcy said. 'We all do.' She checked with the barman which of the drinks was hers as he placed two identical-looking glasses on the bar, and took a sip.

'There's no need to make excuses for me.' Con scowled at Beatrice. 'I'm off the drink. This,' he said, sweeping his hand across the bar, 'is literally poison to me. I'm an alcoholic. So yes, just a soda water please.'

'Sorry,' Beatrice said, 'how was I to know?' As Conor turned away, her expression changed, a smile playing across her lips. Darcy was deep in conversation with Tristan, and when no one was looking, Beatrice switched the two glasses on the bar.

Darcy picked up the nearest glass to her, and took a sip, leaning in to Tristan. Just as she realised it was the wrong drink, Conor spat out the mouthful of vodka and soda. 'Jaysus,' he said. 'Darce, you took the wrong drink.'

'I didn't, I'm sure—' she said, frowning. She handed him the glass.

'Maybe you think it's funny?'

'No,' she said, flushing. 'I wouldn't do that.'

'Easy mistake to make,' Beatrice said, smiling. 'No harm done, is there? Not like one little sip will set you on the road to ruin?'

Conor took a swig of his water and set the glass down. 'What would you know?' He raised his chin to Fergus. 'Fancy a spot of fishing one morning next week?'

'Sounds like a grand plan,' Fergus said.

'Moody, isn't he?' Beatrice said quietly to Darcy, watching Conor push his way out of the pub just as the fiddle player struck up a tune. Darcy ignored her, and went after Conor.

'Lovey, may I have a word?' Tristan said over the music and singing, leaning towards Beatrice. She turned to him. 'I saw you,' he said. 'I saw you switch the glasses.' Her smile didn't falter, only her gaze hardened. 'Don't mess with these people. I care about them, OK? For whatever reason, Di wants to give you a chance, but my gut instinct is that's a mistake. However, I will do everything I can to make sure the filming goes as smoothly as possible for her and I'm not going to tell Diana what I saw.' He pointed his finger. 'But watch your step. I've known people like you before, and I am keeping my eye on you, do you understand?'

'Conor?' Darcy walked into the darkness, waiting for her eyes to adjust. She could see the dark figure of a man up ahead, recognised his powerful stride. She ran after him. 'Conor, wait!' He stopped walking.

'It's been a long day, Darce.'

'Look, I'm sorry. It was a mistake, OK?' Darcy stopped a few steps from him, caught her breath. 'I think it's amazing what you've done, Ma told me.'

'What I've done?' He cupped his hand over the end of a cigarette, and lit it, exhaling. 'You know what I'm thinking now? Would it hurt, really? Would it hurt to go back in there and order a pint or two, or maybe a wee drop of Bushmills? Would it hurt to really relax?'

'You know the answer to that.'

'I know, I know,' he said. She couldn't make out his face at this distance, but she could hear the frustration in his voice. 'It's like a hunger, Darce, gnawing away at me.'

'Conor . . .' She stepped towards him, touched his arm.

'Look, I'm going home. I'm knackered, and my back is killing me.'

'You should see someone.'

'Nah, show me a chef whose back isn't banjaxed.' He laughed. 'Go on with you, go back and have some fun. You always enjoyed a good ceilidh when you were a kid.'

Oh God, is that still how he thinks of me? A kid? Darcy looked at the ground. 'Sure you don't want me to walk back with you?' she said. 'Just in case you need someone to lean on?'

'Give me a break, I'm not ready for a Zimmer frame just yet.'

'If you're sure?' She longed to walk beside him in the quiet and the dark, with only the rush of the stream and the lap of the water in the night around them.

'Get on with you.' He stooped down and kissed her on the cheek. 'Night, Darce, sweet dreams.' She watched him walk alone into the darkness, the silhouette of the Castle up ahead against the silent, silver bay. *Look back*, she willed him. *Look back at me.*

13

Darcy gave up trying to sleep, and ran herself a bath. She sank back into the water, submerging, holding her breath. She walked her feet up the chrome pipe of the shower, the arches flexing, lean tanned calves extended. She lay flat on the floor of the bath, feeling the tension in her body unravel in the hot water. Darcy surfaced, and wiped her face with her hands. She hugged her knees, looking back towards the narrow single bed in her old schoolgirl bedroom. *Not like the films, is it?* she thought, wondering idly what Diana had done with all her childhood toys and posters. *Only been gone a year and Ma has hijacked my room.* Half the room was now taken up with boxes of foreign editions of Diana's books.

Darcy wrapped a towel around herself, and walked over to the window, drying her hair. She flung open the window halfway up the tower of the Castle, and a cool, delicious breeze embraced her. It was raining, and she listened to the pattering of drops on the leaves beneath her, the rush of water heading down to the bay. Darcy looked out across the moonlit hills towards the lake – her lake, as she thought of it, hidden from view by the dark woods. She missed her small apartment in Berkeley, the life she had just begun to carve out for herself, but she was happy to be back. She had always loved the Castle at night, the silver magic of the light on the water, the peaceful rooms sleeping. She thought of Conor. *Is he asleep now?* Darcy smiled. Beneath her, she saw the bedroom light go out in his cottage.

She thought of the filming that lay ahead the next day, of going through the motions, pretending to be the perfect family, in the perfect home. She had seen the figures, the mortgages, the bills, the wages. *Got to keep the show on the road, that's what Ma said.* She would do it, for them, and then once Diana was better she could choose whether she was going to stay, or go home to Berkeley. *It's not too much to ask, is it? Just a chance to be happy, that's all.* She laid the flat of her palm above her belly button, felt it rise and fall as she breathed. *I want to be happy.*

She felt the steady sleeping heart of the Castle beating in the night. In the basement, the dusty bottles of Diana's famous twenty-year-old essences waited patiently, dark vanilla pods macerating in vodka. Jars of jam and pickles gleamed like jewels on their shelves in the pantry, clean linen lay folded in on itself, contented, lavender fresh in the laundry. The wound clocks ticked on, marking the hours, and the warm radiators hissed, breathing and grumbling while the fire glimmered on in the empty hall. Darcy knew every stretch and crack of the timbers in the house, from the cellar to the silent loop of the bats around the jolly roger still flying from the battlements. It smelt exactly the same. Damp dog and wool, mustiness and waxed jackets, wet earth and bonfires. She knew at that moment that however far she travelled, this was home.

In the morning she set about making more space for herself in the bedroom, stacking heavy boxes of German and American editions of Diana's cookbooks. Among the boxes, Darcy found a trunk of childhood mementos that her mother had packed up when she left. She flicked through the old school books, tattered rosettes from pony shows and faded certificates for swimming widths and lengths. In the bottom of the box she found her old yellow Walkman, a C90 tape still inside. She clicked the batteries out of the alarm clock on the bedside table, and slipped them into the casing, and tried it, smiling as the opening bars of an old REM track crackled into life.

She jogged downstairs, grabbing a trowel and basket from the boot room, and walked to the kitchen garden, her feet falling in time to the tune. It was early still, mist rising off the hills, and she was alone. She had always loved the walled garden. Neat rows of produce and raised beds of herbs lined the earth. She walked along the paths, breathing in the smell of cool soil, the sweet air. She had decided to make a gratin to go with the Sunday roast, and stopped beside the potatoes. She dug gently, easing them from the earth, brushing them clear with her palm, and tossing them into the trug. She was lost in the music, and remembering, and the simple pleasure of digging in the earth. As she worked her way around the garden gathering a fresh onion, garlic, a handful of parsley, the sun rose and she looked up in surprise at the sound of church bells between tracks.

'Are you not off to Mass, then?'

'My God,' she said, hooking the headphones around her neck. 'Conor, you made me jump.' She placed her palm flat against her chest and laughed. 'You've not been running again?'

'It's getting to be a habit,' he said, catching his breath. 'Sorry for startling you, I just wanted to apologise for last night.' He squatted down beside her, and picked up a pod of peas from the trug, shucking them. 'I was out of order, I'm sorry,' he said, popping the peas one at a time into his mouth.

'Apologise? There's nothing to apologise for.'

'I didn't need to jump down your throat.' He offered her the pod of peas, and she sat back to look at him. 'You were just being kind, and your ma's not the only one around here who finds accepting help difficult.' He looked at his hands. 'It's all still new, you know. It's all right when you're in the clinic and they're taking care of you like a baby, but when you're out . . .'

He glanced up, uncertain. 'I'm wary of everything. I mean, I hadn't had a drink for six months, and now what do I say? Do I go back to one day?'

'Did you swallow?' He laughed, but she felt the tension in him. 'I think you just say what you want,' Darcy said. 'Who are you proving something to, except yourself?'

'When did you get so wise?' He tossed the pea pod into the basket and stood, stretching. 'Shouldn't you be off to church?'

'Yeah, I'll run down now. What about you?'

Conor shook his head. 'Your ma gave up on me years ago. This is my communion and my prayers,' he said, waving his arm across the garden. 'My God's here, right now, in the earth and the sky. Why would I want to be indoors on a morning like this?'

'Fair enough.'

'Don't be missing the choir. That's how your ma met Fergus, you know?'

'Ah, I wondered about that. I take it they're . . .'

'Lovers?' Conor laughed. 'Yeah, I don't know how serious she is, but he's fallen hard for her. She's never got over losing your dad, that's what I reckon. It's a shame, he's a good man if she'd only let him into her heart.'

'I don't remember Fergus. I mean, from when I was a kid.'

'He moved here a few months ago, took over the antiques place in town. You should go and have a look, he's got some amazing stuff. I spend a fortune every time I call in.' Con glanced at her. 'I'm building a place not far from here.'

'Really? That's exciting.'

'Yeah, it's all very well living in one of the estate cottages but you never feel like you get away, you know, for your sins? I bought a bit of land from the estate, a bit further out. It feels time for a fresh start.' He stood and cricked out his back. 'Better get on, I'm doing lunch today.' He tilted his head, looking down at her. 'So what are you cooking for Di?'

'Nothing complicated,' she said, blushing. 'Roast beef, gratin of potatoes, fresh peas. It's a bit simple, compared to your stuff.'

'Sounds perfect to me.'

'It's amazing what you've done with the garden here,' she said. 'At Chez Panisse we only used the best organic, local food, you know.'

'You can't get more local than this. What, ten paces from the garden to the kitchen?' He looked around the tidy rows of vegetables, his face softening. 'That's the secret, you know? Let the ingredients lead the way, see what's at its peak each day, and write the menu around that.' He squatted down beside her again. 'Good food isn't complicated. Don't think it needs to be. It's about kindness, and generosity, and making people welcome. Use your imagination. Take the best ingredients you can, and take your time.'

'Slow food?'

'Exactly. Let the ingredients shine.'

She looked at the vegetables in the basket. 'It's kind of like I'm looking for the magic ingredient, you know?'

'The one that will make it all right?' He smiled. 'You're just looking for home like the rest of us, Darce.'

'Listen, would you let me cook for you tonight?'

'Tonight?' he raised his eyebrows.

'Don't worry,' she looked down at her hands, rubbing the earth from her palms, 'I'm sure you're busy, I just wanted to try this gratin out on you, too. I was thinking of cooking it for the show.'

'No, I'd love that,' he said. 'I'm taking Chris fishing this afternoon, so with any luck we'll have a salmon or trout and a bit of watercress to go with it.' He rolled his shoulders, and checked his watch. 'Right, better get on. See you at the cottage about six?' he said, jogging backwards before turning and breaking into a run.

*

73

Darcy picked her bike up from where it leant against the warm brick of the kitchen wall, and freewheeled down the Castle driveway. Terracotta pots frothed with lavender and alyssum, perfuming the air with the scent of honey at the edge of the car park, and sunlight filtered through the rustling green leaves of the trees lining the drive.

She cycled down a narrow path frothing with ferns, a patchwork tunnel of leaves shifting above her in the amber evening sun. She passed a couple of pastel-coloured cottages, with undulating roofs of warm tiles. In a gateway, Darcy paused to look back at the Castle. She could hear a lawn-mower somewhere, caught the scent of fresh cut grass on the air. A steady stream of cars snaked their way along the main road, pulling off at the turning. She could see the tower, the house, the walled gardens beyond, the stable block. *Home*, she thought. *Or is it?*

Darcy cycled on down the steep hill towards the bay, dragonflies and butterflies tumbling in the rosy evening sky above the hedges. She could make out the boundary of the Castle's estate, see the sheep and dairy herds kept on their land by local farmers. The restaurant was a beating heart that drew people to the town, filled the B&Bs, kept a steady stream of customers for the stores and petrol station, and put donations in the church box. She realised what it was her mother was fighting for.

The trees reached out to one another across the path, and she sped noiselessly through a dappled tunnel of green light, the sky opening above her. She threw down her bike on the grass beside Conor's truck, and glanced at his gleaming Triumph motorbike and sidecar as she walked on through the long grass of the meadow. Crimson poppies swayed among the golden stalks, and the hillside hummed in the silence – insects, bees, the distant sound of a tractor somewhere. It was still and quiet, birds calling above the long yellow grass. Darcy shielded her eyes and looked up at the keening sound of a bird.

'Grey wagtail, I think,' Conor said, walking out of the shadows of the trees, his dog at his side.

'How do you know?' Darcy said, smiling.

'You see them down by the rivers when you're fishing,' he said, and stopped just in front of her in the meadow. He hooked his thumbs in the belt loops of a pair of faded khakis, the breeze billowing against his old white linen shirt. 'Reckon you've cracked it?' he said, nodding at the covered bowl in Darcy's hands.

'No complaints from Ma, but then no praise either.'

'What's new?' He smiled and took the bowl from her.

'We'll see what you think.' She walked at his side towards the cottage. 'How was lunch?'

'A bit slow. Sunday lunch crowd, but no complaints.' He flexed his hand, and Darcy saw a fresh burn among the scars of many years. She took his hand in hers, inspected the wound on the fleshy part of his palm.

'You should put something on that,' she said.

'I did, came off while we were fishing.' The small blond boy ran from the cottage to greet them. 'Chris, Darcy's brought us some supper.'

'Did you catch anything?' she asked him.

'Yes, it's huge,' Chris said, flinging his arms open wide.

'Might be a bit of an exaggeration,' Conor said, ushering her inside. Their rods were standing in the cottage's porch beside a pair of waders, drying in the evening sun. 'I hope you won't be disappointed.'

Darcy glanced at the simple round table by the galley kitchen. It was laid for three. Conor put the gratin in the oven to warm through, and whistled. The old greyhound loped through from the meadow, and nudged his hand with his snout.

'Hello, Jake,' Darcy said, reaching out her hand so that the dog could give her an exploratory sniff in his own time. 'What happened to his leg?'

'Accident of some sort. They didn't know at the refuge.' The hound looked at them both before retreating to the deck overlooking the river, nimbly hopping down to the grass on three legs. 'We haven't been together too long, but he's a good dog.' Conor folded his arms. 'It was . . . well, it was a bit lonely when I came back. God knows, even when you're fighting like cats and dogs it's company, you know. When Alannah left, she took Chris with her at first.'

'But the courts gave you custody? Isn't that unusual? They must have thought you were the best option?'

'Something like that. Poor Chris, couple of kids for parents, I tell you.' He uncorked a bottle of Sancerre, and raised it just at the moment Darcy pulled a bottle of elderflower cordial from her bag. 'Will you have a glass?'

'Are you sure?'

'I can't drink it, but I can enjoy watching you,' he said.

'Thank you.' Darcy took it from him, and waited as he poured a glass of cordial for himself. 'We should make a toast.'

'To new beginnings.'

'New beginnings.'

'The salmon's ready, if you are?' Conor reached over for a bowl of salad. 'Would you give this a toss?'

'Does everything you say sound like an innuendo?' Darcy trickled olive oil across the leaves.

'Nah, you just have a dirty mind.' He threw her a bottle of wine vinegar, and padded outside. Darcy smiled to herself as she washed her hands. She coated the watercress leaves with the oil and vinegar using her fingers, making sure each leaf was covered. From outside, she heard the sound of a griddle shaking down, the lid of a barbecue clanging shut. Conor carried through the grill, and turned the salmon out onto a platter.

'My favourite,' she said. 'I haven't had fish this fresh for years.'

'Simple, three-ingredient high – fish, lemon, butter. Perfect.

I always reckon the taste is tied up with the weather and the air, you know. Today was a good day.' He looked at her. 'Is a good day. Come and sit down,' he said, taking the plates to the table.

Darcy looked out through the open doors to the river. 'It's so peaceful here.'

'I think we both like being by water.'

'Thank you,' she said, taking a piece of sourdough bread. 'Don't tell me you had time to bake this yourself too. I'll start to get an inferiority complex.' She hesitated. 'You didn't, did you?'

'Nah, we stopped off at the Bridge Street Co-op,' Conor said, laughing.

'Thank God,' Darcy said. 'I thought you were perfect for a minute.'

'Me, perfect? Aren't you meant to be the new domestic goddess?'

Darcy put down her fork and sat back. 'That didn't last long, did it?'

'You didn't think I could resist looking you up, did you? I had no idea I was working with an internet star.'

Darcy laughed and ran her hand through her hair, shaking her head. 'No. I'm no star. The writing was just starting to take off in the States, that's all. My flatmate, Lyn, works at a publisher. She liked the columns I'd written for a few sites, and showed it to a friend of hers who publishes cookbooks. She got me a book deal . . .'

'Hit TV series here, cookbook in the US? If you're not a star, you're going to be one.' Conor watched her as she sipped her wine. 'Did I say the wrong thing?'

'No, no, it's fine.' She felt him waiting for her to talk. 'I just – I mean, it's great being back but I hate all the filming. Is that awful and ungrateful?'

'Not at all.'

'It was different, before. I was always in the background,

with Ma. Sure, I can cook basic restaurant food, or at least I'm learning to. It was hard not to learn when watching Ma.' Darcy paused. 'I knew she always wanted me to take on the Castle so it was always understood that eventually I'd train, and come back, but . . .'

'Go on.'

'When she brought you in to run the restaurant, I managed to dodge a bullet. You were so successful for such a long time, she forgot about me.' Darcy raked her hand through her hair. 'It hasn't been easy lately. I did something stupid, messed up, big time.'

'In the States? Darce,' he said gently, 'if it makes you feel any better I have more baggage than Lost Property at Connolly Station.' He took a sip of his cordial, and beckoned for Chris to come to the table. 'As much as I hate it, Di's right. It's time for a new approach. Fresh blood. Everyone's had enough of all the swagger, with the chefs pissed half the time, effing and blinding at the staff.'

'But when you're cooking at your level, the kitchen is like a pressure cooker,' Darcy said. 'They made you look a lot worse than you are. I mean, you never actually reduced anyone to tears – you didn't humiliate them, not like some of the others.'

'People loved it. The first series is on repeat in half of Asia, still,' Conor said, taking some of the fish off the bone for Chris. 'But the thing is, when they turned up last year to film the final episode of my last series, I was too drunk, too stoned, too . . . whatever, to go on camera. I'd still managed to cook lunch for the crew that day, but Tris just said, 'Right, lovey, you're coming with me and I'm taking you to the Priory. And he did.'

'He's a good man. I know he needs to get the programmes made, but he cares, too.' Darcy smiled. 'The first time I saw one of Ma's shows I couldn't believe it. It all looked so perfect.'

Darcy went to get the gratin from the oven, remembering an interview she had sat through with Diana as a child.

'Diana Hughes is the kind of elegant, witty woman you want to please,' the journalist had murmured into a tape recorder, watching Diana and Darcy being photographed in the kitchen. 'You want to be around her, hope that some of the effortless magic will brush off on you like glitter.'

Darcy remembered sitting at her mother's feet pretending to mix cake batter in a bowl, while Diana posed in a pair of leather trousers and a billowing white silk shirt. 'It is as much about creating a welcoming setting as the food,' her mother said, leaning conspiratorially towards the camera. She had gestured for the journalist to follow her out to the conservatory, leaving Darcy sitting alone on the kitchen floor.

'When I looked at the programme,' Darcy said now, 'I couldn't believe it was my home, it all looked . . .'

'Idyllic?' Conor said.

'Exactly. And they managed to keep it up – they took her off for a series to France, then Italy.'

'Tris even had her cycling round Provence,' Conor said, laughing. 'It was aspirational. People loved it.'

'Dad, Dad, please can we swim? Please?' Chris said, tugging at his sleeve.

'What do you say? This will all keep for a while,' Conor said. 'Let's eat in a bit. The light's fading and it's the best time of day for a swim. Did you bring a costume?' Darcy pulled a blue strap from beneath her sundress to show him. 'Spoilsport.'

Out on the deck, Conor pulled his shirt over his head, and unbuckled his khakis. Darcy slipped out of her dress, and shook back her hair. She caught him looking at her, and smiled.

'I warn you, it's a bit fresh,' he said.

'I remember.' She walked to the edge of the jetty, and dived into the clear gilded water. The cold took her breath from her, and she surfaced, floating on her back, gasping. Chris and Conor leapt from the jetty hand in hand, whooping with laughter, crying out at the cold.

She left them playing and splashing around, and swam out sure and strong across the water. She turned after a while, treading water, looking back at the man and his son, at the low white cottage in the setting sun. She had a moment of absolute clarity then. There was nowhere on earth she would rather be than there. She saw them head back to the jetty and she swam towards them. Conor offered her his hand, and Darcy climbed out, lying back on the warm boards, her arms behind her head.

'Bracing?' he said.

'You forget how cold it is,' she said, laughing.

'California's made you soft,' he said, nudging her leg. 'We'll soon toughen you up.'

'Yeah, I think that's what Ma's hoping.'

'Why are you so hard on yourself?' Conor raised himself up. 'From where I am I see a beautiful, funny, kind young woman.'

'Careful, Conor Ricci,' she said, a warmth spreading through her. 'That sounds dangerously like a compliment.' She smiled. 'I'm my own worst enemy. Always wanting everything to be perfect.' Darcy rolled towards him, her head crooked against her arm, wishing he would reach out to her. He leant over her, dripping cold water onto her warming skin, rivulets running across her chest.

'Come on, let's go and see how good your gratin is.' He jumped up, offering her his hand, and she hid her disappointment behind a smile.

'Do you ever think there's more to life than this? Than cooking?' she said as they walked barefoot across the grass.

'I work every day from the moment I get up,' Conor said, pulling his shirt on. 'Even though I'm shattered, I'm still awake at four most nights.'

'You too? Why don't you call me the next time that happens?'

'I'll bear that in mind, Hughes,' he said, running his fingers through his wet hair. She wondered how it would feel to do that, to trace the hard bone of his skull, the nape of his neck, the valley of the tendons, flexing. Conor swept Chris up in his arms, swinging him round, and roughly shook his hair dry. She was touched by their ease and closeness, the boy's pale gold limbs against the strong, hard body of his father. She tried to remember if she had ever felt that relaxed with her mother. 'There are clean towels in the bathroom. Help yourself.'

She dried off, and wriggled into her dress, her skin fresh and alive from the cold swim. She checked her reflection in the shaving mirror and cleaned a smudge of mascara. The bathroom was simple – only painkillers and shaving kit on the shelves, and two toothbrushes, one adult, one child, in the mug beside the sink.

In the kitchen, she picked up her glass of wine. She could hear them laughing and fooling around outside, so she flicked through the iPod on a dock on the counter, and played an old BB King track, dancing to the tune as she moved between the sink and counter. She took a teaspoon and tested the gratin to see it was still warm, glancing across, aware suddenly that Conor was watching her from the doorway.

'You enjoy eating,' he said.

'Are you saying I need to lose weight?' She glanced back at him as she bent into the fridge.

He stretched out and patted his stomach. 'Who am I to talk?'

'You? You're in great shape,' she said, and placed the bowl on the table.

'I've always had a sweet tooth, but since quitting the booze I'd do anything for a bar of chocolate. Chris,' Conor called, and the boy tumbled through the door, followed by the dog.

'That's the difference between hunger and appetite,' she said. 'If you're hungry, you need to eat.' She spooned the potatoes onto his plate. 'Appetite has the lure of pleasure. That's always interested me more.'

'Explain.' Conor leant forward in his chair, picked up a fork.

'If you read the really good food writers, like Elizabeth David, it's all about being alive – really alive.' She licked the spoon. 'Choosing things with care, a lack of pretension. Food that's sensual, and juicy—'

'Juicy?' He held her gaze for a moment, then took a mouthful of the gratin.

'So?'

'Well.' He nodded, took another forkful. 'Maybe I have got some competition after all.'

14

'Checking out the competition?' Darcy said, squeezing under the shelter of the kitchen's French windows, out of the rain. The summer storm had washed the morning clean and the air smelt alive and green, rain pattering on the leaves of the oak tree beside them. An empty wooden swing on the lowest branch drifted to and fro in the wind.

'Jaysus, Darcy, you almost gave me a heart attack.' Conor turned his head to her, laughing. She squeezed in behind him, standing on tiptoe to see what was going on in the kitchen.

'So? How's she doing?'

'She's running that kitchen like a battalion, that's what's going on. Listen.'

Darcy frowned, leaning back against the stone doorframe. 'I can't hear anything.'

'Exactly,' he said. 'No chatter, no music, nothing.' He peered through the steamy window.

'Do you not notice anything else?' Darcy said, looking closer, her cheek close to his. 'The hair, Con, she's dyed her hair dark.'

'Is that what it is? I thought it was you in there for a minute.'

Her brow furrowed. 'That's a bit . . .'

'Weird? Telling me it is. I mean, imitation is flattery—'

'No it's not. It's damn annoying.' Darcy folded her arms. 'What's she up to?' Her gaze followed Diana walking across the kitchen to Beatrice, their animated conversation. As Diana laughed, Darcy felt a twinge of envy. 'Where's Tris? Shouldn't they have started filming?' She checked her watch, and looked up to see Diana marching towards them.

'What are you doing?' her mother said, rapping on the window. She slid back the bolts. 'The pair of you look like drowned rats. Conor, should you not be in the kitchen for lunch? And Darcy, make yourself useful in here. Bea could do with an extra pair of hands.'

Darcy glanced at Conor and shrugged before he strode off towards the restaurant kitchen, his shoulders hunched against the rain. At that moment, a tow truck rolled into the yard, dragging the TV crew's van behind it. Tristan and the cameraman jumped down from the cab.

'What happened, Tris?' Darcy said, holding open the door for him.

'Bloody van,' Tristan said, striding into the kitchen. He took his faded NY baseball cap off and shook the rain from his thinning nicotine-blond hair. 'Just as well I drive like a geriatric – the brakes went.' He flexed his hand, rubbing at his arm. 'We ended up in a ditch outside Kenmare.'

'My God, is everyone OK?'

'Fine. A bit shook up. The sound guy took a bump because he wasn't strapped in. We've dropped him at the hospital, just in case.'

'Tristan? What happened?' Beatrice said, rushing over with Diana. 'Are you OK?'

'I'm fine, fine,' he said, shrugging off his Puffa waistcoat. 'Sorry, Di, it's buggered up our schedule today.'

'Nonsense,' Diana said. 'Filming can wait.'

Tristan beckoned to the cameraman, who was setting up the equipment and lights already. 'Rubbish. I've never let you down and I'm not going to start now. The show must go on,' he said, raising his voice. 'Darce, you know how this works. If we set everything up can I get you to hold the mike for me?'

'Sure, no problem,' Darcy said.

'Good girl; you look a bit of a mess but Bea is ready for the camera so we'll get to you later.'

'Fine,' Darcy said, glancing at Beatrice. 'Nice hair,' she said to her.

'Thanks, do you like it?' Beatrice said, smoothing down the deep chocolate-brown bob. 'I just thought there would be more continuity if we all looked—'

'The same?' Darcy said.

'I was hardly a natural blonde, sweetie,' she said, smiling. 'I'm going back to my roots.'

'Well you've buggered up the shots we have of you in the can,' Tristan said, and chewed at his lip.

'I'm sorry,' Beatrice said. 'I didn't think—'

'Too late now. Right, are you ready to go?' Tristan checked his file. 'We'll film you cooking the Black Velvet cupcakes first, then move on to cheesecake, OK, and then we'll see what else we can get in the can today. We'll do the location shots at the local dairy tomorrow, if it ever stops raining.'

'Know what they say,' Darcy said, taking the mike from the cameraman. 'If you can see the mountains round here it's about to rain; if you can't it's raining.'

'And *that* is why it is so beautiful,' Diana said, settling down on a kitchen chair to watch the filming.

Hours later, Beatrice stood spotlit in the darkening kitchen, a pale pink mixing bowl under one arm. 'Naughty, naughty eggs,' she said, looking at the camera. 'Gosh, the number of times they have curdled on me at this point.' Beatrice rolled her eyes, and leant towards the camera as if she were sharing a secret. 'What you need to do is help them a little bit. You think I'm bonkers, don't you, Phil?' she said to the camera- man. 'But if you give your eggs a good talking to, blend a little cornflour and mix it in gently ... gently, *there* you are, no scrambled eggs.'

'What's she doing?' Diana whispered to Con.

'Acting.' He paused. 'I think.'

'Ohhh,' Beatrice sighed, lifting the bowl of chocolate mixture. 'Couldn't you just drink it?' She raised an eyebrow. 'But we won't. We can resist the temptation, can't we?'

'Bloody hell,' Conor said.

'Cut,' Tristan shouted. 'Bea, love, tone it down a bit. It's not *Carry On Baking*.'

'What do you mean?' Beatrice snapped at him.

'I'm not being critical—'

'I know exactly what I'm doing,' she said. 'Why don't you do your job and I'll do mine.' She turned to the camera, and her face softened. Tristan signalled to the cameraman. 'Now, to the icing,' Beatrice said, sauntering across to a glass bowl with icing sugar which the home economist had prepared. 'I always say to my boys in the bakery, your icing needs to be stiff.' Her cheek twitched with a smile. 'No use at all if it's all soupy. It needs some body. Now, beat in a little water with a firm hand—'

'If she licks that spoon . . .' Conor began.

'Mm,' Beatrice said, her eyes closing. She bit her lip. 'It's a hard part of the job, but someone has to do it.'

Darcy glanced over at Conor, who was trying to stifle a laugh. She shifted position, her arms aching from holding the microphone boom, and watched as Beatrice chattered on, swinging her hips as she walked to the oven. She turned out the individual chocolate puddings, and the camera switched to a cooled rack of perfect ones baked by the home economist earlier. 'Oh, yum,' Beatrice said, sampling a mouthful. 'Look, look how lovely and gooey they still are in the middle.' She drizzled icing over the top, the camera zooming in on the viscous, white liquid. 'Heaven,' she said, fairy lights twinkling behind her, reflecting in the steel bowl of the pink Kitchen Aid mixer at her side.

'It's as simple as that,' Beatrice said, her voice low and even.

'Baking a cake for someone is like giving them a big hug. My mum always said the best sauce you can give your family and friends is a happy expression on your face, and heartfelt hospitality. Just take the best ingredients you can, and mix with love.'

'And cut,' Tristan said. 'Great, Bea, we've got everything we need for today.' Diana clapped her hands, and a round of applause echoed round the kitchen. Tristan leant towards Darcy as he took the mike boom from her. 'Where the hell did that come from? The minute the camera rolled it was like she was a different person. Who does she think she is?'

'It's an act,' Conor said, picking up a perfectly iced cupcake from the counter. 'That was just ... well it was weird. Like someone flicked a switch and she was all of a sudden ...' He struck a coy pose, and licked his fingertip.

'Get on with you,' Darcy said, nudging him. 'How was lunch?'

'Half full. Could be busier.' He tossed the cake back onto the stand.

'What we need is more publicity,' Beatrice said, joining them. 'You'd be fully booked every day, then. Maybe we could hire a publicist, get some press coverage before the series goes out?'

'Di has a team of people who've always handled that for her. She knows what she's doing.'

'I don't know.' Beatrice pursed her lips. 'It's a different world, these days. The public loves a competition, and there's nothing like a bit of scandal for a story to go viral—'

'Leave it, Bea,' Conor said.

'OK, OK. Anyway, help yourself.' Beatrice gestured at the tiered plate of cakes.

'Nah, you're all right,' Conor said. Darcy held up her hand as Beatrice offered her the plate. 'What is it with girls and cakes? I mean, is it ironic? All this hipster housewife shite?'

'Shite?' Beatrice said, breathily. She straightened her

shoulders. 'Conor Ricci, cupcakes are part of our history.'

'Fairy cakes, that's what we used to call them . . .' he said.

'Darcy, back me up here.' Beatrice's voice dropped a notch, threatening. 'They have been around for centuries, they are just having a moment.' She straightened her posture. 'Vienna cakes, queen cakes, fairy cakes – different names, different trends at different times. We are simply in the business of making people happy.'

'They're sugary little time bombs, that's what they are,' Conor said, folding his arms.

'Deadly? Someone did call them sweet poisons, you know?' Beatrice took a step towards him. 'Pretty and deadly. Just like those gorgeous little barbed flies you use for fishing. You're catching fish, I'm catching diners.' Beatrice pressed her lips together in a tight smile. 'Listen, if you're not working, why don't we all go for a drink, see if we can't come up with a few ideas to get more people in the restaurant?' Beatrice said, sauntering over to the dresser and picking up her iPad. 'Aperol spritz, that's your poison, isn't it, Darcy?' she said, scrolling through the pages. 'I'm sure I read it on your blog. Here we are, I bookmarked the recipe.' Beatrice's eyes sparkled. 'I wonder who you could be talking about in this post: *But then one night when he sang in the pub with his band, and I sat on the bar swinging my legs, drinking lemonade through a green and white straw, I saw him kiss a girl. Really kiss her. I was happy for him, don't get me wrong, that he had found someone his age and all, but my heart broke a little that night.*'

Darcy felt lightheaded. She raised her chin, furious and embarrassed, and glanced at Conor. She took a step towards Beatrice. 'Funny. Really funny.'

Beatrice watched her walk away, her face impassive. 'Some people have no sense of humour at all,' she said as the back door slammed.

Conor ignored her, and strode after Darcy. 'Hey, wait,' he called, jogging to catch up with her, his feet crunching on the wet gravel. 'Jaysus, Darce, don't make me run.' He winced as she turned to him.

'Your back again?' she said, and Conor nodded.

'Think I've been overdoing it with the running.'

'I'm sorry,' she said, the colour high in her cheeks. 'I can't believe she did that.'

'Hey,' he smiled, dimples forming in the dark stubble of his cheeks. 'I'm flattered.' He paused. 'Besides, I'd read it already.' He glanced back. Beatrice was standing in the doorway of the kitchen, her arms at her sides, watching them.

'Why didn't you say anything?' Darcy said, punching his arm softly. She exhaled. 'I didn't think anyone over here read my column.'

'Told you, didn't I? Stayed up half the night reading your columns. Don't go getting ideas though, I'm just checking out the competition.' Conor winked. 'It's good, Darce, you've a way with words.' He waited for her to look at him. 'Don't be embarrassed, she was just trying to get a rise out of you, you know. Besides, it's flattering. I never knew you had a crush on me when you were a kid.'

Darcy turned to walk away, and glanced back over her shoulder. 'Thing is, Con,' she said. 'Like I told you, I'm not a kid anymore.'

FORBIDDEN FRUIT

....

London or Rome, New York or Paris – it doesn't matter where I am in the world, one taste of an oyster and I am home in Ireland. Next month all the big oyster festivals kick off, and I'm planning to honour the humble mollusc in my own way. You never forget where you first ate something memorable. Food conjures up other times and places. France to me is smoked duck and honey-comb, eaten in a stone-walled restaurant located off a dirt track you won't find in any of the guide books. Spain is paella, with glistening socarrat. Singapore is Hainanese chicken and Tiger beer consumed on the humid streets in a hawker stall bathed with fluorescent light. Japan is noodles and hot coffee tins and Thailand is pomegranate and coconut milk, and the Middle East is moutabal and baba ganoush, shawarma and lemon mint, za'atar. Wherever you are, seize the moment, try something new, before the moment goes. Years ago, when a friend shucked an oyster and held it to my lips, I found the food that meant home to me, the taste of the sky and the sea, and I lost my heart.

Darcy Hughes, *Appetite* Tumblr

15

Conor sat on the bench outside the restaurant kitchen at sunrise, reading the paper with his feet resting on an empty milk crate. As Darcy walked towards the porch, all she could see was a plume of blue smoke rising from behind the broadsheet.

'Morning,' she said, stamping the mud from her Dubarry boots on the mat.

'Darce, have you seen the papers yet?' Conor said, without lowering the pages.

'Why? Is there some coverage of the show?'

He lowered the Irish *Daily Mirror* and frowned. 'It's . . . You'd better take a look.' He handed the paper to her and she sat beside him, scanning the article. She smelt good to him, of vanilla and the rain.

'*Domestic Goddess Love Child Shocker*?' she said. The piece was illustrated with photographs of her mother and father in their prime, standing by the shore of the bay with the Castle in the background, and a more recent photo of Diana taken at the previous year's *Top Chef* final. A grainy photograph of Darcy, pulled from her blog, had been added at the side.

'Why are they dragging that up?'

'Ma and Kavanagh were getting married,' Darcy said, her voice tight. 'But he died.' She handed the paper back to him and went in to the house.

'I don't like it,' Conor said, following her.

'What? That I'm illegitimate?' she said.

'Nah. I've just got a bad feeling about this. When the papers went after me over the divorce, they started small, you know, just to start stirring trouble, and then—' He stopped himself. 'Ignore me. I'm probably talking shite.'

Conor watched Darcy walk away. He was unsettled, his stomach tight at the memory of the non-stop calls when the papers found out about his divorce, the cameras lurking beyond the walls of the rehab clinic. He busied himself with getting the lunch menu under way, delegating tasks to his sous chef and the chefs de partie. The newspaper story had troubled him, and he wondered what Diana's reaction would be.

An hour later he stood at the kitchen window staring at the firm-fleshed salmon on the counter before him. He ran his index finger over the scales, testing it.

'So? What do you think?' The wiry little Welshman beside him tilted back his black straw trilby, and twitched his nose, his pencil moustache trembling.

'Fresh, firm. You reckon you can get a regular supply?' Conor looked up as a red Mini careened into the driveway, parking just in front of the window. He smiled at the sight of one of the teenage commis chefs arriving for his shift. The young redheaded girl at the boy's side turned off the engine and entwined her arms around his neck. They kissed, lost in one another, her hands in his hair, his reaching hungrily beneath her loose white vest, tangling in the strings of her bikini top. 'Bloody hell, that makes me feel old. When did we get old, Daffyd?' The little Welshman stood beside him. 'Do you remember that?'

'What are you two looking at?' Darcy said, joining them. 'Oh God, stop perving, Conor.'

'I'm not.' He stepped away, but glanced back at the young couple as the fishmonger went out to the van.

'I think it's lovely,' Darcy said, sorting through some paper-work. 'God, what I wouldn't give to be seventeen again, when you just had to have a pulse to exude sensuality.' She paused, gazing into the distance, an invoice half opened. 'Do you remember how that feels? When days are long and golden, and you're light with life.'

'Do I remember?' Conor took a step towards her.

'Even Ma has a better love life than me.'

'Get your fiddles out, boys.'

'Shut up.' Darcy laughed.

'You're talking like you're an old woman, Darce. How old are you now?'

'Twenty-six.'

'See? Ten years younger than me. Plenty of time for you yet.'

'Yes.' Darcy looked down at the papers in her hands. 'It makes me happy to see people in love.'

'In lust more like, with those two,' Conor said, gesturing towards the Mini.

'Cynic.' Darcy glanced at her watch.

'Expecting someone?'

'Ma wants me to go into town for her and sort out some stuff at the bank. One of Tristan's guys is going to give me a lift.' At the sound of a car horn, Darcy looked up.

Conor followed her outside and whistled, gesturing to the young chef to get inside and start work.

'Aiden,' he shouted across the yard. 'Get your arse in the kitchen. I want fresh tarragon and dill from the garden.'

'Yes, Chef,' the boy called, scrambling out of the Mini.

The car pulled away in a shower of gravel, a pale, slender arm waving languorously from the driver's window, silver bangles catching the light and coloured friendship bracelets fluttering. An attractive man in his twenties jumped down from the cab of Tristan's battered van, and came to open the passenger door for Darcy. 'Morning.'

'Jamie, this is Conor,' she said, her arm brushing his as she turned. He stood up to his full height as Conor sauntered towards them, glaring at Jamie from beneath a lowered brow. 'Conor, this is Jamie Sinclair. He'll be working with Tris for the rest of the show.'

Conor didn't blink. 'Darce, if you're going in to town, would you pick me up a couple of cartons of Marlboro from the cash and carry?'

'Sure. Have you got the card?'

Conor patted his pockets. 'Damn, must be on the board in the kitchen.'

'I'll get it.' Darcy turned to Jamie. 'Won't be a minute.'

Conor waited for her to be gone. 'Hope the brakes are safe on the van.'

'Perfectly fine.' Jamie didn't move. 'The brake fluid was leaking. I mean, look how knackered this thing is.' He glanced at the van. 'The hose had cracked, that's all.'

'You make sure you drive carefully, you hear?'

'Who are you? Darcy's dad?'

'Here it is,' Darcy said, walking out of the kitchen just as Conor stepped towards Jamie.

Darcy sensed something going on. 'What? What is it?'

'Nothing.' A smile flickered over Jamie's lips and he put his arm around her, helping her into the cab, challenging Conor. 'Nothing at all.'

Conor stood, watching Jamie drive away with Darcy, still staring up the empty driveway even after the van had disappeared from sight on the Kenmare road.

'Conor.' Diana's voice echoed across the yard, and he frowned, lighting a cigarette.

'You're smoking too much,' she said, storming towards him. 'Have I missed Darcy? I suppose you've seen this?' She brandished the paper and he nodded. 'What's the matter? You've got a face on you like you're chewing wasps.'

'Nothing,' he said, glancing up the driveway, surprised by how protective he felt towards Darcy.

Diana stopped to check the bins as they walked inside. 'There's far too much waste, Con. We need to look at the menus again.' She wiped her hand on her thigh. 'Come in the house for a minute, will you?'

By the coat rack in the corridor, Conor paused, looking in the mirror as Diana walked on. Conor raked his hair back from his face, ran his hand along his jaw, turning his face this way and that. He turned sideways, sucked his stomach in, hands on hips. 'Ah, feck it,' he said, exhaling, feeling the tug of his waistband.

'Shall we have some breakfast? I need a glass of champagne. No, a Bellini,' Diana said, drying her hand at the sink. She went to the fridge, took an open bottle of Moët from the door, and tossed the fork in the neck into the sink. She scooped a teaspoon of peach puree into the bottom of a champagne coupe, and squeezed a dash of lemon juice in, topping up with the last of the champagne.

'Celebrating?' Sunlight poured through the tall windows, dust motes dancing like glitter in a snow storm around Diana as she sat on the old blue sofa, glass in hand.

'Fergus had me out dancing until the wee hours. I've barely slept, I feel quite giddy. Will you have a tea?' Conor leant against the back porch. His broad shoulders filled the space, his head lowered, dark curls tumbling over his strong brow. 'You always make me think of a bull when you're in a mood like this.'

'Proud, muscular?' he said, pouring himself a cup from the pot on the side.

'Unpredictable,' she said as he half turned to her. 'It's your father's Italian looks. Roman nose and full lips—'

'About all I inherited from him.' Conor splashed milk into the tea. 'But I got my mammy's grey eyes, didn't I?' He leant against the counter. 'What's up?'

'We have a problem.'

'The papers?'

'Not that. A load of nonsense. I've never hidden the fact that Kavanagh died before we had a chance to marry. Besides, no such thing as bad publicity. No. Some ... some person has been sending anonymous emails via the website. Horrible, hateful things.'

'Like what?'

'Photographs.' She shuddered. 'Obviously some person with a screw loose.'

'Shall we call the Garda?'

'No. There's no need for that. I mean, they haven't made any threats. It's just unsettling.'

'It'll be the ads for the new show. It's bringing a few fruit loops out howling.' Conor grimaced and tipped the rest of his mug into the sink. 'Set Beatrice on them. She's good with all that online stuff. I'll be getting on now—' As he turned fully to her, Diana pursed her lips.

'Con, get some bigger whites before you film your segments.' Diana strode over to him, tugging at the flap of his jacket. 'The idea is that they button up.'

'Leave it, Di.' He pushed her gently away. 'Stop fussing. I've started running again.'

'I didn't want to say anything—'

'It's my Elvis in Vegas stage.' Conor exhaled, patting his stomach.

'That didn't work out so well for him, did it?' Diana backed off. 'It's just after Jonny—'

'Maybe there's more to life than the kitchen.' Conor folded his arms. 'Seeing what happened to him, it makes you realise life's short.'

'You'd be lost without cooking.' Diana shook her head.

'I promise, Di, losing JJ has shaken me up. I'm getting back in shape. For me, for the Castle and for Chris. This job screwed up my marriage, but now the divorce has gone through, it's a fresh start, and I'm clean, you know, gold stars from my counsellor at the Priory.'

'You big kid.' Diana held his grey-eyed gaze, saw the hope there. She drained her glass, and scooped up some papers from the table. 'Walk with me. I want to show you where I think the marquees should go for the contest.'

Conor held open the heavy baize-covered door in the kitchen corridor, and they stepped into the Castle. The air smelt of newly applied beeswax polish, and a team of cleaning women were busy at work vacuuming the deep green hall carpets, and buffing the walnut tables to a shine. Diana greeted each woman by name as she strode through the Castle, Conor at her side. At the entrance, she stopped to dead-head some lavender in the stone urns, crushing the flowers in her hand, breathing in the scent.

'What a glorious day,' she said, walking on, the gravel crunching beneath their footsteps.

'Now, would that have anything to do with Fergus, who I saw lolling around in your pink dressing gown earlier?' Conor's eyes crinkled. 'He's not much of a talker in the morning, is he? Anything you want to be telling me?'

'No there is not.' Diana brushed her fingertips on her tweed skirt.

'Shall I be buying a hat then?' Conor put his hands in his pockets.

'No you bloody won't,' she said, punching his arm. 'And don't go blathering in the kitchen.' She glanced over her shoulder to make sure they were alone.

'Ah, good for you and Fergus.'

'I've always had a high sex drive,' she whispered. 'It just feels good to be wanted again. To feel, well—' She jogged down the shallow flight of stone steps to the lawn. 'Alive. Desired.'

'I'm happy for you. Fergus is a good man.'

Diana glanced at him. 'It would do you good, just find someone for a bit of fun.'

97

'Me? Friends with benefits?' Conor felt the loneliness in him well up.

'Is that what they are calling it these days?'

'Nah, not for me. Who'd want me, anyway? Single parent, workaholic, recovering alcoholic. I'm washed up.' He smiled. 'As you said.'

'Find a good local girl and woo her,' Diana said, turning to look back at the Castle.

'*Woo* her? What century are we in?'

'Seduce her then.' Diana threw her hand in the air. 'By the way, has Tris given you a copy of this?' She took the sheaf of papers from under her arm.

'The filming schedule?' Conor flicked through the pages.

'The crew is going to spend a day with each of us, recording us gathering our ingredients and inspiration, and then there's another day recording the cooking of our dishes.' Tristan and the producer had planned to the last detail what they wanted to film, matching each ingredient with a scene – elderflower panna cotta with picking elderflowers from the estate hedgerows, fresh oysters with a trip out to sea. Conor glanced through the list of people who would be working on the programme, and checked they had credited the home economist who would be working with him.

'Would you look at all this – director, producer, PA, home ecs, lights, sound . . . make-up.'

'They'll have their work cut out with you,' she said.

'Thanks.' Conor looked at her impassively. 'No wonder Tris is focusing on Bea and Darcy. It's not like people are going to tune in just to go: feck, is that Conor Ricci? He's let himself go, hasn't he—' Conor took his cigarettes out and lit one, exhaling a sharp puff of blue smoke.

'Con, you are going to behave, aren't you?' Diana took the cigarette.

'Darcy will kill you if she catches you.'

'Don't you dare.' She pushed the cigarette back at him,

flicking her head as she blew a smoke ring. 'It's going to work, isn't it? She's young, but it's time for her to take over the business.' Diana paused. 'The thing is, she's agreed to sell off some shares her father left her to help cover some of our ... well, expenses here.'

'Expenses? You mean running costs, don't you, Di?' Conor folded his arms. 'She does know how bad it is?'

'Between us, we will ensure that the Castle prospers.' She called to the cat stalking across the lawn towards them, and picked him up.

'His nibs is back, is he?'

'Managed to get himself locked in one of the sheds, didn't you, Kato? Silly puss. Lucky that Bea heard you miaowing.' The cat butted her hand with his head, rubbing his teeth against her jaw in a frenzy of purring. But as Conor went to stroke him, he lashed out, hissing.

'Little bastard,' Conor said, sucking at his hand.

'Don't like men, do you? Poor Fergus. Kato was rather put out to be locked out of the bedroom last night. He laid in wait for him on the landing. When Fergus got up for a pee, Kato launched himself at him like a missile. I found Fergus hopping around naked with the cat hanging from his thigh.'

'That's quite a picture you're painting,' Conor said. 'Typical of you to adopt a cat nobody else wanted.'

'I always had a soft spot for hopeless cases.' Diana waited for Conor to look at her. 'Men included.' She let the cat down onto the freshly cut grass, and he slunk away through the flower beds, a white flash along the beds of lavender beneath the stone wall.

Conor stared at her. 'Tell me the truth. How long have we got?'

Diana glanced over at the sound of voices on the terrace, and she lowered her voice. 'Two, three months if nothing changes,' she said without looking at him.

'You have to tell Darcy,' Conor said quietly. 'God knows

she's given up enough without throwing good money after bad bailing my restaurant out.'

'Our restaurant,' Diana snapped.

'It's all I've got,' Conor said. 'This show has to work.'

'What about Chris? Your ex? Are you still in love with Alannah?' she said more gently.

'No, not anymore.' Conor shook his head. 'There was only ever her, from the moment I met her.'

'That's a lie.'

'You mean the drink?'

'And the drugs.' Diana waited for him to look at her. 'Do you blame her, divorcing you?'

'No.'

'That girl supported you a hundred per cent while you built your reputation, and raised your son.' Diana folded her arms. 'What did you do? Go off and shag a groupie who wasn't so shattered she had the energy to raise the great soufflé of your ego.'

'Di, I'm not proud of myself . . .'

'You're damn lucky you didn't end up like Jonny.' Diana pulled her cardigan around her angular frame, and stared back at the Castle, clouds rolling overhead. 'You have a chance, Con, to make good. This show will secure the future of the Castle. I can retire, Darcy will have her inheritance, and you will be chef patron of the Castle, just as you've always wanted.'

'What about Bea?'

'What about her? The moment I saw her, I knew she'd be perfect. She's so hip it's painful.' Diana shuddered. 'I hate it, Con. I hate it all. This twee nostalgia for cake tins and bunting, and fifty-euro floral ironing-board covers. The whole nation is in some sort of narcoleptic nostalgia trip back to their idea of fifties domestic bliss that never existed.'

'You're a sly mare,' Conor said, shaking his head. 'I thought you'd gone mad.'

'This will be the best show yet. I think the marquees should go here, this year. That way you get a full view of the Castle and the bay.'

'Sounds good to me.'

'We will all benefit from this,' Diana said, turning to him. 'Bea is what the public wants. It will launch her career.'

'And Darcy?'

'People will buy in to her because she's real. She's one of those golden people that seems to vibrate at a higher level than the rest of us – clearer, kinder.'

'Got it in one.' Conor looked out across the water, the breeze lifting his hair, sunlight sparkling, the shadows of clouds scudding across the bay. Something clicked in that moment. He thought of Darcy, running towards him dragging her suitcase, her face lit up with joy. He thought of her in the wedding dress, the skirt swinging in slow motion as she turned. He thought of the sudden, surprising jealousy he felt when Jamie drove her to town. He remembered her face in the rain: *I'm not a kid anymore.*

Breakfast is without question the best meal of the day. I am often happy with a simple, well-made cup of tea served in fine porcelain and a fresh orange, but there is nothing better than a seductive feast, a celebration of the day to come and if you are fortunate, the night before.

Be good to yourself. Get up. Greet the day on your terms. Dust off your favourite teapot and that special box of loose-leaf tea you never have time to use. Squeeze an orange or two. If it has been a memorable night and you are making the moment last with breakfast in bed, shave a truffle or pop a dollop of lumpfish caviar onto your scrambled eggs. Or if you are full of self-loathing and remorse (we have all been there), and hoping to pluck a hair from the black dog, try this:

101

Bloody Mary

Blend 150 g chopped tomatoes, quarter tsp of salt and a slug of tomato juice in a blender. Add a splash of vodka, a squeeze of lime juice and a spot of Worcester sauce to a cocktail shaker with ice. Fill up with the tomato mix. Shake. Serve. Add sunglasses and Jacques Brel's 'Ne Me Quitte Pas'. Face the day – it can only get better.

Diana Hughes, *Hughes at Home*

BREAKING BREAD

What do your kitchen cupboards say about you? That old guy, Brillat-Savarin, said: 'Tell me what you eat and I'll tell you who you are.' He had it wrong. It's not just what we eat that shows who we are, it's what we buy but don't eat that says more about the people we think we are. Or want to be. Look at the ingredients in your cupboards. All those hopes and dreams.

Brillat-Savarin reckoned there were six senses at play with food: taste, touch, hearing, sight, smell – and desire. On that we agree – food is desire. For me, as a kid with a working mother and no dad, breakfast was a DIY affair. I envied a friend whose mammy made a loaf of soda bread each day for her family without fail. Sleeping over at their house, I'd wake to the smell of fresh baking, and breakfast would be a glass of warm, unpasteurised milk straight from the cow (they were a dairy-farming family), and a slice of bread with salted butter. Oh, God, I loved it. That smell, that simple food was like an embrace, and I leant in to it the way a flower does towards the sun. I desired their life. Her ma was a big hugger, too, unlike mine, which helped. We're creatures of habit. We all just want to go home. Bake that bread.

Soda bread

Mix 450 g plain sifted flour, 1 tsp salt, 1 tsp bicarbonate
of soda and make a well in the centre. Gradually pour in
400 ml buttermilk and mix. Turn the dough out onto a
floured board, and make it round. Cut a cross on top. Bake
for 45 minutes at 180°C until the loaf is golden brown.

Darcy Hughes, *Appetite* Tumblr

Naked Lunch

'Good cooking is like love, needing both tact and variety.'

French adage

16

Darcy paused beneath the red frontage of the architectural antiques store and looked up at the sign, *Fergus Fitzgerald*. Like every shop in town, Fergus had stuck a poster for *Ireland's Top Chef* in the window, and her mother's face beamed at Darcy above a plate of cakes, Conor smouldering at her shoulder. A bell on a coiled metal loop shook and rang as she pushed open the door, but there was no one in the store. She wandered through, letting her hand drift across the polished surface of an old mahogany door, the warm sandstone of a carved mantelpiece. She could hear music, an old Sarah Vaughan song playing faintly, and followed it to a door leading to the courtyard. A handwritten note: *Free-range pig, close door firmly please*, was pinned to the frame.

'Hello?' she called, stepping out into the cobbled yard. The music was louder, but above that she heard an excited squeal and snuffling. A large pink and black pig waddled towards her from the derelict barn at the heart of the yard. Darcy laughed as the pig nudged her calf with his snout, nuzzling at her Converse.

'Darcy, what a grand surprise,' Fergus said, stepping out from a red door, raising his hand in greeting. 'I see we've met Christmas. Watch that one; he's a bugger for shoelaces. Get away with you, leave the poor girl alone.' He strode over and batted the pig away.

'Christmas?' Darcy shook his hand.

'Christmas the third, to be exact. Though this one's a sweetheart so he might escape the pot. Number two was a little bastard, didn't mind him going. Now, will you have a cup of tea? Come on in.'

Darcy followed him into a warm kitchen at the side of the shop, and Fergus fetched down a fine porcelain cup and saucer for her. 'Thank you,' she said, taking a steaming cup of tea from him. The porcelain was so fine that as she raised the cup to the light it gleamed opaquely, and the gilt edge tasted clear to her.

'Are you doing a bit of shopping?'

'Just been to the bank for Ma,' she said. 'And I was hiding from someone.'

'A young man?'

'Came on a bit strong.' She blew on her tea.

'Chancer, was he? A girl like you must have a string of suitors from Kenmare to San Francisco.'

Darcy laughed, looked down at her cup. 'No, there's no one.'

'I was just reading the paper,' Fergus said, raising his chin towards the kitchen table. 'Are you all right, darlin'?'

'Tomorrow's fish and chips?'

'That's the right attitude. God knows your mother is a celebrity around here, and publicity is all well and good but it must hurt to rake up your private life?'

'Oh, everything is a drama around Ma. This story – it's not really about me, it's about her.'

'It must be difficult for a child, growing up in such a long shadow,' Fergus said, settling back in an old red armchair by the stove, and he gestured for Darcy to sit opposite him.

Darcy sipped her tea. 'Do you have children?'

'And grandchildren! They're all away: Dublin, London, my youngest is in New York. Dreamers the lot of them, and I'm glad they're following their stars. But they'll be back, you'll see.'

'You must miss them?'

'Aye, I do that. But there's the computer, and Skype. My wife would have loved that.' He looked at the fire. 'We were together forty years when I lost her five years ago.' He blinked, his face softening. 'I'm glad to have found some happiness with your mother.'

'Does she make you happy?'

'She . . .' Fergus laughed. 'She's a different woman from my wife. She makes me happy, she makes me mad.' He looked at Darcy. 'At my age I'm glad to feel that alive.'

'Excuse me,' Darcy said, feeling her phone vibrating in her pocket. She checked the screen. 'Talk of the devil.' She slid open the screen. 'Hello, Ma?'

'Darcy, where are you?' Diana said, the tension in her voice setting Darcy's hackles rising.

'I stopped off to say hello to Fergus.'

'Ask him to use the computer. In fact, put me on speaker-phone, would you? Fergus, can you hear me?'

'Hello, my love. What can we do?' he said, standing.

'Fire up your computer, darling.' Diana reeled off the address of a celebrity website, and Fergus typed it in. 'Darcy, you'd better prepare yourself.'

'Oh my God,' Darcy said, feeling as if someone had punched her in the stomach. She gasped, the air tight in her throat.

'I . . . oh, I shouldn't,' Fergus said, turning his face from the screen. 'I'll be outside if you need me.'

'Conor was right,' Darcy said, staring wide eyed at a grainy photograph of herself, lying in long meadow grass. Her white summer dress was unbuttoned, falling open, revealing her tanned shoulder, the hollow of her collar bones, the curve of her breasts.

'What do you mean he was right?' Diana said.

'He told me the story about you and Pa in the papers would be just the beginning.'

109

'Where has this picture come from? How could you be so stupid?'

'Me? My God, someone has leaked a private photograph, from years ago. Who could have done this?'

'More to the point, who took them?'

Darcy hesitated. 'JJ.'

'JJ?' Diana cried. 'Jonny?' Darcy heard the phone muffle, her mother talking quickly. 'Conor, wait—' A door slammed.

'Ma, please tell me Conor didn't just hear that?'

'You have some explaining to do.'

'I'm on my way.'

Rain lashed the windows of the 270 bus, and Darcy huddled in the back seat, watching the countryside rolling past. She thought back to June when her mother had called her apartment in Berkeley.

'No? Are you sure?' Darcy had paused, halfway out of her white vintage sixties dress. She gestured urgently to her roommate, Lyn, who waddled from the en suite bathroom, her hand cupped around her swollen stomach. Lyn flopped back onto Darcy's bed, adjusting the plump goose-down pillows against the antique French headboard. Darcy covered the receiver. 'JJ's killed himself.'

'No?' Lyn whispered. '*The* JJ?' Her face was transformed by shock.

'Listen, Mum, I've got to go if I'm going to get to the restaurant on time.'

'I didn't realise you knew Jonny.'

'I didn't, not really,' Darcy said, grimacing at Lyn. 'I . . . we bumped into him when he was over here filming a while ago.'

'Con and I are going to fly over to London for the funeral. I'll keep you posted,' Diana said. 'And I'll send flowers from all of us. His poor wife and kids.'

Darcy clicked off the mobile and tossed it onto the bed.

'When? How?' Lyn said.

Darcy struggled with the zip. 'Sleeping pills, last night. They haven't released a press statement yet.' She yanked at the zip; the brittle cotton tore. 'What a waste.'

'I'm sure they'll send you another one. Their sales have shot through the roof since you've been wearing their frocks for your vlogs—'

'Not the dress, Lyn. JJ. What a bloody waste.' Darcy caught her breath.

'My God, when I think of the state you were in over him when I first met you.'

'I was young, and stupid, and he . . .' Darcy frowned. 'What does it matter now? He had such joy about him, you know? Such energy.' Tears pricked her eyes. 'Those poor, poor, children. Whatever he's done, they idolised their dad, and he loved them. I don't believe he'd leave them. When I spoke to him last week, he was still hoping his wife would take him back—'

'Hold on? You spoke to him?' Lyn's mouth dropped open in surprise.

'I didn't tell you, because I knew you'd not approve. He rang out of the blue a couple of months ago. Apologised for everything. We've spoken a few times since.'

'Too damn right he needed to apologise, and too damn late,' Lyn said, rubbing her hand over her stomach.

'I'm glad, you know, that he got in touch. After everything, JJ was a good friend.'

'Bit more than that, wasn't he, once upon a time?'

'It's all in the past.' She glanced at her watch, grabbed a pair of faded blue jeans from the wardrobe, and pulled on a white T-shirt. Darcy hugged Lyn, and planted a kiss on her cheek. 'You're a good friend, too. I'm lucky to have you.'

'Someone has to talk sense to you. You're too kind, always were.' Lyn heaved herself off the bed. 'Now get on with you. Oh, and the contract for the new cookery book deal is in the manila files on the dining-room table for you to look through. Caroline needs it faxed through to the agency by tomorrow.'

'Sure, sure,' Darcy said, as she dragged a hairbrush through her chestnut hair. 'Do you think I've made a mistake going with Ma's agent?'

'Nah, keep it in the family. She's good, isn't she?' Lyn tapped her watch. 'You need to get going.'

Darcy stopped off at the restaurant kitchen, looking for Conor. Her heart was pounding, and she felt nauseous, uncertain what his reaction was going to be.

'Are you all right there, Darcy?' Seán the gardener said, carrying a tray of camellias past the yard door as she came out.

'Have you seen Con, Seán?'

'He's walking that dog of his, I think,' he said, raising his chin towards the woods, and Darcy jogged away across the lawn, rain plastering her hair to her face. Among the trees, the air was still, the patter of the raindrops on the canopy overhead muffled. She walked swiftly, glimpses of the silver bay flashing past her through the trees. Her senses felt keen, listening to the rain, her breath coming hard and fast. Then she heard it, a whistle up ahead on the path, and she saw the greyhound race out of the ferns and the bracken.

'Conor,' she called, breaking into a run. 'Con?' She saw him then, just ahead of her on the path, in Wellingtons and a dark reefer coat, the collar turned up against the rain. His hair was wet, hanging about his stubbled face. When he saw it was her, he stood straighter, and his expression hardened.

'Well, aren't you full of surprises?' he said, flicking the stub of his cigarette into the ground, and grinding it out with his boot.

'I can explain,' Darcy said, standing her ground, her hands on her hips.

'Damn it, JJ?' Conor frowned. 'Seriously? I thought more of

you than that.' He shook his head. 'How could you? A married man, with kids.'

'That I had no idea about,' she cried, opening her palms. 'Did it ever occur to you that JJ lied to me? I was eighteen, Con. And he rocked up in California to film a show, and I had no idea that he had a family in London.' She closed her eyes, remembering the first time she'd seen him in a friend's restaurant. They had all finished the night's service and it was open after hours, a gathering of chefs and waiters from the neighbourhood. JJ walked in to the bar with all the gold beauty and swagger of a conquering hero. A head taller than everyone else there, tanned, relaxed, and at home in his own skin.

'I fell for him,' she said quietly, and looked at the ground. 'I fell for him, big time. Nobody told me, you know? That's what I still find amazing. Maybe they assumed that JJ had, and I didn't care, but I would have cared. I did care.' She looked at Conor with tears in her eyes. 'When I found out – not from a friend, from someone who had tried to get off with me and failed – another bloody chef who knew him from London, funnily enough – I finished it with him.' She flinched, remembering the day Jonny had photographed her after they'd made love in a summer meadow near Ojai. She took a step towards Conor. 'I was an idiot, OK? It was just a summer romance.'

'From the look on your face it was more than that,' Conor said.

'I was naive, and trusting.' Darcy scuffed at the earth with her heel. 'He broke my heart.'

'Oh, Darce . . .' Conor said, his face softening.

'And now – now some, some sick person has stolen the photos he took of me.'

'You mean there's more than one?'

'Oh God,' Darcy said, pressing her hands to her face. 'You've seen it, haven't you?'

113

'It's beautiful,' he said quietly. 'If that's any consolation.' He put his arm around her, gave her shoulder a squeeze before walking on. The Castle appeared in the distance, the white tower gleaming in the mist. 'JJ was a fool to hurt you.'

'That's what he said, the last time I spoke to him.'

'He rang you?' Conor looked up at her from beneath his fringe.

'Yeah, we spoke a few times. He called out of the blue a few months back.' Darcy hugged herself, shivering. 'He said he wanted to apologise.'

'Too right. Here,' he said, taking off his jacket and tucking it around her shoulders.

'Thank you.'

'It'll be OK, you know.' Conor whistled for the dog, who appeared on the path ahead of them, racing home.

'It's all going to come out now, isn't it? That JJ took the photos, that we had an affair?' Darcy's voice shook.

'We've got to think clearly. Who'd have access to the photos?'

'His wife?'

Conor shook his head. 'Why would she want this dragged up? They divorced, she's got JJ's money, or what's left of it. Besides,' he said, nudging her, 'you look too good in that photo for her to want the world to see the woman who stole JJ's heart.'

'Hardly,' Darcy said, looking down at her feet.

'But you did, you see,' Conor said, pausing at the edge of the woods. 'We were close, you know. We lost touch when I moved back to Ireland, but I'd see him in London once in a while and we'd pick up where we left off. He told me he'd met a girl in the States – I had no illusions about him, I just didn't know it was you.' Conor laughed softly. 'He probably guessed I'd have had a few things to say to him if I knew he was carrying on with the boss's daughter. Thing is, he said he fell in love. He was talking about leaving his wife for you.'

'You're kidding me?'

'When you dumped him, you broke his heart.' Conor watched her closely. 'Nothing more than he deserved for playing around, mind you.' The deep silence of the woods enfolded them. 'I was surprised,' he said finally. 'When I heard you talking to your ma this morning, and you said it was JJ . . . I thought you were better than that, to fall for a married man. But you didn't know.'

She sensed the question in his words. 'I promise.' She raised her face to him. 'I couldn't bear it if you thought badly of me.'

Conor stepped towards her. 'Darcy, I—'

'Darcy? Darcy!' They turned as one, hearing Diana's voice bellowing across the lawn towards them.

'I have to go,' she said, handing his jacket back to him.

'Listen, Darce. Diana told me you've put some of your inheritance into the Castle. Thank you.'

'The least I could do, now Ma is talking about retiring.'

'Are you really prepared for all this?'

'You think I'm not?' Darcy put her hands on her hips.

'It's just, you know how your life has been, with your ma. The photographers, and the newspapers. You know that's what it will be like, don't you, once you're on TV?'

'I know.' Darcy looked back at the house. 'You think I've forgotten what it was like with you, too?' She raised her chin, as the sun broke through the clouds, shafts of golden light filtering through the leaves above, cloaking them. 'What choice is there? We have to save the Castle.'

'I'm here, if you need me,' he called as she walked away. He watched her run across the lawn to the Castle, and lowered his lips to the still warm collar of the jacket, inhaling the ghost of vanilla, breathing in her fragrance.

17

Silver moonlight spread across the purple mountains like a cloak as Conor walked from his cottage through the misty valley to the hotel. He'd barely slept. His head was thumping from too many cigarettes, and he wanted a drink so badly it gnawed in his stomach like hunger. The gentle rain was cool on his face, the silence a blessed relief. He unlocked the hotel kitchen and turned on the strip lights, which flickered and hissed into life. He went to hang his jacket on the rack, and paused, his hand halfway to the hook. Someone had stuck a badly printed screenshot of Darcy's photo on the corkboard. Conor unpinned the page of paper. Darcy's face smiled up at him, unguarded, trusting. *Beautiful*, he thought. It was the same image he saw in his mind every time he closed his eyes through the night. He carefully folded the paper, unable to just screw it up, and tossed it into the bin.

As he waited for the kettle to boil, he unhooked the kitchen phone and dialled a New York number. 'Howya, Mammy,' he said. 'Were you in bed yet?' He took down a mug and spooned in some coffee. 'Nah, nothing special. Just felt like hearing your voice.' He listened to her talking, and took a bottle of milk out of the fridge. 'Yeah, it's fine, business is picking up with the new show. I'll send you a photo of Chris I took yesterday – he had his first ride.' Conor listened for a moment. 'Well, news does travel fast. Did she? That was helpful of my sainted sister to show you.' He took a deep breath as his mother chattered on. 'No, she's not a dirty whore, Ma. She's a fine girl, just like her mother, and she's been tricked by someone.' Conor closed his eyes and pinched the bridge of his nose. He remembered how the news that it was JJ hurt him like a physical blow. 'Ma, you can't believe everything you read on those gossip sites.'

He flicked through his iPod and set it down in the dock on the counter. The full notes of BB King's 'Sweet Sixteen' echoed through the empty kitchen. *Sweet eighteen*, Conor thought, *what's the difference?* He couldn't reconcile the child he'd first met with the woman she had become. He was restless, his blood quickened. *Jealous?* Every time he thought of the photograph, he thought of her with JJ, in that meadow. *I'm not a kid anymore*. Conor looked up at the sound of the outer door banging open. 'Got to go, Ma. You've enough money until the end of the month? Good. Love you too.' Conor hung up just as Beatrice walked into the kitchen.

'Up early, or is it late?' she said, shaking the rain from her umbrella in the corridor. She slid it into the stand and sauntered over to him. Conor caught the scent of ripe fruit, melon and berries in her shampoo, and her hair was still wet from the shower.

'What are you doing up at 4 a.m.?'

'Couldn't sleep.'

'I just thought I'd crack on with the day,' he said, turning away from her. 'Go back to bed.'

'I saw the kitchen light turn on, so I thought I'd see if I could help you with anything.' She rested her hand close to his on the counter as Conor scanned the printout of reservations for the day. 'Shame about that photo, eh? Poor Darcy. Have you seen her? She must be so upset; I know I would be. I wonder where they got it from. Maybe an old boyfriend with a grudge?'

'We'll sort it out,' he said, not looking up from the book.

Beatrice laid her hand on his. 'Con, you just have to ask, you know. I know Tris wants to drum up some competition or rivalry between us for this silly show, but I like it here. I want to stay, to help you.'

Conor looked at her hand on his, and pulled away. 'Competition? We'll see about that.' Beatrice banged her shoulder against the beam as she stepped aside to let him pass, and winced. 'Are you all right?'

'Fine. A little sore. You want to see what I did on my day off?' She began to slip her shirt over her shoulder, turning.

'Nah, you're all right.'

'Spoilsport.' She pursed her lips, looked up at him through sooty lashes. 'We could have some fun, you know? Come on, Con. I know you. I know all the rumours—'

'That was then, this is now,' he said, holding her gaze. 'All I want is for this place to be a success.'

After lunch, Conor sat hunched over the kitchen table, scanning through his laptop. His brow was furrowed, and his gaze flickered quickly across the text reflected in the lenses of his reading glasses.

'Whatcha up to?' Darcy said, nudging him as she walked by to the dishwasher, a plate and mug in hand.

'Sorting out a few of these feckin' eejits,' he said, his fingers jabbing at the keys. 'There are some sad, spiteful bastards out there.'

Darcy peered at the screen. 'Oh no, Con. You're not responding to the comments on the photo, are you?' She put her hand on his shoulder. 'I mean, thank you, but you don't need to. I'm a big girl. You can't please everyone, and some people are just going to get a kick out of saying online what they wouldn't dare in the flesh.'

'Comments? Bugger that – I started off knocking a few of the trolls back on the site and then I checked my books for the first time in ages.' He laughed manically. 'Look at this little bastard. I bet I know him, from what he's written. What kind of review starts "Hahaha . . .?" I've had a look at his profile, too. He had the cheek to tag along on every post the PR office had put up about my last cookbook to plug his own – I bet it's him . . .'

'Let it go, Con.' She squeezed his shoulder.

'Little git. Listen to this: "More cooking, less photos of Mr Ricci's perfect life."' Conor's jaw flexed. 'Perfect life? Bloody sock puppet with his one-star reviews, not brave enough to face me himself. In the old days you could take a bad review and wipe your arse on it. Now—' he said, jabbing at the screen with his finger, 'they're there in perpetuity. When something goes up online, it's like some stranger walking into your own house and punching you in the face.'

'Tell me about it,' Darcy said under her breath, loading her plate into the dishwasher. She came and sat beside him, reading with her chin cupped in her palm. 'They're not all bad, Con.' Darcy scrolled through. 'You've got some wonderful reviews – look at all those five stars.'

'You don't remember them, though, do you? That's not human nature.' He looked at Darcy. 'Don't you get it? They're in our home. Like bloody vampires, we invited them in and now these . . . these *parasites* are in our lives.'

'Take it easy, Con.'

'They take something beautiful, that's taken years to create, and they suck it dry.'

'What are you two talking about?' Beatrice said, wandering in with Diana. She picked up an apple from the fruit bowl.

'Trolls, sock puppets . . .' Darcy said.

'We should sue that site,' Diana said, taking a seat at the head of the table. 'I've got my lawyer looking into it.'

'This guy's the worst,' Beatrice said, scrolling through her phone. She held up the screen so that Darcy could see. 'He calls himself Mr Creosote.'

'Like the Monty Python character?'

'Exactly. Prides himself on being boorish, goes after all the celeb chefs and food presenters. He has a bit of a soft spot for you, though. Calls himself your biggest fan.' Beatrice's nose twitched. 'Didn't stop him spending most of the weekend slagging Conor off.'

'Let me see,' Conor said, reaching for her phone.

'People like that are a waste of oxygen.' Diana frowned. 'Can't we do something?'

'Would you like me to take care of it?' Beatrice stared at her.

'Yeah, set all your followers on him, that would really sort him out,' Darcy said, laughing.

'They are terribly loyal,' Beatrice said, straight faced. 'They would do anything for me.'

'I just don't get the online world,' Diana said. 'These people you've never met before treat you like you're their best friend. Like they're part of your family.'

'That's weird, right?' Beatrice watched her.

'Totally,' Darcy said. 'There's no privacy anymore – they know all about your intimate life. It's like they are stealing your life, getting under your skin.' Darcy shivered. 'Sorry, I didn't mean to go on. I've just been through the ringer a bit.'

'It's OK. You can all trust me.' Beatrice smiled sweetly. 'It's good to talk.'

'Thanks. It just feels sometimes like you can't get away. I reckon half the people in at lunch were here today because of the press coverage. I looked around the dining room and they were all staring at me. It was like a nightmare, knowing some of them had seen me naked.' Darcy hunched her shoulders, pulled the sleeves of her sweater down over her hands.

'If anyone gives you any trouble, you just come and tell me,' Conor said.

'Thanks. It's like being in a fish bowl, isn't it? Because everyone knows the Castle, they know where we are. When I was little, even with some of the doors marked "Private", we had people walk into the house kitchen while we were having dinner, like we were exhibits at the zoo, or something.' She shook her head. 'I can't tell you the number of times that I looked up to find some stranger staring through the window.'

'Stalkers?' Beatrice said.

'A few have been . . . over interested. Nothing serious.' Diana laughed. 'I'm not Lady Gaga.'

'Is that why you're building a house by the lake, Con?' Beatrice said. Darcy glanced at her, surprised. 'I'm sorry. I didn't mean to pry. I just overheard Conor talking.'

'The lake? My lake?' Darcy said, turning to him.

'Your lake?' Conor said, puzzled. He thought of the peace he felt there, the deep silence of the still water and the steep wooded land enclosing it. 'I told you I bought a piece of land?'

Darcy looked at her mother. 'Not the lake, though.'

'After the divorce I just . . . I just wanted to build somewhere safe, and quiet,' he said. 'Somewhere of my own. I've never had that.'

'I feel like I've said the wrong thing,' Beatrice said, smoothing down her skirt as she stood.

'No. Though I don't know how you heard about it,' Conor said. His face softened as he turned to Darcy. 'Listen, come and take a look, if you like.'

'I didn't think anyone else knew about it,' Darcy said, frowning. 'It was my secret place, when I was a kid. I used to make camps down there.'

'Well you should have said something,' Diana said.

'Kind of defeats the point of it being a secret,' Darcy said. 'You could have asked me before selling off part of the estate.'

'You weren't here. Besides, it's too late now.' Diana pushed her chair back. 'Enough of the sentimental trips down memory lane. We had better get going. We're filming up on the coast this afternoon.'

'Do you need me?' Darcy said.

'No, but we're short staffed, so I want you in the kitchen tonight with Conor. I'll be fine with Tris to help me.'

121

'I could come out with you,' Beatrice said.

'Thanks, but I can manage,' Diana said. 'You've been great through all this. I don't know what we would have done without you.' She tilted her head. 'What are your plans, long term?'

'Me?' Beatrice blinked.

'It's not a trick question. I know you are ambitious.'

Beatrice relaxed. 'The usual, I suppose – I want to be you, really.'

'Oh?' Diana raised her chin.

'I'm going to write the Bible of Baking, supply supermarkets internationally, run boutique shops – like Lavender Cupcakes but bigger, better. And retire as a multimillionaire by the time I'm forty.'

'Is that all?' Darcy said, laughing.

'It's good to think big, to have dreams,' Diana said.

'Dreams? This TV show is just the first step on the road to world domination,' Beatrice said, deadpan. When she saw the look of alarm on Darcy's face, she smiled. 'Just kidding.'

'Come on, Darce, let's get to work,' Conor said, leaving his laptop open on the kitchen table. He helped Diana to her feet, and stepped aside to let her and Darcy pass.

Beatrice waited until she heard the back door close, then she swivelled Conor's laptop around and clicked on the direct message symbol: *Mr Creosote*, she typed. *Recording new series with Diana and Darcy Hughes. Would like to feature you as top food blogger. Interested? Email me at . . .* Beatrice paused and typed in one of her own email accounts. *Thx. Conor Ricci.* A couple of minutes later, she heard her smartphone buzzing in her bag, and she picked up the reply. 'Bingo,' she said under her breath. She deleted the message from Conor's account, and closed down the laptop.

18

At first light, Darcy swam. She surfaced at the centre of the lake, dark water rushing behind the flick of her slim leg, droplets clinging to her face, her slick hair. It had rained through the night, and Darcy breathed in the scent of the damp earth and wood, her eyes closed, feeling the fresh dawn air fill her like wine. The sun rose through the trees, shifting carpets of light gilding the grass. This lake was Conor's now, but here she felt she had come home.

She turned at the ring of her phone on the shore, and slipped into a fluid crawl, cutting through the water. The lake was encircled with trees green and full with summer and time. Here and there, birds awoke, disturbed by the phone, heralding the day, calling up the sunrise bruising the sky apricot and gold.

'Hold on,' she murmured, 'hold on.' She covered her chest with one arm as she reached the shore, and leapt across the pebble-strewn flats. She grabbed her sweater and pulled it over her head, rummaging in the basket.

'Hello?' she said, clicking on the phone. She held it with one hand as she towelled off her legs with her white T-shirt.

'Darcy?' She could hear the noise and chatter of an office in the background, felt glad she wasn't there. 'Were you sleeping? I'm in Dubai with Sasha – it's only six with you?'

'Lyn? Don't worry, I'm up.'

'Oh, God, love. I heard about the photo. Those bastards. Are you OK? Has your mother gone mad?'

'At first.' Darcy glanced around, letting the silence seep in to her. She stepped into a short floral skirt and pulled it up, wiggling her hips, before sitting on the grass to dry her feet and put her pair of silver Converse on. 'It's good to hear your voice, Lyn. I have missed you.'

'You too, darling. I can't wait for you to see the little man. That outfit you sent was adorable.'

'Why don't you stop off on your way back to the US?'

'Really? Wouldn't we be in the way?'

'No, there's loads of room, and it would be fun for you to meet everyone.'

'How's Mr Rock 'n' Roll?' Lyn said, laughing.

'Conor?' Darcy hugged herself. 'He's ... He's been great with all of this. I had to tell them it was JJ, in case it comes out in the papers.'

'It will, just you wait and see. Bloody parasites.'

'Catering isn't a career, it's a disease,' Darcy said, looking out across the lake. 'If I'm going to make a go of it here, I need somewhere to get away from it all.' *From them all.* Darcy smiled, crooking the phone under her jaw, and leant down, picking up a smooth oval stone from the lake shore. She turned the stone in her fingers and stood, rubbing the surface with her thumb as she walked to the edge of the lake. 'Talk to Sash, promise you'll think about stopping off here?' She tucked a snaking tendril of glossy dark hair behind one ear and looked out across the glimmering surface of the lake, the mirror of the sky.

'Will do. Call me anytime if you need a shoulder, OK?'

Darcy hung up, and slipped the phone in the pocket of her skirt. She swung her arm back, and sent the stone skipping across the water in a series of elegant arcs.

'Not bad.'

She spun round at the sound of a man's voice. 'Conor?' He

stood a few feet from her, leaning in the shade of a tall oak. Her eyes widened. 'How long have you been there? And what on earth are you wearing?'

Conor walked into the light, and gave her a twirl. 'Utility kilt,' he said, the heavy black fabric flaring as he faced her. A tight black T-shirt defined his broad shoulders, and a battered pair of biker boots finished off the outfit.

'I like it,' she said. 'I think.'

'You know how it is. You spend all day sweating in the heat of the kitchen. It feels good to get a little air.'

'Chef's arse?' Darcy covered her mouth, trying not to laugh.

'The glamour.' He grinned, squatting down on his heels to pick out the perfect stone. 'There's an art to this, you know.' He glanced up at her. The morning sun gleamed on his black curls, and his eyes were the same grey as the silver lake beyond. Darcy felt her stomach freefall, watching him.

'Reckon you can do better?' she said.

'Reckon I can.' He threw the stone across to Darcy, picking up another stone for himself. She realised she was staring. 'Nice swim?'

'I couldn't resist,' she said, blushing. 'It smelt so wonderful out here.'

'Petrichor,' he said, filling his lungs. 'The smell of the earth after the rain.'

'Doesn't it mean something about coming back to life?'

He cocked his head. 'I love it too. Love swimming in the rain.'

'It was too tempting.'

'No law against skinny dipping.'

'I wasn't! I kept my knickers on . . .'

'Did you now?'

'They're nude.' She cringed inwardly, felt the heat rising in her neck, her cheeks. 'Were you spying on me?'

'I was up on the hill brow, checking the site.' He held her

gaze. 'Voices travel here, have you not noticed that?' Conor flashed her a quick smile. 'Ready? Count of three . . .' They stood side by side at the edge of the lake, arms flexed. A warm breeze played at the hem of her cotton sweater, whispering against the skin of her stomach. Darcy glanced at him, waiting. 'Three!' The stones arced across the lake, skipping in tandem together. Conor shielded his eyes. 'Well I never. Damn, you're good.'

'Lot of practice. Told you I love it here.'

'Funny, isn't it? Back when I started working for Di I came out here most days.'

'So did I, as a kid.'

'How come we never bumped into one another?'

'Maybe it wasn't the right time,' Darcy said, watching him. As Conor turned to her she looked away. 'Tell me about this house you're building here.'

'I just want a place that's . . .' He frowned, thinking. 'Simple.'

'Authentic?'

'Exactly.' He gestured towards the lake. 'A refuge. When the view's this good, you don't need much. I don't need much,' he corrected herself. Conor strode back towards the woods and opened a leather saddle bag on the side of his motorbike, which she hadn't noticed parked up among the ferns in the shadow of the trees. He pulled out a sheaf of blueprints.

Conor unfolded the plans, smoothing them out against the bark of a fallen tree, green and soft with moss. As she stood at his side, Darcy picked up the faint scent of clean laundry, toothpaste. He smelt of the morning.

'You're planning to live here? I mean, full time?'

Conor nodded.

'But the Castle's huge. Diana's planning to retire to her place in the Maremma, in Italy you know? You can take over her suite in the tower; I don't need it.'

'Nah, I've given over fifteen years to the place, I don't need to live there too. How big do you think a house needs to be?'

He gazed out across the lake. 'I need this, some peace and quiet, not a Castle.'

'Fresh start?'

'Something like that.' Conor relaxed, his shoulders falling.

'Good. That I can understand. Now I know where you're coming from. I thought this was some kind of . . .'

'Folly?' Conor held her gaze. 'No. I want this to be my home.'

'Would you like some coffee?'

'If you have some?'

She swung a backpack up onto the tree, and pulled out a silver Thermos. 'Muffin?'

'Yes, dear?' A smile played across his lips. 'Muffin? What kind of pet name is that?' Darcy held up a blueberry muffin, still warm and fragrant from the oven. 'Thank you. Did you make this?'

'Of course. Couldn't sleep.'

'So you're practising your baking, are you?'

'If the competition is strong, you raise your game.' She flashed him a quick look. 'Now, Mr Ricci, why don't you tell me about this house you're building?'

'This is what the architect has drafted,' Conor said. 'You can see it's pretty basic.'

'Just as I'd do it.' Darcy sipped her coffee.

'Where we can have some fun is with the finishes, the interiors.'

'You're a decorator now?'

Conor glanced up at her, amused. 'More of a tip surfer than chintz and swags. Fergus has been helping me.' He pulled out a pencil from his pocket, and began to sketch over the blueprint. 'If I get them to extend the deck out here, into the water, you can sit there and watch the sun come up. I think you want to maximise the light here . . . and here.' He deftly marked up the plans. 'I think they should put in some skylights too. Look.' He strode down towards the water, and lay down on a soft patch of sunlit grass. 'Come on,' he said, patting the ground beside him. Darcy laughed, and put her coffee down. She joined him, lying back with her head resting on her arm. 'Imagine. This is where the bed will be. What do you see?'

'Sky. Clouds. Trees.'

'If we put in skylights, it'll be dark enough down here at night time for you to see the moon, shooting stars . . .' Conor turned to look at her. 'Imagine waking up to this view every day.' He saw her relax, a slow smile warming her face. *Imagine.* She turned over to face him.

'I love it. Do it.'

'What else would you do?' Conor propped himself up on his elbow. 'Listen, we're not working tonight. How about dinner? You can help me with some ideas. I've never done anything like this before, and you've always had good taste.'

'Sure, come over this evening if you like.'

'No, that's OK. I'll cook.' He jumped to his feet. 'Be good for you to get out of there. Whole place is crawling with paparazzi this morning; the *Sun*, the *Mirror*, even the *Kenmare News* has sent along a man,' he said and winked. Darcy felt nauseous.

'Can I bring anything?' she said, as Conor gathered up the plans.

'Just yourself,' he said, striding away. He kicked his leg over the bike.

'Steady on,' Darcy said, laughing as she watched his kilt swing into place.

'Bring your togs if you're feeling prudish.' Conor glanced back at her and grinned. 'But we don't stand on ceremony, as you know.' He kicked down on the bike and rode off along the forest track, raising a hand in farewell.

19

After dinner, they drove west in Conor's truck along the coast towards Sneem, the bay shimmering in the evening light at their side. Conor leant one arm on the open window. A fresh breeze blew through Darcy's hair, and she settled back in her seat, replete after the delicious meal, relaxed by the glass of champagne she had enjoyed with the oysters. She glanced down at Conor's hand as he changed gear, at the pale line on his ring finger, fading already into his tanned skin. She imagined reaching out, lacing her fingers in his. It took her a moment to register that an old love song had come on the radio, and the words of longing and desire made her feel awkward.

'I'm going to nod off if we listen to this,' she said.

'Boring you, am I?' Conor glanced at her, smiling.

'No.' She nudged him. 'It's just been a long day. Mind if I change it?'

'Help yourself.' He accelerated uphill, reaching across Darcy to the glove box. 'See if you fancy anything.'

Darcy flicked through the CDs, the heat rising in her cheeks. *See if you fancy anything.* She stopped when she found one by Conor's band, *The Brigade.*

'I didn't know you'd put out a CD.'

'It was just a bit of a laugh for Christmas last year,' he said. 'Keep it, if you want.'

'Thanks. So where are we going?' Darcy said, turning up the volume.

'I thought it might help you to visualise the house to see something the guy's done before.' Conor's truck pulled off the main road, and bumped along a rough track leading towards the coast.

'The architect?'

'Yeah. I'm planning on doing a lot of work myself but his builders will get the structure up.' He pulled in to a gateway, and switched off the engine. Darcy opened the truck door, letting the cool, sea-scented air drift in. 'Look, Darce, I think after everything that's happened in the last couple of days I should be completely honest with you.'

'Sure.' She settled back in the seat, giving him her full attention. The setting sun was warm through the windshield, and she felt drowsy, happy just to be away from the Castle. To be close to him.

'The reason all the articles and biographies gloss over my early years,' he said and paused. 'It always says we travelled a lot with Da's work.'

'Oh?'

'But Da ran out on us when I was still a kid. I was a juvenile offender, Darcy, in England.' He watched her, gauging her expression. 'A Borstal boy, as they used to say. I was banged up.'

'But you came back here, afterwards?'

'Yeah. I went to live with my granddad in Dalkey when I was seventeen. Ma had gone to the States with my sister by then.' He looked out across the line of the land, to the sea. 'People ask me why I've stayed at the Castle so long. Why I didn't open my own restaurant.'

'Why didn't you?' she said, and Conor turned to her.

'I fell for the place. My heart's here. I've travelled all over the world, but I always come back.'

'Do you want to tell me why you were locked up?'

'I hit a man who hurt someone I cared for a lot.'

'And they prosecuted you for that?'

'I hit him badly.' Conor looked down.

'But you were just a kid?'

'That's no excuse. I'm not proud of myself, but I'd do the same again, if anyone tried to hurt someone I loved.'

'Was it a woman?'

'A girl.' He glanced at her and smiled. 'First love. You think the sun rises and sets with them, don't you?' He shook his head. 'She was young, and foolish, and she was at a party. I wasn't there to protect her, you see? She got drunk, or someone spiked her drink, I don't know, either way she had no memory of the night. This so-called friend of hers screwed her.'

'Jesus. Poor girl. How did you find out?'

'The idiot bragged about it, didn't he? Think he'd wanted her for a long time and he saw his chance. A friend of mine told me he was in the pub bad-mouthing her a couple of days later, and I . . .' Conor took a breath. 'I had a bit of a temper on me in those days. I went round to have it out with him, accused him of lying. Unfortunately my fiancée—'

'You were getting married?'

'Didn't I tell you that bit?' Conor let his head fall back against the seat. 'It was crazy. We were so young, but I was very . . .' He searched for the right word. 'I was very serious. I wanted to do the right thing by her. Unfortunately, my girl turned up in the pub just at the moment I laid into him. I was half cracked by then, raving. I told her to deny it, and she couldn't.'

'What happened?'

'I took the guy outside and beat him unconscious.' Conor turned his head to look at Darcy. 'I thought I was defending her honour, you know? But I just lost it. I could have killed him.'

'He raped her. What you did wasn't right, but it's under-standable.' Darcy put her hand on his. 'What happened to the girl?'

131

'She was devastated. She hadn't wanted anyone to know, you see? Now everyone knew ... she couldn't stand the shame. Couldn't cope with what I'd done. She came to see me once, while I was locked up. I'll give her that.' Conor looked at her. 'It's a small world, you know, and I wouldn't want you to hear half-truths from anyone else now the press are digging around in our pasts. I was sixteen, but I was locked up because of my own actions, and I did my time.'

Darcy squeezed his hand, and nodded. 'Why don't we go and see this house?'

They walked in silence along the brow of the hill, seagulls wheeling overhead. The land gave way to rugged coastline, and a group of chestnut ponies gathered at the edge of the cliff trotted away as they approached. Beneath them, the water sparkled.

'I'm glad you trusted me enough to tell me,' Darcy said finally. 'Thank you.'

'I just don't want there to be any more surprises if we're going to be working together,' he said. She leant in to Conor's shoulder, enjoying the nearness of him. 'There. That's the house,' he said, pointing across the headland. She stepped forward, squatting down on her heels.

'It's beautiful,' she said, settling back on the grass. She stretched out her hands behind her, feeling the warm earth beneath her palms. Conor sat beside her.

'That's what I want to do with the front of the lake house, do you see? Glass from ground to roofline, so you feel like the lake comes in. What do you think? I reckon if they bring the roofline forward you'll have a natural canopy—'

'Like a veranda?'

'You'll be able to use the deck even when it's tipping down.'

'I love that idea, of sitting out watching the rain on the water.'

'If I get them to put a balcony in at first-floor level, you could leave the doors open all night,' he said, looking at her.

'Walk from the bath, to the bed . . .' The idea, the possibility hung between them.

'It's perfect,' Darcy said, 'just what I'd do with that plot if it was mine.'

'Are you mad about that? That Diana sold it without talking to you?'

Darcy shrugged. 'The Castle's hers to do with as she wants. I mean, I know one day all that will be mine,' she said, waving her hand in the direction of Dromquinna, 'but for now none of us has a say, not really. Diana's always done whatever she wants.'

'And to hell with the consequences?' Conor leant in to her, their arms crisscrossing. 'Can you picture it now?'

'Yes, yes I can,' she said.

As they drove back to the Castle, she was lost in thoughts of nights at the lake with the silence and black velvet sky, and gentle rain falling on the trees and water, and kissing him. She wondered what it would feel like to kiss him. Conor pulled up outside the back door to the house.

'Thanks, that was a lovely evening.' She turned to him. 'Good luck with Tris tomorrow,' she said. 'You're going to be great, Con. I know it.'

After he drove away, Darcy searched her bag for her keys, and found they had gone. She tried the French windows to the kitchen, but they were locked, so she strode around the house looking for an open window. She noticed the one to the old playroom was open a crack, so she slid it up and took her shoes off, tossing them through the window before she swung herself up onto the sill. She jumped down noiselessly into the room, and closed the window securely behind her. Picking up her silver Converse in her hand, she tiptoed across the room. A sharp pain in the arch of her foot made her cry out. She stifled it, hopped over to the old sofa, and cradled her foot. The lights flicked on, and Diana appeared in her heavy blue wool dressing gown, brandishing an iron poker.

'Darcy?' she said. 'What on earth?'

'I couldn't find my keys, and this window was open.' Darcy peered at the floor. 'Bloody Lego.'

'There's no pain like it. I remember you used to leave piles of it around the house like booby-traps.' Diana stooped down and picked up the bright yellow brick, tossing it into the old wooden box by the window. 'I bet it was Kato. He likes flicking the bricks around if he can get his paws on them.'

'Sorry I disturbed you,' Darcy said.

'No, I was up, cooking drop scones.' She ran her hand through her hair wearily. 'Couldn't sleep.'

'You're worried, aren't you? It's the Castle . . .'

'All we can do is our best, and hope the show is a success. Shall we have a nightcap?'

In the kitchen, Diana poured half a glass of hot water each from the orange kettle on the range, and stirred in a teaspoon of sugar. She sliced a lemon and dropped a couple of cloves into each glass, topping up with whisky.

'Thanks,' Darcy said, as her mother sat down at the table, the low lamp spilling a pool of light in the dark kitchen. Through the tall sash windows the moon lit the garden, painting the trees a shimmering silver filigree.

'Where have you been?' Diana said, and blew gently on her drink.

'Con cooked dinner.' Darcy picked at a warm drop scone. She sensed her mother tense. 'Well, when I say cooked, it was perfect – a dozen oysters, watercress salad, an apple and a glass of champagne.' She smiled. 'He wanted to show me a house designed by the guy he's using for his place by the lake.'

'I am sorry about that,' Diana said, putting her glass down. 'I had no idea it was such a special place for you.'

'Like I said, that's the point of a secret, isn't it?' Darcy said, yawning. 'Come on, we've an early start tomorrow. Let's get to bed.' She stood and followed her mother out into the dimly lit hall. 'It's going to be beautiful, the lake house.'

'Darcy . . .' her mother began, and paused. 'I don't want to speak out of turn.'

'Then don't.' Darcy folded her arms.

'Darling, I know you had a pash on Conor when you were little.' Diana smiled. 'You were so sweet.'

'Ma, we're just friends, OK? I'm enjoying his company, that's all.'

'Good, I'm glad. I was a little worried. First JJ, and now . . . Don't get me wrong, I adore Con and he's a genius in the kitchen but a complete screw-up in his personal life.'

'Ma—'

'His marriage was a disaster, he's newly out of rehab, and God knows his background is hardly—'

'He told me all about that this evening. I know he was in trouble when he was younger. I know he had, has, a temper.' Darcy started to walk away towards the stairs. 'I know he's a mess, but aren't we all?'

'Darling, I happen to know that the last thing he is looking for is a relationship.'

'He told you that?' Darcy stopped dead. She tried to hide her disappointment as she turned to her mother.

'Yes, in those exact words. He's concentrating on work, and taking care of his son and this place.'

'Just as well I'm not interested, then.' She stood on tiptoe and kissed Diana's cheek. 'I don't need warning off, or protecting. Honestly. I can take care of myself.'

20

'You're sure you're happy cooking in here?' Tristan said, looking around the restaurant kitchen. The lights flared as they were switched on one by one, and the cameraman checked the shot. 'You don't feel like a change?'

'Yeah, you're all right,' Conor said, tying a black and white bandana around his forehead, pushing his curls away from his face. He nodded towards the house. 'What'd I be doing with all the feckin' bunting and motivational quotes Ms Cupcake has strung up over there?' Conor picked up the remote for the iPod dock, and 'Sweet Sixteen' began to play. He quickly flicked on through the menu until the Rolling Stones' 'Gimme Shelter' started. He unbuckled his leather knife roll, and cricked his head from side to side.

'Make-up?' Tristan said, checking his clipboard.

'Feck off, what do you think?' Conor glanced at his reflection in the mirror above the sink, buttoning up his new chef's whites. 'What you see is what you get. Sixteen-hour days made this face.' He flexed his hands. 'Scars and burns, and endless nights. I'm a chef. It's just food. I want you to film a normal lunchtime at Castle Dromquinna, show the folks at home what it is a chef really does every day. And while that's going on, I'm going to cook something special for you.' He turned to the kitchen, and tied a blue and white striped apron around his waist. 'Right, are you ready, lads?'

'Yes, Chef,' they chorused in unison.

'Let's show these amateurs what they are up against.'

Hours later the kitchen was a seething inferno of steam and flames, Conor's knife flashing as he shucked the oysters. Shouts reverberated across the kitchen from the pass: *one lamb, two salmon, two beef* . . . He threw the samphire into a pan of boiling water, and wiped his forearm across his cheekbone, stemming the sweat pouring from his brow.

'Let's go again,' Tristan said, checking the shot.

'Tris, you're a bastard,' Conor said, wearily. He cricked his back and grimaced. The home economist took the pan off the heat, and prepared another batch of samphire.

'All right, let's give you a bit of a break. Just plate up the dishes and we'll do the close-up shots.' Tristan checked his clipboard. 'I want a bit of chat, to go with the gastroporn. We can re-record in the studio if it's not clear enough, add it in over the shots of your dishes.' He raised his hand, and counted down with his fingers.

'Conor, how old are you now?' Tristan said, signalling to the cameraman to zoom in on Conor's face. 'How long have you been cooking?'

'Thirty-six,' Conor said. 'And too bloody long.'

'Where did you start out?'

'Ballymaloe Cookery School, over in Cork,' Conor said, leaning on the counter. 'Saved my life.'

'What do you mean?'

'I was eighteen,' Conor said, his eyes creasing in a smile. 'I'd flunked every exam at school, but I'd learnt a bit about cooking.' He paused. 'Summer job. While we were travelling with my da.' He cleared his throat. Well, my grandfather saw the way I was going – just a wild boy in a band. He ran a café on Castle Street in Dalkey. He told me if I came over and worked the summer for him, he'd put me through the twelve-week certificate course at Ballymaloe.' Conor's face softened. 'I loved it there, loved their passion, the warmth and sense of welcome. Darina and Rory taught me more than how to cook. I was a mess, but they gave me back my joy in life. That was it, I was hooked. In my own small way, it's what I've been trying to do here, with organic produce and using simple beautiful ingredients. That's why my menu has watercress from the stream, and elderflower from the hedgerows, you know?'

'So who would you say is your biggest influence?' Tristan said, out of shot. The freshly cooked salmon was laid up with a place setting in front of him as if the viewer were experiencing Conor cooking for them alone.

'That's about the only thing Di and I agree on, you know? Elizabeth David.'

Tristan stifled a surprised cry. 'I was expecting Marco,' he said.

'Yeah, I know. I mean, I'll never forget saving up to eat at the Oak Room. I had to borrow a pair of shoes and I hitch-hiked from Fishguard ...' Conor went to get the dariole moulds out of the fridge. 'Marco was like a god to me, still is, and that's why me and the boys wear the blue aprons. It's a salute to Marco.' He turned the elderflower panna cottas out onto simple white plates, and arranged a fragile nest of spun sugar, leaves and flowers across the top. 'God, I've never forgotten that meal.' He lowered his gaze to the level of the counter, checking it was perfect. 'Millefeuille of crab and tomato, terrine of foie gras with Sauternes gelée ...' Conor's eyes softened at the memory. 'The wing of skate with capers and parsley ... God, people could write poetry about a dish like that.' He nodded his head, satisfied with the panna cotta. 'I had three puddings that day. Never done that before or since. Lemon tart, tarte tatin of pears, and a caramelised spiced pineapple that if I ever find myself in front of a firing squad will be my last request.' He exhaled. 'And the room – God, those gorgeous bleached oak panels, and the chandeliers. There was a drama to it, you know, a plush and a hush about the place. I sat in the lounge after shelling out over a hundred quid, with a cigar and an espresso, and I had never before felt like that. Still, replete, satisfied. Not sex, not booze, nothing has ever touched that meal.'

'You've been sleeping with the wrong people, Chef,' Tris said, and Conor burst out laughing.

'Marco has class,' Conor said. 'Everything I've done since then I've been trying to better that meal, and I haven't done it yet.' He pointed at the camera. 'Yet.'

'Did you not do a stage at El Bulli?'

'Yeah, '97, the year they got their third Michelin star.' Conor plated up the oysters, his hands deft and steady. 'There I learnt there are no limits to your imagination, I learnt about the beauty of food, how the eyes feed the soul even before you take a bite out of something. Jaysus, all those foams and globules – it was like science, you know? They made a new language.'

The frenetic activity in the kitchen continued beyond Conor, his number two shouting out the orders, cries of 'behind you, hot pan, watch your back'. The men and women moved like dancers along the long and narrow line, waiters standing ready on the other side of the pass. The air was full of noise and familiar banter, born from years of working together in a confined and pressurised space. But Conor leant against the counter growing still and thoughtful. 'We're not El Bulli, but we're off the beaten track. If people are coming over from London or New York, they have to really want to come here. To hell with "worth a detour", I want my third star – it's my job to make it worth a special journey. But if you ask me who my biggest influence is, I'd still say David. I read her cookbooks the same way other lads read *Playboy*, you know. She turned me on.' He glanced up to see Darcy at the window, her hands cupped around her face. She poked out her tongue, and he smiled. 'Funny, isn't it, how suddenly your life can change.'

Conor blinked, looked at Tristan. 'David changed the whole face of cooking in this country for ever. Someone said she was like sunshine – you know, she lit up the whole scene. Olive oil. Pasta. All these gorgeous ripe vegetables.' Conor beckoned to Darcy through the window. 'Come on, let's ask someone who knows. Hey, Darcy,' he called out, as she appeared at the kitchen door. He pointed to the camera. 'Tell Tris about Elizabeth David.'

'The Sainted Elizabeth? Her books are sacrosanct in this house. And boy, she could write,' Darcy added. Conor dragged across two stools for them, and they sat opposite Tristan.

'Here, try this.' Conor leant across to the cutlery tray and scooped out a teaspoon of the elderflower pudding for her to try. Darcy's eyes closed and she let out a soft moan as he held the spoon at her lips. Tristan winked at the cameraman and signalled he should keep filming.

'I may as well give up now,' she said. 'Is that fresh mint I can taste?'

'Like it, do you?' Conor's face creased, dimples forming. 'Yeah, the little leaves are made with infused sugar.'

'Is there any more?'

'Ah-ah, you only need a little. Small bites are enough. If you eat too much it desensitises you.' He licked the spoon clean. 'Thing is, I reckon David was the first of the great food writers with real personality.'

'If my work is half as good or influential as hers one day, I'll be happy,' Darcy said.

'What about the future, Con?' Tristan said. 'You've fulfilled the dream of a lot of chefs – nice, busy little boutique hotel restaurant, kitchen garden, organic farm, the Michelin stars. What's left? What plans do you have?'

'Yeah, well I burnt out on the booze like a lot of chefs, didn't I? But I've learnt my lesson, and thank God I've been given a second chance. Di's been good to me.' Conor straightened up. 'Know what I think? Every chef I know had an unhappy childhood. They're trying to recreate something in the kitchen that they never had.'

Darcy inhaled sharply. *He's right*, she thought. *I haven't been unhappy, but I never knew my dad, and Mum was always so busy. With cooking, I'm trying to make people feel nurtured, and happy.* She looked at Con. *Loved.*

'We're trying to make something perfect. But it never is.' Conor flexed his hand, rubbed at the fading burn on his palm. 'What do I want now? More balance,' he said, looking at Darcy. He glanced at the camera. 'I haven't done anything but cook, I haven't had a social life since the 1990s.' He rubbed his face with his hands. 'Forty covers each sitting. I must be a masochist. It's why all chefs look so knackered. I want to keep my stars, but I just want some freedom back.'

'Is that why your marriage fell apart?'

Conor paused. 'It didn't help. We tried to keep going, for a long time, but Alannah didn't really want me – she wanted the idea of me, you know? Mr Michelin stars. And once she had me, she always felt second best to the kitchen. But Alannah's the mother of my son, and he's the world to me, so I love her for that, for always.' He looked at his hands. 'I'll get it right, next time. It's not enough to have talent, you have to work your arse off too, but you have to know how hard to push yourself, keep a bit in reserve. If I become chef patron, I'm going to make this place a proper partnership. I'm not a businessman, but I want to take care of my people, for them all to have an investment in the Castle.'

'What about you, Darcy, what would you change?' Tristan said.

'I . . . oh, I—' She blushed. 'I was going to say the wallpaper. All the vines and stencilling is a bit nineties, isn't it?' They all burst out laughing. 'No, seriously. I love what Con has done here, and the food is only going to get better.'

Conor turned to the camera. 'I never give up, and never give in. You watch, the best is yet to come. It's a luxury for people to eat here. I'm innovating – who wants things to stay the same? Above all, I'm serving plates full of heart and personality.'

Conor glanced across the kitchen. A new commis chef was reaching for Conor's knives. 'Oi, you!' Conor yelled, storming over. 'Cop on! Get your hands off my knives!' The boy recoiled, his pale, acne-scarred face colouring.

'I'm sorry, Chef,' he said. 'I didn't know.' Conor beckoned over his number two.

'Give this boyo a place to work and a couple of knives,' he said, ruffling the boy's hair.

'Fifteen seconds . . .' came a shout across the kitchen from Conor's sous chef at the pass.

'Right, stop blathering and listen to the man!' Conor shouted to his chefs. 'Taste, taste, taste!' The kitchen was a blur of white figures, steam, plates sent by the chefs de partie from their stations to the pass. 'Ready to dress in ten seconds.' 'Where the hell are the potatoes?' 'Five seconds.' 'Ça marche.' 'Don't wait for me, lovey, out it goes . . .'

'And cut,' Tristan said.

'You never filmed that?' Conor said.

'You have a reputation to maintain, love.' He leant in and whispered. 'We can't disappoint the girls who watched your show in the noughties and thrilled at the idea you all cooked commando under your whites—'

'No one wears underpants,' Conor said, adjusting his apron. 'Chef's arse, Tris, the heat's a killer.'

'Let's not shatter their illusions by revealing you're more disco naps and Tiger Balm for your bad back these days, eh?'

'Tris, you're a gent.'

Tristan cleared his throat. 'Well done, Con. You came across really well. Now, Darcy, this is the first time we'll be seeing you on the programme since the opening segment we filmed the other day, so they'll add in your name on screen as you come in. Conor's going for the natural look so if you're happy we'll just roll straight on without hair or make-up, OK?

142

And . . .' Tristan rolled his finger in the air to signal the next question. 'So you are a chef too?' he said, beckoning to the cameraman to focus on Darcy.

'Me? I will be, but I'm still learning. I'm nothing compared to Ma and Con.' Darcy blushed, pushing a tendril of glossy dark hair behind one ear. 'They're the stars.'

'Don't put yourself down, Darce.' Conor uncorked a bottle of wine and filled Tristan's glass. 'She's a fantastic cook—'

'I did an internship at Chez Panisse after college,' Darcy added, taking a glass from Conor. 'But there's still so much I want to know. Like how did you think of doing that?' The camera panned in to Conor's dish of local oysters. They were set on a samphire-fringed glass plate above an iPad playing a looped image of the west coast. 'You can taste the sea and the spray before you even eat one.' She took a slice of lemon, and squeezed it over an oyster, lifting the shell to her lips, Conor watching her. 'Damn it, they're perfect. How do you do it?'

'Contacts. Fresh off the boat this morning.' Conor raised his glass of water to her. 'You watch. You're going to be spectacular.' He turned to Tristan. 'Darcy is like this place – the real deal. Not that experienced yet, but she's already read more about cooking than I've forgotten, and she's travelled the world, haven't you?' Conor tapped his notebook. 'That's what makes Castle Dromquinna special – it's real, you know. Everything that goes out from the kitchen came in from the garden, or the fields around here, or the sea. Our food is part of the land.'

'Quality ingredients are everything,' Darcy said. 'That's what Ma always taught.'

'Strikes me you two make rather a good team,' Tristan said, picking up his fork to try the samphire. 'Mm, perfect. Con's all rock 'n' roll and magic, and you're all beauty and poetry.'

'Beauty and the beast, eh?' Conor said, leaning back with his arms crossed. 'I thought we were just trying to produce the best food we could.' Conor glanced at Darcy, catching her eye.

'What do you make of your other new judge?' Tristan said, sampling the oysters with a sprinkle of mignonette sauce. 'Oh God, that's good. Shallots?'

Conor shook his head. 'Sweet onion, fresh out of the garden an hour ago.' His brow furrowed. 'What do I reckon? Beatrice knows I think what she's doing is a fad, a phenomenon. Why eat a cupcake loaded with sugar when you'd be better off buying a kilo of local strawberries and cream?'

'But who doesn't love a bit of cake? It makes life a little sweeter.'

Conor took a breath, and leant towards Tristan and the camera. 'I believe living well means making real food from the region you are cooking in.'

'Is that it? That's your philosophy?'

'Yes.' Conor looked at Darcy. 'It's simple. Find your passion and follow it. As we say on the show, we're all looking for the dish which means home.'

IN THE SOUP

(feature for NomNomNom.com – only known piece by all four chefs)

When I first arrived in the South of France, the moment I stepped down from the Blue Train I smelt the most delicious fragrance. I followed this enticing aroma to a small café on a side street near the station, and a young couple eating hearty bowls of Bouillabaisse beneath a dusty yellow awning. It is still my favourite soup, and simplicity itself to make - enjoy:

Fry off 1 small onion chopped, 1 clove crushed garlic, a medium bulb of fennel, chopped, in 1 tbsp of olive oil. Add

2 bay leaves, 500 ml fresh fish stock, a pinch of saffron
and 200 g chopped tomatoes. Heat. Add 200 g fish,
200 g mussels and 50 g prawns and simmer until cooked
through.

Recipe adapted from Diana Hughes, *Hughes at Home*

I am a philistine. I love vinyl, and proper books and newspapers,
and running on the beach or in the rain, not on a treadmill. I am
hooked on a feeling, when most people are hooked into a virtual
world. It's not about ownership but instant access for them.
There's no hunger, no building appetite, which for me is half the
pleasure of delayed gratification. For the ultimate feel-good
lunch you can't beat a simple roast chicken. By the time it's
ready to eat, everyone will be mad for the delicious smells
coming from your kitchen.

Heat the oven to 200°C. Massage an organic chicken with
a bit of butter and season. Squeeze over a lemon, and shove it
inside the cavity with a handful of thyme and tarragon. For a
five-pound bird, roast for an hour and a half, basting once in
a while, until the juices run clear. Add a glass of half wine, half
stock, and a splash of cream if you want to make a sauce.

Serve with salad, veg, whatever you feel like. This time of the
year I enjoy serving a tabbouleh: cover a cup of bulgur wheat
with boiling water and leave to sit. Once the grains are soft
stir in a handful of fresh parsley, 4 spring onions, fresh mint,
garlic, and tomato (all finely chopped). Drizzle with olive oil and
lemon juice. Now don't be throwing away that chicken carcass.
My nana once travelled from Dublin to Kenmare with a tinfoil-
wrapped chicken under the car seat rather than waste it. This is
her go-to recipe for nettle soup. It even heals man flu, trust me.

To make a chicken stock: sling a chicken carcass, a roughly
chopped onion, two cracked celery stalks, a chopped leek, bay
leaf, parsley and seasoning in five pints of water and simmer
for two hours, skimming off the fat occasionally. Strain. In a

clean pan melt 2 oz butter. Chop and sweat 8 oz of potatoes,
a medium onion, and 4 oz of leeks. Season. Add 1 ¾ pints of
the chicken stock, and 6 oz of young stinging nettles. Boil and
simmer for eight minutes. Liquidise. Add ¼ pint of cream. Serve.

Recipe adapted from *Rock 'n' Roll Ricci*

I adore cold soup. Gazpacho is *so* refreshing. Wash and rough
chop: half a cucumber, a couple of tomatoes, half a red onion,
a yellow pepper, a clove of garlic, a chilli, a sprinkle of parsley
and coriander – put in a food processor with olive oil, sea salt,
pepper, a pinch of paprika and 1 tbsp of cider vinegar. Blitz, and
serve with love!

Recipe from forthcoming *Bea Happy*

The cook at our primary school was known for two things:
the gin bottles she threw with gay abandon from the kitchen
window into the stinging nettles below, and her Chicken
Supreme soup. It was supreme – if not in nature (it's really a
rice-thickened stock), then in its place on a menu otherwise
populated by liver, sago and semolina. Chicken soup came to
mean comfort. It reminded us of home.

Make a chicken stock (*ed: see Rock 'n' Roll Ricci method
above*). Shred white meat from chicken carcass, and reserve.
Cook a cup full of long-grain rice in the stock, add the chicken,
season and serve. For variation, you can add a couple of cloves
of garlic, crushed, or a thumb-length of fresh ginger, shredded,
and a few fresh scallions, chopped.

Recipe adapted from Darcy Hughes, *Appetite* Tumblr

Honey for Tea

'The critical minute is less difficult to be hit in
the boudoir than in the kitchen.'

Launcelot Sturgeon

21

The next evening, Conor stepped out of the restaurant kitchen to take some fresh air, and he leant back against the warm stone of the doorway, easing the dull pain in his back. He could hear a man's voice drifting from around the corner, and he listened as he lit a cigarette.

'Yeah, I'm going to go for it tonight,' the man said. 'Sure she's up for it. I was just speaking to that other girl, what's her name, Bea? She said not to take no for an answer. Darcy's just a prick tease—'

Conor threw down his cigarette, and strode round the corner to find Tristan's assistant, Jamie, nursing a glass of vodka at one of the terrace tables, his mobile phone clamped to his ear.

'Got to go,' Jamie said, clicking off his phone. 'Well, well. If it isn't the great Conor Ricci.'

Conor grabbed him by his collar. 'I will not hear you talk about her like that,' he said, his grip tightening.

'Steady on, old man,' Jamie said, shoving him away. He stood, stepping towards Conor. 'What's the matter? Got the hots for her yourself, have you? I was reading about you in the papers this morning – quite the player, weren't you? Even your fucking name sounds like a venereal disease.'

Conor roared, ploughing into Jamie. They fell to the floor

kicking and thumping, struggling to find a break. Conor pinned Jamie down, and raised his fist.

'Stop it!' Diana said, striding across the terrace towards them. 'What on earth do you think you're doing, brawling in front of our guests?' Conor looked up to see all faces turned towards him, the firefly glow of mobile phones filming.

'For feck's sake, man,' Conor said, wiping at his lip with the back of his hand, smarting. He scrambled to his feet, Jamie following.

'I do apologise, Mrs Hughes,' Jamie said. 'I have no idea what I said to offend him—' Conor pushed him hard against the wall.

'Conor, leave it,' Diana barked, marching back to the restaurant. 'Whatever it is you were arguing about, this is neither the time nor the place. The papers have dug up quite enough scandal without giving them fresh copy.'

'Jaysus, woman.' Conor thumped at the side of his head. 'Use your wits. This little arse was . . . he was—' His brow furrowed as he looked at Jamie. 'Never mind, you're not worth it. But you stay away from her, do you hear?'

'From what Bea told me, she'll come to me,' Jamie called after him.

'Meddlesome girl.' Conor turned to him, his hands on his hips. 'Been winding you up, has she? I know her type. In the old days, they'd send people like her to live away from the villages.' Conor tapped his head. 'Look at her eyes, man. There's nothing there. Nothing at all. No feeling.'

'But, she—'

'She reflects back at you. Like a mirror. Sure, she's good at reading other people, bouncing their emotions – jealousy, anger, whatever, back. But people like her are dead inside.' Conor leant against the wall, catching his breath.

'You mean she set me up?'

'Sure she did. Oh, all sugar and spice on the surface but she's ambitious, that one, and I've watched how she uses people.' Conor held his side, panting. 'I don't know what her game is, but I'm going to find out.' He looked up at Jamie. 'How old are you?'

'Twenty-three. What's that got to do with it?'

'You're young, you'll learn.' Conor strode away towards the old stable block. The staff quarters were quiet at this time, everyone busy with the evening service, and a civil partnership celebration in the banqueting hall. Conor looked up to the battlements where a rainbow flag billowed, the colours brilliant against the blue sky. Kato wound himself around Conor's feet as he stopped to punch in the security code at the front door. 'Shoo, Kato,' he said, and the cat stared up at him. Conor leant down to scratch the top of his head, and the cat hissed. 'Fickle bloody animal,' he said, pushing the door open.

Conor's nose wrinkled at the smell of stale smoke and beer leaching from the empty staff living room. He pressed the timer button at the bottom of the staircase and sprinted up the old stone steps of the stable block to the bedrooms. 'Beatrice,' he bellowed, striding past the shared bathroom with its strings of damp washing. He heard the tinny sound of music coming from the bedrooms, so he followed it along the corridor. The lights overhead flickered. 'Beatrice?'

Conor paused outside the door. A 'Do Not Disturb' sign stolen from the hotel swung on the door handle as he knocked. He heard the sound of a chair scraping back, and the door opened.

'What do you want?' Beatrice stood before him in an old vest and underpants, her hair unbrushed, dark circles of mascara smudged beneath her eyes.

'May I come in?'

'Be my guest, boss,' she said, stepping aside to let him in to her narrow room. The bed was unmade, dishes and coffee mugs piled up beside it. On the table, a speaker pulsed out 'Celebrity Skin'.

'That's from the kitchen,' Conor said, pointing at it. 'I've been looking for it.'

'Oh? Di said I could borrow it.' Beatrice unplugged it and handed it to him. She took a cigarette from a packet on the nightstand and lit it, sitting back on the single bed, one leg hugged to her chest.

Conor turned to her, his hands on his hips. 'Lying comes easy to you, doesn't it? What else will I find if I search this room?' He kicked at a pile of dirty clothes with the tip of his boot. 'Jaysus, it's mankier than the lads' rooms. Tidy up.'

'I'm really not feeling well,' she said, resting the heel of her hand against her forehead. 'You have no right to storm in here—' she said, drawing on the cigarette, the coal glowing in the gloom.

'I have every right, as your boss.' He took a step towards her. 'Listen, what the hell do you think you're doing setting Darcy up with that arse who works for Tristan?'

'Me? I didn't do a thing. She fancies him rotten, didn't you realise that?' Beatrice blinked, impassive. 'Ask her if you don't believe me. I think it's fun she's found someone her own age. He looks rather like JJ, don't you think?'

'JJ?' Conor checked himself, clenched his fist tight at his side. 'You get a kick out of meddling, don't you? I know your sort.'

'You just think you do.' Beatrice stood, moving close to him. 'Relax, it's just a bit of fun. You know you could get to know me a lot, lot better.'

'Like that, would you?'

'I think we both would.'

Conor took the cigarette from her, and stubbed it out in the overflowing ashtray. Beatrice moved in to him, her stomach pressed to his hip. He took hold of her arms and held her for a moment as her lips raised to his.

'I don't think so,' Conor said, thrusting her back onto the bed. 'I came here to give you your notice.'

152

'What?' Beatrice rounded on him.

'It's not working out. Once we've filmed the contest, you are out of here. There's no need to work your notice out. I'll give you your month's wages and you can leave immediately.' He looked around the filthy room. 'It won't take you long to pack, I imagine.' He swung back the bedroom door and strode along the dim corridor.

'Diana needs me,' Beatrice said, stalking after him, barefoot, silent.

'No she doesn't.'

'She does. She needs me.' She grabbed Conor's sleeve, and he turned to her at the top of the stairs. 'I won't leave her.'

'What is it with you and her, eh?' He yanked his arm free. 'You're obsessed.'

'Diana is my mentor, my friend, my best friend. I adore her, and Darcy.'

'You hardly know them. I'll tell you this for nothing – you don't deserve to breathe the same air they do.'

'Jealous, are you, Con? Jealous that Darcy got off with Jamie?'

'She didn't.'

Beatrice leant closer to him. 'I heard that they are going to go all the way tonight. Imagine that. As if Darcy would be interested in a washed-up old has-been like you. JJ, now – he was something else; any girl would love to have an affair with JJ.'

'Darcy didn't know he was married.'

'Is that what she told you?' Bea licked her lips. 'And what about you? Is that why you've come storming in here, trying to protect her, just like you did with that girlfriend of yours when you were a kid, Conor? Does Darcy know about that, eh? Does she know you were banged up?' She stepped so close to him that Conor could feel her breath on his face. 'Enjoy that, do you, Conor? Is it a release, hurting people?'

'Of course I told her. And Diana knows, though God knows

153

how you do.' He thought for a moment. 'JJ is the only one who knew. JJ told you, didn't he?'

'I know all about you, Conor. I know that you screwed up your marriage and that every single day is a fight with that gnawing ache for a drink you have in the pit of your stomach.' She tilted her head. 'Always unsatisfied, always thirsting for something.'

'I won't forget this.' He lowered his gaze. 'Never forget what people do for you or to you.'

'Quite the philosopher chef, aren't you Con? Did you get that in a cracker? Hm? What's it for, Conor? What are you hungry for? Whisky? Sex? Darcy? She doesn't need you anymore, now she has me.'

'She doesn't even like you, you stupid feckin'—' Conor stepped onto the steep stone staircase, and glanced up as the lights went out automatically, plunging them into darkness. The last thought Conor had before he stumbled and his head hit the stone steps again and again was one of surprise. How someone so small, who looked so sweet, could be so strong.

22

Beatrice stood at the head of the stairs, listening in the darkness. She stepped down, tread by tread, sensing her way. The old stone steps were cool against her bare feet. She opened the front door a crack, not switching on the light, and looked at him. Conor lay on his back, perfectly still, his head rolled to one side, one foot still raised up on the bottom step. Beatrice crouched down on the ground, laid her head beside his, watched in fascination at the pool of blood seeping towards her. She sat back on her heels and folded her arms, running through the options, calculating which if any had any advantage to her.

How could he be so mean? she thought. She picked up the broken speaker from the floor and turned it over in her hands. As if she would steal a poxy old speaker. *It hasn't even got Bluetooth.* She tossed it back on the floor. She would buy a new one, buy it with her own money, not on the cash and carry account.

A wave of self-pity surged in her, and tears pricked her eyes. She deserved a treat, she'd been working so hard helping Diana. *And what thanks do I get from you?* she thought, looking at Conor with blank eyes. *Now, if I raise the alarm, I could be the hero of the day.* How much would he remember, though? Would he remember why he came to the staff quarters, that he had sacked her? *If I leave it for a bit, while I freshen up, perhaps someone* else will find you, and we can just forget you ever came upstairs. She tilted her head. *Maybe you'd been on the booze again, Con? Missed a step?*

Beatrice liked that idea. She could picture herself in the pub that night, huddled around a table with Darcy and their friends, saying in a concerned voice: you don't think . . .

Yes, that's what I'll do, she thought, getting up from the hard, cold stone floor. She stepped over his legs, and walked slowly up the dark staircase. *Let's leave it to chance, shall we, Con?*

23

'Tris, be a love and lift the Dutch Oven up onto the Aga,' Diana said, pointing at the polished wooden kitchen shelves.

'Which one?'

'That one, the old blue one at the end. Thank you.' She lifted off the lid, filled the casserole half full with stock, and set it to heat through on the boiling plate. 'What do you want from the filming here?'

'I'd like a few linking segments which we can splice in with the shots of you with the contestants, if we need them. You talking about the Castle and what it means to you, how you came to be here, your influences and so on.'

'But people don't want me rambling on about myself.'

'No, I'm hoping for something a bit more fly-on-the-wall,' Tristan said, handing her the bulb of garlic she was beckoning for. 'A bit of humour. I want to put segments with the four of you showing how it should be done next to shots of the contestants panicking as the clock ticks down, ballsing up, dropping their tarts. Audiences love to see people trying.' Tristan checked the shot. 'If you keep your back to us, half turned to the camera, we can keep your cast out of view. When's it coming off?'

'Not soon enough,' she said, closing her eyes as the make-up woman touched up her powder. 'Thank you.' She glanced at

Tris. 'OK, shall I just potter about as usual and you ask me questions?'

'Perfect.' Tristan rolled his finger in the air to signal the cameraman. 'Di, tell me about your love affair with Italy.'

'It really began in the late sixties,' she said, scooping some freshly chopped vegetables into the stock. 'I read every one of Elizabeth David's books, but something about *Italian Food* really chimed with me. I had a little windfall when I came of age, and I just set out like a pilgrim. Of course, everyone feels *French Provincial Cooking* was her masterpiece, but I still have a soft spot for *Italian Food*. I think she really laboured over it, and I admire that.'

'Was it usual for a young woman to travel by herself like that?'

'Usual? Who cares about usual?' Diana said, her glossy grey hair swinging as she laughed. 'I travelled in luxury on the Blue Train as far as the south of France, then hitch-hiked across Italy. I explored the whole country – Venice, Florence, Rome, Naples. Then one day, I arrived in Porto Ercole.' She turned and stared out of the window, her hips resting against the bar of the stove. 'Oh God, it was glorious, after the rain and the cold here. You know when you feel like you have arrived home? I still have the same little cottage I bought in my twenties, and I plan to retire there.'

'What were you doing before you went to Italy?'

'Hm?' She glanced at him. 'I was washing up in a tiny kitchen in Dublin, and doing prep work, learning my trade from the bottom up, which is the right way to do it, not like today when these kids expect everything to be handed to them the minute they put on chef's whites.' She shook her head. 'I remember jumping down from that train the minute it arrived in the station at Nice. Oh, the colour, and the light, the heat. I had ballet pumps on, and a black polo neck down to my wrists.' She hugged herself at the memory, how the full circle of her coat spun out around the slim legs of her cigarette pants. 'God, I thought I was the bee's knees. So me and my little white suitcase set off. "Merci," I said to the porter, sliding my cat's-eye sunglasses down from my cropped black hair. I had a little pixie cut in those days – *très* chic. The station smelt of new beginnings, you know, and possibility – of sea air and black tobacco, fresh coffee. I walked along that platform looking straight ahead, chin raised, ignoring the heads turning after me, the low whistles. In the distance I caught a glimpse of the coast and I set off in that direction, not knowing where I was going to end up.'

'That must have felt pretty daring.'

'It was as if someone had turned up the colour on a television set – shades of grey gave way to Technicolor – blue skies, flaming bougainvillea, green palms, and there was the sea. I stopped at a tabac on the sea front and bought a packet of Gauloises and a box of matches.' She paused, remembering how she had glanced at an English newspaper on the counter, with the headline 'Young Mother Drowns: Suicide' and a photograph of a baby in the arms of a police officer.

'And then you hitched to Italy?'

'Yes, it was blind luck, really. I could smell the most amazing scent of cooking near the station, and I followed it to a little café on a side street. I ordered a bowl of bouillabaisse and a carafe of rough red wine. It was glorious.' She gazed into the distance.

'Di? Then what?'

'Hm? Sorry – so I was sitting in this café and a lovely old couple of chaps saw I was reading *Italian Food*, and they offered to take me with them.'

'What, to Italy?'

'Yes, I know. You wouldn't dare these days, would you, but it seemed like a grand adventure,' Diana said and laughed. 'One of them was a publisher with a string of magazines, and he commissioned me to write a column for one of his glossies about my travels in Italy. The magazine was swinging, you know – a real feminist, boho magazine, so I suited the image perfectly.'

'You really landed on your feet,' Tristan said.

'Time and time again. More lives than Kato.' Diana leant down as the cat came running into the kitchen miaowing, and scooped him up in her good arm. 'What's up with you?' She looked at the kitchen door, aware suddenly of Jake's frantic barking.

24

Diana stood in the driveway, waving off Tristan and his crew for the day. She turned to the house and stopped to dead-head a rose. She ran her hand over the weathered surface of the stone pot. *We bought this in Italy*, she thought, memories filling her mind like a projector illuminating the screen in an old cinema. She smiled, remembering how Kavanagh had lifted it in his great bear-like arms, and carried it from the market in Porto Ercole to his car, all because she had admired it. She looked across the driveway now at the old white Lancia Integrale. She had kept Kavanagh's last car. *All these years*, she thought. *We're both on our last legs.* She cupped her hands around the pot, imagining his hands there. She remembered lying in bed with him the first morning, comparing hands, the sunlight dancing through the sheer drapes at the window overlooking the bay in Talamone. Her slender, long fingers were dwarfed by his dark hands.

'You're the chef? My God, when I asked to see the cook I was expecting a little Italian,' he'd said to her. His first words, at the dark wood-panelled bar in the restaurant she was cooking for in Porto Ercole. He had been sitting alone on the stool, waiting to use the telephone. The light was like amber, gold as honey, an old chandelier gleaming above a curved glass display of desserts. A local boy, drinking a cup of strong espresso, was having an argument with his girlfriend, and while Kavanagh waited he had asked to see the chef to compliment them on the meal. The party of people he was with took up half the restaurant with a long table, and they were rowdy and joyful, several empty bottles and bowls on the table. Diana had decorated the room with simple trestle tables, covered with starched white linen, fresh vine and olive branches winding among the storm lanterns with white candles. The wine glasses gleamed, the old stone walls radiated the warmth of the day. It was the TV crew's last night in Italy, and they were celebrating. Diana had perched on the stool at Kavanagh's side, resting her elbows on the bar.

'Tell me, do you enjoy all that?' he said.

'All what?' She'd looked up at another crash from the kitchen, another pot thrown by her then boyfriend, the owner.

'The drama, the fighting?' Kavanagh leant towards her, giving her a light. A pistachio-coloured Lambretta pulled up on the street outside, and a young couple joined their friends at a table near the window.

'Do I enjoy the fighting? No, not particularly.' She cupped his hand in hers, inhaled. 'Thank you.'

'Then why put up with it?' He leant closer still. 'Is it that your man's as wild in the sack?'

'God, no,' Diana said, and laughed. She remembered the amusement in his dark eyes. 'I love it here. I love the country, the cooking.'

'But not him?' He raised his hand to the bartender. 'Champagne.'

'Are you celebrating?'

'I am now.' Kavanagh held her gaze. 'Well, well. How does a slight, elegant girl like you from . . .'

'Dublin.'

'A beautiful girl from Dublin, like you, cook Italian food better than a native? Those courgette flowers in batter were

162

the most delicious thing I've eaten in years.' The champagne popped, and Kavanagh handed her the first glass.

'To surprises.' She raised her glass in a toast.

'Now, tell me, have you ever seen the south-west of Ireland, Mrs . . .'

'Miss Hughes.'

'Thank you,' he said, raising his gaze and glass to the ceiling.

'Call me Diana,' she said, and laughed.

'Have you ever seen heaven, Diana?' He chinked his glass against hers.

'And where might that be?'

'Why, Kerry, of course!' He leant towards her. 'Come with me away from this place, and I will show you such beauty—'

'I'm perfectly happy here.'

'Do you not miss the rain?'

'Never.' She smiled, sipping her champagne.

'What about a decent glass of the black stuff?'

'Sometimes.' Her eyes sparkled as she looked at him.

'Come away with me, Miss Diana Hughes.' He lowered his voice. 'We'll have such adventures. And with your skill in the kitchen, and mine in the b—' She raised her eyebrows. 'Boardroom, I was going to say boardroom.' Kavanagh held her gaze. 'Trust me, I will make you a star chef, and if you come with me to Kerry, in a sky full of stars, yours will shine the brightest.'

She remembered he had written the name of his hotel on a matchbook, and handed it to her, like a dare. Early the next morning, on the way to the market, she found herself parking her orange Fiat 500 F opposite the hotel beneath the green shade of a cypress tree. She stared at the building for a time, fighting the temptation to go in. A tap on the passenger window made her jump, and she looked across to see Kavanagh, stooping down to look at her over the top of his sunglasses. She leant across and opened the door for him. 'Where are we going?' he said, folding himself into the small car.

'The market,' she said.

They drove through the narrow streets of the whitewashed town. 'I didn't think you'd come,' he said.

'I almost didn't.' She glanced at him.

'Tell me something: what would happen if you just cleared out of town?' he said.

'You're very sure of yourself, aren't you, Mr Kavanagh?' She changed gear, accelerating up the hill.

'Ah, for sure the Italians have their way with food and wine and girls,' he said, his hand trailing the air through the window. 'But style, speed and passion can be very overrated.'

'You think so, do you?'

He stretched his arm across the back of her seat and turned to her as she parked up in a side street near the market. 'What would you be wanting all this sunshine for? Don't you miss the green, the rain . . .' He leant closer. 'A warm fire on a cold night, a whisky and a woollen jumper—'

Diana laughed in surprise. 'Come on,' she said, jumping from the car. She lifted her shopping basket onto her arm, and waited for him to join her.

'What are you buying?' he said, lighting a cigarette. He swung his dark jacket over his shoulder. A tabby cat watched them from the warm sun spot on the wall at the end of a garden tangled with bougainvillea and jasmine. 'Ingredients for tonight?'

'It's my day off, didn't I say?' She glanced over her shoulder as they pushed their way through the crowd, and he smiled, understanding. They strolled slowly from stall to stall, feeding one another morsels of warm bread, prosciutto, parmigiano cheese, slivers of raw porcini mushrooms. After shopping, she drove out towards the Maremma coast, and they picked wild arugula for their picnic. They laid down blankets overlooking

164

the sea, and spread out their haul, eating and talking.

There was no hurry, she remembered, not with him. It felt like they had all the time in the world.

'The thing I love about this place is that everything is quality over quantity. The local producers operate on a small scale but everything is done to the most exacting standards,' he said. 'That's what my restaurant is going to be like.'

'You're opening a restaurant?' she said.

'Did I not tell you?' His eyes creased with amusement. 'It's just the beginning, you see. There will be a chain of restaurants one day, cookbooks, television series—'

'Ambitious, aren't you?'

'Why not? A Mediterranean place. I reckon Dublin's ready for it, don't you? All I need is a good chef.'

'Do you now?'

'Don't suppose you know of anyone?'

Diana heard a whining from Conor's truck, and she strode across the driveway, still thinking of Kavanagh. *He loved to watch me cook*, she thought, remembering a night in their first flat in Dublin. She was massaging a lamb joint with garlic, oil and rosemary, chatting to him from the galley kitchen. He sat on the sofa in the dimly lit living room, smoking, watching. She remembered the weight of his gaze on her, how she felt her blood quickening, hot, even now. Diana touched the nape of her neck, blushing, remembering how he had walked to her, kissed her, the smell of the oil and herbs on her fingers, how he had made love to her against the kitchen counter. She sighed with longing.

It took us years to work our way up to this, she thought, turning back to look at the Castle. *All through the seventies, and the eighties, all those cookbooks and tours, the ever larger restaurants.* She frowned, tucking her good arm across her stomach, holding her purple cardigan down against the wind. *It was his dream, to come home to Kerry. Was it mine?*

She opened the passenger door of the truck, and Jake bolted out. 'Honestly, fancy leaving you locked up in here. No wonder you were barking your head off. What's Conor playing at?' She strode after the frantic dog, and saw it race around the corner towards the stable block.

She remembered arriving here with Kavanagh for the first

time. April 1988. He had rented a boat, and brought her across the bay, mooring at the rickety old jetty. The driveway was impassable then, choked with weeds and fallen trees, the rusted gates chained at the road. He'd brought a picnic, and they sat among the bluebells by the shoreline, looking back at the Castle, drinking an Haut Brion 1959 he had been saving for a special occasion, their plans for the future unfurling across the grounds to the Castle like a sparkling field of stars.

'Let's do it, Di. You only ever regret the things you don't do.' Kavanagh had waved his hand like a magician, conjuring the future for her as he talked. From a distance, the Castle looked solid still, the Georgian end in need of a paint but not too bad. Only when they ventured in through a broken window did they discover the roof had caved in, and much of the old building was water damaged.

Diana laughed to herself. 'Ah, it's not so bad,' Kavanagh said to her. 'We live a charmed life, you and me, Di, and we'll bring the old girl back to her glory days.' She remembered the months of hard work, and stress, making the money stretch again and again. But they were content, living a simple life camping in the grounds in an old caravan. She remembered it all – the smell of the woodburner, the sound of the rain on the tin roof at night. She had never been happier. Diana touched her stomach. And in the middle of it all, she had found she was pregnant. Diana slipped her phone from her pocket and dialled Darcy's number, but it went straight to voicemail. She stood in the stable yard and looked around, trying to find where the dog was, barking frantically.

'Jake?' she called him. 'Jake?' The dog raced from the entrance of the staff rooms, running backwards and forwards until she joined him. 'Who left this unlocked? How many times do I have to tell them about sec–' She broke off, seeing Conor's arm extended on the floor, his hand in the half light. 'Oh God, Conor, no!' She fell to her knees, reached out to him with a shaking hand, and rang for an ambulance.

'No, I do not want to be the face of a Japanese whisky company, Caroline, and I'm definitely not posing in the nude ...' Darcy swung her bag over her shoulder and locked the car door. 'I don't care how much—' She broke off as she heard a siren rushing along the lane towards the Castle. 'I have to go, something's up.' She clicked off her phone just as Diana hurried out from the staff quarters.

'Thank God!' Diana waved her arms, directing the ambulance towards the stable block. She noticed Darcy, and ran over to her. 'Where have you been?'

'I'm sorry, I was—'

'Never mind.' Diana waited for her to jog over, and took her arm. 'There's been an accident, I'm afraid.'

'Who?' Darcy paled as she saw Conor, lying prostrate on the flagstone floor. She dropped her bag and ran to his side, pushing the crowd out of the way. 'Conor? Con – can you hear me?' She took his pulse. 'No one has tried to move him, have they?' She checked his airway, her eyes closing as she felt a faint breath against her skin.

'No. Everyone was busy in the restaurant; God knows what he was doing over here.' Conor's eyelids trembled. 'Thank heaven the animals raised the alarm.'

'The animals?'

'I knew Kato was bothered about something, so I let him

out and then I heard Jake barking in Conor's truck. When I opened it, he just shot in here, wailing.'

'Con? It's me. Can you hear me?' Darcy held his hand. 'He's like ice.'

'Let us through,' the paramedic called, pushing through the crowd. 'How long has he been here?'

'We don't know,' Diana said. The last time I saw him was an hour or so ago.' The paramedics stabilised Conor's neck, and lifted him onto a stretcher.

'I'll go to the hospital,' Darcy said. 'Will you tell Chris's mammy what's going on?'

'I'll ring Alannah now. Call me, the minute there's any news,' Diana said.

Darcy walked at his side and waited for the stretcher to be lifted into the ambulance. She stroked his hand, talking softly to him. 'Oh Con, you bloody idiot. You idiot. What have you done now . . .' She searched his face for any sign of movement, any tremor. 'You're going to be OK, you hear?'

From an upstairs window, Beatrice watched the lights of the ambulance flash and twirl, waiting to hear the siren wail up into the fading evening sky. She plucked at the hem of her vest, humming softly to herself, her fingers working.

'There you go,' she murmured. 'Hush, now. There you go.' She tidied her hair, her make-up, and slipped on a red silk dressing gown. Once the ambulance was safely on its way, she ran downstairs. 'My God, Di, what's happened?' she said, grabbing Diana's arm.

'It's Conor – he had a fall.'

'Is he going to be OK?'

'I don't know.' Beatrice noticed Diana's hand tremble as she pushed her hair away from her face. 'He ... I don't know how long he's been unconscious.' Beatrice saw one of the chambermaids hug a friend as they walked back to the Castle, so she put an arm around Diana's shoulder. She shivered, overcome with shaking as the shock finally hit her.

'You poor thing,' Beatrice said, guiding her towards the house. 'What a terrible ordeal for you. Conor is in good hands now. Let's take care of you, and get some sweet tea, shall we?' She called across to a couple of the restaurant waitresses and told them to bring tea for Mrs Hughes.

Beatrice led Diana to her private sitting room, and settled her in a faded gold brocade armchair by the fire, tucking a mohair blanket over her knees. 'There, now,' she said, her voice soft and low. 'You relax, close your eyes.'

Diana settled back in the chair, and Beatrice looked around the wood-panelled room. It was too cluttered for her taste, every chest and table top littered with photographs of Kavanagh, Diana and Darcy, porcelain trinket boxes and shining glass paperweights which gleamed a wash of jewel colours in the sunlight filtering through the stone mullioned windows. Heavy ochre velvet draped around the frames, and Beatrice could imagine how cosy it would be on a winter's night beside the fire. She pictured herself, standing at the carved stone mantelpiece, wearing her favourite midnight-blue evening gown. *One day*, she thought. She looked at the coffee table, littered with old copies of *National Geographic* and *The Caterer*, and the sagging sage-green sofa with its liberal coating of white cat hair. *Disgusting*, she thought. *Why doesn't someone tidy this place up?* At a knock on the door, she glanced up. 'I'll take that,' she said, reaching for the tea tray the waitress was carrying in.

'Are you sure I—' the girl began to say, but Beatrice swung the door to in her face.

'Here we are, Di,' Beatrice said, kneeling on the pink rug before the fire, and setting the tray down on a tapestry stool. 'You're lemon, not milk, aren't you?' She poured a steaming cup of fragrant Earl Grey, and stirred in a couple of spoonfuls of sugar.

'You dear girl,' Diana said. 'Thank you.'

'Feeling better?' Beatrice settled back on the floor, tucking her legs beneath her. Her red silk gown pooled around her, a sheen of firelight rippling over the fabric.

'It . . . I found Kavanagh, you see. It brought it all back.'

Beatrice's eyes widened. 'How awful for you.'

'I was pregnant with Darcy, and he died at my side in bed one night.' Diana blew gently on her tea, cupping it in her palm. 'No warning, no nothing. Sudden death, they called it. His heart went, they thought. I just remember him lying there like Con. One minute he was with me, and the next . . .' Diana's voice cracked. 'It was— I've never gotten over it.'

'Poor you, and poor Conor,' Beatrice said, her face etched with concern. 'He can't have been out for long. He came up to my room.' She paused for effect, letting the implication sink in. 'It was nothing, really.'

'What was he doing in your room?' Diana's voice hardened.

'Well, he said he was coming to get the speaker he'd lent me.'

'He said?'

'Look, it's nothing. I'm a big girl. I can take care of myself if the boss makes a pass at me.' She smiled sweetly. 'It happens, doesn't it? I think he'd been . . .'

'Drinking?'

'I don't want to speak out of turn.'

'Con, you idiot,' Diana said quietly.

27

Darcy paced the hospital corridor, sipping at a cup of coffee as she talked to Diana on her mobile. 'He's still unconscious, Ma. I'm going to stay here overnight. No, it's fine. I can sleep in the waiting room, and freshen up in the morning.' She glanced into Conor's dimly lit room, at the monitor glowing red and green, tracing the course of his heart. 'You spoke to everyone? Did no one see anything?' She listened, her gaze still on Conor. 'OK, I'll call you later.'

Darcy frowned, clicking her phone off. She scrolled through the music she had downloaded until she found Conor's band, and she set it playing quietly on the nightstand, hoping the melody would reach him somehow. She perched on the pink vinyl chair at the side of Conor's bed, watching his face in profile, willing him to stir. In the distance she could hear the noise of the hospital, phones and voices, shoes squeaking on the lino floor in the corridor, a stretcher being wheeled along. Here, it was quieter, just him and her, the beat of Conor's heart. Darcy took a sip of water from the bottle in her bag, and pulled a face. It had grown warm, tasted stale.

She ran through the conversation she had just had with Diana, troubled that Beatrice had told her mother Conor had come on to her. *You wouldn't, would you?* she thought, watching the steady rise and fall of his chest, her breath falling into the same rhythm. 'Wake up, Con,' she whispered, taking his hand in her own. 'Wake up.' She thought of him at work, his intensity, shoulders hunched over the kitchen counter, dark brow lowered. She remembered him singing at the pub, the energy that flowed from him. 'Come back to us,' she said softly. She lowered her forehead to their hands and closed her eyes for a moment. 'It's funny, you know, when I was little I never wanted to be the princess, rescued by some prince on a white charger. I wanted to rescue the prince.' She laughed softly and sat back to look at him. 'I was queen of my own little castle, and I wanted to save the man of my dreams.' She brushed Conor's hair away from his forehead. 'What do you make of that, Con?' An image of Beatrice touching his face, kissing him, came to her.

Darcy forced the thought of them together out of her mind, but Beatrice had laid a seed of doubt, and it was there, growing in strength. She thought of the conversation she had had with Beatrice that morning as they drove into Kenmare together.

'I love this time of the year,' Darcy had said, trailing her hand from the window of the Beetle as Beatrice drove. Blackbirds twittered in the hedgerow. 'Everything feels golden and ripe.'

'I don't know what you're on but I'd love some,' Beatrice said, gazing at the countryside from behind her large black sunglasses. The song on the radio finished, and the theme tune for *Ireland's Top Chef* began: 'Coming soon, the grand final at Castle Dromquinna. What dish to you says "home" . . .' Beatrice flicked off the radio. 'There's no escape, is there?' she said, laughing. She slowed the car, and three alpacas watched them over a frothing green hedgerow, turning their heads in unison. 'Has there been any more press coverage overnight? I'm waiting for them to come after me next. It just doesn't seem fair that they are going for you and Conor.'

'Tell me about it.' Darcy reached into her bag for her phone, and flicked through her Tumblr account, checking up on recent posts. 'Thank goodness people can't troll on here.'

'Is that why you chose it?'

'Yeah, I just don't get all that negativity. I mean, I made the mistake of looking at some of the articles online. My God, the comments. Do these people really have nothing better to do in real life? Why don't they get out and talk to people, look around them?' She clicked on one of the gossip pages and scrolled on, flicking the screen impatiently with her fingertip. 'Look at this: *Who was it said "to eat is to fuck"? Ms Hughes is taking the adage literally.*'

'Lévi-Strauss?'

'As quoted by someone called *tweetiepie2000*.' Darcy frowned, looking at the account. 'She's cooking her way through Ma's last cookbook, if you can believe it.' Darcy put her head back against the car headrest and rubbed her eyes. 'It seems she has strong views about premarital sex and she has *seen a different side to the Hugheses.*'

'Ignore it. For every one like her, these photos will bring you ten, fifty, a hundred true fans. Trust me.' Beatrice sped through the centre of Kenmare, where brightly coloured houses and shops lined the road. The copper-covered spire of Holy Cross Church soared above the square, and she swung into a parking space on Henry Street, cutting up an old man who had been waiting for the space. Darcy grimaced, and waved in apology to him.

'I feel so guilty with people like that,' Beatrice said.

'The old man?'

'No, silly. Girls like tweetiepie. I mean, between us, half these people who use their own pictures for avatars really shouldn't be eating cakes, bless them.'

'Bea, you can't say that,' Darcy said, aghast.

'It's their choice, isn't it? I'm just stating a fact.'

Darcy looked out of the window. 'Did you see that new bakery that's in town? All chaises and chandeliers – Ma took one look and said it looks more like a brothel than a bakery.'

'Sex and food always sell. That's what my mother always

said. Be a cook, an undertaker or a whore – you'll always have a hungry audience.'

Darcy laughed and looked down at her phone, ready to switch it off. A headline caught her eye. 'Bloody hell, Bea – look at this,' she said, clicking on a link to a newspaper article. 'Wasn't that the food blogger you said was being so horrible to Conor?'

Beatrice glanced over. 'I don't know, there are so many of them. I think it comes down to jealousy. I mean, Conor is gorgeous, single, successful—'

'Yeah, it is,' Darcy said, cutting her off. She sensed Beatrice was waiting for a reaction about Conor, but she wasn't going to rise to her bait. *Or perhaps she really does think he's gorgeous?* The thought unsettled her. 'I remember the name – Mr Creosote,' Darcy said, and read on, scrolling through the article. 'Blimey, not what you'd expect at all – I was imagining some big bloke, not a nerdy lad.'

'I know. Surprising, isn't it?' Bea hesitated. 'I mean, really. It's amazing how you can't take people at face value online, how much people are hiding.' She glanced at the photo. 'From his name, you'd not expect a geek with bottle-top specs and a cagoule.'

'He's not hiding behind the name anymore. Apparently he's been arrested.'

'No?' Beatrice looked up in surprise.

'Seems someone had been trolling him, and he went too far.' Darcy looked at the picture. 'He's only nineteen. He looks terrified.'

'Not as tough as he thought he was, maybe,' she said, a tiny smile on her lips.

28

Darcy stayed at the hospital overnight, curled up on a chair in the waiting room, hoping for Conor to wake up. At breakfast time, a commis chef sent by Diana to relieve her took over the vigil. Darcy returned to the Castle and showered, and then unable to rest she went out to the kitchen garden to work for a while before returning to the hospital. Tending the plants calmed her, and she wandered out to the meadow to gather the morning's eggs from a clapperboard hen house in the pen. The birds clucked on, oblivious, around her feet as she searched the nesting boxes. Darcy carefully laid two speckled brown eggs on top of the fresh green spinach she had gathered in a basket, her mouth watering at the thought of omelettes for breakfast. She locked the chicken coop, double checking the bolt, and walked towards the Castle. The meadow was still and quiet, dew-laden grass rolling down to the bay, and she breathed the cool sweet air in. It was a relief to be out of the hospital, but she wanted to get back to Conor. *Conor and Beatrice*, she thought. She was lost in her thoughts and it was a surprise when she looked up to see two men in plain suits walking towards her.

'Good morning,' she said. 'Can I help you?'

'Morning ma'am,' the elder of them said, showing her his badge.

'Garda? Has something happened at the hospital? I have to—'

'No, ma'am, your Mr Ricci is still out for the count last we checked. We're just talking to everyone to check if anyone saw or heard anything.'

'It seems like a straightforward accident but we can't be too careful,' his partner said.

'I'm sorry, I don't know anything. I arrived back here at the same time as the ambulance.'

'If you think of anything, give us a call.' The policeman handed her his card.

'There was one other thing,' the elder man said. 'I understand you've all been experiencing some problems with the press because of this new show?' Darcy nodded. 'Have you heard of a food critic who styled himself Mr Creosote?'

'Yes. I think he had it in for Ma and Conor, but lately he'd gone after me and Beatrice, too.'

'We found an email exchange from Conor's account with the young man. Do you know if they had arranged to meet?'

'No. No, I didn't know anything about this.' Darcy frowned, thinking of everything Conor had told her about his past, and how he had gone for Jamie the other day. 'When were they supposed to have met?'

'Last Tuesday,' he said.

'That's not possible. Conor was with me that night.'

'Are you sure?'

'Yes, a hundred per cent. Look, I'm sorry I can't help you. It's very sad that this young man was obsessed, but I've never met him or communicated with him. I just don't get it, I have to be honest, how fanatical people get.'

'It's a growing problem, unfortunately. Crimes relating to social media have shot up. Hundreds of people are being charged each year for abuse and violent attacks provoked by posts.'

'Harassment, obscene messages,' his partner said.

'Stalking?' Darcy said. 'I remember Bea saying this person was well known online?'

'A troll. He liked provoking people but he had never crossed over into defamation before. Seems someone had been winding him up and he went too far. Maybe a couple of years inside will make him think again before posting abusive messages.'

Darcy walked back to the kitchen, and set some butter to melt in an old blue frying pan. Polyphemus, the Castle's peacock, hopped up onto the kitchen windowsill and tapped at the glass, waiting for Diana.

'What are we going to do?' Darcy cracked the eggs into a glass bowl, and rummaged in the cutlery tray for a fork to beat them with.

'We coped when Con went off to rehab, we'll cope again,' Diana said. 'But that was a month; this could be much, much longer.' Diana opened the window and placed a bowl of bird food on the window, watching as Polyphemus dipped his head, turquoise feathers iridescent in the morning light. 'Do you want some apple, darling boy?' She fetched a grater from the kitchen counter and shaved some fresh apple over the pellets.

Darcy snipped some chives from the pots by the sink and cut them finely into the egg mixture, which sizzled as she ladled it into the pan. 'Have you had breakfast?' Darcy said. 'You're welcome to share this.'

'I had some porridge with Fergus, earlier.'

'Did you now?' Darcy shook the pan until the egg cooked, then slid the omelette onto a plate. She sat on the kitchen counter, eating, leaning back against a wall stencilled with a faded lotus-blossom design. 'We'll have to call off filming,' she said, watching the peacock feeding at the window.

'We will do no such thing,' Diana said. 'That's the last thing Conor would want.'

'Ma, he's out cold still. Until they get the results of the CT

178

scan they don't know if there will be any permanent damage.' She paused, cutting off a forkful of omelette. 'He will wake up, won't he?'

'He has everything to fight for. Conor wants this restaurant, and for his son to be secure financially. That much I do know, OK?' Diana sat gingerly at the table, holding her ribs. 'He'll bounce back, you'll see. Meanwhile, you have to go through with this. I've seen too many people try and fail in my life. It's a ghastly thing to try to be somebody and not pull it off.' Diana poured herself a glass of orange juice. 'You have a chance to be somebody, Darcy, in your own right.' She thought for a moment. 'I think we should go ahead with filming Bea's segments, give you a chance to get your head together for your part of the show.'

'Talking about me?' Beatrice said, carrying a tray of fresh bread rolls into the kitchen. 'Eugh,' she said, spotting the peacock at the kitchen window. 'That bird kept me up half the night screeching. Did you not hear him?'

'No, his coop is over by the stables,' Diana said.

'I wonder what roast peacock is like . . .' Beatrice said.

'Bea, that's a horrid thought,' Diana said.

'Only joking.' Beatrice smiled sweetly. 'How are you? I was so sorry to hear about Conor.'

'You didn't see or hear anything?' Darcy asked her, jumping down from the counter.

'No.' Beatrice blinked, her gaze unwavering. 'The door of my room was locked. You know how heavy those fire doors are over there.'

'And yet you heard a peacock?'

'Oh, I had the window open last night.' She poured herself a mug of tea and sat down at the kitchen table near Diana, spreading one of the warm rolls with peanut butter. 'Listen, the phone in the restaurant has been ringing off the hook. The press have found out about Conor's accident. What do you want me to put up on your pages online, Di?'

'I don't know,' she said. 'Whatever you think. Something like we thank you for your support at this difficult time?'

'Not everyone has been supportive,' Beatrice said, biting into the roll.

'What do you mean?' Darcy said.

'Oh, Conor's accident has brought out the worst of the trolls,' Beatrice said, her voice thick. 'People are saying he must have been pissed or stoned.'

Diana fiddled with the pile of papers in front of her. 'The thought had crossed my mind.'

'How can you say that?' Darcy said, throwing her plate into the dishwasher and slamming it shut. 'Conor needs us.' She glared at Beatrice. 'Ma told me what you said, and I don't believe it.'

'Look, I didn't want to upset you, or I'd have told you myself.' Beatrice turned to her. 'It's obvious you have a huge crush on him. I didn't want to make you jealous.'

29

'I thought I might find you here.' Diana paused in the new door frame of the lake house. The wind whipped against the plastic sheeting covering the window frames. 'Are you OK?' She walked over to where Darcy sat on the half-finished steps down to the deck, and put her hand on Darcy's shoulder.

'I just needed to clear my head before going back to the hospital. Bloody Beatrice. As if I'd be jealous of her. I don't believe a word she said.'

'We'll see. It will all come out when Conor wakes up.'

'I don't know what to do, Ma.' Darcy hugged her knees. 'I'm so worried about him.'

'You don't have to *do* anything.' Diana leant on her as she sat down beside her. 'You just have to be there.' She put her arm around Darcy and laid her head gently against hers. 'You're right, I'm sorry. He has changed. I'm very proud of the way he's turned his life around.' She sighed. 'God, I must have the patience of a saint to have put up with his nonsense over the years. The booze, and the drugging, and the girls.'

'The kitchen groupies.' Darcy breathed a laugh, shaking her head.

'There's always a woman more willing and less tired than you. Kavanagh always said a wedding band puts off very few women, children a few more.' Diana looked at Darcy. 'Of course now Conor's clean, it might be different.'

'You think? I mean, I want him to be happy. If Bea is what he—'

'I wish you'd listen to me. You don't need Conor. You need a grown up.' Diana glanced back at the house. 'But I must say he's doing a good job with this place.' She ran her hand across the smooth sanded planks. 'It's gone up incredibly quickly.'

'That's the beauty of a timber frame. All the pieces are made off site, so it's just like putting a big puzzle together.'

'Well I never. Some people have a knack for putting things back together, making them better than they were before.' She waited for Darcy to look at her.

'You're talking about me, aren't you?'

'The scandal will pass. The public will move on to the next story. The only life, the only happiness you have any control over is your own.' She got to her feet, and leant down to kiss the top of Darcy's head. 'Make it a good one.'

That evening, Darcy parked Diana's white Lancia outside the hospital and fed the meter. At the shop she bought a chilled bottle of water and a stack of magazines, ready for another long night. Her boots squeaked on the floor of the corridor walking to Conor's room, and she stopped to answer her phone.

'Darcy? Are you there?' Diana said. 'I tried to call you to warn you, but the signal must have gone.'

'Warn me?' Darcy turned to Conor's room, and her hand fell to her side. The bed had been stripped and the room was empty. She could hear her mother calling down the phone: *Darcy, Darcy . . .*

'What happened?'

'He came round,' Diana said, elated.

'Oh, thank God,' Darcy said, pressing the bottle of water to her pounding heart. 'Where is he?'

'He checked himself out, the fool, said something to that lad from the kitchen about needing a couple of days by himself.'

'He's not at his cottage, or the lake?'

'No, that's the first place we checked. We'll just have to wait until he's ready to come home.'

'But I have to see him,' Darcy said.

'Oh, and a delivery of Blue Mountain has just been dropped off for you.'

'I didn't order any.'

'No, Con did. The note said he didn't want you running out while he's away.'

30

Conor walked out of the hospital lift, blinking in the bright lights of the lobby. He stopped beside a vending machine. Someone had taped a note to it: *The light inside is broken, but I still work.* He sorted through some coins in the palm of his hand, and selected a Coke. He opened the can and drank thirstily, his gaze on the note. 'Know how you feel, mate,' he said, wiping his lips on the heel of his hand. 'Know how you feel.'

'Mr Ricci?' Two men in plain suits strode towards him from the reception desk. The elder man held out his badge.

'Garda?' Conor narrowed his eyes.

'We won't keep you long. I'm sure you must be wanting to get out of the hospital.'

'You could say that.' Conor finished the can of drink and crushed it, throwing it into the bin. He walked to the office beside the two men, and the noise of the hospital reception fell away as the door closed. 'How can I help you?'

'Firstly, do you remember anything about your accident?' the younger of the men said.

'No . . .' Conor rubbed his temple. 'I don't. The last thing I remember was a . . . a disagreement with one of the staff at the Castle.'

'So you have no idea how you ended up at the foot of the staff stairs?' the policeman said. Conor shook his head. 'It's very common. Even mild concussion can cause memory loss.'

'Yeah, that and a bastard of a headache.' Conor felt weak, and his body smelt sour, of medicines and stale sweat. All he wanted was to book into a hotel room somewhere, shower, and sleep for days in a clean bed. 'Was there anything else?'

'As a matter of fact, there is.' The younger man pulled out a photograph of the food blogger from a file. 'Do you recognise this young man?'

'No.' Conor looked closer. 'Never seen him.'

'But you have corresponded with him?'

'What?' Conor felt his anger rising. 'No I haven't.'

'The computer records show otherwise.' The policeman slid across a printout of the man's messages. 'That is your account?'

'Yeah, but I didn't message the lad.' Conor tapped the paper. 'That's not my email address in the message, and I certainly didn't meet up with him. Is he one of these nutters?'

'He was known for trolling chefs and food writers, it seems. Mr Creosote?'

'Is that who he is? I remember Di talking about him.' Conor paused. 'Hold on, did you say "was"?'

'The gentleman was arrested recently. We won't trouble you with all the details now,' the policeman said, clearing away the papers. 'It seems the lad met his match. Hundreds of messages targeting him from accounts which have been deleted now. They're hard to trace, but we'll do our best. We know from his last online comments that whoever it was arranged the meeting with you never turned up. His last posts were . . . troubling, to say the least.' The policeman stood. 'We just wanted to check if you had communicated with him. I'd suggest, Mr Ricci, you check all your email and social media accounts when you have a chance, and change the passwords. It seems you have been hacked.'

31

Sleepless nights rolled into restless days as Darcy waited for news of Conor. She went through the motions of filming with Tristan, visiting local farms and markets for the ingredients for her dishes. One afternoon as they were driving back towards Kenmare, Jamie let his hand fall from the gearstick to her knee. Darcy pushed him away.

'Come on,' he said quietly so that Tristan and the rest of the crew in the back couldn't hear. 'It could be fun.'

Darcy glared at him. 'You really don't take a hint, do you?' She looked past him to the tree-lined banks of the Roughty River, and spotted Conor's motorbike parked up on the verge by the old stone bridge, Jake lolling in the sun in the sidecar. 'Stop the van.'

'Hey, don't take it so seriously,' Jamie said.

'Stop the van!' she yelled, opening the door even before he'd stopped. 'Tris,' she called into the back, 'I'll make my own way back to the Castle, OK?' Darcy slammed the door and ran back up the road to the turning where she could get down to the river bank, her flowered skirt rising up around her thighs. 'Hey,' she called to a fisherman nearby. 'Have you seen a young guy, six foot or so, dark curly hair?'

'Yer man Conor?' he said, pointing downriver with his rod. Darcy raced along the bank, her shoes beating a steady pace on the earth path. She saw him then, at a bend in the river, the water swirling around him. He had his back to her, casting his line in an elegant arc like a whip. Darcy kicked off her shoes and took off her jacket, scrambling down onto the shore. She ploughed into the water, gasping at the cold, wading out to him. She embraced him without a word, laying her head against his back, and he stumbled forward in surprise.

'Darcy?' He laughed. 'You're mad.'

'Left my waders at home, didn't I?' Her skirt floated around her like the leaves of a flower. 'Where have you been?' Relief and longing spread from her across the river, new currents flowing in the water.

'Just needed a bit of time.' He turned to her, his free arm holding her steady in the water.

'Thank God you're OK.'

'You're not getting rid of me that easily.' He kissed the top of her head. 'The doctor said as long as I don't fall into a coma or die in the next few days I should be fine. No lasting damage.'

'I could kill you myself for going off like that.'

'When a man's life is in the balance he might as well get a last bit of fishing in.' Conor winked at her. 'I heard you saved my life. Thank you.'

'It was nothing. Just checked you were still breathing.'

'Jeez, did you give me the kiss of life? Shame I can't remember a thing about it.'

'Nothing at all?'

He shook his head and frowned, trying to piece together the remembered fragments of his conversation with Jamie. 'Nope. Bit of a headache. Bit dizzy.'

'You should be resting.'

'Listen, this is a lot better for me than lying in bed all day. They did a CT scan, there was no bleeding on the brain, just a concussion, and a nasty cut here.' He touched the stitches in his hair. 'No broken bones, either. Riccis always bounce. Been useful over the years, falling out of pubs.' He smiled, but winced as he lifted the rod.

'You sure you're OK?'

'Yeah, just a few bruises.'

'You had me going the other day. When I went in to the hospital and they'd cleared your bed, I—'

'You thought I was a goner?' Conor said. Darcy let her head fall to his shoulder. 'I heard the nurses talking. You sat with me for hours, didn't you?'

'Been earwigging, have you? Maybe I did,' she said. 'I was worried.'

Conor put his arm around her, pulled her close. 'I'm right here.' He resisted the temptation to kiss her. *Washed up*, he thought, remembering Diana's words. Darcy looked so beautiful to him at that moment, it seemed impossible she would ever feel the same about him.

'Thanks for the coffee,' she said.

'Least I could do after you've been drinking that dreadful stuff at the hospital for days.'

'Con, I have to ask you, were you with Bea when it happened?'

'No,' he said, his brow furrowing. 'I don't know.'

'That's OK, it's all I wanted to know.' She started to wade to shore.

'Not like that,' he said, picking up on her tone. 'I wasn't *with* her. How could you even think that?' He looked at her, his eyes full of passion. 'What about you and that Jamie? He seemed to think he was getting lucky with you. That I do remember.' Conor looked away down the river, winding in the reel.

'Nothing happened,' she said. 'Believe me.' Darcy scrambled onto the bank, and dried off her legs with her jacket.

'Darce, wait,' Conor said, turning after her. 'I'm sorry. I feel like I'm going mad. How about a truce? I'll take you for dinner tonight.'

'No, I'll cook.' She paused, looked back at him across the river. 'Come to the lake house tonight at seven thirty, OK? And come hungry.'

32

Beatrice sat in a silent, shadowy corner of Fergus's showroom on East Park Lane, curled up on an old leather Chesterfield sofa. Through the window she could see the copper spire of Holy Cross. She looked at her watch, her red lacquered nails tapping on the arm of the sofa. *What on earth is taking him so long?* she thought. She unfurled her legs, walked slowly across the room, her full skirt whispering. The dusty boards creaked beneath the light steps of her Louboutins. Beatrice's fingers traced the furniture – a gleaming marquetry table, a velvet chaise longue, a rattan Lloyd Loom chair. She wrinkled her nose in distaste, rubbing her index finger and thumb together. *I hate antiques.* She shivered, repulsed by the thought of where the stock had come from, who had sat on the chairs and eaten at the tables. She glanced at an old four-poster bed in the corner. *Let alone what someone has done in that bed.* She strolled to the window and looked down at the street, daydreaming about what she was going to do to the Castle once she was in charge. She imagined stripping the house clean, like a carcass, filling it with brand new, modern furniture. *New, clean, expensive.* At last she spotted Fergus on the street, a crowd around him, and she ran downstairs to the office.

She settled back in Fergus's wooden captain's chair, and spun around at the desk, inspecting the cluttered pinboard.

There were old concert tickets, cuttings from magazines, a scattering of family photographs. She leant closer, looked at the smiling faces, and pulled her own into a rictus grin, imitating them. *What is it with people?* she thought, hearing the street door open, the jangle of the old bell. She unpinned a picture of a gummy, smiling baby. *Why do they need photos of their relations around them? Is it to prove they belong somewhere?* She considered ripping the photo up. But Fergus would notice and she was the only one who had been in the office. She held it up to the board, her palm obscuring the child, and jabbed a pin back in.

'Come on, come on now . . .' she heard Fergus saying. Beatrice marched through to the shop, her high heels clicking on the tiles.

'There you are!' she said brightly. Fergus was backing through the door, rattling a pail of food in his hand. Christmas the pig waddled after him, wheezing and snorting, its snout nuzzling the cast iron bucket.

'Ah, Beatrice, isn't it?' Fergus said, glancing over, red faced and sweating. 'Won't be a moment.'

'OK,' she said, laughing. Once Fergus had passed by her smile cleared, and she watched with distaste. *Honestly, Diana, you could do so much better.*

Fergus slammed the yard door behind the pig, and secured it with binder twine. 'There we are,' he said, checking the door was firm. 'Can't people read?' He flicked the sign. 'Some eejit left the door wide open. The pig was galloping down the middle of the road, merrily on his way to St Pat's by the time I caught him.' He dusted off his hands. 'Now, can I help you with anything, my dear?'

'Hm?' Beatrice said. 'No, I was just popping into town, so I said to Diana I'd call in. She picked up your message on the answering phone, and she'll meet you at seven thirty in the Lansdowne Arms.'

'Splendid, splendid,' Fergus said, rubbing his hands together.

'Hot date?'

'It should be a special night, yes.' Beatrice saw his expression change. What was that? Worry? Wariness? *God, you're an old fool,* she thought, impatient now. 'Will you tell Di I'll be at the bar?' he said.

'Sure.' Beatrice smiled sweetly. 'It must be tough for you.'

'Sorry?' Fergus put his hands in the pockets of his old sage cords.

'I mean, you're a brave man to try to fill Kavanagh's shoes.'

'I'm not try—'

'Don't get me wrong, I know how hard it is to love more than you are loved.' She changed her expression to one of sympathy. She could see Fergus's face colouring. *It's working.* 'It's a shame she still loves Kavanagh. She always will, I suppose.'

'What would you know?' he said. He strode over to the street door and yanked it open. Beatrice tried to calculate his reaction. Hurt, she hoped. *I want him gone,* she thought. It was far too complicated. There was no room in their lives, hers and Diana's, for him and all his jolly smiling relatives. They didn't need a ready-made happy family. *All Diana needs is me.*

Fergus turned to Beatrice, his eyes blazing. *He's angry,* she realised. As she passed by he held out his hand, stopping her. 'You've had your fun. I won't mention this to Diana. I know she's fond of you, for some reason.' Beatrice's eyes narrowed. 'I am sure of how I feel about her, and how she feels about me. Perhaps when you get to my age you will understand the importance of that. I think you should run along now, don't you?'

Beatrice paused by the window display. 'You really have her on a pedestal, don't you?' she said, lifting her hand slowly. A fine Lalique glass bowl gleamed opaquely in the sunlight on top of a simple wooden display stand. 'The trouble with pedestals is they are so easy to fall from.' She gave the bowl a nudge, and it rocked over the edge. Fergus leapt forward, catching it. 'Oops,' she said, glaring at him. Close to, she saw uncertainty in his eyes and she smiled, satisfied. 'See you soon.'

33

Conor's ex-wife, Alannah, buckled Chris into his car seat in the back of her BMW, and tucked her son's favourite cuddly toy under the strap.

'Just got off the phone with Ma,' Conor said. 'She sends her love.'

'No she doesn't.' Alannah looked up at him over the top of her drizzle-flecked Chanel sunglasses.

'Ah, you know her,' he said, his shoulders hunched against the rain. 'Bitterness and disappointment keep her going. Don't they always say selfish people live longest? The news about my accident should give her another ten years at least. If she could reach down the phone line from my sister's apartment in New York and knock me about the shins with her walking stick, she would.' Alannah laughed. '"Hello, Ma." *Whack.*'

'Will you be taking Chris to see her in the Christmas holidays?' she said. 'It's just, I hoped—'

Conor put his hand on her shoulder. 'It's fine with me if you want him this year for Christmas.'

'Are you sure?'

'Yeah, I'll take him for New Year, OK?' Conor put his hands in his pockets. 'Besides, why drag him all the way to New York when a few hours with my rellies is enough to make you want to gnaw your foot off?'

Alannah smiled sadly. 'I always thought we'd be different.'

'Every mother thinks or hopes that.'

'Are you sure you're all right?'

'Yeah, right as rain.'

'So who's the lucky girl?' she said, eyeing his fresh blue shirt.

'Girl? Nah, it's just Darcy, you know, Di's daughter.'

'That wee thing? Used to hang around the kitchen all the time?'

'Yeah,' he said, remembering. 'She's cooking for me tonight.' Alannah raised her eyebrows. 'Nothing like that,' Conor said, leaning in to kiss Chris on the cheek before he closed the door. 'Thanks for bringing him over; I'd missed him. I know it's your turn and all.'

'It's nothing,' she said, squeezing his hand. 'We just wanted to check you were OK. When I heard you had a fall—'

'You thought I was back on the booze?' Conor smiled, ruefully. 'You're not the only one.' He glanced down at the large diamond sparkling on her ring finger. 'Are you happy?'

'Yes. Yes I am.' She jumped into the driving seat and started the engine. 'He's kind, and loaded, and there in the evening and weekends . . .'

'Must be novel.'

'Go on then, don't keep Just Darcy waiting.'

The woods were deep and quiet as Conor walked to the lake, a shifting canopy of a thousand greens above him, around him. He ached, his body bruised and sore, and he was bone tired, but he didn't want to let Darcy down. *Darcy.* He frowned as he walked, trying to remember. The fight. His fist clenched again now, thinking of Jamie. What was it Bea had said? Was Darcy seeing him? He stopped at the edge of the trees, his palm holding his back. Every breath hurt.

The lake was washed gold and amber by the sunset. At its edge, the timber frame of the house was going up fast, and he saw the shape of it for the first time, the deck and the simple

A frame. And there, in the middle of what would be his house, Darcy was preparing a meal, a paraffin lamp glowing, guiding him home. She looked up as the dog raced past to the water's edge, and raised her hand when she saw Conor.

'I can't believe how much they've done,' Darcy said, walking towards him. Her glossy hair shone in the evening sun, and through the thin cotton of her dress he saw the shape of her illuminated. He had never wanted anything more than to take her in his arms and find somewhere still and quiet to lie beside her.

'Timber frame,' Conor said, clearing his throat. He ran his hand across the rough timber of the beam nearest him. 'Once the foundations are in, they go up fast.'

'You look great,' she said. 'That shirt suits you.'

'Not going to be a pin-up in *The Caterer* anytime soon, but thank you.'

'Get on with you. Want to know a secret? When other girls had posters of Justin Timberlake, I had pictures of you torn out of the *Radio Times*.'

'Did you now?' he said, laughing.

'Well, you and ponies. Lots of ponies. Hope you're hungry,' she said, turning to the house, pulling her hair back into a mother-of-pearl clip.

'As they say around these parts, hunger is the best sauce. What are we having?' Conor said, standing behind her. The table was laid simply, with a plain white cloth and a gleaming bottle of olive oil beside the glasses. 'Do I smell truffles?' He reached past her, inhaled the fragrance.

'I got them from Daffyd. Seems he's branching out from fish.' As she lowered her head, concentrating on chopping the truffle, he watched the curve of her neck, the soft hair falling at the nape. He longed to place his lips there.

'Can I help?' he said, leaning against the counter.

'Set the table if you like? Or just relax. You must be tired.' She walked over to the fire she had laid at the lake's edge, and carried back a steaming griddle, rib-eye steaks sizzling.

'I can run a Michelin-starred kitchen. It'll take more than a bit of a fall to finish me off.' He laughed. 'What a pair we make, me and Di. Your turn next for a fall – they say things come in threes.'

'Me?' Darcy glanced at him and smiled. She gestured at the lake with her knife. 'I fell years ago, for this place, for cooking.' *For you.* The words hung between them, unspoken.

'There's a magic to it, for sure.' Conor shrugged. 'Wine?'

'Thanks.'

He took out white plates from the open basket, and set them on the rough scaffolding planks Darcy had laid across the builder's trestles to make a table. He carried over the salad bowl, deep green leaves glistening with oil in the circle of lamplight, and laid Laguiole steak knives and forks, two places side by side, on a simple bench facing the lake. 'Darce, you do believe me about Beatrice, don't you?' He poured her a glass of wine, and filled the tumblers with water. 'Come to think of it, I'm sure I went round to have it out with her. I heard the rumours she'd been spreading.' He frowned. 'I wish I could remember.' He carried the wine to Darcy and she took a sip. 'How's Di?'

'Having an early night,' she said, adding the truffle to the sauce, pouring it over the steaks.

'Is she not out with Fergus?'

'No, why do you ask?'

'I bumped into him earlier. I have a feeling he's going to pop the question.'

'Already?' Darcy looked up from her wine. 'I'm not sure how I feel about that. I mean, isn't it a bit soon?'

'They're old enough to know their minds.' Conor winked at her. 'Good for her, that's what I say. She's been so focused on her career and this place all these years, she hasn't been interested in a relationship. But now she's retiring she has time. Kavanagh wouldn't have wanted her to shrivel up and waste away, would he? He wouldn't want her to be alone.'

'I guess not. This was a good idea,' Darcy said, stretching out her legs as she sat down beside Conor. She reached over and clicked on the radio.

'You used to love that song, remember?' The opening bars of 'Angel' drifted across the water. He looked at her, his shadowed face touched with gold in the lantern light. 'I remember your ma made you get up on stage in the pub one night and sing it, when you were a kid.' He sighed. 'Feels like a lifetime ago, doesn't it?'

'It's Sarah McLachlan,' Darcy said.

'Di still loves it,' he said. 'I've caught her sometimes over the years, having a listen and a little weep when she thinks she's alone in the office. I reckon it always reminded her of you.'

'Who'd have thought Ma's sentimental?' Darcy smiled as Conor topped up her glass.

'At least we don't have to search around for a bottle opener,' he said, screwing the cap.

'Seems a shame,' Darcy said, cupping her chin on her palm. 'Less romantic, less beautiful.'

'More useful.'

'What are you having?' she said, lifting bottles of still and sparkling water onto the table.

'Badoit, thanks.' He raised his glass. 'To use and beauty.' Conor took a bite of the steak and rolled his eyes. 'God, woman, those truffles. Anyone would think you're trying to seduce me.' A heartbeat of silence hung between them.

'Would that be such a disaster?' she said, taking a sip of wine. She raised her gaze to his, and his breath caught.

'Look, Darcy—'

'Mm,' she said, swallowing her mouthful of food. 'I forgot the bread.' She walked down towards the fire and he watched her, running his thumb against his lower lip. It was beginning to rain, and the surface of the lake shimmered and rippled beyond her, the wind blowing her hair free. She returned with a foil package from the edge of the fire, and unwrapped warm soda bread.

'God, it's good to sit down,' she said. 'The restaurant's been manic without you. We're fully booked for the next month.'

'Scandal sharpens the appetite.' He blinked, thinking of the photograph of Darcy again. Rain pattered on the tarpaulin above them, the haunting music rising up. 'I saw they named JJ. It's all come out.'

'Yes,' she said, lowering her head. 'We knew it would. I had to change my mobile; somehow the press managed to get hold of my private number.'

'Don't worry, just face it out. They'll move on to the next story soon enough.'

'Is that what happened with you?'

'Yeah. I don't think they're interested in me anymore, though.' *Washed up. Has been.* 'Darce, am I losing my touch?'

'You? Your cooking's better than ever, I think.'

'Not in the kitchen. I mean ...' He shook his head and looked away, uncertain.

'No. Not from where I'm sitting,' she said, and waited for him to look at her, holding his gaze clear and strong. He grew still.

Conor set his glass down then, and kissed her. It was a visceral shock, a jolt of desire coursing through him. Her hand slipped, the glass tumbled to the ground, and still they kissed, no air between them. He felt the lithe weight and strength of her, urgent desire flowing between them like ripples on the dark lake beyond. Darcy's fingers laced through his hair, and Conor winced.

'I'm sorry,' she said, breathless. 'Did I hurt you?'

'Be gentle with me.' He grinned, resting his head against hers.

34

Beatrice tucked herself in a booth at the back of the café in Kenmare, away from the view of Bridge Street, and waited. The light was falling, headlights and shop lights washing the wet road. The windows were steamy, and the café full of people chattering to their friends. She watched them, detached and curious. Beatrice checked her watch. *He's late*, she thought, irritated. The waitress brought over her pot of tea, and Beatrice smiled brightly.

'Cha?' the girl said.

'Thank you,' Beatrice said, her smile evaporating the moment the girl turned her back. Beatrice reached into her bag and pulled out an old brown leather notebook. She flicked through the pages of yellowed newspaper cuttings and recipes, printouts from *Appetite*, glossy images ripped from *Hello!* She paused at a photograph of Diana and Darcy from the nineties. Darcy leant in to her mother, her head resting against her waist. In the background, the Castle stood freshly painted, the bay gleaming beyond. *Diana Hughes' Charmed Life*, ran the headline. *Charmed*, Beatrice thought, picking up a fork from the table. Charming. She drew a heart around them, piercing it with an arrow.

'All right, Bea,' one of the young chefs from the restaurant said, slouching through the café towards her. He sucked at the straw of a glass bottle of Coke. Beatrice quickly closed the book and shoved it into her bag. 'What's that, then?' He gestured at the book, and slumped into the seat opposite her. 'Pictures of Mrs Hughes?'

'Never mind that, it's just research.'

'You're obsessed, you are.' He smiled like he had just put two and two together.

'I am not.' She pursed her lips. 'Aiden, you're late.'

'Yeah, sorry. Maeve had a strop. She's hanging out with her friends by the bus stop on Main Street making me suffer.'

'Silly girl.' She held out a slim hand, took his in hers, running her thumb against his. 'Some girls just don't understand what men want, do they?' She licked her lips. 'What men need.' The neon lights of the café sign blushed her bunches pink and gold. She leant against the wall, and tilted her head. 'I wanted to thank you – you're doing a good job. Just make sure you don't post too often, or too obviously. We don't want them realising there's a mole in the kitchen.'

'Glad to help,' he said, looking down at Beatrice's thumb working against his hand. He licked his lips and shifted in his seat. 'They have it coming to them, so they do. Diana's a bossy mare, and Con's a bastard in the kitchen. Never worked so hard in my life.'

'Anything worth doing is hard, and you catch more flies with honey than vinegar,' she said, staring at him. 'We need to keep them thinking you love working there. Smile. Be polite. Work hard. Talking of which, we should really be heading back.'

'They filming again today?' Aiden said, closing his coat over himself, and picking up his drink as he followed Beatrice from the café.

'Which one's Maeve?' she said as they strolled towards the bus stop. 'I bet you are with that pretty redhead over there.'

'Yeah, that's her, the one with a puss on her. Pretty but stroppy. Maeve's . . . well, I thought I was going to stay over at hers in Killarney after the pictures tonight, but—'

'Silly girl. If I was dating a good-looking fella like you, I wouldn't mess you around. You could have any girl you wanted.' Beatrice glanced over her shoulder, made sure Maeve and the group of teenage girls were watching. 'Why don't we have some fun? Make her jealous.' She laughed, stroking Aiden's arm.

'Why are you laughing? I didn't say anything.'

'C'mon, play along, she's watching.' Beatrice looked up at him from beneath sooty lashes as she slipped off her denim jacket. She was bra-less beneath the light summer dress she was wearing, and Aiden blinked, unable to look away. 'That's more like it,' she said, stepping closer to him. 'Now, if you were trying to chat me up, what would you do?'

'I don't . . . Buy you a kebab?'

'Ooh, last of the great seducers.' She took his bottle of Coke and sipped at the straw, the tip of her tongue catching a drop on her lips. She stepped closer. 'Does that turn you on, Aiden?'

'What do you think?'

'Is Maeve watching?'

'I don't care.'

She leant in to him, stretched up to whisper in his ear. 'Do you like my breasts, Aiden? You can't stop looking at them.'

'God, I'm sorry—'

'No, I like it.' She licked at the lobe of his ear, tasted fresh sweat. 'What if I told you I'm not wearing anything under this dress, Aiden?'

'Seriously?'

'When was the last time Maeve let you give her a really hard shag, Aiden?'

'She hasn't . . . I mean, she won't.'

Beatrice pushed him back into the darkness of the doorway, her mouth against his. Aiden lifted her up, her legs around his hips, and he ground against her, pushing, hard, until she felt him shudder, muscles rigid.

'Bloody hell,' he said, pressing his palm against the cool wet brick.

Beatrice extricated herself, and rolled her head from side to side. 'I like you. That was fun.' She kissed her index finger and pressed it against his lips. 'This can be our little secret, can't it, Aiden?'

'Yeah. But . . . what just happened?'

'Think of it as a thank you,' she said, blowing him a kiss as she walked on into the night. She checked that Aiden wasn't following, and made a beeline for Maeve and her friends.

'Which one of you is dating Aiden?'

'That would be me,' Maeve said, tossing her head.

'Do you know who I am?' Beatrice said, and Maeve shrugged. 'I am the star of that,' she said, pointing at a fluttering banner for *Ireland's Top Chef* strung across the street. 'I work very, very closely with Aiden.'

Maeve stood, squaring up to her. 'You keep your hands off him.'

'Don't you dare threaten me,' Beatrice said. She lowered her head until her eyes were level with Maeve's. 'Take my advice. Stop being such a little prick tease.' She sauntered away swinging her hips, the sound of Maeve's outraged cries punctuating every step.

35

'What's wrong with Aiden?' Darcy said, lifting a tray of chicken breasts onto the counter in the restaurant kitchen.

'I have no idea, I can't keep up with the children,' Conor said, stealing a kiss when no one was watching.

'You don't think Maeve has dropped him, do you? I haven't seen her around for a while.'

'I hope not. She's a good girl – brought a bit of life out in him. He's so easy going, he needs someone to chivvy him along a bit.' Conor grinned. 'Then again he's always had seven sisters to do that, hasn't he? Poor boy doesn't stand a chance surrounded by strong women.' Conor untied his apron and rubbed at his temple.

'Is your head hurting?' she said, and Conor nodded. 'Go home and rest. We can manage without you.'

'That's what I'm worried about,' Conor said, glancing at Beatrice tidying up her station.

'Aiden, is everything OK?' Darcy called as he walked back into the kitchen.

'Yeah, why wouldn't it be?' he said, red-eyed.

Darcy set down a steaming mug of coffee beside him. 'Talk to me. What's up?' She leant back against the counter, cradling her cup of tea.

'It's . . .' He frowned, looking at Beatrice. 'Not here. Outside.' Darcy followed him into the yard. It was drizzling, and the stone wall felt cold through her T-shirt as she leant against it. 'Maeve dumped me.'

'Oh, Aiden. I'm sorry. You'd been going out since school, hadn't you?' She reached out and squeezed his hand. In the silence, she heard a tractor across the valley. She waited. Aiden finally yanked off the bandana covering his hair and leant next to her, looking out across the yard.

'I thought we'd get married soon, you know? I don't get it, Darce. She came over to see me last night, and I thought we were going to make up. We ...' Aiden blushed, the colour rising in his cheeks. 'We were in bed, and she got up to get some water.' He reached into his pocket and pulled out a pair of black pearl earrings. 'She found these in my bathroom, and she went ballistic.'

Darcy pursed her lips. 'I don't mean to pry, but has anyone else been in your flat?'

'Girls? No.' Aiden's lips parted. 'Shit.'

'What?'

'I'm so stupid.' He glanced back at the kitchen. 'What's her name, Beatrice, came up to see me a couple of days ago.'

'Why?'

'Nothing. No reason.'

'Aiden?'

'Oh God, look, don't make a big thing out of this but Maeve had been holding out on me.'

'Holding out?'

'She said she wasn't ready or something. I bumped into Beatrice in town one night and we had a bit of a snog.'

'And?'

'And that's it. She came up to apologise, that was all.'

'And conveniently left an earring behind? I'll talk to her. Aiden, you're to have nothing to do with her, do you understand? I can appreciate her attention might have been ... flattering. But she's almost twice your age.'

'Is she?' Aiden frowned. 'I didn't . . . I mean, she seems so much younger—'

'Look, would you like me to have a word with Maeve? I won't mention the snog bit.' Darcy hugged him. 'Don't worry, I'll sort out Beatrice, too.'

'Bea, can I have a word? I've been looking for you everywhere.' Darcy strode across the test kitchen towards her.

'Everything OK, Darce? I was just having a quick practice before tomorrow.' Beatrice lifted a tray of warm, fragrant Black Velvet cakes from the oven, and set them down on the stainless steel counter. 'Tempt you?'

'No thanks. Look, I'm going to come straight to the point.'

'Ooh, this sounds serious.'

'I talked to Aiden.' Darcy put her hands on her hips. 'I know what you've been doing.'

Beatrice's face stilled. 'Know what?'

'Maybe it's a game to you, but he's a seventeen-year-old boy, Bea.'

'I was just helping him out, Darcy.' Beatrice's blue eyes opened wide. 'You know, treat them mean to keep them keen. I thought if Maeve saw him with an older woman . . .'

'A lot older, Bea. I don't feel comfortable with this, OK? He had no idea what trick you were playing.'

'Trick?'

'The earrings. What was the idea, make Maeve jealous? It's worked – she's dumped him.'

'Earrings?' Beatrice touched her ears. 'But mine aren't pierced.'

Darcy paused. 'I didn't say they were pierced.'

Beatrice blinked impassively, and spooned champagne icing into a piping bag. 'I just assumed. Everyone's ears are pierced these days, aren't they?'

'Yes. I . . . I suppose so.' Darcy dug in the pocket of her jacket, and put the pearls on the counter beside the cakes.

'Look, Aiden said you left these behind. I don't know if they are yours or not, but the point is I don't want you messing him around, OK?'

'OK, I'm sorry.' She lowered her head. 'It was just a bit of fun.'

'Look, don't take it personally. We've got to have some boundaries, you know? It gets ...' She exhaled. 'It can get messy at the Castle, with everyone living and working on top of one another.'

'I understand,' Beatrice said. She wiped a speck of flour from the immaculate stainless steel counter with her fingertip. 'Like you and Conor, you mean?' Darcy's jaw set. She wasn't going to rise to the bait.

Beatrice waited for Darcy to walk away. She took the first pearl earring, and looked at its sharp metal point. She felt for the long-healed scar on her earlobe and drove it in, her eyes narrowing at the sharp pain. She cricked her neck, and did the same with her left ear, rubbing the spot of blood between her thumb and forefinger, then licked it clean.

36

'Mrs Hughes,' the maître d' said, popping his head around the office door, 'I'm sorry but we have a situation with one of the guests on the terrace.'

'Can't you deal with it, Niall?' Diana looked up at him over her half-moon glasses, the phone clamped to her ear against her shoulder. She sat at a wide mahogany desk piled high with brightly coloured folders, a calculator at her side. Kato was curled up in the middle of the desk, smiling in his sleep in a sunspot on a pile of invoices. Diana had painted the office a deep turquoise for Kavanagh when they first renovated the Castle, and she had never changed it. Heavy copper silk brocade curtains were tied back from the open French window; the sunlight glinted on an old painting of the bay in a gold leaf frame behind the desk and a collection of lustreware bowls in the alcoves framing the fireplace.

'I'm sorry,' he said. 'They are asking to see the owner.'

Diana waved him away, and threw down her pen. She held the phone. 'I'm sorry, Fergus, I've got to go.' She closed her eyes wearily. 'Are we all right now? I promise, I knew nothing about meeting you at the pub. I wouldn't have stood you up.' She paused, listening. 'Beatrice? She said she left me a note, but the cleaner must have tidied it away.' Her face softened. 'Darlin', I swear. I'd never hurt you.' She closed her eyes. 'Yes, I'm fine. Just going through the books.' She sighed. 'If there's a good turnout and plenty of votes for *Top Chef* we'll be all right.' Diana rubbed her forehead. 'You're a good man, Fergus Fitzgerald, and I'm lucky to have you. I promise, I'll make this up to you.'

She hung up, and strode through to the restaurant, her velvet leopardskin loafers clicking on the polished wood floor. She braced herself for the confrontation with the customer. *This is when I really could do with a partner,* she thought. *Darcy could handle this, I'm sure of it. She has a way with people.* She paused at the restaurant entrance. Front of house, everything was seamless – local businessmen filled the restaurant, finishing up the 1–2.30 slot. *A few long weekenders, too,* Diana thought. *Banker? Hedge-fund manager?* she wondered, looking at a man in his forties glued to his Blackberry while his caramel-glossed wife gazed into space at his side and their picturesquely tousled children ran around the garden in their new wellies.

'Oh, hello, Beatrice,' Diana said. 'I didn't hear you coming.'

'Everything OK, Diana?' She shifted the tray of cakes in her arms. 'Looks like we're in for a busy weekend.'

'Thank God. All the Masters of the Universe down from the City,' Diana said vaguely. 'Bloody banks. Do you think the world would be a worse place if we slipped a bit of rat poison in their foie gras?'

'No. But there are simpler ways than rat poison,' Beatrice said. 'I could do that for you, if you wanted.'

Diana snapped out of her reverie. 'Bloody hell, Beatrice. I was only joking. Look at your face.'

Beatrice looked at her, deadpan, and broke into a peal of laughter. 'Only kidding.'

'Take those around the back, will you?' Diana said. 'It doesn't do to go through the restaurant.'

'Of course,' Beatrice said, her smile tight.

Diana swung open the door to the terrace, the breeze lifting her cashmere cardigan. Niall, the maître d', pointed at a couple sitting by a low box hedge at the end of the terrace, and she strode over. 'I am Diana Hughes. May I help you?' She towered over them, looking with ill-disguised distaste at the young man's heavy gold watch, his tapping fingers.

'You're not the owner?'

'Yes, I am. How may I help you?'

'What about that Conor Ricci? Thought he owned this place?' The man dismissed her with a wave of his hand. 'Get him.'

Diana forced her face into an accommodating smile, felt the muscles in her jaw clench. 'I can assure you, if you have a complaint about the food, you are better off talking to me.'

'Your peacock relieved itself on our table,' his companion said, pressing a linen napkin to her lips with her crimson acrylic nails. 'Shat it did, right here. It's disgusting, unsanitary.'

Diana looked across the lawn to see Polyphemus stalking among the topiary. *I wish I'd seen that*, she thought, forcing herself to stay straight faced. *Extra apple for you for supper.* 'We do warn our customers when they book the terrace that there are peacocks in the grounds.'

'Yeah, well I thought they were ornamental, didn't I?' He squared his shoulders. 'Didn't expect the bloody thing to jump up and shit on us, did we? What you going to do about it then?'

'I see the incident didn't put you off your meal,' Diana said, stepping back to allow the table to be cleared.

'Health hazard, it is.' The man stubbed his finger on the table. 'Should report you to health and safety, we should.'

'Some people find the peacocks romantic,' Diana said, ignoring him. 'I know I do.' She glanced at the woman, imagining how much she had compromised. *Is it worth it?* she wanted to ask.

'If you don't sort this out I'm going to give you a one-star rating on that Trip site, what's it called?'

'I don't believe there's a category for being shat on,' Diana said, folding her arms. 'Was the food adequate?'

'Yes,' the woman said. 'It was lovely—'

'Shut up,' the man hissed at her.

'Did you get the table you asked for?'

'Yes.'

'Did we warn you about the wildlife?'

'Yes – but that's not the point.'

'It is precisely the point.' Diana took the bill from the leather binder on the table and tore it up, flicking her hands into the air. 'If you get your jollies from bullying people,' she said loudly, every head on the terrace turning to them, 'then who am I to stop you? You were given exactly what you ordered, you've enjoyed Michelin-starred cuisine and it's still not good enough for you?' She leant towards the man, fists on the table. 'May I suggest next time that you choose more carefully.' She looked at the woman. 'I feel sorry for people who find no satisfaction in life.'

Diana stormed through the restaurant, swinging open the doors to the bustling kitchen. She spotted Conor through the window. He was outside, a towel around his neck, smoking. 'What on earth are you doing here? You should be resting.'

'Can't stay away, can I?'

'Listen. You and I need a word,' she said, beckoning to him to follow her. They walked to the kitchen garden, Polyphemus crossing the path ahead of them dragging his swishing tail of feathers.

'Everything OK out front?' he said.

'The usual arses,' Diana said. 'It's not the restaurant I want to talk to you about. Judging from the way Darcy is floating around the kitchen with a smile on her face things have progressed with you two?'

'Floating?' Conor looked at the ground, smiling.

'She's radiant, glowing.' Diana stopped and put her hand on her hip. 'God knows, I think she's adored you her whole life. Stop grinning.' She poked him in the chest. 'If you hurt her—'

'Di, I'd never do that,' he said, looking her in the eye.

'I tried to warn her off. I said you are—'

'What? A washed-up, burnt-out, recovering alcoholic divorcee.'

'Do you take anything seriously?'

Conor took a step towards her. 'I take Darcy seriously. Why do you think I tried to hold off for so long?' His voice softened. 'You know I can still remember the first time I saw her? You'd taken me on as the hot young chef to get this place on the map, and I was strutting round the place like some fucking rock star, like that ruddy peacock,' he said, pointing across the garden. 'I was high on booze and coke, and Darcy—' He closed his eyes for a moment. 'She was so light, and clean, and good. Just a little kid, hanging around the kitchen.' *She smelt of vanilla even then*, he remembered. 'I didn't – I mean, I never thought of her like that—'

'Romantically?'

'I couldn't see the woman she'd become, until she went away. All the time she was in London at college, and in the States, I still thought of her as a kid.'

'She's not a child now, she's a young woman with her whole life ahead of her. She could do anything.'

'Rather than saddle herself with me, you mean?' he said. 'God knows, I don't deserve her. She'll eclipse me now, her star's flying higher, but her heart's true and she's got her feet on the ground. She really cares about people. Look at the way she dropped everything to come and help you.'

'Do you love her?'

Conor thought for a moment. 'You know, I was out running the day she came home. The bus stopped at the end of the driveway, and she jumped down with her case. I saw her feet first, through the wheels of the bus – this pair of silver pumps – you know, not trainers, just these knackered old glittery silver pumps, and as the bus pulled away, there she was in this simple little white sun dress, with the sun shining through the cotton, and the mist on the fields, and she looked

211

as if she'd just woken up.' He looked at Diana. 'And I lost my heart to her then. I never felt more ruined, or wasted, but I wanted to be better, and clean for her. I wanted to be worthy. She looked like this . . . like a deer when it wakes, you know. Big eyes, those big beautiful dark eyes, and her hair all messed up. And she ran up the driveway, dragging her suitcase, and she was so happy to see me. Me!'

'Oh, Con. God knows I am not one to give advice about the way to the heart.'

'Fergus?'

'Yes. I've never seen him like it. He was so hurt.'

'What happened?'

'It seems I stood him up. Lord knows what was so important, it was only going to be a drink at the pub where we went on our first date,' Diana said, and laughed. 'Look at me, dating at my age. It was just a silly misunderstanding. I never got the message. Bea—'

Conor laughed and shook his head. 'Might have guessed she was involved.'

'Anyway, never mind. I'm mending fences with Fergus, but we'll be all right.' Diana kissed his cheek. 'If you love Darcy, this is a fresh start for both of you. I admire you hugely as a chef and a person, Conor, but the jury is out on you as part of the family. You've screwed up once, my lad. Don't make the same mistake twice.'

Conor watched Diana walk away, his eyes narrowing. He strode towards the terrace and jogged up the flight of stone steps, signalling to the maître d'. They spoke quickly, huddled together, and Conor turned to the table of diners who had complained. 'Excuse me,' he said, walking over to them. 'I understand you have a problem with your meal?'

'You're that Ricci, aren't you?' The young man puffed up his chest.

'We're huge fans—' his partner began to say.

212

'Shut up,' he hissed. 'Even if we ignore the sodding peacock shitting on our table, this food was not fresh.' He pushed his plate away.

'Not fresh? Come with me, pal.' Conor pulled out his chair, and gestured towards the kitchen garden. He led the way, and could hear the heavy footsteps behind him as the man struggled to keep up with him. 'Here youse are,' he said, grabbing a fork on the way past the shed, and tossing it to the man. 'Dig,' he said, pointing at the rows of potatoes.

'Dig? These are handmade shoes.'

'For God's sake, man,' Conor said, grabbing the fork from him. He felt the earth give as he pushed down with his foot on the fork, the rich soil crumbling. He leant down and shook the tubers free. 'Not fresh?'

'Well, I—'

'The meal you just ate was still growing a couple of hours ago.' He threw the fork down like a challenge. 'That's how feckin' fresh it is.'

'Listen, I'm sorry—' The man crumpled.

Conor took a deep breath. 'Big date is it?'

'How can you tell?'

'I'm a chef, man, not a saint.'

'Look,' he said, his shoulders dropping. 'I've been working too hard, you know. I just wanted to give her a treat, show her I care.'

'Maybe it would have been more of a treat if you hadn't behaved like a total arse?'

'Fair play.' He looked at Conor. 'I like a fella who stands up to me. Listen, what are you doing hiding yourself away down here? You should be up in Dublin. A couple of friends and me, we're looking for a restaurant to set up, someone to invest in.'

'Nah, you're all right.' He thought of Darcy, of her face when she saw the Castle again. 'It gets under your skin, this place. Besides, Diana's like family.'

'Don't be a fool, mate.' The man brushed off the sleeve of his suit. 'Do the wrong thing and you'd be out on your ear, like that.' He clicked his fingers. 'This is a business, not a family.'

37

Conor stood behind the empty reception desk, checking the bookings for the day. The phone rang, and he glanced up looking for the receptionist. 'Good morning, Castle Drom-quinna,' Conor said, hooking the phone beneath his jaw. He flicked through the reservations book and picked up a pencil. He listened to the person on the other end, watching Darcy reaching up to place a vase of freshly cut flowers above the mantelpiece. The scent of the stocks was intoxicating. Darcy's light shirt lifted above the waistband of her cut-off jeans, and he focused on the glimpse of smooth, curved back, the shadowed hint of the dimples at the base of her spine. 'Sorry?' he said, looking down at the book. 'Did you say today? I'm afraid we are fully booked for lunch. Tonight? Let me see.' He ran the pencil down the reservations. 'Yes, he will be cooking. How do I know?' He laughed. 'Because you're talking to him.' He listened, a smile wrinkling his eyes. 'Do you now?' At the change in his tone of voice, Darcy glanced over. 'We've just had a cancellation so you're in luck. I've pencilled you in for eight. If you're staying in town, they can book you a car. Why don't I take your number?' He paused, pencil hovering. 'Room seven?' he said, and laughed. 'Yes, I'm sure that's a grand room, but I meant your phone number.' He jotted it down and listened, smiling. 'Maybe I will,' he said, and hung up.

'Booking for tonight?' Darcy said, throwing a couple of fallen leaves into the bin behind the desk.

'It would be if I wanted,' Conor said.

'Good for you. See, you've still got the old magic.' She was surprised at the tug of jealousy she felt, pushed it down.

'Hey?' he said, catching her by the waist. 'You know what it's like, Darce. It's all part of the game to flirt with the customers. They're just lonely, that's all it is. Though . . .'

'Though that hasn't stopped you in the past. That's what you're going to say?'

'Play nicely, children,' Diana said. 'Everything OK?'

'No, not really. I'm feeling a bit off colour,' Darcy said, placing the flat of her hand against her stomach.

'You're not pregnant are you?' Diana hissed.

'Ma!'

Conor checked there were no guests around, then put his arm around her, pulled her in close. 'I thought we were careful?'

'We are careful!' she whispered, turning her face to him, Diana watching every move.

'Not that I'm complaining.' Conor held her close. 'The thought of you—'

'Shall we all get on with some work?' Diana said, banging the bell on the front desk repeatedly to summon the receptionist. 'Where the hell is everyone? We've a busy day ahead.'

'Yes, boss,' Conor said, walking away.

'Con, don't go overdoing it. I want you back at a hundred per cent for the show final, do you hear?'

'Yes, boss,' he said, raising his hand.

'Well?' she said to Darcy.

'It's nothing. He was just flirting with some guest.' Darcy shook her head. 'I'm sorry. I have no right to feel—'

'Jealous? Of course you do. You're in love with him, and love isn't rational. But if you're going to have a good relationship, you have to trust him. It's time for you both to move on. You can't start a new chapter—'

'If you insist on re-reading the last one?'

'Am I getting repetitive?'

'A little.'

'It just goes terribly fast.' Diana sighed, hugging the ledger to her chest. 'It feels like I should be the one who is young and free.' She gazed through the open door to the bay. 'I still remember what it's like to date boys whose hair is thick, and full, and dark. But then there's a lot to be said for a man with experience.' The sound of a truck pulling into the courtyard caught her attention. 'Talking of which,' she said. She pulled a gold tube of lipstick out of her pocket and rubbed it across her bottom lip, pouting and smacking her lips.

'You're incorrigible.'

'I'm planning to rage, rage,' she said, winking. Diana gestured at an old couple crossing the reception area, arm in arm, shuffling. 'I don't feel old, you see, but then I look at people the same age as me, and I am. It's ghastly.' She stood a little taller and waved. 'Good morning, Fergus.'

'Diana.' Fergus strode into the reception, cradling a box of tiles. 'Darcy.' He stopped before her.

'So?' Diana touched her hair. 'Did you get the stone samples for the bathrooms?'

'Aye. I just wanted to check with you before ordering. Do you have time to come and have a gander?'

'I should really be—'

'Go on with you,' Darcy said, shooing her out from behind the desk. 'I can hold the fort for an hour or so.' The phone rang, and she cradled the receiver under her chin. 'Good morning, Castle Dromquinna,' she said. 'Lunch today? I'm afraid we're fully booked.'

217

38

Darcy rose before first light, leaving Conor sleeping peacefully in his bed. She borrowed a clean set of chef's whites, rolling up the trousers above her silver pumps, and walked to the kitchen from his cottage, cutting across the lawns. As she passed the staff quarters she noticed Beatrice's light was on, a pale glow leaching from the edge of the curtains. Darcy frowned, thinking over the past days. She couldn't put her finger on it exactly. *What is it with her? Why do bad things seem to happen around her?*

Yesterday's fully booked lunch turned out to be empty. Tristan had planned to film Darcy cooking for the restaurant, but none of the diners showed up. When they traced the phones used for the bookings, every single line was dead. Darcy thought back to the eerily quiet, empty restaurant with a nagging feeling in the pit of her stomach she just couldn't shake. She remembered the first time she saw Beatrice. *Trouble, that was what I thought. I had a hunch I couldn't trust you the minute I saw you.* She thought of JJ's suicide – but she just worked with him, didn't she? Then there was Conor's accident. But all he could remember was talking to her in her room – he'd been defending Darcy against gossip, that was all, wasn't it?

She frowned, thinking of the past few weeks – of Tristan's van, the food blogger. *It just seems to be one thing after another since she showed up.* Darcy shook her head. *I'm just being paranoid,* she told herself. *It's a run of bad luck, that's all. It will change.*

Darcy pushed open the kitchen door, and forced herself to concentrate on the work ahead. She timed every part of the postponed meal Tris would film her making tomorrow, perfecting the preparation, cooking and presentation.

'Jeez, Darce, you're worse than me,' Conor said, padding through the kitchen to her. His eyes were languid from sleep, his face bruised with dark stubble. He put his arms around her and cradled her from behind, looking at the dishes on the counter, the immaculately clean kitchen. His hair was damp from the shower, and he smelt of vanilla.

'You're using my shower gel now, are you?'

'I like it, smells of you.' He kissed her neck. 'Wish all my chefs smelt as good as you. And were as tidy as you.'

'Clear up as you go along, that's what my home ec teacher taught us in school,' Darcy said, turning to him. She tucked her head beneath his jaw and closed her eyes, letting the tiredness wash over her, enjoying the warmth of him, the strength of his arms. 'I could sleep on my feet.'

'If you're knackered, tea and eggs is your only man,' he said, reaching for the kettle. 'Go on, sit down.' He dragged over a stool for her, and clattered around fetching mugs and plates. He cracked a couple of eggs into a bowl. 'Scrambled?'

'Please.' Darcy laughed. 'You weren't tempted with the old joke?'

'How do you like your eggs for breakfast?' He poured the mix into the frying pan, and leant across to kiss her. 'You know, if you were pregnant I wouldn't mind. In fact, it's made me think.' He stirred the eggs.

'Conor . . .' she said, 'let's just take it easy, hey? All I want to do is enjoy this time with you. There's no hurry.' Darcy carved off two slices of fresh soda bread. 'Are you having some?'

'Nah, you're all right. I want to try your apple pie.' He placed a steaming plate of eggs in front of her, and a cup of builder's tea. 'Look, I'm not working until dinner. I think you should take a break. We can get out for a bit, have some fresh air.'

'What have you got in mind?'

Darcy woke in the cab of Conor's truck, her feet tucked up beside her and her head resting against the window. 'What did I miss?' she said, yawning.

'Only the most beautiful scenery in all of Ireland,' Conor said, reaching out his arm to her. Crowded House was playing on the radio, and the windscreen wipers looped to and fro. 'Moll's Gap, MacGillykuddy's Reeks. I stopped at Muckross in case you woke up for a walk but you've been out for the count.' She moved closer to him, laid her head on his shoulder, and he kissed her hair.

'I dozed off, sorry. Where are we heading now?' she said.

'Well this, my dear, is the scenic route,' he said, putting on a local accent. 'The Ring of Kerry, this most magical land of sea and sky.' He laughed as Darcy dug her fingers into his stomach. 'Dingle. We're going to Dingle. You haven't lived if you've not swum with Fungi.'

An hour later, Darcy found herself in a tiny fishing boat bobbing around the harbour on a choppy grey sea.

'Sure I can't convince you?' Conor said, lowering his diving mask.

'I'm fine. I'll just keep my eyes on the horizon.' Darcy was pale, her hair lashed to her face by the wind and the rain.

'This was a bad idea,' he said.

'No, it was a lovely idea, I'm just not up to swimming in that today.' She reached up to him and planted a kiss on his cheek. 'Go on then, go and find your dolphin.' Conor and a couple of other divers leapt off the side of the boat, and Darcy gingerly leant over to check he had surfaced. 'Does the dolphin come here every day?'

'Aye, or your money back,' the boatman said, steering a course around the divers.

A wave of nausea swept over her. Darcy settled back in the boat, and took a gulp of cool air.

'Darce! Darcy!' Conor shouted, waving from the water as a large bottlenose dolphin breached at his side. She laughed and waved back, snapping photographs on her phone.

Later, in a pub near the harbour, she showed Conor the photos. The rain lashed the windows, rattling in the wind, hissing on the open fire. Darcy was glad to be off the boat. Sitting on a red velvet sofa beside the hearth, she still felt like she was rolling to and fro on the sea.

'Chose a good day for it, didn't we?' Conor said. 'I'm sorry, I didn't know you get seasick. You should have said something.'

'Didn't want to spoil your fun.' Darcy sipped at her glass of sparkling water, the ice and lemon fresh and delicious.

'I guess there's a lot I have to learn about you.' He glanced up as the landlord plugged in the jukebox. Conor searched his pockets for a few coins and wandered over. He flicked through the tracks, and chose 'Angel', reaching out his hand to Darcy. 'May I have this dance, Miss Hughes?' They danced slowly together, her head resting against his chest. 'Feeling any better?'

'Much, thank you.' Darcy closed her eyes, listening to the steady beat of his heart.

'Tell me something I don't know about you,' he said. 'Tell me something you love.'

'Dromquinna.' Darcy smiled. 'Strawberries, shooting stars, silver Converse.' She thought for a moment. 'The light in late summer in Italy with Ma. Spaghetti with olive oil and garlic. Beds with fresh white sheets. The smell of frangipani. That moment in a song where they miss a beat before the melody goes on—'

'Me?' Conor said. Darcy heard the hope and uncertainty in his voice, and she looked up at him. 'No pressure or anything. We can take it slow. I know spaghetti's important but—'

'Yes, I love you,' she said, and her lips brushed his. Conor cupped her face in his hands, kissing her tenderly. 'I think I've always loved you,' she said, smiling, resting her head against his.

'I don't know what I've done to deserve you, but once this contest is out of the way and the restaurant closes down for a couple of weeks I am going to take you somewhere far away from all this nonsense.'

'You mean Beatrice?' she said.

'She's trouble, that one,' Conor said. 'God knows what happened when I fell, but bad news follows her around.'

'Have you asked her?'

Conor shook his head. 'She's keeping out of my way and I like it like that. The sooner the filming is done and we can send her on her way the better.' He held Darcy close. 'I don't want anything coming between us.'

They danced on, lost in the music and one another. But something troubled her. Darcy realised that Conor hadn't said he loved her too. Could it be that everything Beatrice had said was true?

39

'How's she looking, Tris?' Diana said, sliding into a chair beside him.

'Darcy's a natural, darling, just like you.' He scrolled through some still shots he had taken that morning. 'It's simple, perfect. Hors d'oeuvres the Colombe d'Or would die for, served standing, with elderbubble.'

'Elder what?'

'Elderflower cordial made with flowers from the hedgerows. We got some lovely shots of her. The recipe's simple but delicious – shot of voddy, top up with prosecco, garnish with mint and cucumber.'

'Then?'

'Cold first course,' he said, checking his notes. 'We've shot that already, like a party down on the jetty by the bay.' He ticked it off. 'Next up we have a perfectly prepared roast chicken as the main course, her gratin of local potatoes, and a simple green salad – but oh, what a salad . . .'

'It's the vinaigrette. Most people mix three oil to one of vinegar. I taught Darcy to do six to one, like Elizabeth. Less acidic.'

'And apple pie with the most heavenly vanilla ice-cream I've ever tasted. Oh, and a gorgeous little earthenware cup of hot fruit salad – redcurrants, raspberries. It sounds simple but there's an artistry and beauty to her dishes.' He leant towards her. 'I tell you what, it knocks young Beatrice's retro menu of prawn cocktail and a fondue into a cocked hat.'

'What does the pudding taste like? Plenty of cinnamon?'

'It tastes like the childhood I wish I'd had.'

'Good girl,' Diana said under her breath. 'I've always said that the sign of a good pudding is that you taste every ingredient in there, and it leaves your palette clear.' Diana's stomach rumbled at the thought. 'Are you hungry?'

'Always, dear heart,' he said, patting his paunch. He followed Diana through to the kitchen, and settled on a stool at the kitchen table.

'Make yourself useful,' she said, tossing him a head of garlic.

'How many cloves?'

'Sixteen.'

'Good lord.'

'There's eight of us for lunch.' Diana cracked five eggs on the side of the mixer bowl, and separated out the yolks. 'Give the garlic a good bash in the pestle and mortar, will you?' They worked in companionable silence for a while, the only sound the hiss of the oil as Diana basted the roast, the steady beat of the garlic being crushed. The air was perfumed with roasting meat, the oil bubbling with spices. 'Thanks, lovey,' she said, taking the heavy pestle from Tristan. She scooped the garlic into the bowl with a pinch of salt, and steadily beat in a pint of olive oil for the aioli. 'Drinkie?'

'Let me.' Tristan hopped down and walked to the drinks cabinet. 'Kir Cardinal?' he said, picking up an open bottle of Pinot Noir.

'Haven't had one of those for years.' Diana smiled. 'You really think she's got it, don't you?' she said, glancing up from the mixer.

'There have been a couple of cooks since Julia Child who took a real sensual pleasure in food,' Tristan said, pouring crème de cassis into two glasses. 'You know, that sexy one with the finger-licking business. But what Darcy has is some of that Barbara Good, girl-next-door, readers' wives appeal.'

'Eugh,' Diana said, wrinkling her nose.

'I know, but bear with me. There's just something quite fresh and sexy and earthy about her – this show is just the beginning. I'm thinking travelogues – like they did with Rick and Keith back in the eighties and nineties, but this time with her. She's got a natural joie de vivre and curiosity about her, you know? We'll start off in America because she has that whole West Coast vibe. People want to buy into her. The books will be sexy, the show's sexy, she's sexy, and as you know—'

'If you're on the telly, it sells the books. I get the picture.'

'I'll make a few calls. We'll get her on the *Late Late* before the final goes out.' He sipped his drink. 'She's a natural, and she enjoys eating – that's still seen as naughty somehow.' Tristan raised an eyebrow. 'Even I can see she looks fit. We've had enough of all this camp, retro nonsense – people are going to want something real, and strong and sexy, like the original supermodels in the eighties. None of this infantilised stuff. People will be tired soon enough of hipsters with their beards and bunting. We want something new. Something of our time. We're going to want to look up to women who look like they can take on the world and feed the five thousand.'

'Steady on, Tris,' Diana said, laughing. 'You think Darcy's it?'

'I know she is. I knew it the minute I saw her when she was ten years old, and she ignored Conor slumped in his bowl of soup at Sunday lunch. She just picked his head up to make sure he could breathe, and got on with carrying the bread around for you.'

'I feel like her pimp,' Diana said. She glanced up as a taxi pulled up outside.

'Guests?'

'Darcy's friends from the States. Her roommate and her girlfriend with their new baby.'

'Very California, darling.' Tristan put down his glass and went to fetch Darcy.

'Hello?' Lyn called, walking through the open kitchen door.

'Lyn!' Darcy cried, sweeping her into her arms. 'How was the journey?'

'Long,' she said, wearily. 'He cried all the way from Dublin airport, and all he wants to do now is feed.' A plaintive wail followed her from outside.

'I am so glad to see you,' Darcy said. 'Where is he?'

'Here we are,' Sasha said, carrying the baby in her arms. 'Hello, Darce, how are you?' She pecked her on the cheek, twice. 'Indigo, meet your godma, Darcy. This place is amazing.' She handed over the child to her, and Darcy cooed, giving him her knuckle to suck on. She looked up and saw Conor watching her, his expression soft and full of love.

'Who have we got here?' Beatrice said, sashaying through the door.

'Lyn, Sasha, this is Beatrice. She's helping with the filming.' Darcy glanced at her, uncertain. 'You've met Ma before, haven't you, Lyn?' Diana raised her hand in greeting. 'And that's Tristan, the director.'

'And you must be Conor,' Lyn said, shaking his hand as he came and stood by Darcy.

'Congratulations,' Conor said. 'How old is he?'

'Just a month,' Sasha said. 'We must be mad travelling so soon.'

'Ah, they just want to sleep at that age,' Conor said. 'Make the most of it. You wait until he starts waking up a bit.'

'You must be exhausted,' Beatrice said, touching Lyn's arm. 'Why don't you go and put your feet up? Look at your poor swollen ankles.'

'No, I'm all right . . .' Lyn watched her, wary.

'Darcy's busy filming at the moment, aren't you, Darce,' Beatrice said, smiling brightly, 'so why don't I take you through to the reception and we can get you booked in to your room?'

Darcy handed the baby to Lyn. 'Thanks, Bea,' she said, something about her friendliness jarring like a wrong note.

'Let me guess,' Beatrice said, guiding Sasha with her hand in the small of her back. 'Model?'

'Actress,' Sasha said, her cupid bow lips pursing into a smile.

'Have you seen the view of the bay?' They stopped at the window, and let the others walk on.

'It is heaven, *so* good to be off that plane,' Sasha said, shaking out her tumbling red hair. 'I feel I can breathe here.'

'I love it. It feels like I've come home,' Beatrice said.

'Don't you ever get bored?' Sasha held Beatrice's gaze.

'I can always find ways to entertain myself.' Beatrice looked over as the baby cried out. 'It must be quite a strain, the baby.'

'I'm not terribly maternal,' Sasha said, leaning towards her as they walked on. 'It was Lyn who wanted children.'

'I can't imagine growing a whole human being.' Beatrice mimed a large stomach. 'I mean, it's not very . . .' She looked at Sasha, gauging her. 'Sexy.'

Sasha licked her lips. 'Don't get me wrong, I adore Teddy. He does rather . . . Well, I always imagined life would be rather more carefree, you know . . .'

'What are you two scheming about?' Lyn said, turning to them. 'Do you know what I did with the muslins, love?'

'More weekends in Naples than piles of nappies?' Beatrice said to Sasha.

'Precisely.' She pointed her index finger, giggling. 'Sorry, darling?' She looked at Lyn.

'Never mind.' Lyn narrowed her eyes, glancing back at them both.

'Oops,' Beatrice said, stifling a laugh. She leant in to Sasha, whispering. 'I think we're on the naughty step.'

'Oh good, it gets *so* boring being well behaved all the time.'

40

Darcy stood on the old wooden jetty, the beautiful bay behind her reflecting the purple mountains, the amber sky. Tristan's team had rigged a simple white pagoda above the table, and were filming as Darcy demonstrated how to season the chicken. Bowls from a local pottery stood on the table, full of bright lemons, bunches of fresh herbs. Darcy was dressed in a long white linen dress, with a simple black apron, and her favourite silver Converse. Her hair had been styled into a looser, edgier long bob, and the make-up girl had come up with a fresh, golden look for her.

'Don't worry too much about the audio,' Tristan called to her above the wind. 'We'll dub everything in later in the studio when you do the voiceover, OK? I just want to get this shot before we lose the light. You look fabulous, darling.' He gave her the thumbs up, and Darcy began to prepare the roast chicken.

'Why don't you tell me about your style of cooking, Darcy?' he said.

'To be honest, I don't have a style yet.' She looked at the camera. 'I'm never satisfied, you know? I'm still learning, always changing.' She gathered up the herbs and inhaled. 'I wish you could all smell this. It smells like summer, like Kenmare, like home.'

'What kind of food do you love?' he said.

'I always think you eat with all your senses,' she said, chopping the herbs. 'What you see, and smell, and taste. And touch – the texture is so important. I mean, look at this.' She picked up a loaf of freshly baked soda bread from the wire rack and broke it open, inhaling, steam rising in a pale cloud. 'The texture is like no other bread, crumbly and warm.'

'When you take over management of the Castle, what will you change?'

'I wouldn't change a thing in the kitchen. There's no hierarchy there, and I admire the way Conor runs it. There's discipline for sure, but they work together as a team, and he's just "Chef".' Darcy smiled, thinking of him – *my brigade of pirates*. She glanced over to the shore where he sat beside Diana and Lyn. 'He's a genius.'

'So you're saying you'll both run the Castle?'

'I've a lot to learn, and I enjoy sharing what I find out with people.' Darcy looked at the camera. 'But am I ready to run a Michelin-starred kitchen? What do you think?'

'You were amazing today,' Lyn said, leaning towards Darcy. The kitchen table was packed with people, a row of simple church candles illuminating the bowls of bread and olives, the platters of salami and bottles of wine.

'Thanks, it still feels strange being in front of the camera, after all those years watching Ma work when I was small.' Darcy glanced down the table to Conor, who was deep in conversation with Tristan.

'Apricot tarts,' Beatrice said with a flourish, sliding a glistening tray of individual puddings onto the table. 'They are so ripe and plump in the orchard right now,' she said, sitting beside Sasha. The candlelight glimmered on the sweet glaze on top of the perfect spirals of sliced apricots. 'I cooked a trio of desserts for the competition. Apricot fool, apricot tart, apricot upside-down pudding.'

'Apricot overkill,' Conor said under his breath.

'Yum,' Sasha said, reaching for one of the tarts.

'Naughty,' Beatrice said, smacking her hand playfully. 'Wait your turn.' Sasha sat back in her chair.

'What's that lovely almondy smell?' Sasha said.

'It's the marzipan,' Beatrice said, passing Diana a plate. 'A special touch. I made it myself. How about you, Darcy?'

'No thanks, I'm full.'

'Go on, I insist.' She handed a tart to her, the candlelight flickering in her dark eyes.

Darcy blinked. 'Bea, I thought your eyes were blue.'

'Blue?' She laughed. 'No, they were lenses, darling.' She glanced at Sasha. 'They suited me blonde, but now I'm brunette I prefer them au naturel.' She held her gaze. 'I find it so dull to do the same thing all the time, don't you?' Beneath the table, Beatrice traced the tendon inside Sasha's wrist. She took the next pudding with her other hand, and gave it to Sasha. 'Tempt you?'

'Why not?' Sasha cut into the tart and ate a small forkful, her eyes closing. As she took her fork from her mouth, her bottom lip caught for a moment, releasing slowly, and she looked at Beatrice. 'How about you? Can I tempt you?' she murmured, offering her the fork.

'Love to, but I'm allergic to nuts,' Beatrice said. 'You enjoy.'

Sasha leant closer. 'It wasn't the tart I was talking about.'

41

Diana reached for an orange from the bowl and began to peel, inhaling the fresh scent of the fruit. 'Thank heavens it's the day of the contest,' she said. 'I can't wait to get back to normal.' She looked out across the lawns to where a huge marquee had been erected. A troop of men were putting up trestle tables inside, and Tristan walked among them with Jamie, pointing out the marks for the cameramen.

'And after the filming, then what? All the chat shows, and roadshows, and book signings?' Darcy said. 'I heard Tris has booked me on *The Late Late Show*?'

'Yes, we can talk about that later. Caroline has some marvellous ideas for publicity.' Diana glanced at her. 'Where are your friends? I thought they were hanging around to see the show?'

'Lyn left a note, said they had to get to Dublin for a flight.' Darcy raked her hand through her hair.

'No? What a shame they're missing all the fun,' Beatrice said, perching on the kitchen table, her sparkly silver ballet pumps glittering in the sunlight.

'I don't know what happened,' Darcy said. 'I know Lyn – she was really upset about something last night, but she wouldn't tell me.'

'Call her later,' Conor said, and kissed the top of her head.

'Morning!' Tristan said, marching into the kitchen. 'Here

we all are, bright eyed and bushy tailed. How are my glamorous judges today?'

'You flatter me, Tris,' Conor said, rubbing the stubble on his chin. 'What's the schedule?'

'Have a shave, will you, love? We've tipped over from designer stubble into hobo.' Tristan stood at the head of the table. 'Right, my darlings, the four finalists have just arrived and are setting up in the marquee to cook their signature dishes for you.' He looked over his half-moon glasses and gestured with his biro. 'As in previous years, you will choose the two contestants who will go forward to the home vote. While everyone is ringing in, we will cut in some of the segments we have pre-recorded of your own favourite dishes.' Tristan folded his arms. 'Between us, of the contestants, it's the bakers, Michael and Kira, who are the ones for us. Brian's crubeens are a bit of an acquired taste.' Beatrice looked blank. 'Salted pigs' trotters, love.'

'Eugh,' she said, wrinkling her nose.

'I'd like him to win,' Conor said. 'They're fantastic with a pint of Guinness. It's what this competition is – or should be – all about. Finding a dish that reminds you of home.'

'Fiona's roasting us one of her own geese, and serving it with apple stuffing from her orchard.'

'I love that,' Darcy said.

'I know, it's fabulous, but she's eighty if she's a day,' Tristan said. 'The sponsors will want a young face for all the publicity.'

'That's outrageous,' Diana said.

'It's the way it is, and we all know baking is having its moment in the sun.' He checked his watch. 'Now the punters will start arriving in a couple of hours, and the contestants are in the main marquee. They are understandably nervous, so I thought it might be nice if we all went and said hello. Make them feel welcome.' Tristan cleared his throat. 'Conor, I don't need to remind you it's a family show.'

'Message understood. There won't be a repeat of last year.'

232

'I want you to focus on the bakers.'

'Seriously, Tris? You're doing this to torture me, you bastard. You know I hate feckin' cupcakes.' Diana pointed at the swear box, and Conor got out his wallet, stuffing euro notes into it. 'I mean it, if I never see a feckin' cupcake again I'll be a happy man.' He shoved another couple of notes into the slot. He gestured at Beatrice. 'Why can't she do it? Make herself useful?'

'The viewers will expect you and Diana to make the final decision,' Tristan said. 'And did I say anything about cupcakes? Kira is baking a tea brack, Michael is doing a traditional apple cake—'

'With apples from his own orchard, probably,' Beatrice said, straight faced.

'Jealous?' Conor said.

'Are you quite done?' Diana raised her voice. Conor nodded, and folded his arms. 'Excuse Conor,' she said to Beatrice. 'We are all a little tense.' Beatrice pursed her lips and shrugged. 'We have hundreds of people arriving in a matter of hours, and they will be parking in our fields, and strolling around our grounds, and enjoying the fine marquee in all its charming glory with its bunting and cake stands, and we are going to make everyone feel good, do you hear? We have marvellous food stalls from all over the country, Ireland's finest producers and cooks. We have family events, the Castle's animals have been set up as a petting zoo—'

'Not Mephisto?' Darcy said. 'You know what he's like if he's in a mood.'

Diana ignored her. 'Children can see a real, working kitchen farm – sheep, goats, chickens, rabbits.' She adjusted her sling, wincing. 'Now, Conor, you will smile as if you are enjoying every bite of cake, and flirt with the girls. Bea, you will be in your element, playing up to the camera, and Darcy, you will be down by the bay doing your cooking demonstration of good, real, local food, and all the time the phone numbers to vote on the favourite contestant will be up on the screen, and the public will ring in their hundreds, their thousands, because they will care, do you understand? They will want Brian, Fiona, Kira or Michael to win, and they will feel invested in you as judges, and professionals. And when I pass the Castle on to Darcy, they will buy your books, and eat meals in your hotel, and your future will be secure. Do you understand?'

'Yes, Di,' Conor said, looking at his boots.

'Good. The future of the Castle depends on the success of *Top Chef*. Let's get this show on the road.'

42

The four contestants stood in front of Diana and Conor, each wearing a black apron printed with *Top Chef* over their whites. Tristan pointed at the cameraman, and Diana stepped forwards into the spotlight as the filming began. A cheer went up from the crowd in the marquee, and home-made signs – *Team Brian*, *Fiona's Fan Club* – waved behind Diana.

'Welcome to Dromquinna,' she said, looking at each of the contestants in turn. 'And congratulations. It is a huge achieve-ment to have reached the final, but as you know there can be only one Top Chef.'

'You are competing not only for the cash prize,' Conor said, joining Diana, 'but the chance to launch your professional career.' A clock projected onto the roof of the marquee began to tick. 'Good luck, and go to your stations!'

'And cut,' Tristan said over the cheers and clapping from the crowd, and the contestants scurried away to their kitchen stations, checking the steaming pots and preparing their next ingredients. 'Right,' he said to the cameraman. 'I want you filming continuously, OK? Get it all, and we'll pick out the choice bits later.' He turned to the wiry dark-headed man at the nearest station. 'Let's check our timings, if we're going to be on target for two o'clock. Brian, love, your crubeens take about three hours?'

'They do,' Brian said, ducking below the counter to the fridge.

'How long have they been simmering for?'

'Two hours so far.' Brian staggered to his feet, mopping his brow with a tea towel. 'Oh God! The thyme, I forgot the thyme!' he said, looking at the herbs wrapped up with the leaves for the salad.

'You're all right,' Darcy said, patting him on the back. 'Get it in the pot now.' Brian's hands shook as he washed off the thyme, and quickly chopped the stalks. 'That smells wonderful,' she said. 'I'm dying to try these.'

'Grew the thyme on my allotment,' Brian said, lifting the lid on the large pot bubbling on the stove. 'And the parsley. I forgot the bay leaf so I nicked one from the garden, hope you don't mind.' Brian looked like a rabbit in headlights as he glanced from Darcy to the camera.

'Good luck, Brian,' she said. Tristan gestured that the cameraman should move on.

'Fiona, how are you doing with that lovely goose of yours?' Diana said, joining a stooped, grey-haired woman who was tossing potatoes in sizzling fat. 'What a fine bird.'

'He's coming along,' she said, weaving slightly as she shuffled to the sink. She heaved a colander of parboiled potatoes up and shook them vigorously.

'Is this goose fat you're cooking the potatoes in?' Diana said.

'It is. Saved it from the bird I cooked for you in Wicklow last month.' The cameraman panned in as the next batch of floury potatoes dropped into the oil.

'May I help you? It's rather a heavy tray,' Beatrice said, striding into shot. She took one side of the roasting dish, and carried it with Fiona to the oven.

'Hold on,' Fiona said. 'The top oven's not on.' The women slid the tray onto the counter. 'Who turned my oven off?' Fiona bellowed, rounding on the other contestants. Michael and Kira looked up from their mixing bowls, wide eyed. 'I bet it was him!' Fiona said, pointing a long, bony finger at Brian, who shrugged, and turned back to his pot. 'I saw him, fiddling about down below.'

'I needed a fork,' Brian said, lifting the lid of the pot.

'Brian,' Beatrice said, 'have you been a naughty boy?'

'Prove it,' he said, under his breath.

'We still have time,' Diana said, turning the top oven on. 'The stuffing's in the cavity, isn't it? The goose will take another good hour. Plenty of time for you to roast these.' She gestured at Conor, who turned to the young woman baking at the station nearest him.

'Now, Kira,' he said, 'I know your tea brack has been a big hit with the folks at home. We've been inundated with emails and messages asking for the recipe.'

'It's all about the tea you steep the fruit in. If I win, I'd be delighted to share the secret with you,' Kira said, her green eyes sparkling. She pushed a strand of red-gold hair behind one ear.

'Is this a family recipe?'

'It is. My grandma made it every Saturday when she looked after me. There's nothing like a slice of this loaf with some salty butter.'

'Not the most visually appealing of cakes, though, is it?' Beatrice said, leaning against the counter as Kira poured the mixture into a cake tin lined with greaseproof paper. 'I mean, bit boring. Is it going to wow us?'

'*Wow* you?' Kira's cheeks coloured. Some of the mixture spilled over the edge of the tin. 'It's ... I don't know.' She gathered up her courage. 'I love it, and so did Mr Ricci and Mrs Hughes, so you'll just have to wait and try it yourself, won't you?' Her eyes glinted, and she raised her chin as she tucked the cake tin into the oven. Beatrice raised an eyebrow and sauntered away, her full skirts swinging.

'Good for you,' Conor whispered to Kira, before moving on to Michael's station.

'Would you look at these apples,' Diana said, bending to sniff the bowl of shiny red fruit. 'Gravenstein?'

'From my orchard at home,' Michael said, looking up from the pestle and mortar where he was grinding cinnamon and cloves. He glanced across as Beatrice tutted loudly, leaving the marquee.

'We grow them here, too,' Darcy said.

'I know.' Michael wiped his hands on a clean tea towel. 'It's my homage to the Castle, I guess.' He smiled, shy suddenly.

'Tell us what you admire about the Castle so much,' Conor said. 'What would it mean if you won the internship here?'

'It would mean everything,' he said, his eyes lighting up with passion. 'I mean, I have so much to learn, and I can't think of any kitchen in the world I'd rather train in.'

43

Beatrice put the finishing touches to a tier of perfect chocolate cakes on a silver stand, a sprinkle of edible glitter spilling from her fingertips as if by magic, catching the lights on the stage. Cameras trained on the countertop projected Beatrice's every move onto screens behind her, so that people at the back of the crowd could see her working. The children gathered at the front of the stage clapped and cheered. 'And that,' she said, looking at the camera, 'is how simple it is to make a magical birthday party for your family. A little bit of imagination, and . . .'

'Mix it with love!' the children chorused.

'Jaysus, she has a catch phrase already?' Conor said, leaning against the marquee pole by Tristan. 'Have you seen the bloody great stall she's got over there?' Conor pointed towards the vendors' set-up a little way from the marquee, selling refreshments. At the heart of them a silver Airstream caravan decked with white and pastel-purple polka dots and floral bunting said 'Lavender Cupcakes'. Young girls dressed in identical tea gowns served customers from mismatched vintage china cups, carrying delicate silver stands laden with richly iced cupcakes from table to table.

'She's ambitious this one,' Tris said. 'She said she had the mobile catering kit in storage so she might as well use it.'

'Free advertising, that's what it is,' Conor said, lighting a cigarette. 'She's building her empire, so she is.'

'You know she's been approached by a couple of publishers already?'

'Who told you that?'

'She did.'

Conor laughed through his nose. 'I'll believe that when I see it.' He watched Beatrice shaking hands with some of the children and the mothers, a rictus grin on her face. 'To be honest as long as she rocks on from here, I don't care what she does.' Beatrice caught sight of them and marched towards them.

'Uh oh, incoming,' Tristan said, feigning interest in his filming schedule.

'Well, that was fun,' Beatrice said, putting her hands on her hips. She turned to Tristan. 'But children, really? If you don't edit this show to give me equal billing with Darcy you will be hearing from my agent, do you understand?' She glanced at Conor. 'I mean, if the bakers make it through to the final, who is more qualified to judge them than the owner of a chain of bakeries?'

'Hm,' Conor said, pretending to think. He glared at Beatrice. 'A chain is it now? Looks like a tarted up caravan to me. How about a Michelin-starred chef who has employed more pastry cooks than you have had hot dinners?'

Tristan checked his watch. 'Conor, calm down, love.'

'It's pathetic, really,' Beatrice said, looking at the crowds milling around. 'I mean, the contestants are amateurs. What are they competing for, really? Now if it was a competition among the judges, with really high stakes, say running the Castle—'

'You're mad,' Conor said. He shook his head. 'The prize they are competing for is good enough. Ten thousand euros and an internship with us.'

'What? At the Castle?' Beatrice looked at him, sharp and alert.

'Did you not know that?' A slow smile broke across Conor's face. 'I thought you said you'd watched the last series of the show.'

'*Hughes at Home*, yes – not *Top Chef*. Why would I want to watch a bunch of amateurs?'

'You might have learnt something,' Conor said, stepping towards her. 'See, if one of the bakers wins you really will have some competition in the kitchen. Come to think of it, we won't need you at all.'

'Right, save it for later, you two. We start filming in five, OK?' Tristan said. 'Conor, I want you over by the judging table with that gorgeous sexy smile of yours lighting up the room and giving the ladies their jollies.' He walked away.

'You think you're really something, don't you?' Conor said, stepping closer to Beatrice and lowering his voice. 'Everything you touch is a disaster. The sooner you're out of here the better.'

'I'm not going anywhere,' she said, smiling sweetly as a crowd of visitors walked past, snapping photos of them.

'You still don't get it, do you? We gave you a chance but you've been nothing but trouble. You're all froth and no substance, Beatrice, and we expect more than that.' He turned to walk away.

'You're lying. Diana wanted me here, she needs me. I'm just as good as you and Darcy.'

'You really think you can compete with us? She's using you, you fool. Look around you. All this?' He pointed at a strand of polka-dot bunting on the marquee. 'Window dressing. A load of overpriced tat. You watch. Just as soon as the cameras stop rolling you are out of here, and it's none too soon for me.' He leant closer to her. 'You like making mischief, messing with people, don't you? You lied about Darcy, and I have no idea what happened when I came to have it out with you—'

241

'You don't remember, do you?' she said, smiling, sly.

'Nothing happened, I know that much,' Conor said, clenching his fist. 'Not between us.'

'Do you honestly think I pushed you?' She stared at him, her face expressionless.

'I don't remember and I don't give a damn. I just want you gone, do you understand?'

Beatrice watched him go. She saw the crowds heading towards the marquee for the final part of the competition, and the filming lights turning on one by one, illuminating the four contestants, their dishes laid out before them. Her eyes narrowed watching Kira wipe a speck of cake from the edge of her plate. 'There's only room for one baker in this kitchen,' Beatrice said under her breath, stalking away from the marquee.

44

Tristan was filming a head and shoulders shot of Darcy, talking about the art of home baking with the bustling marquee in the background, when Conor took his place behind the judges' table at her side. Immediately a group of women in summer dresses gathered round him, brandishing cookbooks for him to sign, and crowding in for selfies which appeared on social media seconds later.

'Ladies, ladies!' Tristan said, signalling to the cameraman to stop filming. There will be a book signing later, plenty of time for you to have some one-on-one time with Mr Ricci. He looked around. 'Where's Beatrice?'

'I don't know,' Diana said, joining them. 'But it's too late. The contestants have served their dishes and it's time for us to choose the two finalists. You'll have to cut her in later.'

The judges began with Fiona's roast goose, sampling a forkful of the succulent meat, the perfectly golden roast potatoes. Fiona stood beside the table, rosy-cheeked and hopeful.

'I love the tartness of the apple in the stuffing,' Conor said.

'Just the right balance,' Darcy said.

'These potatoes are perfection,' Diana said, breaking one open with her fingertips.

'Don't burn yourself, Mrs Hughes,' Fiona said, offering her a plate.

'Asbestos fingers,' Diana said, waving the plate away. 'Too many years in a kitchen.'

'Well done, Fiona,' Conor said, before they walked on to Brian. An artfully arranged pair of pigs' trotters sat on a frothing bed of parsley. 'I'm looking forward to these,' he said. Brian handed each of them a fork.

'Do you think this is a winning dish, Brian?' Darcy said doubtfully, picking at the meat.

'I don't think so, I know so,' Brian said, puffing out his chest. He handed a fork to Beatrice.

'Where have you been?' Diana hissed.

'Just in time,' Conor said, gesturing that Beatrice should help herself. 'Tuck in.' She pressed her lips together, gouging at the dish with a fork.

'The mustard is homemade,' Brian said, his voice full of desperation. The four judges chewed thoughtfully, until one by one their expressions changed. Darcy gestured to Tristan for napkins, and spat her food out.

'I don't understand,' Brian said, his face colouring.

'Did you salt these yourself, Brian?' Conor said, grimacing as he swallowed.

'I did.'

'Did you check it was salt you were using?'

'Eugh, they're sweet,' Beatrice said, gagging.

'Who—' Brian's eyes widened. 'Which one of you bastards switched the salt and the sugar?' he said, pointing at the other contestants. Fiona whistled quietly, wiping down her station.

'Keep rolling,' Tristan cut in. 'Family show, love, we'll beep you out later.'

At Kira's station, the judges tried the rich and delicious tea brack.

'Mm,' Darcy said. 'The sugar glaze gives a gorgeous crunch.'

'Did you make the butter yourself, Kira?' Beatrice said, her voice sweet and sly.

'I did,' Kira said, defiant. 'I live on a dairy farm,' she said to Diana.

They moved on to Michael's station, and each of the judges took a slice of warm apple cake. Michael drizzled cold double cream over each plate.

'Thank you,' Conor said. He took a forkful of cake, and closed his eyes. 'That's amazing,' he said. 'I remember my ma cooking this by the open fire. How have you captured that smokiness?'

Michael tapped the side of his nose. 'Trade secret. I'll share it with you after the show.'

'Lovely firm bottom, Michael,' Diana said.

'That's the way we like it,' Conor said, winking at Darcy.

'Behave, Conor,' Diana said. 'This is quite the best apple cake I've ever had.'

'Very good,' Beatrice conceded. As she talked on about the importance of baking together with your family, how nurturing and calming it is, how much fun, a scream went up from the crowd. The judges turned, and a look of horror crossed Diana's face.

'Oh my God, I hope you're getting this,' Tristan whispered to the cameraman. 'It will be worth a fortune on the blooper shows. Imagine how well this will go down in Japan.'

Mephistopheles leapt nimbly onto the nearest table, kicking over a floral display and sending pastel tea cups crashing to the floor. By the time he was dragging a festoon of bunting behind him like the fallen rigging of a schooner, people had stopped running and had their phones out, filming the chaos. Pausing to snatch a bite of Kira's fruit cake, the goat raced onwards, with Aiden and a couple of the young chefs in pursuit.

'Mephisto!' bellowed Diana, pushing her way through the crowd. 'You are a very naughty boy. How did you get out of your pen?' The goat stopped in his tracks, turned to her and bleated. She unravelled the bunting from around his neck, and picked him up. 'Aiden, would you mind awfully taking him to the stable? These people are scaring him.'

'He should be locked up!' a man called from the crowd. 'We should call the council. Bleedin' hazard it is, having wildlife around here.'

'Wildlife?' Diana rounded on him. 'Wildlife? This is his home. He has far more right to be here than you do, you odious little man. If you don't like it, bugger off.' She waved her hands, shooing the crowd from the marquee. She paused for a moment, unnerved by the ranks of mobile phones filming her outburst. She turned to Tristan and mimed 'cut', running her index finger over her throat. 'Go on, all of you,' she shouted, 'clear off. There's nothing to see here.'

Tristan grabbed a megaphone. 'Change of plan, folks.' He gave Diana a gleeful thumbs up. 'If you'd like to follow the girls with the clipboards, we're going to film the next segment of the show down by the bay. While the judges deliberate about their choice of finalists, Darcy Hughes will be giving a cookery demonstration, and Conor Ricci will announce who will be going through to the phone vote . . .'

'Are you OK?' Beatrice said, strolling over to Diana. The marquee fell silent as the last of the crowd left

'Shouldn't you be at the bay?'

'No, Darcy will be fine,' Beatrice said. 'In fact, I think you rather enjoyed that.'

'What on earth do you mean?'

'Now you're handing over to the next generation doesn't it thrill you to see how badly everyone is messing up?' Beatrice shrugged off her pale pink cashmere cardigan, and flexed her shoulders. 'I know I'd love every moment.' Blue wings rippled beneath the straps of her summer dress, willow pattern designs snaking down across her back, her arms. She picked up a string of bunting.

Diana turned her back on Beatrice, gathering up fallen plates from the grass. 'You really don't know me at all, do you?' Beatrice stepped closer, running the bunting between her hands, looping it round. 'All I've ever cared about is nurturing talent, and making a success of this place.'

'I don't want you to retire, not yet. We're just getting to know one another.' Beatrice's voice was soft. 'If anyone should go, I think Conor—'

'Do you know what you are, Miss Lavender?' Diana's eyes flashed open. She caught a glimpse of movement in a silver platter she was lifting on to the trestle table. 'A cuckoo in our nest.' Diana swung round and Beatrice stumbled back in surprise.

'What? What do you mean?' she said. 'All I've ever done is try to help you. I love you.'

'Love?' Diana hesitated. 'You barely know me—' Her face contorted at the sight of the intricate, sprawling tattoo across Beatrice's back. 'What have you done?' She looked down at the delicate, pale birds on her own wrist, and then at Beatrice. 'You – you copied my tattoo.' Diana curled her lips in distaste. 'It's monstrous. You're like some sort of cuckoo or chameleon, taking whatever shines.'

'Copying?' Beatrice threw back her head and laughed. 'I don't want to *be* you. I belong here. I want to help you, take care of you. We don't need them.' She smiled sweetly. 'You still have no idea who I am, do you?' She stood straight, cricking her neck from side to side. 'I feel sorry for people like you, I really do, so caught up in your little dramas, your . . .' Her upper lip lifted. 'Emotions. I'm no monster. There are people like me everywhere.' She edged closer. 'I'm the guy with the toupee you think is so sad until he steals your cat and dumps it miles out of town. Or the PTA mother with the American tan tights who you think is rather pathetic to take it all so seriously until you realise she's engineered for her child to be head girl and win the scholarship to the university you had picked out for your child. I'm Beatrice Lavender of Lavender Cupcakes, all sugar and spice, and I despise every last one of the suckers who paid me three pounds a pop for a confection of sugar, and flour, and aspiration to a life beyond their reach. I despise them all. But you . . . I know you. You owe me.'

'What have I ever done to you?' The look on Beatrice's face chilled Diana's blood. She glanced around the tent. They were completely alone.

'Where to begin, Colleen . . .'

Diana gasped. She felt nauseous. The moment she had feared her whole life was upon her, sickening, inevitable. 'Who . . . who are you?' Diana clasped the pearls at her throat, her hand shaking.

'I'm Beatrice Lavender of Lavender Cupcakes.' She smiled, sweetly. 'I want to be just like you, you see. When I look at everything you've achieved, I want that. It just doesn't seem fair that Darcy should get all this when you had another daughter, didn't you, Colleen?'

'Fair?' Diana rounded on her, the fight rising up in her. 'Is it fair that your parents are killed when you are still a child? Is it fair that one of the doctors who is supposed to be looking after you singles you out. Gr-grooms you? Moulds you into the perfect wife?' She took a step towards Beatrice. 'I came from a good family, did you know that? I was a happy, strong and confident girl, once. But my parents died, and he chose me. They are very good at that, you see, singling out vulnerable victims. Or should I say people like you are.' She sniffed the air. 'I smelt it on you immediately. I should have listened to my gut instinct, rather than feeling sorry for you.' She leant in to her. 'But you made a mistake. Colleen Smith is dead. Diana Hughes is strong, and Darcy is strong. You bought in to the whole illusion, didn't you? All sugar and no spice? You underestimate us.' She started to turn away. 'I played you just as much as you think you've been playing us. I don't know who you are, or how you dug up this . . . this dirt I have so successfully hidden for nearly fifty years, but you are not welcome here.' Diana began to walk away. From the folds of her skirt, Beatrice lifted a silver rattle. As it chimed, Diana froze. She turned to her, ashen. 'Where did you get that?'

'Mummy gave it to me,' Beatrice said in a little-girl voice, pouting. She strode towards Diana, who flinched as she raised it to her face. 'Well. Darcy may be strong, but underneath all this you are still afraid, aren't you, Colleen?' She shook the rattle gently by Diana's ear.

She screwed her eyes shut. 'Stop it. Stop it now.' She pushed hard and Beatrice fell back to the floor, but she scrambled forward, grabbing Diana's ankle as she tried to run, and Diana stumbled. She fell with a cry, landing on her broken arm. Beatrice crept onto all fours. 'The thing is, I don't really care. If I destroy Darcy at the same time, that's even better.'

'You leave Darcy out of this, do you hear?' Diana made a lunge for a cake slice which had fallen beneath a nearby table, holding it out ahead of her. Beatrice threw up her hands in mock fear, her dark eyes dead, focused.

'Give up, Diana. You're too old.' Her eyes narrowed as Diana clambered to her feet, cradling her broken arm. 'How old are you, anyway?'

'I'm sixty-five and I'll take you out any day.' Diana was breathing heavily, her hair askew.

'She was just eighteen months, then, when you abandoned her,' Beatrice said, doing a quick calculation. 'You see, it was Mummy's dying wish that I find you. She told me so many stories about this beautiful woman who loved to cook. She had all your books. She was sure it was you. You were like something out of a fairytale. She was too afraid to seek you out, to meet you.' Beatrice smiled, her canines glinting. 'She always had a soft heart.'

Diana froze. 'You mean . . .'

'Oh yes, Mummy was, what's the word, *normal*.' Beatrice flicked the rattle against her skirts. 'Unlike most of the men she was attracted to, including my father. Unlike me.' She stared at Diana, cool and focused. 'I know exactly who I am, and what I am. Which one of us is the more authentic do you think, Diana? Which one of us is living a lie?'

'Oh God—' Diana pressed her hand to her lips.

'You call me monstrous? *You* are the monster,' Beatrice said, striding towards her. 'What kind of a woman abandons her baby? All Mummy ever wanted was the perfect family, and you took that from her. She wanted to be loved so badly, you see. Spent her whole life feeling she wasn't good enough, all because of you.' Beatrice sneered. 'You broke her heart. It made her very easy to manipulate, I can tell you.'

'What do you want?' Diana said, her face pale.

'Don't even think about sacking me after the show. If you don't give me an equal share of this restaurant, I'm going to tell them everything,' Beatrice said. 'You owe me. You owe me big time.' She blew Diana a kiss. 'Here's to happy families.'

45

'Hello!' Darcy waved from the stage, spotlights glinting on the crystals in her tiara. She wore a long black evening dress, and her hair had been swept up into a Holly Golightly chignon, streaked with gold. The tiara tugged at her hair. *What the hell has this got to do with local food?* she thought again, remembering her argument with Tristan. 'Trust me, lovey,' he'd said. 'People always love a bit of Audrey Hepburn glam.'

'Welcome to our *Breakfast at Tiffany's* demonstration.' She raised her voice above the wind lashing the shoreline. The crowd clapped and cheered above the strains of 'Moon River'. Darcy adjusted the microphone. 'I love a theme – it gives a real sense of occasion to any meal,' Darcy said, reading from the autocue. *I don't*, she thought, *there's nothing worse*. She felt her throat dry, the expectant faces of the crowd swimming before her. *I'm going to kill Tris when this is over.* She wished she was away from here, with the cameras staring at her, with all these people wanting her to be something she wasn't. 'Who can tell me what Holly was eating the first time we … we see her?' She felt a tremor in her lips as she smiled and the crowd fell silent. All Darcy could hear was the patter of rain starting to fall on the canopy above her.

'Croissant?' a woman's voice called out from the back row.

'Well done,' Darcy said. 'It's easier than you think to make your own croissants at home.' Darcy picked up a spatula and backed towards the gap in the curtain at the back of the stage. 'Bea?' she whispered out of the corner of her mouth. She glanced behind the curtain into the prep kitchen. No one was there, and none of the bowls had been set out with the ingredients.

Darcy felt nauseous; she heard coughing and low voices from the hundreds of people watching her on stage. One by one brightly coloured umbrellas opened above the crowd. She thought about lying, pretending it was all part of the show, and she looked around the faces hoping to see Conor. She saw the four contestants in the front row, waiting, expectant. Sweat prickled at the nape of her neck, and she put the spatula down on the counter, laying her palms flat to steady herself. She calmly turned on the oven. 'Well,' she said, 'it looks like my glamorous assistant has failed to turn up.' She took off the tiara and stood straight, with her hands on her hips as the first roll of thunder shook across the bay.

'Damn it,' said Tristan. 'Beatrice had one job after her poxy kids' demo. Come here and put the oven on for Darcy, and get the sodding croissants ready. Darcy's screwed. She set her up.' He glanced at Jamie out of the corner of his eye and caught him smirking. 'And you're fired.'

'What? Why?' Jamie said, his mouth falling open.

'Because, dear boy, as decorative as you are to have around the place, your job was to check each demo area before the chefs arrived to make sure everything was ready for filming. So instead of chatting up that gorgeous bunch of girls serving the teas at Beatrice's stall, you should have been down here making sure Darcy was ready to go.' Tristan took his clipboard. 'Your last pay cheque will be in the post.'

'Do you want me to keep filming, Tris?' the cameraman said, watching Jamie march off towards the Castle. The storm was rolling in across the bay, steel-grey clouds sinking low across the hills, rain driving hard. He tucked his camera beneath an awning, and focused on the stage.

'Yes, we'll edit it later, make it look like it was all planned.'

'Right,' Darcy said, her voice echoing from the speakers. 'What we are going to do instead, is take the kind of ingredients we all have lying around the kitchen to make a quick and healthy breakfast you can rustle up in the same time it takes to fill a bowl with sugary cereal or toast a piece of bread with all the nutritional value of cardboard.'

A camera onstage filmed Darcy's every movement. 'We're going to rustle up a quick omelette.' She thought of what Conor had said to her that day in the kitchen. 'If you're feeling knackered, eggs are your man.' A few people in the crowd laughed, and she began to relax. As she cooked, she talked lyrically about the kind of food she loved, and completely forgot her nerves. The camera on stage beamed close-ups as she deftly chopped bright red peppers and grated a cheese from the dairy up the road. She beckoned to a little girl in the front row to come up and try the food, and a couple of the men helped her up onto the stage to cheers and clapping. Darcy adlibbed with the girl, talking to her about her favourite snacks, and at the end slid the sparkling tiara into the girl's hair.

'Now,' Darcy said, 'I think we're about ready to announce which of the four contestants will be going through to the final.'

Conor joined her on stage. 'Where's Diana?' he said, covering his microphone. At that moment, a cry went up from the marquee and everyone turned to see a St John ambulance racing towards the tent. Darcy saw a figure in a flowered tea dress and cardigan running across the lush green lawn towards them, waving her arms frantically.

'Darcy, I'm so sorry,' Bea said, catching her breath. 'I was . . . I was trying to help Diana. She's had a fall.'

'Ma?' Darcy gathered up the skirt of her dress and leapt down from the stage with Conor, running ahead of the crowd.

She saw Fergus up ahead, walking at the side of the stretcher, holding Diana's hand.

'Ma,' Darcy said, running forward. 'Are you OK?' Beatrice stood behind her, out of sight, her face an impassive mask, watching.

'No, no I'm not,' Diana said, her face contorted with pain. She looked not at Darcy, but at Beatrice. She shook her head, warning Beatrice not to say anything. 'I fell. I'm such an idiot.'

'It was an accident, it can't be helped,' Fergus said, wiping the tears from Diana's cheek with his thumb.

'Come with me,' she said, her voice choked with tears. She cupped his hand in her own. 'I need you.' He lowered his head and kissed her hairline.

'I'm right beside you, my love,' he said.

'Ma, we're coming too,' Darcy said.

'No you're not, you need to announce the winners,' Diana said. She waved regally at the crowd as she was wheeled away, and cheers and clapping rose up.

'Will you be all right following with Conor later?' Fergus said. 'I promise I'll take care of her.'

'Of course,' Darcy said, and Conor put his arm around her.

'Con,' she said, watching the ambulance drive off, 'I'm scared. It's like the Castle is cursed.' They turned at the sound of someone tapping the microphone on stage. Beatrice was looking out across the sea of faces, her hand shielding her eyes from the lights.

'May I have your attention,' she said. 'Diana Hughes has sadly had to be rushed to hospital. She asked me to apologise, and to announce the winners—'

'What the hell is she up to?' Conor said, pushing his way through the people.

'Con, wait,' Darcy said, grabbing his arm. 'It's too late. Not in front of all these people.'

'All four contestants produced wonderful dishes, but only two can go through to the live phone vote in a week's time.'

Beatrice pointed at Brian, Fiona, Kira and Michael in turn. Tristan signalled to the sound man for a drum roll. 'Congratulations, Fiona and Michael!'

'That's wrong,' Darcy said under her breath. 'Kira should have gone through. Bea just can't take the competition.'

'I don't believe in curses,' Conor said, watching Beatrice drop the microphone and walk off stage. She looked across the crowd, seeking them out, and raised her chin defiantly. 'But I do believe in evil.'

MEMORIES ARE MADE OF THIS

I learnt to cook at my mother's side. She often talked of the kitchen she grew up in, with its woodburner, and dogs sleeping beneath the table, and the scent of madeleines cooking for tea. It always made her nostalgic when we cooked them together. She had a bottle of sloe gin steeping in the pantry, too, because she remembered the glistening restfulness of the bottles in her own mother's kitchen. Ma would have a nip of gin with a warm madeleine while I drank my milk and ate the tea we'd cooked together.

It's a good lesson: set your children to work, early on. Even the smallest hands can manage garlic bread – rubbing slices of toasty baguette with garlic, salt and a drop of olive oil. Somewhere along the line we lose the playfulness of cooking. Let them throw the spaghetti against the wall to see if it is cooked, let them squish the tomatoes for a simple sauce. Let them drizzle honey on their madeleines:

Set the oven to 190°C. Melt 60 g unsalted butter, and whisk in an egg and 50 g caster sugar. Sift 30 g plain flour and 20 g ground almonds into the mixture, stir in with the zest of one lemon. Rest for 1 hour. Spoon the mix into madeleine moulds, filling each shell ¾ of the way. Bake

each batch for 8–10 minutes until they are plump and
golden. Reminisce.

Darcy Hughes, *Appetite* Tumblr

LAVENDER CUPCAKES
recipe card #6 BLACK VELVET

At Lavender Cupcakes we like to take things one step further than the Red Velvet cakes you see everywhere (yawn),
with our signature Black Velvet cakes. What could be more
decadent, more indulgent than champagne and edible gold
leaf? Can we tempt you?

Pop the oven on at 180°C. Put 100 g soft butter in your mixer
(I love my pink Kitchen Aid!). Add 175 g of dark brown sugar,
1 egg, 100 g lightly sifted self-raising flour, half a teaspoon
of bicarb, 5 tbsp of good dark cocoa powder and 150 ml of
Guinness. Give them a jolly good beating. Pour the cake
mixture into cupcake cases – I love gold ones for this recipe.
Bake for 20 minutes, or a bit longer (poke a toothpick into
one of the cakes – if it comes out clean, you're done!). Now,
while those yummy cakes are cooling, simmer 125 ml of
champagne until it is reduced to 2 tbsp. Let it cool to room
temperature, and whip up 250 g sifted icing sugar, 125 g soft
butter and 1 tbsp of champagne from the bottle to make the
frosting. Add in the cooled, reduced champagne until you
reach the consistency you prefer. Fill a piping bag with the
frosting, and swirl your gorgeous, fudgy cakes with snowy
peaks. Decorate each with a whisper of gold leaf, and voila!

eBay: rare recipe card from Lavender Cupcakes
Linked to *Hughes at Home* scandal

'EFFORTLESS ENTERTAINING'

Teas and Suppers

There are few rules with cooking, and those there are can be bent or broken. The last thing your guests should feel is that they have put you out – arriving at the door to greet them with your hair awry, and shiny faced from the stove is simply not done. Choose a no-fuss menu, serve them a simple omelette and salad, even (thank you, Elizabeth David), but make your guests welcome, and enjoy the event yourself. It is better to ask your guests to peel the spuds or dress the salad than to spend the whole evening sweating in the kitchen, missing out on all the conversation and fun.

Easy omelette

Beat three eggs with a pinch of pepper. In a hot frying pan, melt a small knob of butter and begin to cook the eggs. Sprinkle over 1 tbsp of a favourite grated cheese, mixed with 1 tbsp of thick cream. Either fold the omelette over and serve once the egg is cooked through, or pop it under the grill until the mixture bubbles, golden. Serve with a salad, wine, water, enjoy the conversation.

Diana Hughes, *Hughes at Home*

Guess Who's Coming To Dinner?

'Appetite, a universal wolf.'

William Shakespeare

46

The next evening, Darcy jogged along the forest path, ferns snatching at her heels as she ran. Her breath was ragged, her heart beating in time with the rhythm of her feet, the pounding bassline of Daft Punk on her iPod.

Out of the corner of her eye, she saw something move beyond the trees. Her heart quickened. She ran faster, powering uphill out of the valley floor. Again, something flickering just out of sight. As she veered round towards the path, and the forest gave way to open fields, she felt strong arms embrace her. She cried out, tumbling to the ground.

'Conor?' She thumped him in the chest.

'Ow. That's some greeting.' He kissed her, rolling on top of her, his hand against her rib cage.

'You scared me.' Jake lolloped over and licked her face. 'Get off me.' She felt Conor lift. 'Not you.' She kissed him, pushing him back against the soft ferns, straddling him. Darcy pinned his arms back. 'Don't do that again.'

'I will if it gets me ravaged by a gorgeous sweaty woman.'

'Eugh.' She released him.

'What's all this in aid of? Don't say I've got you running now.'

'Health jag.' She squeezed her hip between thumb and forefinger.

'Don't be losing that,' he said, sliding his hands down her waist, pulling her nearer to him.

'I saw Tristan's shots of the finals in the editing suite today. The camera adds ten pounds.'

'To hell with the camera.' He reached up to her, his mouth seeking hers. 'I like what I feel.' At the sound of voices, evening walkers coming down the valley, they looked up, startled.

'Come on.' Darcy leapt up and he took her hand. 'There's time before dinner.' They ran back through the forest together towards the lake, the dog at their heels, cutting across the valley floor.

An old melody from the radio bloomed like a flower across the water. Darcy dozed in Conor's arms on the mattress they'd put on the half-finished mezzanine of the Lake House. He kissed the top of her head.

'Hungry?'

'For you? Always.' She raised her face to his, her hand tracing the line of his stomach.

'Later. You're insatiable, woman,' he said, smacking her on the backside. Darcy sat up, scooping her hair onto the top of her head in a loose bun. His face softened. 'God, you're beautiful. If I was an artist, I'd paint you like that, with the lake in the background, and the line of your back.' He traced the dip of her spine with his index finger, placed his thumb in the dimples at the base like a benediction. He bent and kissed her there. 'Let's grab something to eat before heading over to the kitchen.'

They cooked together. Darcy pounded four cloves of garlic in a pestle and mortar, grinding them to a smooth paste ready for a simple dish of spaghetti. She relaxed, washing the bright vegetables, trimming the celery, cucumber, radishes – there was a simple pleasure in their fresh beauty. She looked out at the grass glistening with fresh rain in the sunset, and put two glasses and the hors d'oeuvres on a tray, carrying them out to where Conor had set a blanket by the edge of the deck. She set the tray down and flopped beside it, crossing one foot over the other.

'Have you seen Beatrice since yesterday?'

'She's had her fun; I've told her she'll be on her way after the show,' Conor said, shaking his head. 'She landed us right in it with the finalists. Tris was in the kitchen this morning with Fiona and Michael filming a few bits which will go out with the live vote. We had to get the old girl a stool to sit on while she worked.'

'Don't laugh,' Darcy said. 'She's a sweetheart.'

'But Kira should have won.' Conor thought for a moment. 'I reckon we should quietly offer her a go in the kitchen.'

'You'd do that?'

'It's what it's all about, isn't it? Passing on your knowledge and passion to the next generation.' Conor stretched. 'But right now, once the show is over we should take a couple of weeks off. Do you want to go away, while the restaurant is closed?'

'Why not just stay here?' Darcy said, looking out across the lake. 'I've travelled the whole world over, and I can't think of anywhere I'd rather be than here, with you.'

'You're right. Let's not leave here,' Conor said, wiping a speck of oil from her cheek, and she leant in to his touch, closing her eyes. *He still hasn't said it,* she thought. *He still hasn't told me he loves me.* Conor lifted her chin, kissed her softly. 'You know in some languages the words for "to eat" are the same as "to fuck"?'

Darcy smiled slowly, hiding her uncertainty. 'Now who's insatiable?'

'I never thought I could be this content.'

'Me neither. I thought after having my heart broken I'd never trust anyone again.'

He tilted his head. 'JJ really hurt you, didn't he?'

Darcy shrugged, and raised her gaze to his. 'Me and my

263

broken heart, you broken open in rehab, maybe we were meant to be.'

'We can mend one another.' He smiled. 'I thought I was the last man in the world you needed.'

'You're all I'll ever need.'

'You're under my skin, Darce,' he said, cupping her face in his palm, taking the weight of her head. 'I'm an addict, a hungry soul, and nothing's filled the hole in my heart before like you have.' He shook his head. 'I feel like I've been a long way from home, and you've brought me back. I don't know what I've done to deserve you.'

'You're you. And I love you,' she said. 'You make me feel like anything is possible, and I love you for that.' Conor's phone alarm buzzed.

'Damn, time to get to work.' He stood and carried the tray inside.

Why won't he say it? she thought as they hurriedly wolfed down the last couple of mouthfuls of spaghetti standing in the kitchen.

'Any word from the hospital?' he said, wiping at his mouth.

'I just checked,' Darcy said, scraping her plate into the bin. 'They've operated on her arm, and Ma's sleeping. They said she'll be able to come home in the morning.' She frowned, crossing her arms. 'Fergus said she seemed troubled about something. She hasn't said anything to you?' Conor shook his head. 'I'm worried,' Darcy said. 'She's hiding something.'

47

That night in Conor's bed Darcy dreamt of flying again. For the first time since childhood, she dreamt that she was soaring above summer fields, the sun casting a shadow of her looping, sweeping effortlessly through the warm air. She felt free. Distant at first, there came a drumming, like hooves, something or someone pursuing her. She fought to stay in the dream, but the sound grew louder, forcing her awake. She awoke, naked, the sheet thrown aside, early-morning sun breaking through the curtains, bruising the full-blown roses into colour, a breeze playing over her body. She blinked, coming to. The drumming continued, insistent, pounding on the door.

Darcy lurched awake, and realised she was alone. She quickly wrapped the sheet around her and ran downstairs. She threw back the lock and opened the door to find Conor, fist raised to begin knocking again. 'Con? What's wrong?'

'Forgot my keys.' He balled the Irish *Sun* newspaper in his hand and shoved it against her chest, pushing past into the hall, gesturing at her to shut the door.

'Have you been crying?' She reached out to him.

'Don't touch me.' He recoiled like her fingers burnt. 'Just don't.' He noticed, then, that she was naked beneath the sheet and his face twisted in anguish. 'You could have told me.'

'Told you what?'

'Look! Look at the bloody paper.' He tore it from her hand and showed her the headline: *Horny Hughes at Home*.

'Oh God.' The strength went from her legs and she sat on the stairs, clutching the sheet to her chest.

'Popular TV food show host Darcy Hughes, lover of recently deceased chef JJ Roche, who was married—' Conor broke off and jabbed at the paper with his index finger. 'Was married, Darce. Was.' He shook out the paper and went on: '. . . has been spotted with a string of mystery men, even making a midnight dash to buy condoms from a petrol station.'

'Thank God.'

'What do you mean, thank God?'

'They didn't know it was you.'

'That would be a disaster, would it, if people knew we are together?' Conor threw down the paper.

'No! That's not what I meant—'

'There's pages of it. Look.' He jabbed his finger at a grainy blow-up of Darcy embracing Jamie on Henry Street in Kenmare. He looked down at Darcy with red-rimmed eyes. 'How long has this been going on?'

'Con, seriously? Do you not trust me?' She sat back against the stairs, hugged her knees to her chest. 'This was ages ago, after he first arrived to work with Tris, way before we got together.'

'To find out like this. I mean, Jesus, Darce.' He balled his fist against his heart. 'I love you, you know that, don't you? I don't want any secrets between us.'

'Con . . .'

'The thought of another man touching you, being with you.' He sat beside her and put his head in his hands. Darcy laid her head against his shoulder.

'I'm sorry. I didn't want you to find out.'

Conor moved away. 'Well I did.'

'You still don't get it, do you?' She turned his head, forcing him to look at her. 'You remember he drove me into town

266

one day? Well, he made a pass at me and he wouldn't take no for an answer. I blew him off, and . . .' She pressed her lips together. 'I was stupid enough to give him a hug, because I felt sorry for him, that's all. What looks like grand passion is that jerk shoving his tongue down my throat.'

'You mean he forced himself on you?' Conor threw the paper down. 'I'll kill him.' He jumped up and pulled on his jacket. 'Where is the bastard?'

'See, this is why I didn't tell you,' Darcy said, calmly. She wrapped her arms around Conor's neck, held him until she felt him still. 'There,' she said. 'OK now?' She kissed his jaw, his neck. 'See, what they cut out of the photographs was the moment I kneed him in the balls. About two seconds after this was taken he was writhing around on the ground singing like a choir boy.' Conor laughed. 'Say it again,' she said.

'Say what?'

'Tell me that you love me.'

48

'Oh, hi, Darcy,' Beatrice said. 'Is it OK if I get a cup of camomile tea to take up to Di?' she asked, popping her head around the door of the house kitchen. Darcy raised her head from her arms, and looked up at her from the table. 'Are you OK?'

'You've heard, then?'

'Fraid so. Everyone in the restaurant is talking about it.' She hopped up onto the kitchen counter, her legs swinging beneath her polka-dot skirt like the stamens of a flower, tipped with red ballet pumps. 'Look, I want to apologise. I was out of order, announcing that Fiona was going through to the final.'

'It should have been Kira,' Darcy said.

'It was *so* close. I know Diana was going to vote for Fiona, and we all know her vote is final.'

'She wasn't—'

'Anyway, how are you feeling?'

'How do you think?' Darcy's head slumped back onto her arms.

'They're filth, these rags. Really they are. Still, today's news, tomorrow's fish and chips, eh?'

'It doesn't work like that anymore,' Darcy said, her voice muffled. 'Every screw-up, every duff photograph is online, for ever.' She groaned at the sound of her mother's voice echoing from the old baby monitor.

'Darcy?' Diana called. 'Darcy?'

'I'll take her that cup of tea,' Beatrice said, setting the tray. 'By the way, the messages are piling up on the answer phone, and there are some photographers hanging out down by the gates.'

'Already?'

'The TV company has been trying to get hold of us, of course. The video of the goat has gone viral,' Beatrice said, laughing. 'I've left a message with Diana's agent Caroline and she's on her way.' Darcy's eyes opened wide in alarm.

'She doesn't need to—'

'Look. The live filming is going out at the end of tomorrow's show for the phone vote. We need to get our ducks in a line, and she's the best agent out there. We're lucky to have her.'

'We?'

'Yes. Did Di not tell you she recommended Caroline to me?' Beatrice smiled sweetly. 'If anyone can turn around all the scandal the papers are printing, she can. Maybe it would be as well if you took a back seat.' She glanced at Darcy. 'Take a break. Just for a while. I can manage while Di is laid up. In the meantime, speak to no one, don't answer the phone if you don't recognise the number, don't go outside.'

'How do you know so much about this?'

'You're not the first person in the public eye to go through this, and you won't be the last. You forget, I saw what happened to JJ.'

'I have to see Conor.' Darcy got to her feet and ran her hand through her hair.

'Be careful. The paps will be watching your every move.' Beatrice took Darcy's hand. 'You're a good person, Darcy, so sweet and trusting. You have done nothing wrong.' Beatrice's eyes narrowed, her face unreadable. She glanced at the baby monitor. 'Tell her I'm on my way,' she said, twitching her snub nose as she smiled.

'Hey, listen, I heard Conor's given you your notice, but you didn't need to move out, not yet.'

'Hm? We'll see about that. Silly misunderstanding.' Beatrice swept out of the room, tea tray aloft.

Darcy pressed the buzzer. 'Ma, Bea is bringing you a cup of tea.'

'Bea? Beatrice?' Diana's voice crackled, the lights arcing.

'Knock, knock,' Beatrice said, pushing open the door to Diana's bedroom. Diana lay in the old gilt four-poster at the heart of the eau-de-nil room, sunlight filtering through floor-length sheer curtains. 'Hello Co—' Diana shook her head, and pointed at the baby monitor. Beatrice put down the tray and flicked it off. 'How are you?' she said, walking her finger-tips along the plaster cast on Diana's arm. 'Rotten luck, eh? Broken again? Maybe it's the universe's way of telling you to slow down a bit.'

'The universe? For God's sake, you're to blame,' Diana said, under her breath.

'Me? What did I do?'

'Who put you up to this? Your mother?'

'Mummy?' Beatrice said, pausing with the steaming cup of tea over Diana. 'Don't you ever listen to a word I say?' She held the scalding tea to Diana's lips, and tipped the cup. Diana's head jerked back, and she pushed the cup away with her good arm. 'Look what you've done, you silly,' she said, putting the cup to one side. 'I told you the first time I came here that Mummy died in May. Honestly, it's like you didn't care enough to listen to me.'

'She died?' Diana's heart beat fast. 'Of course I care,' she said, her voice gentle, placatory.

'Yes. Your daughter died alone and penniless in the corridor of a hospital because there was no bed for her. I was with her.' Beatrice leant in, her breath against Diana's cheek. 'I saw how she suffered.' She sat back and composed herself. 'Now. Perhaps you're tired. We can talk about the future later.'

'We have nothing to discuss.'

'Then perhaps I can talk to Darcy,' Beatrice said, her eyes cold.

'No,' Diana said firmly. She softened her voice. 'No. You are not to breathe a word of this, do you understand? I will not see you destroy my life's work.'

'It really is the work of a lifetime, to create a person, isn't it?'

'What would someone like you know?' Diana forced herself to smile. 'I bet you change who you are, what you are, every year. I'd love to hear all about it.'

'We can talk later, as I said.' Beatrice stood and smoothed down her skirt.

'What is it you want, Beatrice? Money?'

'Money?' She blinked and shook her head. 'But, Diana, you're my family. Don't you understand? Now Mummy is dead, you are all I have left.' She smiled sweetly, her eyes blank. 'Con can carry on running the restaurant if he wants, but don't you think Darcy should really go back to California, where she's happy?'

'Is that what she wants?'

'She's just too afraid to tell you.' Beatrice smoothed the blanket on Diana's bed. 'You don't need to worry about a thing. I'm here to help, and I can look after you.'

At that moment, Darcy pushed open the door. 'Hi, Ma, just thought I'd check you're OK; the monitor was off.' She glanced at Beatrice as she leant in to hug Diana.

'I'm sorry,' her mother said, holding her close.

'Sorry?' Darcy said, laughing, her voice muffled by Diana's shoulder.

'I love you, darling, and I want you to be happy.' Diana paused. 'That's all I've ever wanted. It's all my fault.'

'What? How do you figure that one?'

'Thanks to me, you've been exposed to the press your whole life, but they – the people who write about us – they are a different breed now. They're not professionals. Everyone has an opinion, everyone is just waiting for us to fall flat on our faces.'

'And I have.'

'What we have to figure out is how to make this work to our advantage.' She sat back and held Darcy at arm's length. 'I think a dignified silence is the best course. Don't waste your words on people who only deserve your contempt.' She glanced at Beatrice and brushed back Darcy's hair. 'We'll get through this. The Castle will survive.' She closed her eyes for a moment. 'You know, I wanted to be the next Elizabeth David. I admired her so much. We ached for the sun, longed to escape the dreadful, cheerless food of the fifties. Her books lit up the world for me. It took me years to realise there could only ever be one Elizabeth David, and all I could do was to be the best version of myself.'

'I don't know what to do,' Darcy said.

'You have to be clear about what you want, Darcy. You'll get through this nonsense, finish the series, but after that you have to decide.'

'If you fail to plan, you plan to fail,' Beatrice said, her voice calm.

'As true now as it has ever been.' Diana sniffed. 'If you don't tell the world, the universe, what you want, how is your destiny supposed to find you? I rather like that idea that what you desire in your heart is also trying to find you.' She paused. 'You love Conor, don't you?'

'I do.'

'Well maybe you have found one another.' Diana looked up at her. 'Most people idle through life, wanting vaguely to be famous or rich and doing damn all to work towards it. You have to meet your destiny halfway, that's what I've always thought. It's about momentum – setting things in motion. Work resolutely towards your goal, step by step.'

'Ma . . .'

'I mean it, Darcy. If you don't you will wake up in forty

years and wonder where the time went, and why your friends have everything you assumed would be yours naturally and isn't. Most people don't stop to think what they really want. I know you love California.' She glanced at Beatrice. 'But you will have to make a choice. What do you want? That's the question.'

Conor. It was the first thought. A new life, with him. She could picture them living at the lake house clearly now. A peace and clarity. Warmth. Love.

'Dreams come true when you set them in your sights and work towards them. Keep them in the corner of your eye, like a wild thing – come upon them gently, firmly. Tell the universe what you want and then let it get on with it.'

'Blimey, what's brought this on, Ma? It's not like you to be philosophical,' Darcy said.

Diana glanced at Beatrice, who stood in silence in the shadows of the bedroom. 'There's too much gone wrong lately. It just feels like the right time to share the benefit of my experience with you. Just in case.' Diana took Darcy's hand. 'I don't know if Conor really has the capacity for peace and contentment, but you do, and you need it. Right now, I want you to go out into the restaurant and hold your head high, do you understand? If you see the staff sniggering or any nonsense you look them straight in the eye, OK? And you show them who is boss.'

Darcy nodded.

'We all will,' Beatrice said, stepping forward and putting her hand on Darcy's shoulder. 'We're all in this together.'

49

Conor stood at the pass, checking the order slips. He glanced up as Aiden walked over from the restaurant. 'What are you doing all tarted up?'

'Night off.'

'Can't stay away?'

'I wanted my girl to see where I work.' He gestured to a slender red-haired girl at the back of the restaurant, and she raised a hand, hesitant. 'Con, can you help me? I really screwed up, and I want to impress her, you know.'

'Laddie, I will make a meal for her to fall in love over.' He punched his arm. 'What's she ordered?'

'She doesn't care, whatever I think is best.'

'Doesn't care? Good God, boy, are you sure this is the one? Never say you don't care what you eat, it just sounds stupid. Tell her to make up her mind. You mustn't spend your life with people who don't care.'

'I think she was just nervous about ordering the wrong thing.'

'All right, boyo, I'll let her off this time. Leave it with me.' His face softened. 'You're serious about her, aren't you?'

'Yeah, I am. I've been an idiot.'

Conor looked over at the girl. 'Take my advice. If you love her, don't lose her.'

Aiden went back to the table, and Conor began to cook. He

gave each chef de partie instructions, and went out to the back room. A few moments later the restaurant plunged into darkness, and the diners let up a surprised 'Oh!'

'Don't panic,' Conor said, appearing with a tray of lit candles and lanterns. 'Just a power cut. Don't worry, we can cook fine with the gas. Hand these out to the diners will you, lads?' He put the tray on the pass and the waiters and waitresses crowded round. Conor looked across the room and winked at Aiden, who moved closer to his girlfriend.

'What are you up to?' Darcy said, joining Conor.

'Nothing. Just helping out a young lad.'

'Are you going soft, you old romantic?' She nudged his arm, but he didn't respond. 'You're still angry?'

'It just pisses me off, the whole thing.'

'It will be OK.'

'What do you think everyone's going to do? Just roll over and adore you?' Conor said, gesturing at the evening papers on the side. 'Tall poppy syndrome, Darce. It's the worst side of human nature. People see something beautiful and they want to destroy it. Kids in the playground screwing up another kid's painting, fucking terrorists blowing up cities which have stood for centuries. The mob mentality.'

'God, that's a depressing way to look at the world.'

'You're too naive sometimes, Darcy. Of course they were going to be salivating, waiting for you to screw up.'

Darcy's phone buzzed into life, Eddi Reader's voice ringing out 'It's Got to Be Perfect'.

'You couldn't make it up.' Conor threw his hands up in mock disgust, rolling his eyes back in his head and laughing. 'You are *un*believable. I can't even—' A horn blared in the courtyard. Conor jumped up. 'It's Chris.'

Darcy scrambled to find her phone, sheaves of paper drifting to the floor. *Caroline,* she thought, glancing at the screen. 'Hi,' she said. She got to her feet and looked out across the yard. Conor was standing beside a blacked-out Porsche Carrera, and the door swung open to let Chris out. She caught a glimpse of a slim blonde woman with expensive, caramel highlights and large black sunglasses, and recognised Alannah as the girl from the bar all those years ago. As Conor leant and kissed her cheek she felt a tug of jealousy.

Darcy paced across the kitchen. The white tiles gleamed in the candlelight. Beside her, three simple wooden shelves held blue Le Creuset, like a battalion.

'Explain yourself,' Caroline said. Darcy could hear she was on the road.

'Someone spotted us. Conor and me, and the condoms.'

'The what?' The line broke up.

'Condoms,' Darcy shouted. 'They took pictures, sold them to the tabloids.' She raked her hand through her hair.

'And the other bloke?'

'He's no one. Worked with Tris, tried it on with me.' Darcy bit her lip. 'It'll blow over, won't it? Does it matter?'

'It will matter to the TV company I'm talking to. The whole concept is built on this wholesome image — Darcy: Julie Andrews-style daughter of a cooking legend, born with a culinary silver spoon in her mouth, tamed and shacked up with a bad-boy chef, living in perfect bohemian rock and roll bliss in their country castle.'

'A bit of scandal didn't do what's-her-name any harm. She came out of her divorce with her head held high, and her cookery programmes were more popular than ever. People still love her.' She looked uncertainly at the two-page spread in the paper, where her face had been superimposed on an angel in fishnets, with a wonky halo and horns pencilled in. *Domestic Goddess Whose Home Life is Hell* screeched the headline.

'Look, we'll sort it, OK? People love you. If you ride this out in style, they'll love you more. No one wants perfect. Flaws make you human, and my guess is that people will be pretty sympathetic.' Darcy could hear the sound of a horn pushed.

'Get out the way, you bloody fool. Right. Who have you spoken to?'

'No one, but—'

'Good. Say nothing. Not a word. Don't go out, don't even poke your head out the door for a bottle of milk or the paps will get you. Silence is golden, as my mother used to say.' The horn blared again. 'We'll sell your story to a rival paper – Conor's health jag, sponsored to lose weight, boot camp, jungle, Darcy bounces back . . .' Caroline broke off from her riff to light a cigarette and Darcy heard the click of the car lighter, then Caroline inhaling deeply. 'There are so many angles. We'll get you dolled up and interviewed by one of the glossies – a heart to heart about the difficulties of being with a chef—'

'Conor's not that bad.'

'No, no, not him, the other one – JJ, keep up,' Caroline said. 'You'll come out of it smelling of roses, an innocent tricked by a married man, who loyally wouldn't reveal her lover—'

'No. It's none of their business. This is my private life. Mine.' Darcy thought of the congregation of photographers waiting at the end of the drive. 'I love Conor. He makes me happy and I'm not going to mess this up, do you understand?'

'All right, darling, don't get your knickers in a twist.'

'What about Beatrice?'

'What about her?'

'She says you've taken her on as a client?'

'Your mother asked me to. There was an email in my box this morning. Frankly, I'm not bothered about her. Strong image, suits the zeitgeist, ambitious, she'll be fine.'

'I'm sorry—'

'Nonsense. There's no bad publicity. Is Tris there? You're filming live tomorrow night, aren't you? With the fireworks? I'll be with you in the morning.'

'You don't need to—' Darcy said, panicking at the thought. But it was too late; Caroline had already hung up.

Darcy looked up to see Conor talking to Niall, the maître d', over the pass. She wandered over. 'Caroline's on her way.'

'Jaysus, I might go into hiding,' Conor said. He watched Niall talking to Aiden and his girlfriend, ripping up their bill. Aiden gave Conor the thumbs up as he left.

'What are you up to?' Darcy said. 'Did you pick up their tab?'

Conor slung his arm across Darcy's shoulders, and looked out into the dark, candlelit dining room as the last of the diners left. 'You have to do what you can for love in this world of ours, Darce.' He kissed her. 'Let's go home.'

50

The next day, Darcy strode through the forest at lunchtime, the cool green silence seeping into her after the noise and heat of the kitchen. She found Conor at work in the lake house, cutting lengths of timber for the jetty. She heard music first before she saw him. Stepping into the shadows of the house, the midday sun gilding the open windows, the gently rippling lake, she heard the bump and scratch of a needle, then the opening bars of 'You Do Something To Me', Conor singing along above the noise of the saw. She watched him working, the rawness of his voice raising the hair at the nape of her neck, a slow honey warmth spreading low in her stomach. Conor glanced up, breaking off mid-bar, and the record sang on. He raised his hand.

'I'll be done soon,' he shouted above the noise of the machine. 'Just needed to get away for a bit. It's bedlam over there.'

'Conor, would you just stop?' She yanked the plug from the socket and the saw wound down. She waited for him to look at her. 'Please. I need to talk to you. I can't do this.'

His face fell. 'I know. I'm not good enough for you—'

'Not you, you eejit.' She stepped towards him, into a pool of rosy sunlight spilling through the skylight. Sawdust danced around her like glitter in a snow globe. 'You're about the only thing that is right at the moment.' She saw the relief on his face, and he laid the palm of his hand on his heart.

'Jaysus, you had me going there.'

'It's . . . I can't cope with all this, the press, all the people arriving for the final show.'

He turned to the workbench. 'You have to. We all do. The Castle is riding on it.'

'There's something else. JJ's ex, Maria, called me. She wants me to meet her up at Moll's Gap this afternoon.' Darcy waited for Conor to say something. 'Con?' She walked towards him, the sound of the song, of the wind rushing in the trees enfolding them. He smelt of sawdust, fresh sweat, soap. 'I knew you'd be upset. That's why I wanted to tell you myself, in case the press are still snooping around.' She came closer still to him. When he didn't move away, she leant in to him, curling against the heat of his back, her lips brushing against his neck, catching, skin on skin, releasing slow. 'I don't know what's so important she has to talk to me face to face, but I love you,' she said, her voice hoarse. 'It's like you're part of me, and when I'm not with you, I need you like air, like water.' Still he didn't reach for her, take her in his arms. 'Conor,' she whispered, moving round between him and the bench, her lips on his ear, eyes closing, cheek caressing cheek. She felt the tension in him, the hard set of his body. 'Trust me. Please.' The trees wept for the golden leaves spinning in the rain. 'I know you're angry, but just let it go.'

Beyond the window, pale silk lanterns that Darcy had bought in San Francisco swung in the breeze from the veranda roof. Without a word, he took her in his arms, pressed his body, his lips to hers, lifting her clear of the floor. She answered his kisses, ready now, breathless, her hands in his hair, holding him to her. They broke apart, eye to eye. Conor swung her easily into his arms, and carried her through the house. She saw him wince as he lifted her.

'Your back?'

'Be gentle, eh?' he said, his stubbled cheeks dimpling. Darcy curved in to him, her head resting against the hard muscle of his shoulder. He padded up the stairs to the mezzanine bed, and laid her down.

Darcy looked up at the new skylights, at the blush of clouds drifting above them. 'It's beautiful, Conor.'

'You're beautiful.' He pulled off his white T-shirt, and threw it down on the floor, slipped out of his old blue jeans. 'I've never seen anyone more beautiful than you are at this moment.' The sun shone high above them as Conor lay down beside her and slipped the straps of her dress clear, easing the fabric over her breasts, her stomach, her hips, tracing its path with his lips.

'I want you,' she said. 'I want you, Conor.' Darcy pushed him back on the soft white duvet, against the full down pillows, and straddled him, dipping down to kiss him again. Conor's hands encircled her waist, guiding her. The rhythm of the music held them, the melody of the wind in the trees, of the birds' chorus, the water lapping against the dock, of their bodies, moving, falling together as one.

THE TASTE OF EXPERIENCE

The first time I had Indian food was one summer night when I dropped by the beach house of an older teenage friend. She had nicked two Lucky Strikes from her mother's pack before her ma went out to a party. We smoked them watching *Purple Rain* while the aroma of chicken tikka and bhajis drifted through from the cottage's kitchen. She seemed to throw the meal together in seconds. It felt like the height of sophistication, and rebellion.

Now I keep a stash of tandoori spices in the cupboard at all times. It's a simple way to come up with something a bit more exciting than plain chicken breasts if you have an unexpected guest, or a new friend sleeping over. Boil some rice, chop some fresh mint and cucumber into plain yoghurt and you have a feast.

The impromptu meals I've experienced with friends are often the best and most memorable. I've a repertoire of go-to quick meals which are my staples. Spaghetti with garlic and oil is one. Another is a simple pastry tart. It's all very well rolling your own, but I admit to keeping an emergency stash of puff pastry in the fridge. That way in seconds you can rustle up a tasty supper.

Get your unexpected guest to open the wine, or wash the salad while you crank the oven up to 180°C. Grease a baking tray, roll out a block of puff pastry, and on the top add chopped tomato, onion, a shake of thyme (or a pluck of basil, fresh is best). Top with whatever cheese you have hanging around in the fridge – or a shake of parmesan – and bake until golden.

Failing that, who doesn't love a simple Ploughman's? If you have a loaf of bread, put it on the kitchen table with ham, cheese, chopped apple, pickles and olives and let people get on with it. After all, they dropped by to see you, not to inspect you for a nascent Michelin star.

Darcy Hughes, *Appetite* Tumblr

51

London

June

In a shadowed corner of the yard behind Lavender Cupcakes, Beatrice leant against the bins, her face cupped in the palm of her hand, staring at a fly struggling in a spider's web on the fence. She blew a perfect pink bubble, popping it with her immaculate French-manicured gel nail.

Beatrice smoothed down her skirt and straightened the white chiffon bow of her apron, rubbing at a slight mark. She took a pink lipstick from the apron's pocket and reapplied it perfectly without the aid of a mirror. 'We open in two minutes. Get in the kitchen,' she called to a young pastry chef smoking by the back door. She tightened her long glossy blonde ponytail, feeling the hair tug her scalp. Her button nose wrinkled. She tugged harder.

Beatrice checked her fine gold watch and clicked her tongue. 'Look at the time. We can't be late, even on the last day.' She marched past the boy to the shop. 'Is everybody ready?' she said, checking over the gleaming chrome and marble counter. 'Yes, Bea,' the café staff answered in unison. She stopped to check the display. 'Perfect,' she said, bending down to give the ranks of identical cupcakes a final check. Beatrice turned and stared at the window, at the faces pressed against the glass, waiting for the shop to open. 'Look at them,' she said under her breath. 'Pathetic. Every day they come. You listen to their conversations: 'Am I putting on weight?' 'Why

283

am I always broke at the end of the month?' Well, it's because you are in here every week picking away at beautiful little time bombs of sugar, flour and eggs that cost pence to make and cost you pounds. Pounds from your purse, and pounds on the scale.'

Beatrice's face lit up with a smile as she waved to the waiting women. 'Stupid, stupid people.' She signalled to the girl behind the till to flick on the retro lounge music, and she walked to the door in time to it. *Everything's been done,* she thought. *Everything's a cover version. That's all you people want. Cosy nostalgia.* She smiled brightly, remembering to make her eyes crease at the same time. Beatrice flicked over the 'closed' sign. 'Come on in,' she said, her hands settling on her immaculate starched apron.

'Is it true?' Two girls at the front of the queue squeezed through the door. 'You can't be closing?'

'I'm afraid so.'

'No!' they cried in unison. 'What are we going to do without your Black Velvet cupcakes?'

Beatrice ran through the available answers: *Lose a few pounds? Try a salad?* 'There's always the chain café on the high street.'

'But their cakes are nothing like yours . . .'

Beatrice bored of them. She stared at their faces and wondered how anyone could care so much about a café. About cake. 'You must excuse me. I have to go.' She walked away as they continued to chatter, joining the growing queue at the counter.

'How can this place be folding if there are people queuing up?' the girl in the cramped office said, looking up from the paperwork.

'Hm?' Beatrice untied her apron, and tossed it into the bin. 'I love baking. Always have. It's simple, scientific. I love . . .' Beatrice looked into the kitchen, at the ordered ranks of baking trays and bowls, at the practised, measured movements of her assistants in their immaculate white aprons. *Love?* She thought. *Is that what it is?* 'I have no interest in business. It's that simple, really. Cupcakes are having a moment so I thought it would be easy money. I didn't pay enough attention to the money coming in. Jonny's restaurants owed us a bit—'

'More than a bit,' the girl said, laughing bitterly. 'It's because of them we've gone tits up.'

'It's been interesting, but to be honest I got bored.' She gazed out into the café, crammed with people now, and wiped a speck of flour from her Louboutin heels. 'Easy come, easy go.'

'It can't have been the same for you, since your mum died . . .'

Beatrice blinked, seemed to zone out of the conversation. She opened the filing cabinet with a small silver key, and took out a pale blue envelope. Her mother's writing was painfully neat, backwards sloping. *Diana Hughes is my mother, I am sure of it. I saw a wedding photo. Her real name is Colleen Smith . . .*

'What are you going to do?'

'Sorry?' Beatrice stuffed the letter into her handbag. 'I've been headhunted, didn't I tell you? Diana Hughes. She wants me to take over the Castle Dromquinna.'

'The one off the TV? Seriously? That's amazing.'

'Sorry, Bea, there's a woman insisting on seeing you.' The girl behind the till popped her head around the door.

Beatrice frowned, her jaw flexing. She walked through to the café, a tight smile breaking over her teeth like latex tearing. 'Can I help you?'

'Are you the manager?' A woman in skinny jeans and a fur gilet swung round. 'I vant to see the manager.' Beatrice tried to place the accent. *Moscow, perhaps?*

'I am Beatrice Lavender.'

'These cakes I bought yesterday are no good.' The woman's freshly blow-dried hair gleamed expensively under the shop's spotlights. 'No good!' she said, flicking her hand at Beatrice.

'I beg your pardon?'

'Look at zem.' The woman flipped open the pale purple box with a manicured nail. 'They are a gift, for a tea party. They are *no good*.' Beatrice watched her carefully. The woman was trying to curl her lip and failing, her full pout immobile.

'I told her the box had been dropped,' the girl behind the till whispered.

'I did not drop it!' The woman rounded on her.

'I didn't say you,' the girl said under her breath, glancing at the three Burberry-clad children racing around the cafe.

'You imbecile,' the woman said. 'I'll have you sacked!'

'That won't be necessary,' Beatrice said calmly. 'The store is closing today.'

'I'm not surprised,' the woman growled, 'if zis is 'ow you treat your customers.'

'It would be my pleasure to replace the cakes for you. Personally.' Beatrice closed the lid. She watched the children weaving among the tables. 'Imagine being that fearless,' she said quietly, 'so blithely unaware that a single act can shatter everything and ruin you for ever.'

'What?' the woman said.

'I won't be a moment.' Beatrice sashayed across the café, nudging one of the chairs near the children out of line. She heard a crash and a cry behind her, and pressed her lips together in a smile.

She carried the box through to the kitchen, and closed the door. 'We've got a dissatisfied customer,' she said, holding the box aloft on her palm. Everyone paused in their tasks and gathered round.

'What's wrong with them?' someone said.

'Nothing.' Beatrice took the four Black Velvet cupcakes out one at a time, and placed them in a row on the marble counter. 'Yet.' She felt a glorious calm settle on her. 'Spatula.' She took the metal blade and scraped away the damaged icing with surgical precision. She squatted down, her eyes level with the marble counter. 'You can all go.'

'Are you sure?'

'Yeah. We're done here.' She waited until the kitchen emptied, and picked up a piping bag of crimson icing, holding it up to the light. 'Now, what can we do to teach you a lesson?' she murmured, thinking through the possibilities. She gathered up the slack of the piping bag, squeezing the icing, and a slow, wicked smile spread across her lips.

Beatrice sauntered through the bustling café, holding the freshly boxed cakes aloft like a cocktail tray. 'There you are,' she said to the woman, handing the box to her. Beatrice tilted her head and pouted, looking at the red-eyed little boy who was rubbing a bump on his head. 'Oh bless, did you trip over, darling? You should be more careful.'

'Red frosting?' the woman said. 'It should be white.'

'No, I gave them a special touch. Just for you.' Beatrice tilted the box towards her. 'And look, edible gold leaf.' She leant towards her, as if she was sharing a secret. 'The taste of money.' The gold cakes shimmered beneath the cellophane lid. The woman's lips parted. She took the box without thanks, snapping her fingers for the children to follow her.

'No, really, thank *you*,' Beatrice called after her, and checked her watch. 'The guys from the bank will be here soon to take the keys.' She slid hers from the ring of her car keys, and tossed them on to the counter.

'Aren't you going to wait for them?' the girl at the till said.

'Nah. You can go, too. Don't bother about closing up the till.'

'But what if someone—'

'Not ours to worry about, is it?' She looked around at the familiar faces of the café regulars. 'In fact, take what you want,' she said, raising her voice.

'Seriously?' a woman said, pausing with her fork halfway to her mouth.

'Yes. Take anything.' Beatrice walked away as every person in the café surged towards the counters, scrambling to grab the last of the cakes. 'I don't need it anymore.'

52

Ireland

August

Darcy parked the Lancia in the car park at Moll's Gap. The drive through the beautiful wooded roads had calmed her. She loved the lanes and lakes, the ancient oaks, remembered watching a herd of red deer with her mother, once. The ring of her mobile broke the silence, and she picked up the phone. 'Lyn?' she said. 'I've been trying to get hold of you. Are you OK?'

'Me? I'm fine now, darling,' she said.

'Are you back home?'

'Yes, we cut short the trip. I'm sorry for storming out like that, but I didn't know what else to do. We had the mother of all arguments. God knows I'm insecure enough most of the time living with someone like Sasha, but just after the baby—'

'Hold on,' Darcy said, frowning. 'I don't understand. What happened?'

'Bea happened,' Lyn said, her voice full of disgust. 'That sly little bitch.'

'Are you saying Bea and Sasha . . . ?'

'Yes, that's precisely what I'm saying.' Lyn clicked her tongue in disgust. 'I didn't want to upset you with everything you've got on your plate, and I would have swung for Beatrice if I'd seen her. It just seemed cleanest to leave quietly.'

Darcy locked the car, the phone crooked against her ear,

and walked towards the café. 'I can't believe it. I thought Bea was seeing one of the chefs.'

'Miss Lavender likes to have her cake and eat it, it seems.' Lyn's voice muffled at the cry of a baby. 'Got to go. Call me later? I just wanted to let you know that we're OK. More than OK. When I threatened to kick Sasha out, it made us have a good heart to heart. We're on the same page now.'

Darcy was early and she browsed the Avoca shop, her hand running over the bright, soft blankets. She picked out one in Diana's favourite jewel colours, and was just paying for it when a young woman with blonde hair touched her arm.

'Darcy? It's Maria, JJ's wife. I'm sorry I'm late.' Her voice was soft, child-like. The women smiled and shook hands. 'Thank you for meeting me. Shall we get a coffee?'

They sat together at a quiet table, and looked at one another in silence. 'I'm—' they said together, and laughed. 'You first,' Darcy said, her stomach fluttering with nerves.

'I'm so glad you agreed to see me,' Maria said. 'I hadn't expected you to seem so . . . well, so young. You must have been a kid when you were with JJ.'

'I was,' Darcy said, looking at her hands. 'I'm so sorry. When I found out he was married, I thought of writing to you, to say sorry.'

'What did you have to be sorry about? He broke your heart too, didn't he?' Maria's eyes glistened. 'Bloody JJ. It would be easier if I could hate him. He was a useless bloody husband, but I loved him.' She squeezed Darcy's hand. 'You weren't the first, and you weren't the last, but you were special. If you hadn't dumped him, I think he would have left me for you.'

'Oh God, I'm sorry.' Darcy looked at her.

'No, don't be. Like I said, it's not your fault.' Maria blinked, and wiped quickly at her eye. 'See, the worst thing about infidelity is that you never completely trust the person you love again. That's the real consequence of an affair, if you manage to hold it together. I stuck it out as long as I could. It all got too much though, you know? He burnt out. Too many women, too much booze, too many drugs—'

'Too much cooking?'

'Yeah, exactly. Cooking's not a career, it's a sickness.' Maria shook her head, and took a sip of her coffee. 'Of course the press have been going on that I banged his business partner while we were still married, but I didn't. I loved him. I'm just . . .' She exhaled. 'Thinking of the future now, you know? He'll take care of me and the kids.'

'Are we stupid?' Darcy said. 'Are we stupid to trust men like JJ?'

'Nah, they're the stupid ones. They have the whole world in their hands – great job, great home, someone who loves only them, and it's still not enough. They'll always have a hungry heart.' Maria looked at Darcy, her eyes bright. 'But JJ wasn't why I decided to email you. The thing is, a friend told me you've been filming a new series at the Castle, with Conor and someone called Beatrice.' She paused. 'It's not Beatrice Lavender?'

'Yes, why?' Darcy felt her blood chill .

Maria shivered. 'She was obsessed with you all.'

'With us?'

'Quizzed Jonny non-stop about you lot. He got sick of it in the end.' Maria sipped her coffee. 'What does she look like these days?'

'What do you mean?'

'She changes herself – becomes whatever she thinks you want her to be.' Maria flicked open her iPad. I mean, look at this.' She pulled up a tabloid column from a year ago, of Jonny on a sun lounger in Ibiza. At his side, a woman with cascading blonde hair and endless tanned legs had her back to the camera.

'Is that you?'

'No, it's her, looking like a younger version of me, in her

291

Page Three incarnation – you know what Jonny was like.' She looked down at her inflated chest. 'I'm going to get these taken out. It was only to make him happy. Didn't work, did it?' She looked at Darcy. 'He always had a soft spot for you. You didn't change for him. I think he admired that. I think . . . I think everyone who came after you had a tough time living up to that.'

'So what are you saying? Beatrice had an affair with JJ?'

'Yeah, but she knew he was married all right.' Maria shook her head. 'She uses sex to get what she wants, that one.'

'She told Ma they worked together.'

Maria threw her head back laughing. 'You can call it that if you want.' She leant towards Darcy. 'Beatrice can faff around with fairy cakes, but she's no businesswoman, and she's certainly no chef. She ran her ma's bakery into the ground. One of my friends was really sick after eating there.'

'But she has a string of qualifications. Ma showed me her CV.'

'About as fake as her D cup,' Maria said, pursing her lips. 'You mean Diana didn't check her references?'

'Well no, I mean, JJ was dead.'

'Yeah, and she was one of the last people to see him alive.' She sipped her coffee. 'It's a classic, Darcy. I've read a lot of self-help books about dealing with narcissists. You've been – what's the word? Gaslit. Just because she said JJ recommended her, your ma attributed his qualities to Bea. Narcissists wear other people's personalities like a mask, because they don't have one of their own, you know – no emotion at all.'

'That's . . . I can't believe it. Why did none of us see what she's been doing?' But as Maria's revelations sank in, Darcy realised she could believe it only too well. It felt like the last pieces of a puzzle sliding into place.

'How's Con? Haven't seen him since the funeral. I see from the papers you two are an item?'

'He's good,' Darcy said. 'We're really happy.'

'I'm glad he's found a good woman. He was JJ's only real friend.'

'Thank you,' Darcy said, standing. 'Thank you for being so generous, for forgiving me.'

'Have to move on, don't you?' Maria flicked her hair. 'If you stay bitter and angry it eats away at you, and the only person you end up poisoning is yourself.'

Darcy thought of the old saying: *it's like taking poison and waiting for the other person to die.* She felt her stomach lurch. *Beatrice was the last person to see JJ.*

'Well, I just wanted to warn you,' Maria said, gathering up her Louis Vuitton handbag. 'If you and Con want to stay happy, I'd watch your back, and kick that cuckoo out of your nest as quickly as possible.'

53

Diana dozed fitfully, propped up against a bank of pillows in her bed in the tower room. As she came to, a ringing disturbed her, and she batted at her face as if she was trying to push away an annoying insect. Her eyes flickered open, but the ringing continued. Bells? Tinkling bells? *A rattle,* Diana thought, her stomach dropping like the fall from a rollercoaster. She listened, her senses heightened. A rattle was being dragged along the banister rods leading up to her tower suite one at a time. Diana reached for the lamp and flicked the switch. Nothing. *Not another bloody power cut.* In the half-light she searched frantically on her bedside table, slid a metal nail file beneath her pillow.

'Hi, Di,' Beatrice said, pushing open the door. She carried a wicker tray with legs on her hip, and settled it on the bed across Diana. 'I thought you might be hungry.'

'No, I'm not. Go away.' Diana turned her face to the pillow. 'You were asked to leave by Conor, I believe.'

'Come on, don't be like that. Someone has to take care of you. You have to eat.' Beatrice tilted her head. 'I only want to help.'

'How did you get in?' Beatrice twirled a set of keys on her index finger. 'Those are Darcy's,' Diana said.

'We're all family. I just borrowed them.'

'I'll scream.'

'Why? You don't think I want to hurt you?' Beatrice said, wide eyed. 'Besides. Who do you think will hear you, Diana?' She sat down on the side of the bed. The firelight flickered in the dim room, gilding her dark eyes. 'Everyone is busy setting up for tonight, Darcy's gone off somewhere and Conor's at the studio with Tris, doing the voiceover. It's just you and me.' She waited for Diana to look at her and then tucked a white napkin into the collar of her pyjamas.

'I said I'm not hungry.'

'And I said you have to eat.' Beatrice smiled. 'Let's not argue.' She lifted the lid from a white soup bowl, and steam rose into the air, conjuring the earthy smell of mushrooms. 'I made the stock myself.' She stirred the chicken soup. 'This is what you need to build yourself back up again. Chicken and mushroom. Mum's special recipe. Here,' she said, adjusting Diana's pillows. 'I can take care of you—'

'I can take care of myself.'

'Mummy used to make this chicken soup for me when I was small.' Beatrice's mind seemed to drift. 'She loved your books. It's your own recipe, really, isn't that funny? She was your biggest fan.' She blew on a spoonful of soup, and forced it into Diana's mouth, the spoon rattling against her teeth. 'Oh dear. What a mess.' She dabbed gently at the corner of her mouth. 'Silly sausage. Open wide.'

'I'm really not hungry,' Diana said, calmly. 'But it is good soup.'

'Do you think so?' Beatrice blinked. 'I'm so glad you like it.'

'You are a good cook, Bea.'

'Thank you,' she said.

'Why don't you leave it on the side there?'

'I'm so glad. So glad you like it.' Beatrice brushed down her skirt. 'I know that the others want me gone from the Castle, but they are just jealous of me, of you.' Her face faltered. 'I was so worried that after your accident, and that silly misunderstanding about the finalists, that you might push me away. I couldn't bear that, Diana. I mean, we belong together.' She jingled the rattle and Diana flinched.

'What a pretty old thing,' Diana said, keeping her voice steady.

'Mummy kept it, all these years.' Beatrice rolled it around in her palm, the silver gleaming. 'I've been dying to tell you, ever since we met at JJ's funeral. I wanted to let you know. Let you put two and two together.' Beatrice stared at her, and the blankness in her eyes terrified Diana. 'I just want you to love me, like you love Darcy. That's not too much to ask, is it?'

'You don't know what it is to feel love.'

'No, but I see it. I see it when you and Darcy look at one another. I see it in Con's eyes when he looks at her.'

'And you want that?'

Beatrice's face trembled. 'I want it all.'

'We can talk about that later, can't we? I'm rather tired now.'

'Of course.'

'Where are you staying now, Bea? They said you'd moved out of the staff house.'

'Not far away,' she said, turning the rattle over in her hand. 'Just needed a bit of privacy, you know? The whole place is crawling with press. It's all Darcy's fault.' She blinked and turned to Diana. 'But you needn't worry, I'm here for you. I won't mess up, like her. I'll be right here, waiting for you.'

Diana waited until she heard the sound of Beatrice's footsteps descending, and the back door close, then she swung her legs from the bed, wincing, and hobbled across to her door, locking it and jamming a chair beneath the handle. She grabbed her phone and dialled Darcy.

'Ma? Is everything OK?'

'No, not really, darling. Where are you?'

'Driving back from Moll's Gap.'

'I think you'd better hurry home. There's something we need to talk about.'

'What is it?'

'It's about Beatrice.'

54

'I will not make a statement just to keep the press happy,' Diana said to Caroline. Her agent stood on the balcony of her bedroom, glass of champagne in hand, holding a cigarillo at arm's length so the smoke drifted away. The sun was setting, washing the open windows rose gold. 'What was it Shaw said? Silence is the perfect expression of scorn? I will not waste my breath on people who only deserve my silence.'

'But, Diana, darling. We have hundreds of people arriving for the live final tonight, and the press are—'

'No, Caroline. The greatest strength is to say nothing. Never explain. Let them go to hell.'

'Ma, are you OK?' Darcy said, jogging into the room.

'Darcy! Darling!' Caroline said, flicking the cigarillo away.

'Caroline, how are you?' Darcy said.

'Look at you, back from the States and all grown up. What a beauty, Di!' She hadn't altered since Darcy last saw her, still wearing her uniform of a sharply tailored black suit with slim trousers, and fierce black stilettos. Caroline's narrow red glasses gave her an air of intelligence and creativity, balanced by the erotic potential her hair suggested. Her glossy black bob would have looked at home on a thirties Berlin torch singer, and the hint of Rigby and Peller lace and silk at her cleavage only enhanced this. She embraced Darcy in a cloud of Chanel No. 5 and champagne fumes. 'What a transformation,' Caroline said, holding Darcy's face in her hands.

'You haven't changed a bit,' Darcy said.

'You are a darling, but we are getting old, aren't we, Di?' she said, gesturing at her.

'I feel ancient,' Diana said, shifting uncomfortably in the bed.

'What did Beatrice want?' Darcy said.

'I felt much better once Caroline arrived,' Diana said carefully.

'Seems the little minx tricked me, pretended Diana had recommended I take her on.'

'That's the least of it,' Darcy said, throwing her soft leather tote bag on the floor. She filled them in on the conversation she had had with Maria at Moll's Gap.

Caroline whistled slowly. 'I've come across some narcissists in my time, but little Miss Cupcake takes first prize.' She topped up their glasses, and turned the champagne bottle upside down in the ice bucket. 'She's met her match this time.' The three champagne flutes chimed and sparkled as they toasted one another.

'I've always admired people who are creating themselves, still changing and inventing their lives,' Diana said, sipping her drink. 'People with the courage to begin something new, on their own terms.'

'You'd know more about it than most, Di,' Caroline said.

'C. S. Lewis said courage is every virtue at its testing point – or something like that,' Diana said. 'It's not about being un-afraid, it's about doing it anyway.'

Caroline took her hand. 'When I think what you went through, Di, losing Kavanagh.' She looked at Darcy. 'But you still went ahead and had this beautiful child, created this extraordinary home and restaurant anyway.'

'I did it for him, for you,' Diana said. 'When I fell for your father, for Kavanagh, I saw a glimpse of the life I'd always wanted, in his family.' She paused. 'I wanted that for you, Darcy, even though we lost him. It's very important for a child, I think, to feel they are the heart of someone's world.' Diana looked up at the high vaulted stone ceiling soaring above the velvet drapes of her four-poster bed. 'But if I'm honest, I wouldn't have chosen the Castle myself.'

'I've always thought your temperament was lighter,' Caroline said, waving a hand. 'Open French windows, Regency, darling. The restaurant end is far more you.'

'I saw it through for him.' Diana folded her arm, rubbing her shoulder. 'When we were tucked up in the caravan at night, with saucepans catching the drips from the roof, he used to say: 'Imagine, Diana, when we are king and queen of the Castle, on the nights when the wind is howling we will be tucked up in our tower on a feather mattress with a fire blazing.' But we never had a chance to sleep in this room together.' She smiled sadly. 'I rather liked the caravan. The simplicity of it. The freedom.' She glanced at Caroline. 'Good God, woman, don't cry.' She passed her a box of tissues. 'Toughest agent in London, this one,' she said to Darcy.

'It's all an act.' Caroline dabbed at her eyes. 'I just feel sorry for you, dear heart, for all you've been through.'

'*We've* been through.' Diana raised her glass to her. 'None of it would have been possible without you.' She looked around the room. 'King and queen of the Castle ...' she said under her breath. 'I felt safe enough here. I thought it would protect us.' Diana laughed softly. 'Didn't work, did it?'

'It's not over yet,' Caroline said, blowing her nose.

'I've been fighting to hold it together ever since I lost him. I've had enough. It's time to hand it over to you, Darcy.'

'Now?' Darcy said. 'But I'm not—'

'Yes you are. I'm not going to just disappear. After a little break in Italy with Fergus, I shall come back and teach you all I know before I retire. All Kavanagh taught me.' Diana gestured towards her dressing room. 'Talking of Fergus ... Darcy, would you fetch my phone for me?'

'Where is it?' Darcy said, sorting through the piles of discarded magazines on her mother's bureau. She followed a snaking pile of chargers from an overloaded socket. 'Found it. Con's right, you mustn't leave this plugged in, it's dangerous. The wiring has always been dodgy in this end of the house—'

'Nonsense,' Diana said, scrolling through her contacts. 'I'll call Fergus, ask him to come over for supper.'

'Are you serious, about Fergus?' Caroline said.

'It's different. But yes. There are similarities between them.' Diana closed her eyes, smiling. 'Kavanagh was a great bear of a man, too. He made me feel safe, and I ... I loved him so much the air vibrated between us like violin strings. He drove me mad, too.' Diana shook her head. 'Honestly, the gloss of history is a varnish that eradicates all the brush strokes, isn't it? Everything looks smooth sailing in retrospect when it was anything but at the time.'

'I don't think we'll look back and think that about this chapter in your careers, girls,' Caroline said, searching in her quilted bag for her silver cigarillo case. 'If you want Beatrice out, we need to be careful how we handle her. She has a lot of people wrapped around her little finger.' She waved the hallmarked case in triumph, and tottered to the balcony. 'However, I have better press contacts than she does, and I have been doing this for a lot longer, so she had better watch her back.'

'Darcy,' Diana said to her once Caroline was out of earshot, 'I need to tell you something.' She patted the bed beside her. 'Come and curl up here, my darling girl.' Darcy felt uneasy, but she did as her mother told her, and waited as she left a message for Fergus. 'Now, I need to tell you a story,' Diana said quietly to Darcy. She looked over at the balcony. Caroline was leaning on the balustrade, barking orders into her mobile phone. 'A long, long time ago in London, there was a young Irish girl who had lost her parents. She was paying for her squalid room in a boarding house by cleaning in a hospital. One of the doctors was so kind, so charming.' She closed her eyes. 'He asked if she'd like to become his housekeeper, instead. More money, and a peaceful, cosy little room in the basement which would be all hers.'

'It sounds like a fairytale,' Darcy said.

'Bluebeard, maybe,' Diana said, her face grim. 'You can guess what happened. He seduced the girl, wooed her with gilded words and bunches of violets, and she married him.' Diana let her head fall towards Darcy. 'That's when he changed.'

'Ma, why are you telling me this?'

Diana pulled back the sleeve of her blue wool dressing gown, and showed Darcy the pale swallows tattooed on her wrist. 'This covers a scar, Darcy, a scar where that doctor held the wrist of the girl down on a scalding hot dish.'

'Hold on? You're saying that you . . .' Darcy glanced across to the balcony. Caroline was still busy on the phone.

'Yes, I am that girl. I am Colleen Smith, or O'Shaughnessy as was. Wife of Doctor Timothy Smith, deceased.'

'He's dead, your . . . your husband?'

Diana nodded. 'It's why I wouldn't marry Kavanagh for such a long time.' She rubbed between her brows and sighed. 'And why I kept on turning down the chance to be on TV until the end of the eighties. I wrote cookbooks, sure, but I couldn't risk him – Dr Smith – seeing me on TV.'

'Did Dad know?'

'I had to tell Kavanagh, eventually, when I fell pregnant with you. I thought his heart would break when I told him I was already married.' She paused. 'When I was in the worst of the grief, I wondered if I had killed him. If the revelation that I'd lived a lie, that I wasn't the person he thought I was, killed him.'

'Rubbish,' Darcy said. 'You are who you are. He fell in

love with the person who was the sum of everything you'd experienced.'

'When did you get to be so wise?' Diana stroked Darcy's hair. 'He'd proposed to me every year on the anniversary of when we met, and the last time, because I was pregnant, I told him the whole story. He hired a private detective to trace Dr Smith. You know what a big heart he had; he even talked about adopting the girl.'

'The girl?'

'My child,' Diana said, taking Darcy's hand. 'Your sister.' She paused. 'Beatrice's mother.'

55

Darcy had to wait to find a quiet time to be with Diana. She was grateful for the distraction of the busy kitchen, glad that Conor was too occupied to ask her what was wrong. Her mind was reeling with questions by the time she knocked on her mother's door. She eased it open a crack. 'Are you resting?' she said, as her mother opened one eye.

'No. Can't sleep for the noise out there,' she said. 'I'll go mad, resting here when there's so much to do.'

'You know what the doctor said.'

'Is everyone here for the final?' She held out her hand to Darcy, who sat on the side of her bed and poured her an icy glass of lemon barley water. 'Oh, that's better,' she said, sipping at the glass. 'I was parched. How are you?'

'Confused,' Darcy said. 'Who knows about this?'

'That's alive? You, me and Beatrice.' Diana's face was grim. 'I have no doubt on reflection that it is she who is feeding these stories to the press, hoping to undermine you. I doubt we can prove it.'

'Undermine?' Darcy swirled her glass, ice chinking. 'Interesting choice of words.' Darcy looked at her mother. 'How could you? How could you abandon your own child?' Darcy shook her head.

'I ... Colleen wasn't well. You have to understand, I was only a child when I met Timothy, and he charmed his way in.

Narcissists can be terribly charming when they want to be, and they pick their victims well. No family, no one to save me but myself – and that's what I did, I saved myself.'

'Not your baby.'

'The child was the spitting image of her father. I did my best to love her, and take care of her, but she seemed so unhappy with me. I thought she would be better off without me. I felt so ashamed; what kind of mother feels like that?'

'It sounds like you were depressed,' Darcy said gently.

'I hoped every day it would get better, that I would do better, or he would stop, and that I'd grow to love her, but it never did. It never got better. I was so afraid, all the time.'

'Surely, that kind of violence, that abuse, it's as much to do with how someone is raised as what they are innately?'

'Do you think so? I still don't know. I never forgave myself, ever, for leaving her. And now . . . well, it's all going to come out in the open, isn't it? Caroline's doing her best to get the press on our side, but I think we can guess Beatrice will sell her story to the papers.' Diana looked at Darcy. 'She has nothing to lose now. Beatrice was holding it over me, threatening to tell you. I wanted to tell you myself so many times. I'm not proud of what I did, but I am proud of who I became. I reinvented myself. I christened myself. I created myself, and all this.'

Darcy gently hugged her mother, careful not to press on her arm. 'I love you, Ma. When I think what you went through . . .' She sat back and rubbed her mother's wrist with her thumb.

'You know, Kavanagh had a matching one,' Diana said, her eyes growing soft. 'We had them done for a laugh, one evening in Naples. He said it was like us, two swallows who chose one another for life.' Diana blinked. 'You know what Beatrice did? She's had the whole bloody willow pattern tattooed on her back.'

'She didn't?'

'She did! She's mad. Can you imagine how that hurt?' Diana and Darcy looked at one another and burst out laughing, hysteria overcoming them. After a few minutes, they lay side by side, catching their breath.

'So what do we do now?' Darcy rubbed wearily at her eyes. 'The press has already got hold of the story that I'm illegitimate,' Darcy said. 'I am – allegedly – a home wrecker and serial seducer of celebrity chefs—'

'Try saying that after a few glasses of champagne.'

'Meanwhile, Beatrice – who may or may not have had a hand in JJ's death, Tris's brake failure and Con's fall, and leaking all these stories to the press—'

'You're forgetting the goat.'

'Do you think she did that?'

'She's bonkers enough to set Mephisto loose just to mess up the final.' Diana chewed her lip. 'But we can't prove any of it.'

'So Bea is getting off scot free?'

'Not if I have anything to do with it,' Diana said.

'I can't get my head around this at all.' Darcy let her head fall back against the soft down pillows. 'You had another life entirely.'

'Darling, it is impossible for you to imagine how grey the fifties were. Postwar Britain wasn't like this,' she said, gesturing at an advert for pastel floral duvet covers in the magazine lying open on her bed. 'It was dull, and dirty, and cold. That's what I remember most, being terribly cold when I was little.' She hugged herself. 'And hungry. Rationing only ended four years after I was born.' Diana paused. 'The sixties seemed to promise so much.'

'Swinging sixties?'

'They may have been swinging, but they weren't for me. He – Dr Smith – he loved me to cook, like a good wife, but not to eat. He wanted me to look perfect too, you see. Whip thin, like a model. I had red hair down to my waist—'

'Red hair?'

'I dyed it brown for years, after I escaped. It went white in my forties.' Her eyes gleamed. 'Dr Smith wouldn't have liked that. He wanted to mould me into the perfect woman.'

'How did you get away?'

'I planned it for months. I had to be so careful. Although the little money I had from my parents was mine, you see, he kept tabs on everything.'

'Is this why you never talked about your parents when I was little?'

'It was too hard,' Diana said, her eyes gleaming. 'I still miss them, even now.'

'Did you grow up here, in Ireland?'

'No, in London, but I spent every holiday here. When my parents died they left me the house in Ireland, in the country. It was smaller than this, but I remember it felt not unlike the Castle. When I walked into the dilapidated old kitchen here, there was something about the proportions which reminded me of my mother's kitchen.' She glanced at Darcy. 'I don't know if the house even exists anymore. I've never been able to go back – too painful.'

'So Dr Smith took all your money?'

'He controlled everything. Places like that went for a pittance in those days, but the good doctor sold it anyway. I think that's why all those years later I let Kavanagh persuade me we should buy the Castle. It reminded me of my childhood, of something wonderful. I wanted that for you.'

'Oh, Ma.' Darcy reached across and took her hand.

'He watched my every move, so it took a while for me to plan my escape. I saved up – a bit of housekeeping here, a bit there. And I had a friend who knew what was going on; she helped me. With that I had just enough for a ticket on the Blue Train. Enough for a new beginning.'

'You didn't think of trying to find your daughter after you found out the doctor had died?'

'No. How could I? I had died. It was better that way.' Diana glanced at Darcy. 'Did I ever tell you that I met Elizabeth David, or Colleen did?'

'No.' Darcy smiled. 'How on earth have you kept that quiet all these years?'

'She was a remarkable woman. My mother adored her – *A Book of Mediterranean Food* was published the year I was born.' She smiled sadly. 'I imagine she read it while she was pregnant with me. It's probably why my middle name was Elizabeth. At least I kept that – Diana Elizabeth. I remember growing up with the recipes, how happy her kitchen was. Elizabeth David always said, and I've stuck to it myself – that a kitchen is a comforting place. It's not just about the food, it's about heart, and love and family.'

'I think,' Darcy said, 'it's about time you told everyone the truth about ours.'

56

London

August 1969

'Mrs David,' a young man said, poking his head into the tiny office under the stairs, 'there's a gentleman here to see you.'

'Is he attractive?' Elizabeth David said, not looking up from the ledger she was writing in. The walls of the office were crammed with reference books for dealing with customers' queries. She had a lit Gauloise in her other hand, and she flicked on the noisy air conditioner to clear some of the smoke.

'Probably just another country reader desperate to have an audience with his favourite cookery writer.'

'Oh, very well.' Elizabeth threw down her pen, and took off her reading glasses. She stubbed out her cigarette and marched into the shop. 'May I help you?' A man in a stiff blue overcoat stood with his back to the cash desk.

'Good afternoon,' the man said, turning and holding out his hand. Elizabeth held his gaze steadily, but there was something about him she disliked on instinct. His brilliantined blond hair reminded her of cheap embroidery silk, and he had the thin, bloodless lips of a corpse. He smiled at her with the superficial charm of a door-to-door salesman. 'My name is Dr Timothy Smith.' *Or a bad doctor*, she thought.

'Yes?' she said.

'I hoped you might be able to help me with this,' he said, taking out his wallet. He unfolded a handwritten invoice from the shop and smoothed it out on the counter. Elizabeth noticed his opaque nails were bitten to the quick. 'My wife bought a casserole dish from you last week.'

'We sell many casseroles, to many women,' she said.

'Perhaps you remember her? An Irish girl, Colleen? Slim, red hair.'

'Frightened?' Elizabeth said, folding her arms.

Timothy glanced over his shoulder, waiting for a couple of women to walk on. 'Did she say anything to you, anything at all?'

Elizabeth frowned, the pieces of the puzzle falling into place. The news headlines about the young mother who killed herself, leaping from the bridge. The girl who abandoned her baby. She remembered the screeching child, the flustered, red-faced girl, how sorry she had felt for her.

Elizabeth's face betrayed nothing; she knew he was watching her like a predator. 'No. I'm sorry, you've had a wasted journey.' She pushed the invoice towards him. 'Wait,' she said, rummaging in the basket on the counter. She shook out a carrier bag, and threw something wrapped in greaseproof paper into it, holding the handle towards him.

'What is this?'

'A gift.'

'Thank you, but it won't encourage me to shop here.' He took the bag. 'I prefer to give my custom to the local supermarket.' He glanced at the artfully displayed shelves. 'I like efficiency, cleanliness.'

'I'm sure you do,' Elizabeth said, folding her arms, her fingertips drumming against her arm.

'But I'll drop in next time I have a patient in Chelsea.' Elizabeth felt her skin prickle with unease as he looked at her, blank eyed. 'Perhaps you'll remember something. I'm very patient, myself.'

'I recall her now,' Elizabeth said slowly, clearly, not backing down at his unspoken threat. 'Beautiful girl. Very brave, I think.' She held his gaze. 'I remember her saying how much

310

she loved cooking. That's all. So there is no need for you to ever come back to my shop, Dr Smith.' Elizabeth David marched through her shop and held the door open, sunlight spilling in across the floor from Bourne St.

'Thank you for the gift.'

'Yes. I imagine you'll be cooking for yourself now, so it's just a little hard cheese.' The mask fell from his face, and he glared at her, before striding from the shop. Elizabeth slammed the door behind him, and leant against the frame, her heart racing. She remembered the large manila envelope the girl had slipped the cookery book into after Elizabeth had signed it for her. She remembered the address in Italy written on it with a neat, schoolgirl's hand. 'Good luck to you,' she said quietly, and smiled.

57

Kenmare

August

Diana tucked the new blanket from Avoca which Darcy had bought her around her shoulders and settled back into the bed, the jewel-coloured tartan bright against her white hair.

'Bloody hell,' Caroline said. 'I don't believe it.'

'Well,' Conor said, his hands resting on Darcy's shoulders. 'You dark horse.' He strode over and gave Diana a kiss.

Fergus laced his fingers tighter in Diana's hand. He sat beside her, his feet hanging off the end of the bed, his pink-toed, black-socked feet crossed at the ankle. 'Colleen O'Shaughnessy, I'll be damned.'

'I've no doubt Beatrice will sell her side of the story now, but I want you all to swear the details stay with us. You're the only ones whose opinions I care about. Let the press and the gossip columns do their worst,' Diana said. 'Poor Colleen. She was only a child. Elizabeth's books kept her going.'

'Kept you going,' Conor said.

'But it's like another person,' Diana said. 'Another lifetime. All those long, dark years my mother's books were like a promise, that somewhere, if I could just find my way, there was colour and life. Dr Smith destroyed most of them. Luckily I had *Italian Food* in my shopping basket the day he went mad and burnt all my cooking books, so I hid it from him. That was the final straw, I think, burning the only things I had left of my mother's. I wanted to meet Elizabeth David, just once, before I disappeared, to say thank you.'

'But you must have had the chance to meet her loads of times over the years,' Caroline said.

'As Diana, yes. But you see at that point I thought I could never risk coming back to London again. So I went to her shop, and asked her to sign my book. I posted it to myself at the address of the boarding house in Porto Ercole I'd arranged to stay at.' Diana lowered her head and smiled. 'I bought a new Dutch oven, too, and put it in the bottom of the pram. In fairy tales you get given gold and jewels. I thought a good bit of Le Creuset was a more practical gift to leave behind for my daughter.' She exhaled. 'It seems it worked. She loved cooking too.'

'So everyone thought you had drowned?' Conor said.

'I had to make them think I was dead.' Diana pulled up her sleeve, flexed her wrist. 'It's faded now, but just before I left, he held my arm down on the casserole.'

'Oh my God . . .' Caroline said, taking Diana's hand in hers.

'It would have got worse as I got older. I wasn't a malleable child anymore.'

'Didn't you worry that he would do the same to the baby?' Fergus said.

'Of course I did.' Diana's eyes glistened. 'I lay awake night after night for years hoping she was safe. But I thought . . . I thought she was so like him he'd never hurt her.' Diana took a breath. 'So I left her in her pram on Chelsea Bridge, and I jumped.' She looked at Darcy. 'I'd been practising that too, you see. He didn't think I could swim, but I was good.' She looked down at her hands. 'I'd been going to the local baths. Where I found the strength and determination to jump is beyond me, but it is amazing what you can do if you have to.'

'Then what happened?' Conor said.

'I had hidden a suitcase in Battersea Park – I was careful that no one saw me, and I was lucky.' Diana laughed. 'You know how superstitious I am. I took that as a sign that I was doing the right thing.'

'I still don't get how you became Diana Hughes,' Caroline said.

'In Nice, when I stepped off the Blue Line, I told them I had been mugged, and all my papers taken.' Diana paused. 'I'm not proud of it, but the old woman—' Diana broke off, laughing. 'God, I say old woman. She was younger than I am now. She lived next door to us, and she had helped me, looking after the baby while I went swimming. She knew. She knew what he was, heard him screaming at me most nights. People like Timothy don't notice women like her – they are no use to them, so they are invisible. He wouldn't have dreamt she was my friend.' Diana took a deep breath. 'In those days, you just had a photo in the passport, which they stamped. She had been an artist, so she helped me change her photo for mine, and fake the stamp. That's how I took her name. Diana Hughes.'

'Was all this why you didn't want children?' Fergus's brow furrowed.

'I worried. I was terrified that they would be hurt.'

'Because of the way you were treated?' Darcy said.

Diana smiled at Darcy. 'But I named you for a strong and decent character, and kept my name for us, rather than taking Kavanagh's for you.' She took Darcy's hands in hers. 'And it worked. You know I've always said that charming people are spoilt – you are the most charming person I have ever known.'

'You're saying I'm spoilt?' Darcy laughed.

'I'm saying, that in spite of what you have been through, you have been blessed: being loved, being surrounded by people who only wish the best for you.' She stroked back a strand of her daughter's dark hair. 'You have been through ups and downs like the rest of us, and you've seen me fight back again and again financially, but you have loved, and you are loved – that's what counts. Kavanagh always said you would be one of life's golden people. He used to speak to you when you were still in my stomach, you know.' Diana smiled. 'Let yourself shine, Darcy. We'll get through this nonsense.' Diana's eyes softened. 'It was the choice I made, when I left for Italy. I wanted the life that Elizabeth's books promised – something vibrant, and colourful, and authentic, and alive.' She laughed. 'It wasn't all breathtaking villas in the hills of Tuscany, but it was real, it had guts, it was . . .' She searched for the word. 'Stimulating. God, even thinking about London in the fifties and sixties I feel claustrophobic. Dr Smith's little rooms, and squeaky-clean linoleum, and the smell of gas and cabbage. I couldn't breathe.' Her face grew hard. 'Sometimes literally, when he tried to strangle me.'

'Oh, Ma,' Darcy said, touching her arm.

'He was very clever. No bruises where they could be seen, rarely anything that required hospitalisation. He could take care of the basics at home, you see, burns and sprains.' She flexed her hand. 'Even a broken bone or two.' Diana lowered her head. 'He was terribly clever, even convinced me it was my fault, the "accidents"–'

'I could kill the man,' Fergus whispered, fighting back the tears. 'I hate to think of what you went through. God, you were a child.'

'I don't regret it. I want you to know that. I don't regret a thing. Even the child . . . Perhaps.' Diana looked at Darcy. 'When you came along, I wanted to get it right, you know? I wasn't afraid, I was just so filled with love for you. Perhaps that's why I've been tough on you sometimes. I just wanted your life to be . . .'

'If you say perfect, I'm leaving,' Darcy said, glancing at Conor.

Diana stroked back Darcy's hair. 'When I look at you, I see him. You had a remarkable father.'

'And one irreplaceable mother,' Darcy said.

'Two women in one,' Diana said. 'I've been Diana so long, it's like I'd forgotten Colleen ever existed.'

Conor's phone rang, and he stepped into the hall to take the call.

'It's almost time for the final show to be filmed. We should leave you to rest,' Darcy said to her mother, and Caroline led the way. Diana settled back beside Fergus.

'He sounds a remarkable man, your Kavanagh,' Fergus said, tucking his arm gently behind her head.

'He was,' she said, laying her cheek against his shoulder.

'You miss him, still?'

'You miss your wife, don't you?' Diana looked up at him. 'We can't replace them. I can't possibly fill the shoes of the woman you loved for forty years.'

'But do you think we are too old to have a little happiness and fun?' He kissed the top of her head, held her close.

'The hell we are!'

Darcy pulled the door to behind her. 'Shall we eat out tonight, after the show?' she said to Caroline.

'The pub? Grand idea. I'll just go and freshen up before I join the audience.' Caroline steadied herself on the banister and headed down the spiral stone staircase. Darcy could hear voices echoing up from downstairs, the sound of the last chairs being set up in the Great Hall for the show. Darcy crossed the hall to Conor, frowning at the tense hunch of his shoulders as he spoke quickly on the phone.

'What's wrong?' she whispered. He shook his head.

'Call the Garda, right now,' Conor said, and clicked off his phone. He looked up at Darcy, his face stricken. 'It's Chris,' he said. 'The childminder said he's missing.'

58

Staff and guests walked the darkening grounds of the Castle, Chris's name echoing along the water. The wind was rising along the bay, rippling the surface, stirring the branches of the trees along the banks. Conor held one of his son's T-shirts to his dog's nose, and let him sniff. 'Come on, boy,' he said, rubbing the dog's ears. 'Go and find him, Jake, bring him home safely.'

'I've called the Garda,' Darcy said, running from the house kitchen. 'They're on their way. How could he have got out of the childminder's garden?'

'It's not her fault, you know what they're like at that age, turn your back for a moment and they're into something.' Conor wrung the little shirt in his hands. 'Besides, that gate is always locked,' he said. 'It takes an adult to open it.'

'You mean someone took Chris?' Darcy touched his arm. 'Oh God, Conor, you don't think? She wouldn't, not a child?'

'I think she's capable of anything. I don't think she'd hurt him, but yeah, I reckon she'd do anything to make mischief.' He strode on. 'How long have we got before Tris needs to start filming?' Conor said.

'An hour.' Darcy checked her watch. 'I'll call him and let him know what's going on.'

'If we haven't found Chris by then, you'll have to hold the fort.'

'Do the show alone?' Darcy said, feeling sick with nerves.

'Di's out of action, Beatrice has disappeared. You can do it,' Conor said, hugging her. 'I'm not giving up until we find Chris. Good luck, Darce.'

The search continued as the moon rose, its silver light reflected in the bay. As cars streamed up the driveway, parking in the fields at the back of the Castle, in the workshops, Conor and the men found as many flashlights and lanterns as they could. He looked up as the lights of a search boat swept across the water.

'Con, there you are,' Aiden said, pushing through as the last of the men filed out of the workshop. 'I'm sorry, I just got here. I didn't know—'

'What is it, Aiden?' Conor flicked his torch on to full beam. 'Can it wait?'

'No, no it can't,' he said, following him out into the yard. Conor could hear voices calling his son's name across the hills: *Chris, Chris* . . . 'Con, I'm sorry.' Tears filled the boy's eyes. 'She talked about teaching you all a lesson, but I didn't think she'd do anything like this.'

Conor gripped his arms. 'Anything like what, Aiden? What are you saying?'

'Bea . . . she got me to post a lot of stuff online for her. You know, stuff on forums and social media, spreading lies about all of you.' He looked at the ground. 'She was . . . well, ages ago she promised me that we'd—'

'You'll not be the first idiot who's been manipulated by his cock, by someone like Beatrice,' Conor said. 'What else do you know?'

'I bumped into her this afternoon, hanging around by the childminder's. I didn't think.' Aiden raked his hand through his hair. 'She's in a bedsit in town, near my flat, Con. It's nuts, you know. Now I've told her I'm not interested, that I'm with

Maeve, she's all over me. I'm supposed to meet her there to-night.' He scribbled down the address.

The Garda went ahead of Conor, crowding up the dimly lit staircase, a bare light bulb flickering above them. Conor paced the landing as they knocked on the door of the bedsit, glaring at the faces of the neighbours appearing from their rooms, curious about the commotion.

'Jaysus, she's not there. Can we not just break down the door?' Conor said. The landlord pushed his way through the crowd, sorting through a hoop of keys. 'Has she changed the locks? Come on, man.' Another key was tried. Conor's heart was pounding. He looked along the shabby corridor, saw the flickering light of someone's television, heard the roar of canned laughter on a game show. He wanted to be away from here, couldn't bear the thought that his son might be hurt, or frightened.

The Garda pushed their way through the open door at last. They found Chris curled up sleeping peacefully on a mattress in the corner of the room, a grubby sheet covering him. A cartoon was playing on the television.

'Is this your son, Mr Ricci?' one of the men said.

'Yes, yes it is.' Conor lifted the sleeping boy into his arms, his face contorted with emotion.

'Da?' Chris said, smiling sleepily, burying down against Conor's neck. 'You found me.' He yawned. 'I told Bea you always win at hide and seek.'

'If she had hurt you,' he whispered, holding him close. Conor pulled his phone out of his back pocket, and rang Alannah before calling Darcy's number. 'We've found him,' he said. He closed his eyes and breathed in the smell of his son. 'Are you OK, Darcy?'

'Me? I'm fine, about to go on.' Conor could hear the nerves in her voice. 'I'm just so glad you found him.'

'All of this would mean nothing without you both.' He

stroked Chris's hair. 'Alannah is on her way. She's going to take him to the hospital for a check-up, just in case.'

'Won't you go too?'

'Now I know he's safe, I'm coming back to the Castle,' he said, cradling Chris in his arm as he walked down the stairs. 'I can't leave you and your ma there with Beatrice on the loose.'

Conor drove back along the bay road to the Castle, the car's headlights illuminating the green verges, the bright flash of a fox's eyes near the turning to Dromquinna. He parked up in the yard, and as the engine ticked in the silence, he noticed the restaurant kitchen lights were on. *Someone's working late*, he thought as he crossed the drive to the house and ran up to Diana's tower bedroom.

'Have you found him? Have you found Chris?' Diana said, stirring.

Conor nodded. 'He was in Beatrice's bedsit, some filthy, god-forsaken place in town. He was a bit groggy, so his ma's taken him to the hospital, just in case.'

'She wouldn't drug a child, surely?'

'Nothing would surprise me,' Conor said, already imagining how Beatrice would try to twist the facts, the excuses she would come up with for taking Chris. 'She was stupid, hiding him at her flat. With Aiden's help, we've got her now. She won't be able to wriggle out of this one.'

59

Darcy walked down the curving flight of stone steps to the Great Hall, her red silk evening dress trailing behind her. The cameras and lights were trained on her, and she couldn't make out the faces of the audience filling the huge stone vaulted room. Her stomach was tight with nerves, but her mother's words came to her: *let yourself shine*. She watched Tristan for the signal that the show had gone live.

'Hello, and welcome to Castle Dromquinna for the grand final of *Ireland's Top Chef*,' she said, reaching the red-carpeted stage which had been set up beside the stone fireplace. Michael and Fiona sat, pale faced and anxious at the side of the stage, smiling as applause echoed around the wood-panelled room. 'On behalf of my mother, Diana Hughes, and myself we congratulate our finalists, Michael and Fiona.' Darcy joined the audience in applauding them both. She turned to the camera. 'Now, having watched our finalists in action, it's time for you at home to cast your votes and decide who will be crowned Top Chef tonight.'

'And cut,' Tristan shouted. 'Well done, Darcy, my love. That was perfect.' He turned to the audience, and pointed at the monitors. 'Right, at this point there is a voiceover going out on screen, with the numbers for people to ring for the phone vote. For those of you who would like to vote, do dial now.' There was shuffling and chatter as people reached for their phones. 'Sit back and enjoy the rest of the show. In half an hour, we will be on air again for the live result.'

Darcy sniffed the air. She was sure she could smell burning, something charred. 'Tris, I just want to check something,' she said, gathering up the long skirt of her dress. She stepped down from the stage, and hurried through to the reception, checking the fire in the hall. Everything was calm. She pushed open the door marked 'Private' and ran through to the house, her heels clicking on the old parquet floor. The kitchen was empty, so Darcy raced back through the lamp-lit passage to the hotel and swung open the green baize door, heading towards the restaurant. The bar was full of people who had helped with the search for Chris, and a local band was playing by the fire. Darcy pushed through the crowd to the bar. 'Niall? Have you seen Beatrice?' she said.

'No, not for a while,' he said. As Darcy started to shove her way through the dancers Niall called after her, 'Darcy! Conor rang earlier – Chris has been sent home from the hospital; he's fine. Con's on his way back.' Darcy strode through the empty restaurant, the tables dark and cleared away for the night, towards the double doors to the kitchen. Light seeped like a knife edge between them. Just as she swung them open, the smoke alarm kicked into life, lights flashing, a high-pitched whine starting up, bells ringing through the Castle. Darcy's eyes smarted, and she covered her mouth as she ran to the corridor to get the fire extinguisher. She dragged it back into the kitchen, and leant down to pull the pin. Someone had cut through the black pipe. Darcy looked up at the oven. Acrid black smoke was escaping from the seal. She flung open the back door and turned off the gas, covering her mouth, coughing. She grabbed a pair of oven gloves, carrying the tray outside, and threw it onto the ground. 'Cupcakes?' Darcy hesitated, then kicked the charred cakes over with her silver shoe, and stepped back.

'What a waste,' a voice said in the darkness.

'Beatrice?' Darcy said. She squinted, and shielded her face with her hand, blinded by the security lights which had clicked on as she came outside. She heard footsteps approaching, and Beatrice stepped into the light. 'What have you done? What have you done?' Darcy yelled, marching over and shoving her, hard.

'Darcy,' Beatrice said, blinking in surprise. 'I don't understand.'

'How dare you? How dare you take Chris. If you have harmed one hair on that child's head—'

'Me? I didn't take him. It was Aiden,' Beatrice said, wide eyed. 'We saw the poor kid, dumped at the childminder again because Conor and his ex were too busy to take care of him themselves. We thought he'd have more fun having tea at my place. We told her. We didn't just take him. I was baking those cakes for him, but I saw that the tower was—'

'You did not tell her, and you left a little boy all alone.'

'Yeah, well, maybe that runs in the family. Leaving children—'

'Don't you dare try and twist this around.'

'I'm not.'

'You tried to blackmail Ma—'

'No, Diana is confused. Are you sure it wasn't the fall? Maybe she banged her head.'

'Like Conor?' Darcy said.

'Conor had an accident. A momentary lapse of concentration. Could happen to any of us.'

'You're so plausible, aren't you? An answer for everything.'

'Who called the ambulance that came for him? Eh?' Beatrice raised her chin. 'I did. I saw Diana running around in the yard like a headless chicken shouting for help.'

'When? When did you call it? Ma saw Conor and she called the ambulance. You said you went back to sleep after Conor left.' Darcy sneered. 'You lied about that, too?'

'I called it first! I had to change – I was only in my under-wear.' She paused just long enough for Darcy to put two and two together.

'You're still lying. You and Conor?' Darcy shook her head, laughing though she felt sick even at the idea of them to-gether. 'I don't believe you.'

'Of course he says now that he can't remember anything.'

'Who are you?' Darcy's face contorted with disgust. '*What* are you?'

'I'm your family, Darcy.' Beatrice smiled sweetly. 'I'm part of your lives now, for ever.'

'Family?' Darcy said, playing for time. She hoped desper-ately someone would trace the smoke alarm to the kitchen and come to help. 'You're not my sister,' she said, frowning. 'You're my half-sister's daughter, so that makes you—'

'Can we go a bit faster, do you think?'

'What is it that you want? Enlighten me.'

'Ladybird, ladybird,' Beatrice recited, twirling her hands in the air like wings. 'Fly away home . . .'

'I'm not in the mood for games. Perhaps you'd rather tell the Garda.'

'Do you think? What do you think they could charge me with? Hm? Do you really think some sort of restraining order will stop me? It didn't stop me seeing Jonny.'

Darcy paled. 'You didn't . . .'

'What do you think? He wanted to let me go, too.' Bea-trice's fingers beat a staccato rhythm against her thumb. 'All I wanted was to *help*,' she said, her voice rising. 'It doesn't work like that, you see. This is over when *I* say it is, not before. When *I* get bored with *you*.'

'You're crazy,' Darcy said. 'Get the hell out of my life, and make your own. This is my mother, my family, my home.'

'*Our* family, Darcy. It's *ours*.' Beatrice stepped towards her. 'You see, Ma told me everything just before she died. That little girl Colleen, or Diana, or whatever she calls herself, grew up all alone, when her parents died. Then she had a little girl all of her own. But Colleen abandoned that child.' Beatrice's voice rose.

'I am sorry for that little girl, and for her daughter.' Darcy held her ground as Beatrice walked ever closer. 'But I know all this. You have no hold on Diana, do you understand? Have you no shame? Look at what you have done – the carnage you've left in your wake.'

'Diana – Colleen – started it. What kind of a woman just leaves her child to fend for itself?' Beatrice's eyes flickered. 'I couldn't escape the bloody woman growing up. Every paper, every time I turned on the TV, there she was. My mother idolised her, the fool. It was like Diana was stalking me. She wouldn't leave me alone.'

'You take no responsibility for what you've done? Feel no regret?'

'Regret?' Beatrice thought for a moment. 'I was caught, once, at school. One of the girls had annoyed me – I can't remember for what – and I cut through the elastic in her skirt while she was at games. I had the peg next to hers so it was quite easy to do. I remember the thrill of waiting for her skirt to fall down as she ran around the playground at break time. She tripped over it. I remember her lying there with her stupid pink knickers showing. Everyone crowded round, pointing and laughing.' A satisfied smile crept over Beatrice's face. 'When she stood up, she wet her pants, she was so ashamed. How we all laughed . . .' Her gaze hardened. 'She ratted me out, of course. The teacher asked me the same question: didn't I regret humiliating her?'

'And?'

'I just regretted being caught.'

'I feel sorry for you,' Darcy said quietly.

'You?' Beatrice laughed. '*You* feel sorry for *me*?'

'Your jealousy's a poison, Beatrice. You try to destroy anything and anyone that's in your way, but the worst torment is your own.' Darcy shook her head. 'After everything you have done, you have no place in this family.'

'You can't just get rid of me. I have every right—'

'Get lost, Bea.' Darcy began to turn away.

'Don't you turn your back on me. How dare you think you can ignore me!' Beatrice cried. 'I belong here.'

'Even your last batch of cakes burnt. You really are a lousy cook.' She glanced across at the blue flashing lights tearing along the driveway.

'I am not a lousy cook – take that back!' Beatrice yelled, her face contorting. 'I will show you. I will have my own programme, and I will be more successful than you—'

Darcy's eyes narrowed. 'This was never about working with us at the Castle, was it? Because then the fight would be over. You're so obsessed with Ma, you just wanted to push your way into our lives like some . . . some cuckoo and destroy us.'

'I want her to need me.' Beatrice inhaled, shakily. 'I want to help—'

'Don't you get it? We don't care about you. You are nothing to me. You think that you've been clever, and maybe none of us will be able to prove anything now, but one day you will slip up, and it will all catch up with you. I do feel sorry for you, I really do, Bea, because you will never, ever know what it is to have a real family, and feel love.'

'I don't want love. I want to win. But now I should go,' Beatrice said. 'Aren't you wondering why no one has come to check the restaurant kitchen?' She pointed back at the Castle and Darcy turned. Flames engulfed the tower, glowing red in the lower windows.

'My God, what have you done?' Darcy cried out.

'Me? It's nothing to do with me. I tried to tell you. I stepped out of the kitchen for some air and saw the tower was on fire.' Beatrice smiled. 'Who do you think called the fire brigade?'

'I don't believe you!' Darcy shouted, running towards the tower.

'Isn't it what Diana wanted?' Beatrice called, backing away into the shadows. 'You heard her. She said she wanted it to go up in smoke. This place is a beautiful monster.'

60

Darcy ran to the crowd of people on the lawn, and grabbed Aiden's arm. 'Where's Ma? Have you seen her?' He shook his head, watching with his mouth open as the flames blew out the kitchen windows. The Garda made everyone move back, but Darcy pushed through to the front of the crowd. 'My mother, Diana Hughes, she's still in there!' She ran past the Garda, glancing over her shoulder to see a stream of fire engines arriving. Darcy choked on the smoke-filled air, cried out, 'Ma!'

'Darce, what on earth are you doing?' Conor said, dragging her to safety. The fire crew pushed past. 'I'm not losing you,' he said, holding her close to his side as they walked across the lawn.

'Con, I can't just stand by and—' Darcy rushed forwards as a dark figure loomed in the doorway, escorted by two firemen. She could see he had a woman in his arms.

'Fergus!' Conor shouted, waving him over. They gathered round, and Darcy took Diana's hand as Fergus laid her gently on the ground, her back resting against the trunk of the oak tree.

'Ma, are you OK?'

'I am now,' she said, gazing up at Fergus's smoke-blackened face.

'This is a nightmare!' Tristan shouted, running towards them with his phone clamped to his ear, the cameraman running after him. 'What are we going to do? We're going live in five!'

'Have the votes been counted?' Conor said.

'Yes.' Tristan listened to his phone, and nodded. 'We have a winner.' He checked his watch. 'Right, get Fiona and Michael over there by the bay, and film towards the firework display.' He took Darcy's hand. 'Everyone is out safely so we'll see this through to the end.'

Tristan and his team hurriedly set up lights, and Conor and Darcy joined the finalists on the lawn. 'Are you OK?' he said, taking Fiona's arm.

'A little shaken,' she said. 'I'm not sure I'm cut out for all this excitement.'

'Not long now,' Darcy said, giving Michael's shoulder a squeeze.

'We're going live in thirty seconds,' Tristan said, watching the time. 'Good luck.' He signalled to Darcy.

'Welcome back to Castle Dromquinna,' Darcy said, smiling broadly. As she looked at the camera, she could see the Castle blazing in the background, the shadowy figures of all the people gathered on the lawns. 'It's been quite a night, but we are just moments away from finding out who you chose to be Ireland's Top Chef.' Conor took a gold envelope from Tristan, and stood at her side.

'And the winner is . . .' he said, opening the note. 'Michael!' he and Darcy said together. As they shook hands with the contestants, fireworks plumed up into the night sky, reflected in the silver bay behind them.

'Thank you for joining us,' Darcy said to camera.

'See you next year, on *Ireland's Top Chef*!' Conor said, raising his hand in farewell as Tristan signalled 'cut'.

The fire crew ran a pipe down to the bay, pumping water up to the hoses, but the fire raged on into the early hours, ravaging the timbers of the old building.

Caroline carried a tray of coffees from the kitchen in the staff quarters to where everyone stood on the lawn in the dawn light. 'Here we are, Di,' she said, handing her a mug. Caroline settled down on the grass nearby, the light from her iPad illuminating her face as she scrolled through the morning papers.

'Is it Nescafé?' Diana said.

'For heaven's sake, Ma,' Darcy said, sitting on the damp grass beside Diana's stretcher, her red dress pooling around her. She leant in to her mother, kissing the top of her head. 'You know she said this is your – our – fault? She must have overheard you talking about the Castle, that it's a monster.'

'People like that weave a fabric of lies, twist the truth to suit their own ends.' Diana stared at the Castle, smoke pluming from the tower where the roof had caved in. 'It was a beautiful monster, but it was ours,' Diana said, her voice hoarse. She coughed, and pressed a handkerchief to her lips.

'They've managed to stop the fire spreading to the hotel and restaurant, at least, but the tower's a shell.' Conor slumped down on the grass beside Darcy, and she leant back against him. 'They think it started in Di's dressing room. If you ask me it was an overloaded socket.' He glanced at Diana.

'I know! I know!' Diana said, throwing her hand in the air. 'You all warned me a hundred times about leaving my phone plugged into that cheap charger. I was just worried the battery would run out.'

'No, Beatrice had a hand in this,' Darcy said. 'I bet she is involved.'

'You reckon? She's mischief itself, that one.'

'I just want her away from here,' Diana said. 'She's done what she set out to do: destroyed everything.'

'She's destroyed nothing,' Conor said. 'Places like this aren't built of bricks and mortar.' He looked at Darcy. 'They're built of dreams. And she can't touch those.'

In the dawn light, Darcy could just make out the smoke-blackened keystone above the archway of the main door, carved with DH. As she listened to Caroline reading out the first reviews of the final show from the papers, in her mind's eye Darcy could already see another stone there, with new initials, for a new beginning.

THE FOODS OF LOVE

There is a magic in distance. Look back at the golden lamp-lit rooms of your home from the road of your life, and it all for a moment is exactly how you hoped it would be: warm, peaceful, safe. Proust had his madeleine, and Ma had her beef daube bubbling away on the stove in her old blue Le Creuset. On a chill day when the ground was hard outside (and there was ice on the inside of the bedroom windows), I loved coming home to the Castle from school to the scent of thyme, rosemary, bay, spices, wine, meat and woodsmoke.

Me? I have a simple loaf of soda bread, a roast chicken, a glass of wine, the rain on the lake and the man I love at my side. What more do you need? There are tastes, and meals, and memories that become so much a part of you, of the story of your life, that you can't imagine a time before. A perfect meal does not, in fact, have to be perfect. It is not about expense, but quality, not finery, but comfort – welcoming people to your home, and generosity and kindness. I think it is as tricky creating recipes as it is falling in love. You can spend a lifetime discovering tastes that balance one another, bring out the best in one another. Some tastes, like some people, complement one another, and everything tastes better when love is reciprocated. Your senses are heightened, your nerves more, firing with renewed vigour and hunger for life. I think to cook is to love – to care for and nurture, and create something beautiful. And few puddings are simpler and lovelier than this:

With a sharp knife, quarter figs, cutting down almost to their base so that the fruit blossoms, arrange upright in an ovenproof dish and drizzle each little gaping maw with lavender honey. Bake at 220°C for ten minutes. Serve with chilled Greek yoghurt or mascarpone.

Darcy Hughes, *Appetite* Tumblr

FOOD FOR BROKEN HEARTS

To make a bitter chocolate sauce:

Boil 250 ml of milk, and whisk in 150 g dark melted chocolate, 80 ml of whipping cream and 40 g unsalted butter. Peel four pears, submerge in 1 litre of apple juice with star anise and 1 tbsp of honey – simmer for 15 mins. Pour over the sinful, bitter chocolate sauce. Forget about the calories: you deserve it, and I promise, it helps.

Beatrice Hughes-Lavender, *Bea Happy*

The thing is, I think you should just experiment. Break rules if they don't work for you. Food is about pleasure, about making you feel good, healthy and alive.

It is real, visceral, it's about family and home and life, whether or not it's perfect. In this messed-up virtual online hidden world of trolls and people who are not what they seem, food is love. It's not about celebrity and showing off, it's about what really matters, and that is kindness, nurturing, friendship and love.

I cook this pudding for Darce, sometimes, if I'm hoping to get lucky. There's something magical and aphrodisiac about zabaglione. I made it once for a young lad who wanted to make a girl fall in love with him. I'm a godfather now.

For each person, whisk 2 of the freshest egg yolks you can get with 2 tsps of sugar in a bowl above a simmering pan of water, until white and frothy. Stir in a sherry glass of marsala wine and keep whisking until the mix thickens but doesn't boil. Be lucky.

Conor Ricci, *Hughes & Ricci On the Road*

Epilogue

Darcy stood in the trees at the edge of the lake, looking back at the house. The windows glowed gold in the falling light, lamps lit, woodsmoke curling from the chimney of the red woodburner she could see in the kitchen, copper pans gleaming above. It was more than she had hoped for. She walked back across the wet grass, copper and yellow leaves whirling and falling around her as Jake ran on ahead. She heard his claws on the jetty, his excited yelp. There in one of the Adirondack chairs he sat waiting for her.

Conor stood as the dog reached him, and squatted down to fuss him, rubbing his ears. He wore a long-sleeved white T-shirt beneath his familiar dark one, and thick socks beneath his boots. Darcy walked along the grey timber jetty, the light of the house behind her, the wind catching at her long black sweater. As she reached him, he took her in his arms, and held her close. He smelt of the cold wind, of the earth, of home.

'It's going to be OK, isn't it, Con?'

'Of course it will. We're young enough to start again.' She laid her head against his shoulder, and looked out across the lake. 'And this time, we'll get it right.'

'Darcy, Con,' Diana called from inside the lake house. 'Come and see this.' They wandered inside, to where Fergus and Chris sat playing chess in front of the fire, and Diana was cooking supper. A wide gold Claddagh ring shone on her tanned finger as she pointed a paring knife at the television in the sitting room. 'Fergie, darling, turn up the volume, will you?'

They gathered in front of the news, and a familiar face filled the screen.

'TV cook Beatrice Lavender, who has been tipped for great things as the next culinary star, has been rushed to hospital today while recording her new series . . .'

Darcy reached across and aimed the remote control at the television, switching it off. Beatrice's face vanished.

'Don't you want to know what happened to her?' Diana said.

'No. Good riddance,' Conor said under his breath.

'Right,' Darcy said, gesturing to the table laid by the fire. 'Let's eat.'

Beatrice moved one of the almond cookies a fraction to the left. She felt the heat of the lights as she leant down to the kitchen counter, her dark eyes level with the tray. They were perfect. She took an icing bag and sculpted white flowers of sugar, petals curving like the smiles of virgins. Behind her, the evening sun sparkled on the Thames, the windows of the loft apartment were open, strings of lights on the Embankment illuminated, the London Eye turning slowly.

'Look, Tris did it before with that contest, when Darcy stepped in for Diana,' Jamie said quietly to the director in a corner of the loft. 'Why can't it work again?'

'It's not *Dr Who*, Jamie. It's not like we can just regenerate the Hughes chefs at the end of each season,' the director said. 'Di and Darcy have said they're not doing any TV for a while, and anyway, they'll only work with Tristan. And Conor's signed a new series with that US station. Road trip across the States I think, lucky sod.' His face fell, watching Beatrice barking orders at the make-up girl. 'Could do with a road trip myself—'

'I know you've got doubts, but why can't Bea work? She's a Hughes, isn't she? Everyone knows that now.' Jamie licked his lips, and caught Beatrice's eye. 'Trust me, this will work. The home ecs are taking care of the complicated recipes; all Bea has to do is perform. She's exactly like Darcy, but sexier.' She blew him a kiss. 'People love a bit of scandal. They eat it up.'

'If you say so. She scares the hell out of me,' the director said.

'What are you on about?'

'Nothing. Nothing – I'm probably just being over-sensitive as you always say. There's just something . . .' He watched Beatrice preening in the mirror.

'She's a natural, look at her. Fun, fresh, adorable. Just like Darcy's big sister.' Jamie stared at her, bending over in a simple white dress, tying the laces of her silver pumps. He sniffed the air. 'Smells great, Bea,' he called.

'It's the almonds in the marzipan,' Beatrice said, 'and just a hint of vanilla.'

'Make-up!' the director called. 'Touch up Bea's lipstick, please.' He leant against the counter and the girl reluctantly approached Beatrice again. Jamie strolled over.

'I told you I'd make it worth your while moving back to London.' He ran his index finger against the zip of Beatrice's dress as the make-up girl slicked a red stain on her lips. 'This is your chance,' he whispered. 'Make it work, OK? And then you make it worth my while . . .'

'Oh, I will.' Beatrice looked down at the tray of sugar-frosted, sparkling cookies.

'Right, first shot. I want you to take a bite out of the cookie on the top, really work it. Think flirty, sexy . . .' The director stepped back behind the camera, checking the shot.

'But I'm allergic—'

337

'Listen, Bea,' Jamie said with an edge to his voice. 'This is what you've always wanted. Your own show.'

'Do you want this or not?' the director said.

'Yes. Yes I do,' Beatrice said, and stared directly into the camera.

THE LAST COURSE

Some say that the qualities which make food delicious are simply flavour, smell, colour, texture and appearance. Sure, they are important, but what about sound? The sound of food is vital, I think. Nowhere sounds like your home, your family, your kitchen. Remember the sound of a bread knife cutting on the board you've had since you first moved in together, the song of the kettle or the clatter of the copper pots you saved up for, and the steady, reassuring weight of the pan lid clunking into place as you boil some water for spaghetti? This is the dish that says family to me. A three-ingredient high, as Conor says: pasta, garlic, oil. It conjures it all – the well-thumbed copies of Elizabeth David on the kitchen shelves, the fall of the light from the deck doors, the meal bubbling on the stove. One of the books which survived the fire, *Italian Food*, is signed. I remember asking Ma about it as a kid. 'I was sent it by a friend,' she said. 'Who?' 'You never met her, she died.' 'I'm sorry.' 'It was a long time ago.' She'd lent it to Fergus, so that was lucky.

Then there's Conor, returning from the hen house with Chris on his shoulders and fresh eggs for zabaglione. And Fergus and Ma, press-ganged into peeling spuds over yesterday's *International Herald Tribune* on the kitchen table, with its headline: *TV cook's narrow escape*. It is the man I love embracing me as I cook, Conor placing his hand on the swell of my stomach, the new life within kicking back defiantly. It is a new beginning for all of us. To cook is to love, to live. My cooking's not perfect, yet, but I am enjoying it, and you can, too. We are all still learning, and I think that's half the fun. We all need a little help along the way, for there is an art to the perfect meal.

Darcy Hughes, *Hughes at Home Part II*

Acknowledgements

My thanks to John Brennan of Dromquinna Manor; Sheila Lovett of White Heather Farmhouse, Kenmare; Robert White of Kenmare Fishing Tours. Thank you to Brigette Carpanini for her culinary expertise. Thank you to Jill Norman, literary trustee of the Elizabeth David Estate, for her advice about Mrs David. Thank you, Darina Allen of the Ballymaloe Cookery School and Hannah Love of Alice Water's office, Chez Panisse, for your generosity.

Thanks to Anneliese O'Malley at Virago/Little Brown for the kind permission to quote from Margaret Atwood's beautiful poem 'Variation on the Word Sleep'. As ever, my thanks to the team at Curtis Brown, especially the incomparable Sheila Crowley. Thank you to all at Orion, and my brilliant editor Kate Mills. Finally, thank you to my ever-supportive, ever-loving family, without whom books, life and meals would be a whole lot less fun.